AA Hasker is the author _____ previous novels
Cows Didn't Graze in Brum and *Eternity Must Wait.*
He lives with his wife in Portsmouth, where much
of this novel is set.

JACOBS' KINGDOM is a fast moving nautical saga
of romance and intrigue in which Captain Aaron Jacobs
achieves wealth beyond his wildest dreams as he
takes his ship *The Golden Falcon* and his loyal crew
(including his long time mistress and ex-Portsea
prostitute – Polly) from one heart-stopping, seaborne
adventure to another.

JACOBS' KINGDOM

AA Hasker

British Library in Publication
A catalogue record for this book is
available from the British Library

ISBN 1- 898546- 07- X

EDWARD GASKELL
The Lazarus Press
Cranford House
6 Grenville Street
Bideford • Devon
EX39 2EA

First published by
Edward Gaskell 1995
© AA Hasker 1994

TM

Set in New Century

Typeset, Printed and Bound by
The Lazarus Press
Bideford Devon EX39 2EA
Great Britain

COVER DESIGN FROM A PAINTING BY NORMA FYNN

Dedicated to
Joan Hasker my wife
whose patience has
known no bounds
over the last
50 years

JACOBS' KINGDOM

Chapter One

Aaron was a short stocky man in his mid twenties. He wore a mop of red unruly hair that permanently looked like it had survived a hurricane. His face resembled what can only be described as a walnut pickled in strong alcohol and a small scar on his lip gave him a slight permanent grin. But his most prominent feature was his nose – shaped like a ripe pear split down the centre making the bulbous tip into two large globes. Yet he couldn't be described as unpleasantly ugly, the way women flocked round him bore testament to that. A fascinating face would be a more reasonable description.

The permanent smile, at times, could be a disadvantage making it difficult to hold a serious conversation. In the latter part of the eighteenth century, in the narrow slum streets surrounding the dockyard in Portsmouth, a slight change of tone in one's voice or a word at the wrong time could send a knife flashing through the air and disfigurement, if not death would result. It just didn't pay to have a grin spread across your face, so Aaron restricted his movements to the taverns surrounding the harbour where everyone knew him.

Born on a thirty foot fishing boat, his mother having died in childbirth, he was brought up by his father. He was not only a good father but a good teacher, he taught him to read and write and to navigate. At ten years old he was left with a French family in Brittany to master the language. This was not to help him in the respectable trade

1

of fishing, but the more lucrative trade of smuggling. Before reaching the age of fourteen he had mastered French fluently. So fluently he, at times, thought in French and spoke with a strong Brittany accent.

A few days after Aaron had left the French family to rejoin his father a simple accident aboard the ship proved fatal. The sail boom swung round hitting the side of his father's head and a few days later he died with a brain haemorrhage.

Aaron was left alone to carry on the nefarious but lucrative trade of smuggling. Good class brandy and silks were both in high demand. As war with Napoleon stretched on and on for what seemed years, so the demand for good class brandy increased, for war or no war Aaron carried on smuggling. He was classed as the finest smuggler along the South Coast. There was hardly an inlet or small out of the way harbour on both sides of the channel that Aaron wasn't familiar with.

The best advice he was given by his father was "To trade only in the best. Don't risk your life bringing in rubbish." The advice was well borne out for he supplied all the best hotels and taverns in the city, amongst them 'The Dolphin', 'The George' and the 'Sally Port' hotels, all patronised by high ranking naval officers including the great man himself, Lord Nelson.

With the war dragging on and on Aaron, much to the relief of his clients, seemed to bear a charmed life. When warned of dangers by his friends, Aaron only laughed and with a tankard of brandy in his hand would shout, "Crossing the Channel these days is no more dangerous than walking down the filthy disease ridden streets of Portsea." He knew what he was talking about, for he had often been forced to draw the slender sword he always carried at his side. The streets, lit only by the weak lights spouting from the tavern, were the stamping ground for every crook and cut-throat. It abounded in prostitutes working from every tavern and dark alley. But the greatest danger came from the notorious press gangs.

Open sewers failed to cope with the refuse thrown from windows, and the corpses of dead dogs and cats were left to rot in the streets with rats feeding on the gas filled bodies. Without warning, an unsuspecting pedestrian could find himself deluged with stinking slops thrown from an upper window and with no redress. Anyone daring to complain would be met with a volley of abuse or worse still physical violence.

Not a street corner was without a tavern of sorts and most of the houses were drinking dens or brothels. With the war in progress it wasn't so bad, as there was more work in the dockyard where most of the locals were employed. The local prostitutes plied their trade quite openly, often for a tankard of rum or gin and would greet passing men with "Drop me kecks for sixpence sailor." And somewhere in the noisy background someone would retaliate with, "You don't wear kecks Moll". Causing an outburst of merriment from the crowd and a rude gesture from Molly.

Dark moonless nights were the favourite times for the press gangs. With the war in progress the demands for seamen were higher than usual. The gang was often led by a Petty Officer or Junior Officer. The technique was to seal off one of the narrow streets at each end and then systematically search every tavern until they filled their quota. A stranger stood as little chance as a snowball in hell. Plied with cheap rum or gin by some unscrupulous landlord until he was legless and too drunk to move, the victim would be dragged unceremoniously through the filth laden streets. Thrown into the bottom of the ship's boat beached at Sally port he would be rowed out to a man-of-war at anchor at Spithead, his life at the mercy of some sadistic Petty Officer with a knotted rope's end in his hand.

For the next two, three or maybe four years he would be at the mercy of the petty officers, ship's officers, and a ship's Captain who held the power of life and death of every member of the ship's crew in his hands. A virtual prisoner with no reward he would live on a starvation diet of salt beef (which could be horse meat if bought from an unscrupulous supplier) supplemented by hard-tack biscuits, often inhabited by families of weevils, and on occasions some mushy peas.

Then there was naval discipline with over one hundred statutes on the books that carried a death penalty at the jurisdiction of the ship's Captain alone. A man's back could be scoured with the cat-o'-nine-tails until his ribs became exposed just for looking at an officer in an insubordinate manner. Was it any wonder that men preferred prison to life on a floating hell?

The word spread like wildfire when a ship was about to sail. The Captain would have to make up a crew and the press gangs were sent out. The regulars had their own exits and Aaron was no exception. He supplied his favourite tavern with good quality brandy, in turn the landlord had, with the help of a shipwright, built a secret cupboard on the tavern's landing. Six feet long, three feet wide and two feet high, secured from the inside by a series of strong bolts which he forced into place when he was safely inside. The landlord kept the coffin like structure in good condition and the bolts well oiled.

Of all the doxies that frequented the taverns Aaron's favourite was Polly an intelligent girl forced into prostitution as most of the girls were, by poverty. In her late teens, she had penetrating brown eyes; her hair, when washed, was a striking blonde with a figure that turned men's heads. It was she that tucked Aaron into his safe cubby hole and it was she that always gave the all clear by three sharp taps followed by two harder taps. Tonight was no exception, he emerged from his bolt hole sweating and gasping for air.

"They were a long time tonight Polly. Looked like they were searching for someone special." Little did he realise at the time it was himself that was the main target.

"One of these days your number will be up Aaron, you would be a great prize for them." Her voice filled with concern, for she too had a soft place for Aaron.

Aaron's perpetual grin turned into a raucous laugh that echoed through the now deserted tavern. The press gang could clear a tavern faster than if lightening struck.

"That will be the day Polly." He gave her a playful slap on her bottom and banged his pewter tankard on the liquor stained pine table causing the other empty tankards to leap in the air. "Fill her up Polly, come on get that arse over to the barrel." He cast a long lingering look at her swaying bottom as she sauntered across the tavern, thinking she would be much prettier if she washed more regularly and took more care of her hair. It was naturally wavy but now it hung in long strands around her shoulders. Frequently, as with other tavern girls, it wasn't unusual to see families of lice exploring the long strands. So prolific were the lice in Polly's hair that at one time, much to the amusement of the other drinkers, he poured a tankard of good quality brandy over her head. When they realised what he had used, their amusement quickly turned to disgust.

"Polly!" Aaron shouted, his legs wide apart and stretched under the table. "The tavern stinks, the street stinks, Portsmouth and the whole harbour stinks, worse of all you stink. Go and get washed, have a bath in the sea. Then if you are a good girl and you haven't got the pox since the last time I was here, you can come and stay on my ship for a few days."

Living aboard Aaron's boat was the highlight of her life. It wasn't very big but the cabin was warm and he always ate the best food. The only thing she detested was the morning swim, both summer and winter. Aaron would strip and dive over the stern, he never seemed to feel the cold and when she was aboard he expected her to do the same. She always made some form of protest.

"Away with you Aaron, it's bitter cold tonight – want me to catch my death of cold? I had a bath in March, don't you remember you tipped me off the end of your boat?"

"It's September now Polly." He laughed. Polly was an exception, he had sought the favours of very many women, but Polly was the only one that was allowed on his ship. He was fond of her and she had saved him from being robbed on more than one occasion and from the press gangs. But she was right, with her woman's intuition, one of these days he would be taken. Tonight for example, he only made it to his bolt hole with seconds to spare. The Press came tumbling through the front door just as he secured the bolts from inside his coffin-like structure.

It was an hour since the Press invaded the tavern and the regulars started to return, cursing that their drinking time had been so rudely interrupted. "See they took old Clements tonight, must be fifty if he's a day." A pock marked sailor sitting across from Aaron shouted to another seaman at the far end of the tavern. "He won't last long that one, he's got the lung fever, spitting up blood by the bucket full." He exaggerated.

"Them navy bastards won't worry about that so long as they get their quota. If the bloody lung fever don't get him, the bloody Frenchies will." Clements was soon dismissed from their minds as they got down to serious drinking, safe in the knowledge that they were unlikely to be disturbed by the press again that night.

Polly brought Aaron another tankard of ale laced with his best brandy, a bottle kept under the counter just for his private use. He tipped it back, emptying it without taking a pause or deep breath, then slammed the tankard down on the liquor stained table. He caught Polly round her tiny waist and planted a kiss firmly on her ruby lips. He clamped her hand tightly in his and pulled her towards the door. She made a limp show of protest but enjoyed every minute of it. She knew what was to come before he allowed her on his ship, but the cold bath in the sea water for a few days freedom from the tavern and prostituting her body would be worth it. He led her into the street amid a volley of ribald remarks from the other drinkers.

Drunks rolled past, most of them seamen from a large merchant that docked recently and had been lucky enough to dodge the press gang. They were singing and dancing followed by women calling out after them. "Drop them for sixpence sailor." Often receiving a slap across the face or a curse. A dog ran towards them yelping at a drunken sailor's leg, he lashed out, catching the dog with his boot and sending it scuttling down the road. Several young women and children accosted Aaron willing to sell their souls for a few coppers for food for the baby or a bottle of gin to release themselves from this misery for a few hours.

Polly was still putting up a formal protest and making a negative effort to hold back. A chill wind was blowing. It wasn't quite autumn yet but the signs were there, leaves blew along the street and there was a haze around the moon. The sky was cloudless and the stars looked brighter than usual. But Aaron's well stocked cabin had that French cheese which Polly adored and that beautiful French wine. What was a dip in the sea compared to that? She couldn't let him see she was going to give in easily, she still struggled. The warm boat beckoned, the good food beckoned and so did the best brandy and wine.

At times her feet slid beneath the shingle along the fore-shore and Aaron impatiently pulled her arms, on towards the Castle so prominent on the sea front. Fed up with her struggling he lifted her as if she were as light as a sack of feathers and threw her over his shoulder, smacking her bottom occasionally as she complained about the rough treatment. Two drunken soldiers shouted out what they thought was good advice to Aaron. Polly retaliated with mouthfuls of abuse usually only heard in their barracks. When it came to swearing there wasn't a sailor or soldier that could match her. Aaron slapped her bottom once more, "Stop that swearing Polly." He broke into a steady trot.

She protested, "My tits hurt Aaron, you are squashing the bloody things."

Completely ignoring her protests he didn't stop jogging until they reached the entrance to Langstone harbour where his dinghy was hidden in amongst the gorse bushes. He dragged it clear until the bows were in the water then lifting Polly he walked into the sea up to his knees and dropped her into the cold water. She screamed as he put his hands on her head and submerged her completely. She came up spluttering. "Aaron you bastard, the bloody water is freezing."

He answered her protests with another push under water, then pulled her ashore. "Now take those filthy clothes off."

Her teeth were chattering as she stood there, the sea water glistening over her naked body. He took a bottle from his top pocket and poured brandy over her head. "Cup your hands Polly then wash round that little Mary of yours."

7

"No Aaron no, that burns like hell and it's a waste of good brandy." She cringed in terror holding both hands between her legs. She was turning blue with cold.

"Come on Polly clean yourself, you are not bringing any of those crabs onto my ship."

Polly's objections fell on deaf ears, he knew it was all sham. To go aboard his vessel for a few days she would go through hell and high water. He poured the brandy over her head again and made her hold her cupped hand forward then made sure she rubbed it where he wanted it rubbed, Polly spluttering protests all the time the operation was in progress. Satisfied she had washed thoroughly he handed her the bottle, she took a long drink then wiped the back of her hand across her mouth. The fiery liquid brought life back into her naked body. He threw his heavy top coat over her shoulders then lifted her into the small dinghy.

Chapter Two

Aaron, competent sailor that he was, let the tide do the work. Rowing in to midstream the current swept the bows of the dinghy round and carried it into the harbour at break neck speed. He only touched the oars now and again to bring the dinghy round into the fast current. Like the French coast where he knew every small harbour and inlet, so he was familiar with the South Coast and especially Langstone harbour. Almost the twin sister of Portsmouth harbour, he knew every nook and cranny and when he wasn't smuggling across the Channel he hid his ship in one of the many inlets. Just when Polly thought the boat would be swept up on the furthermost foreshore, he grabbed the oars and propelled it to where his ship was hidden from view from the land side and most of the seaward side of the harbour itself. They bumped alongside his lugger to be greeted by a tired voice from inside the cabin.

"Is that you cap'n?"

"Of course it's me, who the hell do you think it was, old Nick himself?"

A youth of eighteen came running on deck and caught the rope end Aaron passed up to him. When he saw Polly sitting in the bows, his heart sank. He knew he would have to move out of the warm cabin and into the small cubby hole where the spare sails and ships ropes were kept.

Willie was the only other member of the crew, and had been since he was twelve years old. Aaron had found him

begging for pennies in the narrow streets round the dockyard.. He was being set on by several elder boys when
Aaron waded in and rescued him.

"Go on son," he gave him a shilling, "go home to your
mom and get that bloodied face seen to."

"I got no mom sir, no home. I sleep in any doorway 'til I
gets kicked out."

There was something about this boy that Aaron took an
instant liking to – beneath that filth a small boy lurked.
He was alone on his boat and sometimes he felt the loneliness.

"Why haven't they caught you for the navy, you would
make a good powder monkey." At this suggestion the lad
shied away from Aaron.

"I run too fast for the Press men sir."

Aaron laughed. "I don't blame you lad, wouldn't you like
to work on a ship?"

"Yes sir, but not a navy ship. I manage here sir, I fetch
things for people and earn money and sometimes they give
me food and the tavern bosses give me a tankard of ale
and I help myself to the scraps when I help them to clean
up."

It was obvious the boy had never known what a real home
was or been shown any kindness. It was over a meal at
Aaron's favourite tavern that he learnt the truth about the
boy. From a filthy cellar that spelled home he had been
battered and bruised by a drunken mother and father – if
he really knew who his real father was, the situation
changed so many times since he was born. One day a 'new'
father, drunk as usual, gave his mother an ultimatum –
"Either he goes or I go", he shouted to his mother. The
speech was slurred and his blood-shot eyes frightened
Willie so much he didn't wait for his mother's answer, but
shot out of the basement room as fast as his feet would
carry him. He hadn't seen his mother from that day until
this.

After the meal Aaron walked him down Queen Street, a
street filled with brothels, grog shops, tailors and slop
merchants. Aaron took him to a friend that kept a slop
shop, a small Jew who sat cross legged on a table at the far

end of the shop. The shop itself was a cavern of worn clothing. Suits and coats hung from the ceiling, piled on shelves and where there was no more shelf space they were piled on the floor and in old sea chests. Every available space was taken up with old clothes.

"Fix the lad up with clothes Samuel."

"Why, Hello ...." he looked at the rags hanging from the boy, "I hope you are not expecting an allowance on this stuff Aaron." Holding the boy's coat by the shoulder, between this thumb and finger, he pulled a face to show his disgust.

Aaron, always happy to join a joke shook his head.

"No Samuel, I think the best thing to do is give the lad a good wash and see what he looks like under the dirt." At the sound of the word wash, the boy shrank away but Aaron blocked his exit. They took him out into the cobbled back yard where a massive iron water pump stood in the centre. It looked like a gallows to the boy as they stripped him and stood him under the pump. Aaron worked the handle up and down until the water shot out in powerful jets, Samuel washed him thoroughly. They fixed him up with new clothes. It was the first new clothes Willie had ever owned.

"Aint a lot of meat on the lad Aaron. What are you going to do with him?"

"I can't let him starve, he wants to work on a ship. He might just as well come with me, we'll soon get some meat on him."

From that day Aaron became Willie's hero, they were inseparable. He hardly ever went ashore and was quite contented living aboard and keeping the ship clean and the tiny cabin bore testimony to that. The small iron stove used for cooking and heating shone like burnished steel. The floor was scrubbed daily as was the ship's deck. Willie was a quick learner, and Aaron taught him to read and write just as his father taught him. He was also learning to speak French and navigation. The cabin was small and oozed warmth. A double bunk ran along one wall, Aaron's father had it built just before he brought his wife aboard. Two shelves above the bed were packed with books of every description. There was also a bed on the far side that folded up when Willie wasn't using it. A table that folded down in the centre, two chairs and two cupboards, one for food, always well stocked, and the other for their clothes were the only other furniture. A huge brass oil lamp hung from the ceiling and another lamp lay above Aaron's bed.

"Shall I move into the sail locker, Captain?"

"Well you can't stop and watch me and Polly. Off you jolly well go Willie."

Willie scooped up his blankets while Polly stripped off the top coat of Aaron's which she wore, "You stop looking at me Willie, you're too young to look at my naked body."

"I seen a naked lady before. I slept with Emma, that dark haired wench."

"Yes and I bet you got the pox from her." Polly bated him, "Everyone knows Emma's poxed up to her eyeballs."

"I got no pox," Willie's face reddened, "Emma's a nice girl."

"She can't be all that nice if she only charges threepence."

"She don't charge threepence – She charges two shillings."

"You been done Willie, everyone knows threepence is her going rate."

Willie was well acquainted with all the hell holes in old Portsea, but to be done by a prostitute for a shilling or so was the last straw. He glared at Polly then grabbed his blankets and, kicking the folding bed into place, rushed from the cabin.

"You shouldn't egg him on Polly, Willie is very sensitive," Aaron laughed, "I doubt if he would know what to do with a woman."

"Don't you believe it Aaron, kids where he comes from know what to do with it from the day they get their first erection."

Polly stood completely naked and unabashed, the faint light from the oil lamp from behind catching her golden hair and creating a halo around her head. Aaron caught her round the waist and ran his fingers over her flawless skin sending a shuddering sensation through her body.

"I don't know why you have to sell your body in those taverns, Polly."

"What else is there for me Aaron? You don't think I like that life do you, those men give me the damn creeps, I always try and think of something else while they paw my body. Why don't you let me come and live aboard here Aaron when you go smuggling? I could cook your meals and do your washing."

"Smuggling is no job for a lady Polly. If we ever get caught they would send you to prison and more than likely transport you. Believe me you would soon wish you were back in the taverns of Portsea."

"Your father took your mother when he went on his smuggling trips."

She had a point there, he never knew his mother but she really must have been some lady. His father told him so much about her there wasn't a thing he didn't know. When his father talked about his mother his voice became subdued and tears would rise in his eyes. No, they were both gone, buried together in Mile End cemetery.

At twelve years of age Polly had been put into service at a big house in the better part of the town. She was already showing signs of her forthcoming beauty, spreading out in the right places. The eyes of the lecherous old owner fell upon her, and from the first day she was hotly pursued by him, and he could run in spite of being in his late sixties. He promised her everything but she was still very innocent. Finally, catching her bending over a bed, he'd walked silently across the room and took her from behind. She had ran screaming to his wife, who wouldn't believe her and threatened to take her to a magistrate who would send her to prison for telling such dreadful lies about her husband, a respected citizen and former mayor. That same night she ran away and went home to her mother, she wouldn't believe her either and threw her out on the street. The shilling a week the lady had given them was stopped and her mother had another mouth to feed. From that day Polly lived by her wits and eventually fell into the same fate as many young girls in the town – prostitution.

"Well I can't take you smuggling Polly, the risks are too great." He started undressing. "One day Polly I shall have a decent merchant ship of my own. I don't want to do this smuggling all my life. When I do get my ship you can be a permanent member of the crew."

It was a dream that Aaron had nursed all his life, to own a decent merchant ship. He dreamt about it, not a large ship but a decent size. Every penny he made from smuggling he would save. Sometimes he would visit various shipyards watching the price of merchant ships both new and old. A new one he preferred, but he knew he would never be able to afford that. One day he was certain he would become a proud ship owner. It was his sole ambition, he lived ships, dreamt about them and whenever he passed a merchant man outward bound to some far eastern port or for an Atlantic crossing, he would positively drool imagining himself at the wheel.

Aaron was the first on deck the following morning. A heavy mist shrouded the harbour and the rising sun gave the scene a ghostly appearance. Gulls screamed overhead, and he could faintly hear the cockle gatherers on the beach talking to each other. The tide was on its way out. If he wanted his early dip he would have to be quick about it, the ship would be high and dry stranded on the mud channel within the hour. He lowered himself over the side then dropped the foot or so, digging his hands into the mud bank and wiping it all over his body, before he slid beneath the water. On deck he didn't dry himself straight away but jumped up and down on the deck before rubbing himself down with a dry cloth.

"Come on Polly, get up and have a good wash down." He smacked the lump beneath the blankets, only to get a mouthful of abuse from beneath.

The fire was soon roaring up the stove-pipe chimney spreading the heat across the small cabin. He made three pots of coffee, gave one to Polly then wandered back on deck after handing one to Willie secured under a pile of blankets and canvas in the small cubby hole.

Aaron sat alone on deck for an hour before he heard Willie coming on deck, shivering and rubbing his arms, the cold morning air biting into his bare chest. He would have loved to emulate his hero, Aaron, by having a dip in the sea, fortunately for him the tide was right out now. The ship itself was upright, held firm in a cradle of thick gooey mud secured in a cast iron grip.

"Did you hear that Captain, someone shouting from the shore." Willie was relieving himself over the stern of the ship. Aaron strained his ears, there were few people that knew exactly where his ship was hidden, so he could only assume it was some friend. It was five more minutes before they heard the shout, much clearer now. He hollered back and a torrent of words came from the shore, all jumbled up. They could hardly make it out, but it sounded very urgent.

"Look Willie, wade through the mud and go and see what it's all about, it sounds like some kind of warning."

"I meant to tell you Captain, there was a lot of activity about in the harbour, the revenue men and the navy were all over the place. Two naval ships were guarding the entrance to the harbour."

"Well I didn't see them and we came right in from the main entrance. Go ashore and see what it's all about Willie."

He watched Willie ease himself over the side of the ship, his legs sinking into the mud just below the knees. Each step was difficult and hard, the mud clinging to his legs then releasing it with a loud sucking noise. He vanished into the mist and although the shore was less than a hundred yards away it was over an hour before Willie returned. He sat down on the cabin top exhausted and fighting for breath, panting he eventually gasped out.

"They are after you Aaron, not the revenue men, the navy, they are offering a reward for information as to your whereabouts."

"What the hell do the navy want me for? The navy men are no pals of mine. What else did he have to say Willlie?"

"They are offering a reward of five guineas for your whereabouts."

"Five guineas, why a man in these parts would sell his soul for that. The best thing we can do is get far away from here, as soon as the tide turns and we have enough sea room beneath us we will make a move. Thank God my father knew this harbour and all these inlets, now the tide

15

is out and in this channel and with these high mud banks no one can see us from the shore. Better put that fire out Willie, we don't want the smoke giving us away. This harbour is treacherous with all these inlets and the way that tide changes around, they won't take many chances."

Polly was more scared than the both of them. "I thought that press gang was acting strange last night Aaron, they were looking for someone special, they wouldn't give a name."

"Well... they wouldn't would they? If they had done so, it would have warned me off. We will try and make a run for it when we are afloat after dark."

To Willie, being chased by the revenue men was a bit of a game. He knew Aaron could outwit and outrun them. But this was the navy, and it must be serious. They would never go to this trouble just for a pressed man. He had already learned that anyone fraternising with the enemy could be hung as a traitor and Aaron went in and out of the French harbours like a man on a pleasure cruise. Perhaps that's what they wanted him for, thinking he was a spy and were going to hang him.

"Let's get far away Captain. How about the small bay down in Cornwall? That place we sheltered when we were blown off course. They will never find us down there."

"Maybe Willie, but we have to get out of here first." He stopped suddenly and held his hand up for silence. They heard a boat passing in a deeper channel, they could distinctly make out the sound of the oars splashing in the water.

"They ain't there sir, that channel is high and dry and no ship could pass in there." The rowing stopped and they listened to the crew talking to each other, it seemed like hours before they heard the talking fade away, yet it couldn't have been more than twenty minutes. Willie's face had turned a dark shade of red through holding his breath for as long as possible.

"Do you think Wilkins told them where you are Captain?"

"I shouldn't think so Willie, Wilkins loves my brandy and it's not very likely he would warn me, then tell the bastards where we are. No, I don't think there is any danger from Wilkins. Over the months he earns more than five guineas from me running my brandy to my customers."

"Look Willie," Aaron's voice sounded more serious, "we only have two or three bottles aboard, you know where the rest of the brandy is stored. Now should I get taken you can sell the brandy a bottle at a time to buy food. Polly can stay with you 'til I return, but as soon as we can we'll make a dash for it."

"No Captain, if they take you I want to come too. If you are going to be hanged I am just as guilty."

This ship was the only home Willie knew and Aaron his only friend, he would sooner be dead than lose both at the same time. He could never go back to the life on the streets and gutters of Portsea.

Although Aaron was flattered he rebuffed Willie, "Don't be bloody stupid, they don't want to hang me, perhaps they want me to teach those itey-titey officers of theirs to navigate." He went below again to cut himself a thick slice of cheese and a hunk of bread. Polly and Willie followed him down.

"Come on you two, cheer up, they haven't caught me yet and believe me, I will give them a real chase for their money." He slapped Willie between the shoulder blades and laughed, trying to make light of the situation. "Nip on deck Willie and keep an eye on things."

Chapter Three

Polly was walking around the cabin dressed in a pair of Aaron's baggy trousers cut down to fit her and a loose white shirt. The sky pitted with cloud and the sun was bright, one of those rare September days. Willie had been laying in bed, he went on deck to join Aaron. The tide was already on the turn and the sea water just lapping along the keel.

Several times they heard boats rowing past in the deeper channel and within hailing distance. There was no need to warn each other to be quiet, they stopped talking instinctively. With more sea water rapidly filling the inlets there seemed to be more activity, it became a cat and mouse game.

Aaron was sat deep in thought on deck assessing the situation, suddenly and without warning a face appeared above the hull. Aaron sprang to his feet, surprised and a little fearful. Not many people knew the whereabouts of his ship and it was minutes before he recognised him as one of the cockle gatherers. It was obvious the man had risked the dangers of the incoming tide to seek them out. The temptation of the reward was too good to miss. Aaron gave the man his hand and hoisted him on deck, water from his wet trousers legs spilling onto the deck.

"I heard someone shouting you and thought I had better warn you."

"What's it all about Mitchell? Why the Navy and the revenue men?" If Mitchell came to warn him, Aaron knew he was in serious trouble, for he was no Samaritan. He was the type of man that would sell his own mother for a few pounds and watch her hang. He had waded out to search out the situation, and to benefit his own ends. Aaron fired several questions at him and was convinced of his guilt. Mitchell put one leg over the side to drop back into the rising water.

"They're after you Aaron, I thought it was my duty to warn you," he lied, "It's the navy Aaron. It's them that wants your blood and the revenue men are glad to help to get shot of you. To them you're a pain in the side. Don't worry Aaron, my lips are sealed, you are safe as far as I am concerned."

"Good lad Mitchell and thanks for going to all that trouble. Have a tankard of brandy with me before you go, you must be freezing with those wet trousers on."

"You know me Aaron, we cockle gatherers are used to the cold water, and the tide is on the way in. Perhaps the next time." He hesitated, Aaron only shipped-in the best brandies and wines from France – not that gut rot they sold in the taverns. He ran his fingers through the stubble round his chin and licked his lips. Free brandy and only the best, the real sort he couldn't afford to buy. A cunning glint crept into the corners of his eyes as he spied the bottle of brandy Aaron was holding in his hand. Fortunately he didn't see the heavy wooden stake held tightly in his other hand behind his back, just in case of a refusal to return to the deck. Mitchell ran his fingers through his stubble once more and licked his lips. Who knows, perhaps someone had already warned the navy, better a bird in the hand than two in the bush. "Aye Aaron, just a tot to warm me old innards."

"Don't worry about the tide Mitchell, it was damn good of you to come out here to warn me. The tide is rising, Willie will row you ashore. Go and pick Mitchell's sack of cockles up Willie, they are by the side of the ship. Give Mr Mitchell another drink of brandy." He tossed the bottle to Willie, who deftly caught it with one hand. "A decent drink Willie, he's chilled to the bone."

Willie filled the tankard with brandy as Mitchell's greedy

eyes fell on the bottle and the tip of his tongue rolled across his lips. He drank greedily, at the third tankard his brain becoming confused and his suspicions growing. It was rare he met with such generosity. His eyes fell on Polly as if just noticing her for the first time and he leaned forward, closer for a better look down her ill fitting shirt, her breasts prominent.

"Nice to see you Polly, you look fine." If he hadn't been looking through bleary drink sodden eyes he would have known he was seeing her fresh and clean, the cleanest she had been for a very long time. She gave him one of her pleasant business smiles. In gratitude he took a long drink from the brandy and belched straight into her face. She got the full blast of his evil smelling breath.

"Much about Aaron?"

"Enough Mitchell, quite enough." He peered down into Mitchell's empty tankard. "Fill his tankard Willie, we can't have our guests going round town saying we aren't sociable, not after Mitchell waded out here to warn us, that just won't do, fill the tankard right to the top." Aaron shook his head. Mitchell placed his hand over the top of the tankard and made a feeble protest, then took it away as Willie held the second bottle over it, free brandy he couldn't refuse and he certainly knew how to hold it. He had drunk enough to make two ordinary men paralytic. After all it was free booze, what's more it was the best that money could buy.

To prove he was sociable and to belay any fears that he was getting him drunk on purpose, Aaron held the bottle to his lips to make believe he was drinking, then burped loudly to prove his point. "Drink up Mitchell, there's plenty more where that came from."

"It's great Aaron, bloody great." He went to grab the bottle from Willie, missed the bottle and grabbing fresh air, lurched forward. Willie held his hand and wrapped it round the bottle, then guided it towards his mouth where it dribbled down Mitchell's chin. His eyes refused to focus. "Thanks Willie." He swayed to and fro on the edge of the bed. "Where's me bloody cockles Willie?"

"Don't worry Mitchell I will put them in the dinghy when

we go ashore." Willie answered. He couldn't quite understand what Aaron was about, two bottle of his very best brandy, the brandy he kept for his own personal use letting a rascal like Mitchell drink it. Not drink it, to relish the flavour, but to gulp it down like a pig that hadn't been fed for days.

"Thanks Willie." Mitchell made to rise from the edge of the bunk but his knees gave way and slowly, with a stupid grin on his face, he sank to the floor. He made one more desperate effort to get to his feet, his fuddled brain sensing something was wrong – but he was too far gone. He pitched forward across the small cabin and his chin hit the iron stove, blood spurting from the wound on his chin and another deep cut in his mouth. Polly cleaned the wound up, Mitchell was out stone cold and they lifted him onto the bed.

"There we are." Aaron said, a satisfied smirk on his face. "Get under weigh Willie, you keep an eye on him Polly, if he comes round pour more brandy into him. If the navy wants Aaron Jacobs they have got him, a bit under the weather you may say, but by the time he comes round we will be at a safe anchorage. What about that place over the Isle of Wight Willie, that little cove we dodged in when the revenue chased us?"

They had sufficient water under them to make it to a deeper channel. Negotiating the treacherous tides and mud banks was child's play to Aaron. Many a time he allowed the revenue to chase him only to leave them high and dry and fuming at the mouth. The stories of his exploits with the revenue were almost folk lore. It was said he could feel his way around by the pressure of the water under his hull.

Cautiously they moved towards the open water where the navy and revenue men would be waiting. The sky filling with heavy cloud, it started to drizzle, a fine rain that sank into their clothing. "Just the right weather for smuggling, eh Willie?"

Willie's eyes, sharper than a cat's in the dark, scanned the harbour. They hoisted the main sail and the fresh breeze filled it with a loud resounding crack. The lugger's bows lifted and they surged forward like a race horse on exercise across open moors. They were instantly spotted and several small boats took up the challenge, like a pack of hounds picking up the scent of a fox. Twice the revenue cutters came within hailing distance but each time he gave them the slip.

They stood at the narrow entrance to the harbour. The lugger had a very small draft and he swung it towards the shore, no navy ship would come in that close. But he hadn't reckoned just how desperate the navy was. The navy ship was less than two hundred yards away, there was a puff of white smoke from one of the gun ports followed by a screech that almost deafened them as a ball passed overhead just missing the mast by inches. The navy ship sailed past – this was Aaron's chance. He sailed in closer and sped between the gap of the ship and the shore. A voice shouted over the narrow distance. "Lugger ahoy, pull alongside or my next shot will be right through your hull."

"Alright Willie, we've made a bit of a show, better go and tell the Captain down below the navy wants him to be their guest. But make sure Willie, that he's pissed out of his tiny mind."

"He's alright Captain, his wife is down there with him and she's crying her eyes out. He's out bloody cold. He won't come round 'til the morning Captain." Willie reported back on deck just as a small pinnace pulled alongside. A young midshipman, half a dozen burly seaman, and a petty officer crowded the small deck of the lugger.

"Are you Captain Jacobs?" The young midshipman asked, a small sword in his hand and trying to adopt an authoritative manner. Aaron didn't think he was old enough to shave and he looked a damn sight younger by the side of the Petty Officer and the seamen.

"No, he's down below, blind drunk and if I were you I wouldn't disturb him, he's like a bloody mad man when he is drunk, he's a violent temper. What the hell do you want him for?"

"None of your damn business." He pushed past them and went below, Polly was sitting at the edge of the bed stroking Mitchell's face and pretending to cry.

"Is that Captain Jacobs?"

Polly threw herself over Mitchell tears rolling down her face. "Oh don't take him away," she screamed. "Please don't take him away. What is to become of us if you take him." She dropped to the floor and threw her arms round the midshipman's legs pleading with him not to take her dear husband. "He wouldn't hurt a fly sir." The tears ran down her cheeks.

The midshipman pushed her roughly away. "Get out of my way you bitch. The navy wants him and he must go, now get out of my way or I will have my men to throw you overboard."

Two heavily built sailors under the guidance of the Petty Officer lifted the unconscious Mitchell from the bunk and carried him on deck.

"His breath sir.... I wouldn't mind a bottle of what he's been drinking." One of the seamen remarked.

"Get on with it Peddy. Get the blighter aboard the pinnace, we have wasted too much time here as it is." They threw Mitchell into the bottom of the pinnace and without another word pushed the boat away from the lugger.

"Right Willie, now they have taken our poor Captain away you had better get down below and let's get some food inside us, I'm starving. And you Polly, that was a fine bit of acting, I was almost believing you were real. How did you do it?"

"I made believe it was you Aaron." She burst out laughing. "Heaven help you Aaron when they find they have the wrong man. And when Mitchell comes round and ever gets his hands on you he will kill you. I wouldn't like to have that head of his when he wakes up in the morning aboard some man-o-war."

They sailed into the open sea and rounded the Isle of Wight anchoring off shore, waiting for the tide to make for the hidden cove. It was difficult to negotiate at any time but not even Aaron, with his knowledge of the area, dare try in the dark. Once they entered the cove he had to bring the tiller round hard, it was like a sharp elbow but once there they would be hidden from the sea and any passing ship. They could only be seen from the cliff tops. Should they have to make a hurried exit, the cove had plenty of water beneath them at any state of the tide. They could stay there indefinitely, having plenty of food aboard that could be eked out with Mitchell's cockles.

Peace reigned supreme for two days. The weather was cold and crisp but stayed dry. Aaron was planning to do a smuggling run in three or four days and Willie became excited at the prospect. Each morning Polly and Willie walked along the foreshore for driftwood and she often went to the village some four miles away to replenish the food stocks. It was then that she must have been spotted as a stranger in the area, which always commanded attention. She learned that word had gotten around of Aaron's escape from the navy's traps and was followed back to the lugger without noticing anyone trailing her. The reward had risen to ten guineas. "Bloody hell Aaron, ten guineas, that's a king's ransom to any poor man round here."

"Don't worry Polly, we will be away from here in two or three days' time. You can stop in the Isle of Wight, and have money to stay in a tavern. When we come back we will make straight for this cove."

"Can't I come with you Aaron, just this once, I will make myself useful. If those navy men catch me they will know I helped you, it was me that pretended I was Mitchell's husband, please Aaron, take me with you."

Polly kept on and on to be allowed to go with him to France, all that afternoon and right through dinner, getting into bed she kept on and on. "There is nothing to lose Aaron, if the navy catch me here they will send me to prison and if you get caught smuggling I will go to prison."

Fed up with her begging he eventually gave in. "Oh alright Polly, but understand this, you didn't ask to come – I made you – and you stick to that story if we do get caught."

"Alright Aaron." Her face lit up and throwing her arms round his neck, she pushed him down on the bed and kept kissing his face and neck. Going smuggling with Aaron had been her one ambition ever since she first met him and the thought of going to France and seeing real

Frenchmen filled her with excitement.

But it had all been to no avail.

Aaron was the first to hear the footsteps running across the deck above his head. He sat up in bed just as the cabin door swung open with a crash and the same midshipman they encountered before came tumbling down the three steps into the cabin. A drawn sword and an angry look on his face, quickly followed by two brawny seamen and a petty officer completely filling the small cabin. "You bastard Jacobs!" The midshipman shouted. The petty officer moved forward and grabbed Aaron by the neck and pulled him from the bunk sending him flying across the cabin. "You tricked me you bastard and made me the laughing stock of the whole ship!" He hit him across the face with the back of his hand leaving a red wheal. "I will give it to you for making a damn fool out of me."

"Leave him be!" Polly screamed. She sat up crying and covered her bare breasts with the blankets.

"Leave him be." The midshipman mocked, "If the Admiralty didn't want him I would run this bloody sword right through him. And you, you bitch, you said the other man was your husband and he was the Captain. I have a good mind to take you with us and hand you over to the magistrates in Portsea – sling you in gaol where you belong. You people are scum." He threw Aaron his clothes. "Get dressed." He turned to the Petty Officer. "As soon as he is dressed tie his hands and feet and then get him into our own pinnace, the sooner we get back to the ship the better."

Aaron started to protest, the midshipman turned sharply and slapped his hand across Aaron's mouth, "Shut that mouth you animal, you almost had me court martialled. As it is you made a damn fool out of me in front of the officers and ship's crew. They warned me you were an ugly bastard – that man Mitchell was ugly, but not as ugly as you – I should have known I had the wrong man."

He was hoisted unceremoniously up the three steps onto the deck, Willie was waiting there. "You know my orders Willie, I leave you in charge." But his conversation was cut short by the bullying Petty Officer who gave him a rough push in the small of his back. The Petty Officer whispered in Aaron's ear. "I would hate to be in your shoes Jacobs, if that man Mitchell gets you. He's threatened to kill you the minute he claps eyes on you. He sails this week for the West Indies and the Captain of his ship is reputed to be the biggest bastard in the navy. He makes Captain Bligh look like a children's nanny – his nick-name is 'Nine-Tails Jimmy' – gives a man ten strokes just for looking at him. And he's madder than usual because he was hoping his ship was going to join Nelson's fleet. You might be in luck, the fever is so bad out there, it may get Mitchell before he gets you."

Chapter Four

After being bundled into a ship's pinnace Aaron was rowed out to a Frigate anchored off Spithead and spent the first night there in a small cabin guarded outside the door by a ship's marine. A hot meal was served late in the afternoon. This puzzled him even more – it couldn't be a press gang that's for sure. He lay on the bunk pondering the happenings over the past three days.

First they had scoured the town searching every tavern and known brothel. Sure that he wasn't there, they had turned their attention to the small harbours along the South coast haunts they knew he frequented. They had been desperate to offer a reward, and this was quickly doubled. They must have had an inkling he was hidden in Langstone Harbour, but that had so many creeks they eventually sealed off this and the surrounding harbours. Their most desperate act had been to request the revenue men to help search for him – and desperate they must have been – for there was no love lost between the revenue men and the navy.

A marine sergeant bought a tankard of ale into the cabin, Aaron plied him with questions, it was a waste of breath. The sergeant's lips were sealed tighter than a monk that had taken a vow of silence, either he couldn't answer because he knew nothing or both the sergeant and the marine sentries were warned not to open their mouths.

The night dragged on, Aaron a heavy sleeper normally just dozed off for an hour or so at a time but the slightest movement on the ship and he was wide awake. The ship's bell, at change of watches, sounded like the bells of St. Paul echoing right through the ship. No one was more happy to see the grey light of dawn than Aaron, at least this day would reveal the fate the Navy had in store for him.

After a good breakfast and a clean up he was taken ashore in the ship's cutter towards Portsmouth dockyard. He was helped up a flight of slippery seaweed and moss covered stone steps to the quayside where an escort of four marines and a sergeant waited for him. Then marched to a large building under the curious gaze of the dockyard workers. The marine sergeant unlocked a heavy oak door and invited Aaron to enter. The room was sparsely furnished with a large wooden table scrubbed white and four chairs, a cot in one corner, and a large open fireplace with a thick pine log burning spilling out warmth all over the room. The one window in the room was so high it was impossible to see outside.

"There you are Mr Jacobs, you have to stay here 'til you are called for. Make the best of it Mr Jacobs, special cell this, only kept for important prisoners. They do say this is the cell where they kept Admiral Byng before they took the poor sod out to Spithead and shot him."

This sergeant seemed more talkative than the other naval personnel he had come in contact since being taken. And the treatment since arriving ashore was almost as good as that received by officers.

"What the hell do they want me for sergeant?"

The sergeant shrugged his shoulders. "I really don't know Mr Jacobs. My orders are to keep you here 'til you are sent for. You are to be treated well but I am not to let you out of my sight for one minute. You have a reputation of being a slippery customer," the sergeant laughed, "If it was up to that middi, that caught you, you would be hung drawn and quartered. You made a right idiot of him, he's the laughing stock of the fleet and his fellow officers will never let him forget it. Is there anything you need?"

"Yes sergeant, and thank you – if you could get me some books I would be very pleased. It will drive me crazy sitting here doing nothing."

The sergeant looked a little puzzled. Books? No one ever asked for books. "Books, Mr Jacobs, I don't know about that. What kind of books, Mr Jacobs?"

"Any books sergeant, anything to read."

Scratching his head and looking rather doubtful the only books he ever saw in the navy were in the officers' quarters. Better go to the officers' rooms, they had plenty of books in there. He had been inside once and the room was stacked with shelves from the floor to the ceiling. He tapped lightly on the door and a worried looking servant poked his head out. "I shall have to ask an officer, sergeant." He closed the door.

An officer opened the door wide. "You say that ruffian, Jacobs, wants a book. Who the hell does he think he is, a bloody Admiral or something?"

"I don't know sir, I was ordered to get him anything he needed within reason, sir." The sergeant stood to attention, his back as stiff as a ram rod and wishing to God he had never been sent on this errand.

The officer turned towards the room and his fellow officers sitting on large leather armchairs, a bright fire blazing in the fireplace. "That damn smuggler-fellow Jacobs wants some books gentlemen."

He roared with laughter as another officer said, "It's that damn rogue who made a fool of midshipman Cleary. You had better send him some, he gave me the best laugh I've had in months."

He took a couple of French books from a shelf and showed them to his fellow officers, one by one they burst out laughing. Little did they know that Aaron spoke French as well as a native and enjoyed reading the French classics as much as he enjoyed the British. It could be said that he was weaned on French books.

It was dark when Aaron's room was disturbed by a loud knocking on the door. As the sergeant opened it a naval officer, much the worse for drink, barged in followed by two of his cronies laughing, the first officer shouting in a drunken slur. "Ah, Mr Jacobs, enjoying those French books I sent you?"

Aaron put down the rich red leather bound book on his bed. "Very much so, although I have read this one before."

The stupid grin turned to surprise, then to one of incredulity as the smile faded.

"You have read it before Mr Jacobs?" He tried to hide his true feelings. Aaron had already made a fool of a midshipman. Surely this gutter snipe from Portsea – a notorious smuggler – dare not make a fool of another naval officer. He would have thought such a man was incapable of reading simple English not the French classics.

"Oh yes, Voltaire is very interesting, but like our Shakespeare he does go a little over the top, using two and three chapters when one would be quite sufficient. Mind you he had several good points, he fought against the many injustices of France even if he did spend a lot of time in England. Pity he didn't visit Portsmouth and watch your press gangs in action, he would have had some real injustices to fight."

"Why you damn young puppy, if you were on my ship I would have your back ribs showing for a remark like that," the fumes from his drink sodden breath, as he pressed his face forward, made Aaron take a step back, "and I suppose you are also fluent in French?"

"Yes sir, and with a strong Brittany accent."

"What are you, a spy? A damned traitor to your country? The greatest country in the world with the greatest navy."

The small scar on Aaron's lip turned a deep crimson, his lips began to twitch. It was several moments before he regained his composure. He glared at the officer with contempt. A glare that, had he been serving on a man-o-war, would have warranted at least twenty five lashes. As a civilian, he bit his bottom lip until he tasted salty blood, clenching and unclenching his fists. Gradually he calmed down. Maybe we did have a great nation but it wasn't built by idiots like the one standing before him. It was built by the common marine; the sailor; and the private soldiers who suffered unmercifully, not only at the hands of the countries' enemies, but at the whims of the officers. Idiots who never knew what a hard days work was or to work on an empty belly, and when the job was done to be rewarded by the lash or rope's end in the hands of some sadistic Petty Officer striking with enthusiasm to maintain his job. And the slums of Portsea bore testimony to those who reaped the benefits of a wider Empire, it certainly wasn't the poor.

Aaron swore to himself that when he owned a real sea going ship no man would receive the punishment meted out to navy men. Was it any wonder that Bligh's ship was taken from him? Aaron had heard tales of the islands in the South Seas, and to the men from Portsea and other large towns they must have thought they had reached paradise itself.

It took a lot to frighten Aaron but the next morning when summoned to attend the large offices under escort he felt his inside surge upwards. As he stepped out into the sunny but cold September morning he felt a tremble pass right through his body. He was placed between four marines, two in front and two behind with the sergeant in charge. They marched into a large building with a long corridor and halted before two double doors that stretched from the floor to the ceiling. After a few minutes they were ordered inside a large room, two of the marines posted outside the doors and two inside as the sergeant marched Aaron to a chair in front of a long table. Seated at the table were five senior officers, the officer in the centre, an Admiral. They all looked at Aaron as he marched into the room and started whispering at each other. Aaron was about to sit down when the sergeant stopped him. The Admiral nodded as much as to say. 'He can sit.'

There was another small table at the side of the room where a young officer sat with a pile of papers in front of him. Above him a large map of the coast line of Normandy and Brittany, a coast line Aaron was very familiar with.

"Are you Aaron Jacobs, Captain of a small lugger?" The officer at the far left side of the table asked.

"Yes sir." Aaron felt the inside muscles of his stomach tighten and sensed a feeling of nausea. This table was set up as he thought for a court martial.

"Do you know this area ?" The officer pointed to the large

chart on the wall. Aaron hesitated, then examined the chart. Yes he knew it. There were the inlets and small harbours he knew so well.

"Come on Mr Jacobs, we know you are familiar with this area, we want no fooling around. We want your answers and we want them correctly. We are well aware that you carry on a profitable smuggling trade in this area. Just give us a plain answer, do you know this area?"

"Yes sir."

"How well do you know it?"

Aaron hesitated once more, were they leading him into a trap? So far he had no idea why he was here but seeing all these high ranking officers was starting to worry him. Meekly he said, "Very well sir."

"Speak up man, do you know this area very well?"

"Yes sir. Very well." Aaron answered in a firm voice.

"That's better, now let's get down to real business. Do you know this small town?" The officer at the small table jumped up and pointed to a small town on the chart. The words on the chart were not very big and Aaron was told to go over and look at it. There was no need, he knew every inch of the land along that coast, especially that small harbour and town, he had lived there on and off for ten years. Everyone in the town knew him. But he was still on his guard and didn't want to incriminate himself until he knew why he was brought here.

"Come on you damn rogue, we know all about your sorties into this area, speak up and no more pussyfooting around. We have some urgent business to get through. You do know this town don't you?"

Aaron nodded his head and in a firm voice said, "Yes sir."

For the first time he smiled to himself, looking at the Admiral's red nose and blood shot eyes. He was probably one of Aaron's best customers. Though still on guard, he couldn't take his eyes off the Admiral's red bulbous nose. The wrong answers and he could find himself hanging from a yard-arm of a man-o-war anchored off Spithead, or at the very least serving on one of His Majesty's ships for life. On second thoughts he preferred the first alternative. This majestic line of top brass and gold braid knew his complete history. Every question they fired at him they appeared to already know the answers. The charts, the questions, the knowledgeable looks they gave him, all pointed to one big mystery question, what the hell did they want him for?

"Now listen here Captain Jacobs, so far you have told us exactly what we knew and after a while your answers were truthful. Now keep this up and we will get along fine. Any lies and I promise, you will pay dearly. We do understand you speak the language fluently. Just speak to the officers in your best French."

Aaron racked his brains for a sensible answer and looking directly at the Admiral with that slight but permanent smile, and in fluent French without a trace of an accent said, *"Dans ce pays ci il est bonde tuer de temps en temps un amiral pur encourager les autres."*

The officer that asked the question stared unbelieving at him for a few seconds. Then he and two more officers, who obviously knew their French, burst out laughing. The Admiral asked for a translation.

Trying to control his laughter the officer addressed the Admiral, "Why the cheeky young bugger has just quoted a passage from Voltaire's Candida, absolutely perfect and without the slightest trace of an accent, let me quote your Lordship : *In this country (meaning England) it is thought well to kill an Admiral from time to time to encourage the others."*

The Admiral stared at Aaron for a few seconds, then burst out laughing. "Why you cheeky young bugger."

Aaron felt a sigh of relief pass through his body, thankful that the old Admiral had a sense of humour.

"Well now that we know his French is as good as we have been led to believe, shall we get on with the job in hand gentlemen, we have very little time to lose?"

The old Admiral wiped the sweat away from his forehead. "What is *that* place Jacobs?" The Admiral nodded towards where the young officer had his finger on the chart on the wall.

"It's a very small town, they use it for victualling and for replenishing the powder and ammunition of the French

33

Fleet. It's very shallow and all the powder is kept in barges out in the harbour. I suppose it's pretty safe from our own fleet sir, no man-o-war could get into that harbour. When a ship wants stores, it's taken out to them by small boats. The entrance to the harbour is very narrow, with a spit of land jutting out from either side. And they have a small artillery battery each, mostly soldiers too old for real front line active service. It would take a very experienced sailor to get into that harbour undetected. When the tide is out the entrance that would take a small boat is barely fifty yards wide. The artillery pieces are secure on the dry land – I think there are two guns each side, not very heavy ones. It's also a small garrison town. The barracks are situated at the far end of town formed into a large square. The quarters for the troops one side, the officers' quarters the other. The gendarmerie was on the third side and the last one is a gaol for the English prisoners and barracks for the guards. There is an entrance to the square at each corner, like a narrow alleyway."

"You seem very knowledgeable about this town. Now you know exactly where the prisoners are kept are there any French civilians in that prison?"

"No sir, only British prisoners, they work on the barges sir and help to keep the streets and barracks clean."

Well if that is what it was all about, Aaron felt relieved. So why go to all that trouble of seeking him out with a big reward? They would only have to ask and he would have given them all the information they wanted without all this trouble and frightening the damn life out of him.

"Have you been there lately?"

Aaron hesitated, was this the trick question, after all he had been out there several times this year and consorting with the enemy was a hanging job. Never mind that he was only doing a bit of smuggling – if they wanted him they could soon put a case together. He didn't have long to wait for the real answers as to why he was brought before this august array of gentlemen.

"In that prison there is a high ranking British naval officer, he has to be brought out before they discover his true identity. Do you think you are capable of such a task? You will be well rewarded."

Aaron was speechless, getting a dozen barrels of brandy out of that harbour was a simple task after the bribes were paid, but to take a prisoner from there and to bring him safely across the channel, that was an entirely different matter.

"I take it you are joking gentlemen." His eyes swept along the row of blank faces waiting for Aaron's reaction. "Why security in that prison is tighter than a lady's corsets. Those prisoners are marched out first thing every morning down to the foreshore and kept under strict guard until it's time to return to their prison."

"Mr Jacobs, that officer must be released at all costs. I am assured you are the only man in England that is familiar enough with that town. I want you to return to your room and think up some plan. You will be here at ten o'clock tomorrow morning. If there is anything you want, just ask the sergeant of marines. I want your answer in the morning."

"What if I don't sir." He looked the Admiral in the eye.

"Well there's always the Fleet. We are in need of good men."

Chapter Five

Safely back in his room, Aaron threw himself onto the bed. So that was it. A bloody suicide mission to bring back some bloody snotty-nosed high ranking officer, who wouldn't give him the time of day if he met him in the street. What alternative was there? Bloody blackmail. Join the fleet and he bet they would make sure he had a dog's life for not accepting the mission. Just how did they expect him to succeed. Getting into the harbour was child's play, really. But to walk three miles from the shore, through a town, get inside a prison and walk calmly back to the lugger with a prisoner? Yes he could do it if the officer was outside, but in a secure prison, why the whole idea didn't bear thinking about.

He lay back on his bed, his head in his cupped hands, staring at the ceiling. The sergeant and the four marines sat around the fire – the sergeant occasionally throwing Aaron a glance, it was like watching a man waiting for his death sentence.

"Who the hell is this high ranking officer they are so keen on releasing from that prison, sergeant?"

"He's an Admiral. His ship was sunk off Brest a few weeks ago, he was washed ashore with about twenty of his crew."

One of the marines, eyes wide open, stared at the sergeant, "Not that bastard Medlam sarge? Let him rot Mr. Jacobs, he's the biggest bastard in the British Navy and one of the youngest Admirals. His old man is also an Admiral and I don't know who is the biggest bastard out of the two of them. I think they must be the most hated officers in the country."

"All right Watkins," the sergeant warned him, "that's no way to speak about an officer. If anyone heard, you would really be in a mess. Cut it out."

"Yes, I've heard of this Medlam," Aaron said, "it was all over Portsmouth. Had a man sentenced to fifty lashes – after thirty the man was dead but he told the bosun to carry on with the lash. The bosun refused so he received the rest of the lashes. Crowds gathered outside the hotel, his favourite was The George, when he came out the crowds booed and hissed him. Yes I remember that bastard all right."

Aaron didn't sleep. All night, he tossed and turned. One of his sentries turned the burning logs occasionally, the bouncing shadows giving movements to the bare walls of the room. By first light he had a plan worked out in his head. He would get him out – but not without the rest of the crew who were taken at the same time. At least it would salve his conscious for getting the Admiral out – a job he hated doing. He had no choice, it was either the Admiral or the rest of his life aboard a naval ship.

When he arrived back at the room another high ranking officer had joined the board. He screwed his eyes up to scrutinise Aaron as he sat down on the chair placed before the board. The newcomer shook his head from side to side his lips pouting in a snarl. "Is this the idiot we're entrusting with my son's life? I don't like it one bit. What's the idiot smiling for?"

The officer next to him whispered in the Admiral's ear. The snarl seemed to deepen.

"Well let's hear what he has to say."

"Gentlemen, my plan..."

At this the newcomer jumped to his feet, "What the hell do you mean *your* plan. This is a navy job. You will take your orders from a naval officer."

"Admiral Medlam, if you want that son of yours rescued let Captain Jacobs say what he has to. If it doesn't sound feasible we will have to find an alternative."

Reluctantly and with a grunt, Admiral Medlam sat down

again, glaring at Aaron, "You call him Captain Jacobs now. He's a smuggler." It was obvious that Admiral Medlam was going to have the last word.

"First the prison must be taken by stealth and not force. A large party would be mown down before they entered the town. I shall need six men. I did think of taking my own ship but it will never hold all the twenty-odd prisoners."

Admiral Medlam sprang to his feet and brought his fist down heavily on the long table, decanters and glasses bouncing up and spilling their contents over the highly polished table, "What do you mean, *all* the prisoners? My five hundred guineas reward is for getting *my* son out. It is *not* for that other scum! As far as I am concerned they can rot in hell!"

The rest of the officers on the board squirmed in their seats, and Aaron almost failed to retain his calm, thinking it was true what everyone was saying about Medlam. One of the worst officers in the British Navy – but with five hundred guineas dangling before his eyes and with a superhuman effort he managed to remain calm. With five hundred guineas and the money he had accumulated from his smuggling he could perhaps realise his ambition to become a ship owner. A ship that could sail the seven seas.

"Sir, I cannot leave these men to remain in that hell hole. We may have to kill some French to get the Admiral out. And if we leave anyone behind it is certain they will be beheaded. I am sorry it's either the lot or none at all."

Realising his last statement had not gone down too well Admiral Medlam didn't immediately speak. For a few moments he just scowled at Aaron until he found a suitable reply, "Well it must be understood – my son gets top priority."

Aaron nodded his head in agreement, "I think we have a fifty percent chance of pulling this off, but first my terms." He didn't bother looking up to see the board's reaction.

"The five hundred guineas must be paid to my lawyers *Harris, Mills and Harris* in the High Street. If I succeed I will collect it. If I fail, one hundred guineas goes to my only crew member – the remainder returned to you. I also want warrants to free us from any naval service, that includes being impressed by any press gang, both for myself and my crew member. We will have to work quickly. I must get my notes from my lugger to be absolutely certain of tide and moon times. It will have to be done in complete darkness, no moon and preferably a starless night. So I will have to collect my log. I think we will have those conditions, except for the clouds they are unpredictable, in about three or four days time. I shall need a ship to take me at least three miles from the harbour. We can lower the ship's boats and row the remainder of the way. I shall need four marines, a sergeant, and two seamen. I prefer marines that are good with the oars. We will need to tow another ship's boat. One boat will not be sufficient for all the prisoners." Admiral Medlam was turning redder in the face by the minute, Aaron was sure he would be having apoplexy at any minute, "I don't intend to leave one man behind." Aaron's eyes never left the Admiral's face as he emphasised the last statement.

The board members whispered amongst themselves as Aaron outlined his plans for releasing the prisoners.

"Well Captain Jacobs, it certainly sounds feasible I must say....." But the officer was rudely interrupted by Admiral Medlam. Thumping the table hard with his clenched fist and pushing his chair back he stood up yelling at Aaron.

"What do you think you will do with the French army? Alone, you intend to penetrate a garrison and release those men?"

"I won't be alone I shall have seven men with me. I stand more chance of getting them out than if you sent a couple of battalions of infantry."

"I don't think you have any choice Medlam." The president of the board said. "We will also send a naval officer to more or less take charge. However, I think Captain Jacobs' idea sounds feasible." He turned his attention to Aaron, "H.M.S. *Swiftsure* is anchored off Spithead, I will call the Captain in today. In the meantime you may go back to your lugger and collect whatever notes you want. The marine sergeant can go with you. Attend this office at ten o'clock tomorrow morning, I will have the Captain of the *Swiftsure* here and you can work out your plans with him."

He turned to Admiral Medlam, "Is that all right with you Medlam?"

"Well, if it has to be, I suppose I have no other choice." He scowled at Aaron.

Once back in his room the sergeant opened up, "Say Mr. Jacobs, how about asking me to join you. I hate this bloody job here – guarding prisoners wasn't my idea, so put a word in for me will you?" The chance for action excited the sergeant, "I can't understand that damn Admiral, you were putting your life on the line for that bastard son of his and he publicly insulted you." The sergeant looked around making sure there was no one within earshot, his four marines had gone about their duties. "That bastard Medlam and his son, are hated throughout the service. Watkins was right, I doubt if there's a man in the navy that would lift a hand to save them, but he's been very lucky so far. If the French knew who they were holding they would put him against a wall and shoot him. When his ship was sunk, him and some of the men clung to an upturned boat and slowly drifted ashore. He was unconscious and naked when he was washed up and suffering from loss of memory. When he awoke a young officer next to him in prison warned him and told him not to tell the French he was Admiral Medlam as the French wanted him badly. Years before he sank a French frigate and those that were rescued he eventually threw overboard, including the son of a high ranking officer. It soon got to the French authorities what he had done and they put a high reward on his head. Since he was captured we've heard he's been working those barges you were telling the officers about."

Aaron wasn't thinking about rescuing the Admiral, all he was interested in was the five hundred guineas, with which he would realise his life's ambition – although he admitted to himself he would miss the excitement of his smuggling adventures. He'd had many narrow misses with the revenue men, but that was what it was all about. He had no hatred of the French. On the contrary he loved them – as one or two of the ladies of that particular French town would testify. Five hundred guineas would be the answer to it all. If he succeeded on his mission, and if anyone from the town recognised him, he would never be able to return. He was determined to succeed.

There had been little point in Willie trying to conceal the lugger, and Aaron saw it long before they reached the harbour. Stood on the foreshore, he shouted across to Willie. Polly was the first on deck waving frantically, and within minutes Willie was pulling hard for the shore in the lugger's dinghy.

"What's up Cap'n?" Willie began bombarding him with questions.

"Wait 'til we're aboard and I will tell you all about it."

"You sod 'em Aaron. Let them do their own dirty work," Polly shouted. "It's dangerous and I've heard all about that Medlam. He's a pig, let him rot there Aaron. It's not all sailors he bullies either. He had that pretty little Angela in his room at the Dolphin Hotel – the next morning she was covered in bruises. I tell you Aaron the man is an animal. Let's up sail and get away from here."

"Sorry Polly, I made a promise, and I am sure you wouldn't want the sergeant here shot."

In spite of Polly's pleading and the disapproving look on Willie's face he refused to listen to any argument that would deter him from the job in hand or to break the promise to the sergeant that he would not make a run for it if the opportunity arose. Inwardly, now he knew more about it, he was looking forward to it. The excitement stirred his insides and in the two days he'd spent with the sergeant they had become friends.

They returned to his room inside the dockyard after giving Willie his instructions and telling Polly she could stay as long as she liked on the lugger and stay forever if he failed to return.

Laying on his bed he studied his log book of tides and the state of the moon. With a more definite plan in mind they returned to the offices. Admiral Medlam listened intently to Aaron's ideas and shifted uncomfortably in his seat, "I certainly hope you know what you are up to Jacobs. How long will the operation last?" He appeared to be more sociable this time. Perhaps he realised, at last, that Aaron was the only man along the south coast, if not the whole of Britain, that was capable of doing the job. He called the young officer at the side of the table over, gave him a note, then nodded towards Aaron.

Aaron read the note. It was a receipt for five hundred guineas paid to his lawyer and a letter with the Admiralty stamp excusing both him and Willie from any further naval service.

"The Frigate *Swiftsure* is at you service, four marines and two seamen and a sergeant of the marines," one of the officers said.

Aaron raised his hand, "I would like the sergeant here to be in charge of the marines. I have got to know him in the past two days. I feel I can trust him and that he won't let me down."

The Admiral noted, "I think that can be arranged. You will also have Lieutenant Saunders. Officially this is a naval engagement although unofficially you have complete charge. Is there anything else you need?"

"No sir, just that I would like to be off *this* point," here he stabbed his finger on the chart, "by ten o'clock at night in four days time. The tide will carry us straight into harbour and this small creek, which will take us further into the town. Allowing one hour to the prison, where we can assess the situation, and leave two hours to release the prisoners. Another hour back to the ship's boats, by then the tide will be changing into our favour for the outward trip. *Swiftsure* will be laying three miles off and will pick us up for the trip back home. So with luck we should be back home in Portsmouth in seven to ten days."

After his last meal ashore both Aaron and an overjoyed sergeant of marines were rowed out to Spithead and the frigate. It was a new ship just brought into service by the navy. A young naval officer greeted him as he stepped on deck, he came forward with his hand outstretched.

"Mr Jacobs, I am Lieutenant Saunders, I believe we have an appointment in France." Like most men his age he could hardly conceal the excitement building up inside him.

Aaron took an instant liking to the man. "I believe we have Mr Saunders." The first question he asked was, "Do you speak French?"

Mr Saunders laughed and let out volumes of fluent French.

"Yes Mr Saunders, I can hear you do."

More officers came on deck to see the man who was leading this expedition. His smuggling activities were well known and the news was around that seeing the top brass and talking to them held no terrors for him. The ship's Captain held his hand out, "Welcome aboard Mr Jacobs, I trust that you will find everything to your satisfaction." He nodded towards two ships' boats that were hoisted on deck, "You have two of my best seamen going with you and the four marines have been hand picked for their skills with the oars. Perhaps you will dine with me tonight and we will discuss the operation. I am sure my officers will be delighted with your company."

Amongst the few possessions that Aaron had brought aboard was a bottle of fine brandy. At dinner he offered it to the Captain who gave the steward orders to serve it.

"Why I declare this is the finest brandy I ever did taste," a young officer said.

Another officer shook his head and touched his mouth with a crooked finger as if deep in thought, "No, I remember I was in the George Hotel in the High Street. The landlord there sells the best brandy in Portsmouth."

Aaron burst out laughing and took a sip from his glass rolling it round and round his tongue savouring the last drop before swallowing it.

"It's the one and the same sir."

"Why you young rogue," the Captain said, "what part of France does this come from?"

"The same place we are going sir. And if I were you I would make the best of it, after this I doubt if I will try again. I am made most welcome there and should anyone have the remotest suspicion it was I that led you, it would be madam guillotine I would be visiting next."

For the remainder of the dinner, and well into the night they heard about Aaron's hilarious and sometimes dangerous exploits into the enemy territory.

"Just one thing Mr Jacobs, if you get a chance to bring a barrel back aboard it will be welcome." The cheer was heard all round the ship.

Chapter Six

At first light the frigate weighed anchor. There was already excited movement along the fleet of ships anchored off Spithead. Nelson's fleet, who within the month would be rejoicing in the greatest victory fought by the British navy, unfortunately was overshadowed by the death of the greatest sailor of them all. The fleet floated in a calm sea on a bed of fine mist like ghostly apparitions, as seagulls lined the yard-arms of the ships. Occasionally seamen rested on the ship's rails idly watching the frigate glide past. This part of the exercise no Captain relished for he knew every officer on watch would be criticising each movement as his ship put to sea.

But soon they were passing St. Catherine's point and out into the open channel. The *Swiftsure* lived up to its name, a strong breeze filling her sails and carrying the ship at a steady speed, the sea splitting apart as the slender bows cut into the clear water gaining speed. They followed the English coast all day long and only moved further into the channel as darkness fell. A fine sea spray covered the deck, Aaron stared at the receding dark smudge of land and wondered if he would ever see it again, but soon dismissed those morbid thoughts from his mind.

The night before the landing the Captain of the frigate had called a meeting. The chart showing the landing spot was spread out across the table.

Aaron explained his plans more thoroughly.

"Drop us about three miles from the harbour entrance, at

nine. There will be a very strong current as the tide charges into the harbour. If it's cold or wet the artillery men will be inside the forts at each side of the entrance. The biggest danger will be hitting one of those barges, the incoming tide rushes in so fast it will be a hell of a job fending them off. There are eight of us here, so Mr. Saunders will take four men in the rear cutter once we are in the harbour, the remainder will come with me and I'll be at the tiller, we can't have any mistakes. It will be much calmer right inside the harbour and we can row the cutters to the creek. Once landed I can cut across the marshes with the party and we come into town from the rear. The two seamen left with the boats will move them up and down with the tide, it's their job to keep those two cutters afloat at all times in case we have to move fast. Two things are in our favour, it's very dark and it's the weekend, these Frenchies love their wine and are usually drunk at this time."

Luck was favouring them, two hours before the cutters were launched from the frigate, a fine drizzle started.

"It will be a long pull to that harbour Mr Jacobs," the Captain said, shaking hands as Aaron stepped over the hand rail.

"The tide will be taking us most of the way Captain, good-bye sir."

"Goodbye Mr Jacobs and good luck. I will be round here at about sun up."

"Don't hang around too long Captain, the French navy is active along this shoreline. If we don't find you we will just carry on across the channel towards Plymouth."

"It's a long way for such small cutters Mr Jacobs."

"So was Captain Bligh's boat sir, but he managed to cross the wide Pacific with no charts or compass, in waters he didn't know. At least I have charts and compass and I do know the Channel."

With a final wave the boat's crew pushed away from the frigate and they plunged into the velvet blackness, within minutes the darkened ship was completely out of sight and they were all alone.

Aaron picked up the familiar dim lights from the shore as

the cold bit into the exposed parts of their bodies. Aaron wished he had his own brandy with him, instead the frigate's Captain had given him two bottles of strong ship's rum, he passed the bottle round.

"In a few minutes men we will be picked up by that tide rushing into the harbour, when I tell you, ship your oars and one of you sit at the stern with me and keep that other cutter from bumping into us, it will sound like a bloody drum and wake those guards at the harbour entrance." He tried to make a joke of it but the men were much too cold to laugh.

"Right lads, ship oars, the tide will do the rest," he ordered in a grating whisper. They felt the tide grip the bows of the cutter and swing it round, "That's it lads, relax now."

Instinctively they ducked down as they sped through the narrow entrance, the juts of land from each side were no more than a few yards away from the cutter. They couldn't see the headlands so it was obvious that the guards, if they were awake, couldn't see the cutter. They were right in the middle of the harbour when a dark shadow loomed up right ahead of them.

"Quick a bloody barge, fend it off quickly Andrews – no, not with your oar with your hands." Andrews and another man hung over the bows of the cutter, their hands outstretched.

Lieutenant Saunders' men were at the ready alongside their cutter, they glided past with just inches to spare.

"Right lads let's row for that small creek," he pointed into the darkness, "It's over there."

They felt the cutter scrape along the sandy bottom and without any orders being given the men leapt onto dry land, happy in the knowledge that at last they had their feet on enemy territory. The cutters were pulled up, they would be afloat again when the tide rose.

"Right now men," Aaron said to the two seamen, "make sure the boats are kept afloat. Keep quiet and don't talk. If anyone does come near here don't give the game away, lay low. If they come too near and you are forced to quieten them, use the butts of your muskets, don't make any noise at all."

Once the main party had departed, the two seamen set about covering the two cutters with gorse bushes which were plentiful, keeping the two cutters afloat but near to the main channel.

Aaron followed the shoreline for the first mile, occasionally casting a glance towards the dark smudges floating in the harbour. "They would make a nice firework display if we could set fire to them Mr Jacobs," said Mr. Saunders, "they would hear the explosions from here to Paris and back, all hell would be let loose. Just two or three in the centre of the harbour and the rest would soon follow."

"Forget it Mr Saunders, our job is to release those prisoners."

But Mr Saunders could not forget it. As he trod in Aaron's footsteps his mind was on anything but the real job in hand. Several times in the dark a marine tripped over the ropes that secured small dinghies to the beach preventing them from floating away when the tide rose. They came upon the path they were looking for, "This circles right round the town, but be very careful, the French army use it for patrols and the men in the barges use it when they return from a night out in the town."

It was a brisk cold September night but that didn't prevent them from sweating as they kept up the sharp pace Aaron was setting. The trailing marine accidentally strayed from the path and cursed as he sank up to his knees in freezing marsh water.

"Alright Norris, cut it out." The sergeant ordered in a harsh whisper, "Do you want to get us all bloody shot?"

The town itself was veiled in silence. The honest citizens asleep in bed but occasionally the men could hear bawdy songs coming from some tavern. They made good progress until they came to the first bend when they heard footsteps approaching from the other directions. "In the marshes quick!" Lieutenant Saunders ordered, and threw himself sideways. The remainder didn't wait for the order to be repeated. Two dim lamps came swinging towards them.

"Looks like two sentries doing the rounds." The two

approaching figures swayed and were clinging to each other.

"No they are drunk out of their minds. Sarge, can you finish them off quietly?" Aaron asked, "We could do with their uniforms.... we'll stand a better chance when we approach that prison."

Just five yards away, as the two drunken soldiers stopped to urinate, the sergeant tapped the two marines next to him. Quiet as a wild animal they sprinted the few yards and before the two Frenchmen knew what had hit them the sergeant had one soldier round the neck and jerked it towards him. There was a loud snap and he sank slowly to his knees. The other two marines had finished the other man with a swing of a musket butt to the back of his skull.

"Two of you change into those uniforms," ordered Aaron, "and be as fast as possible – we have no time to lose."

"What shall we do with the bodies sir?" The sergeant asked.

"Well we can't take them with us, drag them out a few yards from the path and dump them in the marsh, they will find them when its light and give them a decent burial. By then we should be well and truly out of the harbour."

They quickened the pace to make up for lost time, one of the marines in the French uniform complaining that the man had lice.

"Right, we are on the far edge of town, we will take that narrow passage, it will lead us into the main square, once there the rest will be all bluff. Form the men up sergeant and we will march in."

Aaron was side by side with Mr Saunders, "Let's hope they don't recognise the other uniforms in the dark." They marched down the passage and into the main square. "Straight ahead, that's the prison." On several occasions a military man or a civilian passed without giving them a second glance. They were used to the military going about their business, as it was a garrison town as well. They were about fifty yards from the prison when a door opened. They stopped dead in their tracks, hardly daring to breath. A fat balding man emerged looking over his shoulder and shouting to someone behind him.

"It's one of the prison guards," whispered Aaron, "He's just told them he will be away for the next two hours." He motioned towards a dark doorway, "Stand in there and grab him as he goes by, we'll find out how many guards are in there and how many prisoners."

The man was muttering to himself and cursing about how long he had been on duty, and not seeing his wife and family for so long. The sergeant's arm shot out like a snake striking its prey. The man was shocked and frightened, his eyes wide and his tongue protruding as the sergeant's grip tightened around this throat. Before he recovered from the initial shock the sergeant's hand moved from the throat and clamped over his mouth.

Aaron whispered in the man's ear and listened intently to the gasping reply.

"Alright sergeant, you can let him go now – There are two guards inside and twenty prisoners. Ten more prisoners have been moved to the barracks, they are being moved in the morning to the next harbour a couple of miles down the coast."

"What shall I do with this man Mr Saunders?"

He knew Aaron hated unnecessary violence so he made it easier for him. Aaron knew there was no other alternative. Even in the dark the man could have recognised him, their faces had only been inches apart. He felt a certain amount of relief when Mr Saunders gave the dreaded order, an order he knew he could never give himself. There was a loud crack as the man's head jerked back and the body slid gracefully to the ground.

"We know what's in there now, I only hope they haven't moved Medlam. Come with me Mr Saunders, and you sergeant. Two more men, perhaps those in French uniform, stand each side of the door. We will go and bang on the door, I will try and mimic the old guard, make an excuse I left something behind. As soon as the door opens the sergeant and two men rush in. This is the layout; there's a small corridor that leads to a large room. Three sides of the room are laid out as three cells with iron bars each side. Then there's a large wooden table and benches in front of a roaring fire. Make short work of it." Aaron's voice lowered. "You will have to kill the two prison guards."

Mr Saunders stood behind Aaron, the sergeant one side of the door and a marine the other. He banged against the solid oak door and shouted a few words There was a movement from inside and he heard someone fumbling with a bunch of keys, the door swung open and a beam of pale light fell on the sergeant's uniform. "I never expected to see a soldier..." But the words faded and the man's face changed to one of fear as the sergeant lunged forward with his bayonet and ran it straight through the prison guard. The officer rushed forward, sword in hand, the second guard was sitting at the table with his back to the fire and the table littered with scraps of food and empty pewter mugs. Awakened from a deep sleep the only thing he saw was the officer's sword flashing through the air, a spout of blood from the guard's neck shot across the table.

The remaining men outside brought in the other dead guard. The smell from the cells was nauseating. Although the marines were used to the stench of the lower deck, it was nothing compared to this.

Each of the three cells were about ten by twelve feet and covered in a foot of putrid straw. A large tub in each corner of the cell was used as a toilet. The sergeant kicked the first man, he looked up with blood shot eyes, completely indifferent, they were used to being disturbed in the middle of the night to carry out some duty or to be marched to the beach to unload a barge. He sat up rubbing his eyes, looked around and saw two marines. He was indifferent and was about to walk over to the tub to relieve himself, when he noticed something different about the uniforms. Suddenly it dawned, they weren't French but British uniforms and they were carrying muskets. He scratched his head and kicked the next man awake. "Eh Evans, there are some British marines here!"

"So bloody what," answered Evans still half asleep. "They have sunk another British ship. Go back to sleep."

"It's the first time I've seen them bring their muskets in with them."

The men shot up straight and looking at the crowd outside the cells, including the two men in French uniform, couldn't grasp what was going on until he heard Lieutenant Saunders giving orders. "Keep quiet if you all want to go home." More men were waking up as each cell was opened. "Is Admiral Medlam here with you?"

"No they moved him down to the next harbour with a few more men. The French navy is getting ready to move. The barges here are loaded with powder. They brought in a new British prisoner the other day, he reckons the French and Spanish fleets are combining."

"Where are the prisoners now?"

"Over at the barracks, they took them over about three hours ago. They always move them over to the barracks the night before. You will never get him out of there. It's well guarded, the cells and the garrisons ammunition store is below ground in the cellars. The ground floor is for the officers and the two floors above are the barracks. Just to get inside the building would be a miracle. The Frenchie sergeant and a private sit at a small table just inside the passage. They scrutinise every person that goes in there. That's after you pass the two sentries. The room behind the table is the guard room, wherever you go in that building they send a guard with you. You have no chance at all of getting in that building, it's a fortress."

So at last Dame fortune had finally turned her back on them. They had negotiated the harbour with time to spare. Apart from the fracas with the two French soldiers, which had taken only a few minutes, they had met with no further resistance.

Aaron was a stubborn man, they had come this far and he had no intention of returning empty handed and he could see his one great ambition of becoming an ocean going ship owner fading fast. After hearing all about that monster Medlam he was surprised to hear he was still alive. Every officer and man that served with him hated the very air he breathed and could easily have informed on him. Perhaps having the privilege of watching him work as a common labourer had given them pleasure, more pleasure than seeing him hanged. That must be it, his men had watched him being worked to death's door and being flogged.

"We'll have to bluff it out Mr Saunders. I suggest we change into the guards' uniforms and with the two men in French soldiers' uniform, walk straight into the barracks and demand we take the prisoners. Make up a story, tell them there is a barge adrift in the harbour and an officer wants every prisoner down to the beach. They want as many hands as possible, say it's lodged on a sand bank. The sergeant and the two marines can make their way back to the cutters with these prisoners."

The prisoners quite rightly guessed that Aaron was the brains behind the operation and tried to dissuade him from such a foolhardy and daring plan, after all it was their necks at risk. Any commotion at the barracks and the first thing they would do would be to search the prison. The chase would be on. They would never get out of the harbour.

"Sir, you have no chance of getting inside that barracks. I implore you, the risks are too great, the place is alive with Frenchies and in that prison the guards are the worse of the lot."

Aaron looked at Mr Saunders as if asking for advice but the officer shrugged his shoulders. "What are your thoughts?" But he just shook his head.

"I am only here as an observer Mr Jacobs and to make sure the men obey your orders."

"Alright Mr Saunders, change into that guard uniform." He pointed to the dead man stretched across the table.

"I will change into the other and as for the dead guard we brought in from outside...." He pointed to one of the British prisoners, an ex-petty officer, who seemed to be in better shape than the others, "....You take his uniform, you will have to point out Admiral Medlam to me."

The marine sergeant was given his final instructions. "Make sure the men keep quiet sergeant, if they catch you it will be the chop for us all." He brought his finger across his throat to emphasise the point.

The cobbled square resounded to the echoes of their heavy boots as they marched towards the large building. He nodded towards the main centre door and proudly marched in — only to be challenged by the two sentries. In fluent French and a superior voice, he asked for the prisoners and told the sentry a barge was adrift in the harbour. The sentry nodded him towards a sergeant sitting at a table inside the main hall who looked half asleep.

"We have come for the prisoners," repeated Aaron.

"What prisoners?" The frown turned to a scowl.

"The prisoners you are holding here. There is an emergency, one of the barges is adrift and causing havoc, if it gets onto a sandbank we will never move it. There is a real panic going on as the Inspector General is due here in the morning. There will be hell if he sees that."

At the mention of the Inspector General the sergeant became more alert — mentioning a high ranking officer is enough make any N.C.O. sit up and take notice.

"Captain Duval is on the beach," added Aaron humorously, "running around like his backside is on fire, you know how H.Q. officers panic."

"Duval?" The frown returned to the sergeant's face and he bowed his head in deep thought, "Duval.... never heard of him. Have you got written authority?"

"Of course you haven't heard of him you idiot! He is on the Inspector General's staff! Now if I were you, I would remove your fat behind from that chair and get those prisoners down to the beach. The last time I saw Captain Duval he was up to his knees in freezing water and not in a very pleasant mood."

"What about the prisoners over in the gaol..." he muttered, "...these here are due out in the morning."

The French sergeant puffed and wheezed as he eased himself out of the chair jangling a large bunch of keys on an oversized ring.

He led them along a corridor and down a flight of stone steps.

Chapter Seven

There was a golden opportunity for Aaron to dispose of the sergeant of the guards, walking a couple of steps in front, his bald head shining brightly as they passed each lantern in the prison corridors. But they still had to get away from this building without causing any suspicion. They stopped at a thick oak studded door with a small iron barred window and the sergeant cautiously looked through the bars. The men strewn around the straw lined floor did not bother to move or look up as he selected a large key and inserted it noisily into the lock.

"Come on you lot get to your feet, you are wanted urgently down at the beach." He was speaking in broad French and Aaron doubted if anyone amongst the prisoners understood. A heavy boot struck the nearest prisoner in the small of the back and brought the carpet of filthy straw to life.

"How many do you want down there?" The guard sergeant queried.

"All of them – they already have the soldiers and barge men working there, but I have to collect as many prisoners as possible."

The prisoners were assembled in the long passage, a more miserable assembly of men Aaron had never seen. Unwashed and unshaven, what pitiable clothes they wore were in shreds. Boots worn by the lucky ones were held together with string.

Next to the cell was the armoury. Mr Saunders tried the

door, it was secure. The sergeant had left his bunch of keys in the cell door and was busy taking count of the prisoners. Quickly and silently he took the keys and tried to open the armoury door, nervously looking over his shoulder. Three keys later he found the right one to fit, turned it and the lock gave a loud click. He looked around innocently but the sergeant was too preoccupied counting and recounting the prisoners. He replaced the keys leaving the armoury door unlocked. The marines had witnessed the officer's move and, sidling towards him, shielded him from the sergeant's view. Silently he slipped inside, the only light came from the passage but he made out barrels stacked high and filled with powder. Several boxes contained muskets and his hand slipped inside one. It was filled with slow match burners and quickly he stuffed a couple inside his tunic, then slid back into the crowd of men in the passage.

The officer tailed at the end of the men as they were marched outside the barracks without any interruption. He touched one of the men and whispered, "Don't speak or look around we have come to get you out of this prison and back to Portsmouth, which one of you is Admiral Medlam?"

For a moment the man couldn't answer, he just stared at him with his sunken eyes. He lifted his arm, "That one." He pointed to a man second from the front.

"Right. Just look to your front, or you will all be dead men."

To allay any fears Aaron had insisted that the French sergeant and two men help to guard the prisoners, but Aaron was having his doubts. The sergeant kept glancing at him and shadows of doubt were beginning to sweep his face as if he recognised Aaron. Half way across the cobbled square the sergeant asked Aaron, "Have you been stationed here for very long, I seem to recognise your face?"

Aaron's heart sank, for the first time since landing his nerves flinched. He had the Admiral in his grasp, surely nothing could go wrong at this late hour. The sergeant had just signed his own death warrant.

"No, only been here a few days, but this is not my first

time here. Two years ago I was here for three months, got
slung out of that brothel." He pointed to the house next to
the prison. "Got blind drunk and caused a bit of trouble.
The girl tried to overcharge me. I wasn't that drunk!"
Both he and the sergeant laughed out loud. For the
moment it put the sergeant's mind at rest. "Better get a
move on sarge that Duval is a right swine when he's
aroused. We will pick up the other prisoners."

Aaron kicked at the small door, it gave slightly, much to
the sergeant's amazement. Aaron pushed him forward.
The marines dealt with the other two sentries that had
escorted them across the square before anyone realised it.
The prisoners looked more startled than the guards as
they lay flat on the cell floor. Without another word, the
marine sergeant ran his bayonet through one man and
Lieutenant Saunders ran his sword through the other.
The prison sergeant's eyes opened wide as he sank to the
ground with a bayonet in his chest and gasped a few
unrecognisable words.

"You did recognise me sergeant, but you were not sure
were you?" asked Aaron.

"Yes... you are the Englishman that smuggles... the
brandy." He clutched at his chest as the marine attempted
to withdraw the blade. Finally he pitched forward with the
bayonet still embedded in his chest.

No one seemed inclined to speak and silently watched as
the party changed back into their own clothes.

"I was glad to get out of that Frenchie stuff, the bastard
was lousy." The sergeant had a wide grin across his face.

A short stocky man stepped forward, from the sound and
aggressive tone of his voice he was a man used to giving
orders, but with his unkempt appearance, ragged clothes
and a large bushy beard it was doubtful if his own father
would have recognised him.

"What the hell is going on here?"

Aaron decided to play along, "We have come to rescue
Admiral Medlam. Does anyone know where he is?"

"I am Admiral Medlam you damn fool. Who the hell are
you?"

The officer now back in his own uniform stepped forward

and saluted. "Lieutenant Saunders at your service sir."

"And pray Lieutenant, how do you intend to carry out this escape?"

"We have two ships' cutters down at the water's edge sir. We intend to take you out of the harbour where a frigate will be waiting to rendezvous at first light. So if you don't mind sir we must make a start, the tide will soon be on the turn and it will help to carry us from the bay. Mr Jacobs here is very familiar with these parts."

The Admiral eyed Aaron up and down and his mouth twisted into a snarl. "Do you intend to take off this scum too? I understand your orders were to release me. Just get *me* out of here – these men can look after themselves."

Aaron could hardly believe his ears. It appeared that all the stories he had heard of this man were true. But to let his own men suffer the consequences for the murder of the guards and no doubt the murder of the two soldiers – the same men who had sheltered him and kept secret about his identity. One word from any of these men to their captors would have removed Admiral Medlam from the naval list permanently. It was time for him to intervene, he stepped forward.

"This so-called scum have kept you alive for the past few months. They come with us or no one goes. I have brought two cutters and we must hurry. Don't worry I will get you out of here." He turned to the ex-prisoners, "Move these bodies into a cell, just leave their heads showing above the straw, then lock the cells. The men with boots must remove them. We will go in parties of six or more. I will take the Admiral – make as little noise as possible."

They took the same route as they came, circling the town. Twice they encountered soldiers and took evasive action. The prisoners enjoyed seeing the Admiral fling himself into the marshes, no one offered a hand to extradite him as he cursed Aaron for being disorganised.

"I will have a coach laid on for you next time Admiral."

They found the two cutters well hidden but afloat.

"Did you find old misery guts?" One of the sailors asked, hoping the answer would be in the negative and not recognising the scarecrow he was helping into the cutter. The

Admiral swiped him across the face with the back of his hand.

"You will pay for that remark. 'Old misery guts' am I! Believe me when you get aboard ship I will have the pleasure of seeing your guts exposed. What ship do you belong to?"

The man sprang to attention trembling at the knees. This didn't look like any Admiral, but that voice he would recognise anywhere, having served with him before. *"Swiftsure* sir".

Seeing the Admiral in action with the naval men Aaron realised there wouldn't be a man in the British navy that would thank him for the rescue. Before Aaron agreed to the mission, the marine sergeant had advised him, "Don't do it Aaron, settle for the hundred guineas, that bastard should rot in a French prison."

Now Aaron was regretting his actions. Seeing him at close quarters, he *was* an 'old misery guts' – the sailor was right but when his rib cage was exposed to the elements the man would regret it for the rest of his life. The other parties were arriving and the first cutter with the Admiral aboard was full.

"Right, come on, we have wasted enough time, we can shove off, the rest can make their own way back."

"Sorry sir, we don't move until every man-jack from that prison is safely aboard," Aaron insisted, "no cutter would be able to find their way from this harbour."

"I am ordering you, get this cutter moving right now!" The tone of his voice made the navy men tremble, "I am not concerned with this scum."

But Aaron wasn't perturbed by his domineering and selfish attitude, "You can damn well order what you want sir, I am not in your navy thank God, and I have made sure I never will be." Aaron was shaking with rage inwardly. With officers like this in the British navy it was little wonder that men would sooner serve time in typhus ridden prisons than go to sea.

The last party arrived with a marine sergeant in charge. "Sorry we are late – met a French party of soldiers, four men and a sergeant – didn't have time duck into the marshes, we almost bumped into them on the path. They became very suspicious, although one of the lads speaks a little French he picked up while in prison. It wasn't much good, so we had to kill them. I finished a couple off with a bayonet and Simpson strangled a couple – a handy man with his hands that Simpson."

Admiral Medlam was still cursing, "So, we are overloaded. This cutter can't take any more, we have less than six inches of freeboard Jacobs. We should make some men stay behind." He raised his voice a little. "Twenty guineas for any man staying behind!"

A voice from the second cutter hidden in the anonymity of the dark whispered loud enough to be heard in the first boat, "Why don't *you* stay you fat, miserable, old bastard, and we could have another six inches of freeboard."

"Who said that?" The Admiral peered into the darkness, "Every man in that cutter will report to the officer of the watch the minute we step aboard the *Swiftsure*!" He was shaking with rage. "I will find out who said that if I have to flog every man there!"

"If you don't stop talking and raising your voice you won't get *on* that ship to carry out your threats. And what's more we will all lose our heads. I hope you realise how many deaths we are responsible for. Sssssshhhh." He held up his hand. Far off in the distance they could hear men shouting at one another. Aaron climbed quickly to the top of the embankment, in the distance he could see the lights from lanterns swinging. He slid back down the embankment and straight into the cutter. "Let's push off. They are searching for us."

Several of the men waded out as they pushed the cutter into deeper water. The tide had started to turn making it easier to row into the middle of the bay. They passed within inches of a barge, which was too much for Lieutenant Saunders and sitting at the stern he attempted to light a slow match. Eventually, after a few hearty puffs, he saw a glow at the end of the match as they passed within yards of another barge. He stood up and swung the match several times then let go, it arched over and landed in the middle of the barge.

Aaron timed it right, the escaping tide caught the cutters just in time, although it was too dark to see them. There were men shouting from the foreshore. A couple of muskets were fired towards them but the balls were well off their mark.

"Prime your muskets men." Lieutenant Saunders ordered.

Flames from each side of the entrance to the harbour lit up the narrow deeper channel, the gunners having lit huge bonfires put there for just such an occasion. Five hundred yards to go, it seemed more like five miles. The men, some of them very weak from months of captivity living on a diet unfit for dogs and expected to do days of hard manual labour, pulled at the oars with a vengeance. They knew their lives depended on it. In the reflection from the fires trailing out to sea, Aaron felt like an actor on the stage.

"Pull lads, pull. Pull like you are pulling a rapist off your sister. Those that can't get near an oar, paddle with your hands. These gunners may be old but they are well trained. The tide is in our favour, but it will be thirty minutes before we are out of range and swallowed up by the darkness."

The cutter took off, with the other trailing behind, and was within yards of the entrance when the first gun fired. The cannon ball came bouncing over the sea, like children playing with flat stones skimming across the water. The opposite gun opened up – they were in the cross fire. The balls from both directions missed the cutters by inches.

They were so close to both guns now that every time they opened up it almost tore their ears apart. Balls were bouncing off the water with tremendous leaps, and as one approached beside them, they heard it whine. Striking the water again between both cutters, it hit the towing rope with a loud twang sending the bows of the trailing cutter into the stern of the first one.

"That was bloody close!" Someone cursed.

"Raise your muskets lads, but no man leave his oars. Take aim at those gunners, let's show them how British Marines can shoot. We must distract their aim!"

Men were now firing muskets from the shore, musket balls were flying in all directions. Then suddenly, as if hell itself was let loose, there was a tremendous crash; orange, blue and red flames lit up the whole harbour, debris spiralled skywards. The barge nearest them went up in flames. A smouldering barrel twisted and turned as it went sailing through the air and landed on another barge which instantly ignited. They could distinctly see crowds running along the foreshore. Another barge, then another went up in flames until it seemed as if the whole harbour was a raging fire of explosions, rattling one after another and reaching a crescendo of one continual blast. For a some minutes the guns stopped as the gunners stopped to watch the hell breaking loose all round them. The two cutters were almost out of the harbour when the guns, the gunners now over their initial shock, opened up once more.

Another ball came racing over, bounced off the water, and struck a man at the oars.

"Barnes has been hit sir. His head has been knocked off, there's blood everywhere."

"Toss him over the side – it will be less to carry!" The Admiral shouted.

"But he's dead sir."

"Well I didn't expect him to be alive with his bloody head off. Heave him over the side." No respect in his voice, just contempt for his seamen. Not *lower* him over the side, *heave* him over the side.

The men muttered amongst themselves as another ball found its mark, taking away a foot of the gunnels and a part of the planking, leaving barely two inches of freeboard. Every few seconds the cutter heaved up and down taking in water on its downwards thrust. One man acted swiftly, he removed his coat and wrapped it over the damaged woodwork, holding it securely in place with his hands.

"Those not rowing move over to the other side."

With just a few inches to manoeuvre it was a difficult task, but it was sufficient to bank the cutter.

"Haven't you got rid of that dead man yet?" The Admiral demanded. "Get him over the side quickly and look sharp!"

While he had been a prisoner he knew he held on to life by the grace of his crew members. No man had informed the

French. This had subdued him, but now freedom was looking him in the face, his old ferocious ways were returning. One man at the oars stopped and crossed himself as the dead man was lowered over the side.

"Damn you man, grab that oar." He lashed out at the man with his clenched fist. The man bent over his oar cursing the Admiral under his breath. In the light from the blazing barges, which had turned night into day, the Admiral glared at the man. "I will take the skin off your back when we board the *Swiftsure* you damn insolent man."

The man stood up, the oar in his hand as if to strike the Admiral, "Oh no you won't sir! For months we covered for you. You selfish bastard! No man told the Frenchies who you were, one word in their ear and you would have finished up like Barnes, without a head! We covered for you, we helped with your work. Barnes himself helped to pinch extra food and share it with you, and how do you repay us? You threaten us with the cat! When you were in prison it was different – but the minute you smell freedom you are back to your old brutal ways. You couldn't even say a few words for old Barnes. I wouldn't serve on another ship of yours.... we were better off in that hell hole." He pointed shorewards. "Keep your bloody navy, and I hope you rot in hell!" The man jumped into the water and slid beneath the waves...

It had no affect on the Admiral.

"That's another gone – that makes the cutter lighter. You men, rogues the lot of you, will pay for this insubordination. You are a mutinous lot. You, Jacobs, you say you are a civilian, when you step aboard the *Swiftsure* you are under my jurisdiction. You and Lieutenant Saunders will be put under arrest. You were given orders to get me out of that prison not to rescue this scum. Setting fire to those barges put my life at risk."

Aaron knew it was little use arguing with the Admiral. He had taken on the task of saving him on condition he rescued his crew. That task he had fulfilled. He had saved the Admiral, and more than twenty prisoners. In fact there had been thirty men of all ranks.

Chapter Eight

Aaron studied his large silver watch, "I make it five o'clock, which means it has taken us exactly seven hours since we left the frigate. All that remains is to find it again." He nodded towards the blazing harbour, "Those fires have stirred up a hornet's nest. It should be light in an hour's time but in the meanwhile we must get rid of some of this water. I know it's cold but bale out with anything you can. Take off your coats and soak up the water. We should be on board shortly, perhaps you will allow us to split the main brace, eh Admiral?"

"I shouldn't worry about that if I were in your shoes. The minute you step aboard both you and this whipper snapper of a Lieutenant will be clapped in irons. I can vouch he will never see further promotion."

Dawn was breaking and a sea mist rising when they heard men shouting to each other. The men could hardly contain their excitement. Aaron growled, "Keep quiet!" The men in the boat looked at each other.

"Surely it's the frigate sir?"

"No, they are speaking in French. Even if it was the *Swiftsure* they wouldn't be shouting at each other. Don't speak, ship oars and lay still. I don't have to tell you how sound carries across the water, especially with such a calm sea."

A magnetic silence fell over the two cutters, the men trying not to move a muscle. They heard an approaching ship slicing through the water, the crew standing at the bows straining their eyes to see what was going on through the mist. Explosions from the shore rent the air and brilliant flashes – reminiscent of the flashes from the northern lights – followed a few minutes later by a low rumble. They had almost passed the French ship when from its deck a man spotted them and shouted excitedly. But by the time other members of the crew came towards him they had vanished neatly behind a screen of mist. Aaron could distinctly hear his mates chiding him and accusing him of seeing things. The French ship never altered course.

It was quite light before they spotted the *Swiftsure*, the crew seeing him at the same time and altering course. They were about half a mile from the cutters when they saw the French ship now laying off the harbour. The *Swiftsure* didn't alter course but crowded on more sail, tacking several times. The men at the oars pulled for all they were worth making straight for the frigate, and it became a race. They came within range of the frigate with the ship's crew lining the rails and shouting encouragement. Ropes were dropped as they came alongside and those fit enough scrambled up on deck. A bosun's chair was already prepared and lowered for the Admiral. When every man was safely on board, the ship turned and headed for home.

The Lieutenant, one of the first aboard, whispered something to the officer of the watch and as the bosun's chair was lowered to the deck the Admiral was piped aboard. The ship's Captain came to greet him with his hand outstretched, the Admiral now back to his formidable self, ignored the hand and grunted, "I trust you have a fresh uniform for me?"

"Yes sir." He turned to a seaman by his side. "My servant sir – he is at your service, as is my cabin."

"I damn well hope so." He turned and pointed to Aaron and the Lieutenant, "I want those two men arrested. They will both face court martial when we arrive at Portsmouth, damn impudent rascals."

The Captain's look of surprise turned to one of embarrassment as he ordered two marines to escort them both to a cabin.

"I will send food and wine straight down to you, Admiral, and of course a change of clothing."

Locked in the tiny cabin well below the water line and the only light from a small oil lamp Aaron could hardly believe this was happening to them. All they could hear was the sea water rushing past as the frigate made for home, and the crew going about their duties. They were near the crews' quarters, for now and again they heard laughter. Twice on the journey across the channel they heard the shout 'sail ahoy', although the frigate never altered course. The instructions had been to get the Admiral home and under no circumstances to engage the enemy.

There was a soft knock on the door, a heavy bolt slid back and the ship's Captain entered. He was a tall man and had to duck down to get through the door. A marine followed carrying a tray. The Captain with a nod of his head dismissed the marine and closed the door behind him.

"I haven't the slightest idea what this is all about, but I am sure when we reach Portsmouth it will all be sorted out. I am sorry I couldn't come down to see you before but there is plenty of activity about on deck. That perishing French ship tailed us all day yesterday, I could easily have blown him out of the water but my orders were firm, not to engage the enemy 'til the Admiral was safely back on dry land. I am so sorry to see you both in this predicament, obviously I will do all I can for you, you are both very brave men. But what the hell did you do in that harbour, to make the Admiral so furious."

"It was too tempting. Old Napoleon's navy ammunition was all stowed there – we just flung a slow match in one barge and that in turn blew the rest."

"The most I can do here is to make sure you are comfortable and well fed. I have sent you down a bottle of my best wine. Is there anything else you need?"

"No sir, except a walk on the deck?"

"I am sorry, Mr Jacobs, but my orders are to keep you locked up until we reach Portsmouth, we anchor off Spithead and then you are to be taken in chains."

"In chains sir?" The Lieutenant raised his voice in a most indignant manner. "I must protest most strongly, we have done nothing to qualify for such treatment. Is this our reward for rescuing the Admiral from that hell hole? Sir, when this stupid charge is sorted out I have every intention of resigning my commission. I feel I couldn't spend another day in a service that treats its officers in such a manner."

"Be quiet Mr Saunders and keep those feelings to yourself. We are not all like..." Here he cut himself short and clamped his lips together. Saluting with a nod of his head, he left the cabin. A few seconds later they heard the door bolts being slid home. They settled down to their meal and wine.

They couldn't read – it was too dark – so for hours they just talked.

"What do you intend to do Mr Jacobs, go back to smuggling? It must be something, to be your own Captain, even on a small ship such as yours. After this I will join the East India company, I cannot live without the sea. I was a middi at thirteen."

"Well... I won't go back to smuggling. I daren't show my face in that French town again, and it's were my best brandy came from. They'll realise this was carried out by someone familiar with the place and I will be the prime suspect. I doubt if anyone saw me but I couldn't take the chance. I've five hundred guineas coming – safe in the hands of my lawyer. They can't do me out of that. I also have money saved from my smuggling, so I will look around and see if I can find myself a ship and go deep sea.... work off the African coast.... do a little trading."

Mr Saunders laughed, "Definitely not slaving, eh Aaron?"

"You've heard me sir, slaving is the abomination of mankind, any man that deals in human flesh is a disciple of the devil himself. I've seen those smug bastards at the dining table – I wonder how many of them derived their wealth from that disgusting trade. The time will surely come when laws will be made against such a trade. Already voices are being raised in the right places. Mr Wilberforce is urging government to suppress it, and prominent people, influential people, are starting to listen and to side with him. And believe me Mr Saunders, when

I do get my ship there will be no rope's end.... no flogging
....and definitely no bullying by officers. My men will be
told, when they join the ship, what will be expected of
them. Should they break the law of my ship they will be
escorted off on the first land we sight, whether it be inhabited or not. They will be treated like men not animals.
Just look at this navy – men would sooner go to prison
than serve aboard a man-o-war. If men were treated right
they would be queuing to join up."

"Well Aaron if you are thinking of recruiting officers
please let me know. I have every intention of resigning.
What is more I could invest in that ship of yours."

Throughout the day they either slept or talked, stopping
only to eat their meals. They heard the anchor drop, pre-
suming they had finally reached Spithead. It was another
two hours before they came on deck, Aaron breathing in
deeply the fresh air. The Captain was on deck to wish
them God speed and to shake their hands, "I convinced the
Admiral not to send you ashore in chains, but you must
give me your word of honour as officers and gentlemen not
to abscond."

Mr Saunders stood erect and saluted, "Sir, you may rest
assured on that matter. I wouldn't miss this for anything."

The Captain shook hands with them once more, "Good
luck gentlemen and be assured I will do anything in my
power to help you in any way I can. I have already sent
copies of my log ashore telling them of your courage."

The marines' landing party and some of the ex-prisoners
were lined up on deck to bid them farewell. Aaron shook
hands with them one by one and all wished him good luck,
the ex-prisoners thanking him for their unexpected
release. The marines sergeant was the last, he gripped
Aaron's hand, "Good luck sir and don't forget – when you
need crew members, come and look me up." There was a
twinkle in his eye.

Aaron laughed, "I thought you said you wanted a tavern
of your own sergeant."

They lined the ship's rails and waved to them as they
were rowed swiftly into Portsmouth harbour. The same
moss and seaweed-covered stone steps to which he had

first been taken before the mission. Under escort they were marched to the same room in which he had been held when they had first caught him. Now there were two beds and a roaring fire was lighting the room – the room itself warm and cosy. Several books were on the table, two quills, some ink and some paper.

An hour later a large tray was brought in covered with a white cloth. Plates of cold ham, cheese, cold beef and chicken and two bottles of fine wine.

"Compliments of Admiral Webster gentlemen," a marine said smiling, "your exploits are all over the town sir. Everyone is talking about it, how you went right through that French town and released the Admiral and all those prisoners, and you a Portsmouth man Mr Jacobs." There was a note of pride, which the man couldn't hide, in his voice.

They were laying on their beds when the door opened and a high ranking naval officer entered attended by a Captain and a young lieutenant. Lieutenant Saunders jumped from his bed and stood to attention, while Aaron slowly raised himself and sat on the edge of the bed. As far as he was concerned he'd had it up to his eyes with naval discipline. He hadn't the slightest idea why he was entombed in this cabin. He had been requested to spring Admiral Medlam from a prison and been rewarded with the handsome sum of five hundred guineas. As an extra reward he had been insulted by the very man he helped to release and falsely imprisoned on some stupid naval charge.

The young Lieutenant made signs for Aaron to stand up which he completely ignored, but when the visiting Admiral came to his bed and shook his hand Aaron stood up, "That was a marvellous job you did Mr Jacobs, the news is all around the town, it's the talk of the taverns and already a great crowd has gathered outside the dockyard gates. Now I have come to find out just what this nonsense is all about. Tell tell me if I am correct – I've heard the story from a petty officer who was amongst the released prisoners. A man named Sharp, a good man who has served with me several times. He has told me how you actually got to the prison, released some prisoners, and then discovered Admiral Medlam wasn't amongst them. He had been moved to the barracks, a barracks full of French soldiers. You bluffed your way inside and released the Admiral with several more prisoners. Then Lieutenant Saunders here broke into the armoury right under the guards' eyes and stole some slow matches. As you left the harbour with all the prisoners, Saunders blew up a barge which in turn destroyed the remainder of the barges. And you lost only two men, its incredible." He slowly shook his head.

"No sir, we lost only one man. The other committed suicide rather than serve under Admiral Medlam again." The Admiral looked sharply at Aaron.

"Do you mean to say that a seaman who had been incarcerated in a filthy French prison, would rather die than return to serve in the navy? Right. You two men – I am sorry you must stay in this room overnight, but in the morning I want you to see the board. Is there anything you need?"

Lieutenant Saunders sprang to attention, "We would like some clean clothes sir, a bath, and a shave."

The Admiral nodded and left the room ordering the officer with him to make sure the two men got everything they wanted.

Chapter Nine

Aaron, always a man to rise early in the mornings, slept rather late. Earlier someone had crept into the room and stoked the fire. The room was comfortably warm and more fresh clothes had been lain by the side of his bed, a meal prepared at the table. He washed and then a seaman came in and shaved both Aaron and the Lieutenant. "Nice morning Mr Saunders," grinned Aaron, " looks as though the navy has forgiven us."

"Don't jump the gun Mr Jacobs, Admiral Medlam is not a forgiving man. Mark my words, it's far from over yet and Admiral Medlam is a man with influence in very high places. You don't think for one moment they would have gone to all this trouble for any old Admiral. They say he has the ear of His Majesty himself. Believe me we are not out of the woods yet."

"Well they didn't lock the door last night and there was no sentry there, we could have walked out at any time we pleased."

It was well past ten o'clock when they were called back to the main building, no escort, just a marine sergeant to show them the way. Men working on the ships around the yard stopped work and clapped their hands as they passed, several men who knew Aaron slapped him on the back. 'Well done Aaron', almost became a chant. Men took off their hats and those not near enough to speak to them, waved and shouted.

The usual high ranking officers sat at the long table and

71

the rescued Admiral had joined them. A dozen more naval officers sat around the room. Two chairs were set in front of the table and they were invited to be seated. The high ranking Admiral they had met before setting out to liberate the prisoners was the first to speak, "We have read both of your reports and now we have gathered here for you to tell, us in your own words, exactly what happened from the day the *Swiftsure* left Spithead. Mr Jacobs can narrate the story and should he miss any part Lieutenant Saunders can correct him. I don't wish you to miss one word."

So Aaron started. He had already written a full report and kept a few notes to which he occasionally referred, ".....then sir, after insisting that we take all of the prisoners,or none at all, we were called scallywags and traitors. The minute we stepped aboard the *Swiftsure* we were placed under arrest like common criminals...." It was at this point that Admiral Medlam interrupted the story for the first time. The Admiral of the board leaned forward and glared at him. "Sir, we earlier listened to you without interruption. Please now be so good as not to interrupt Mr Jacobs."

"What made you set fire to the barges and put the whole operation in jeopardy?"

"Well sir, it was Mr Saunders' bright idea and I agreed. As well as having the effect of distracting the gunners from the foreshore, it was the most magnificent sight you ever saw – the whole harbour was lit up."

The officers all started laughing and the Admiral said, "I bet it was."

"Well I think we have heard all we wanted to hear, have any of you gentlemen anything to ask Mr Jacobs and Mr Saunders?"

An officer sitting at the side of the room stood up.

"Were you at any time insubordinate to Admiral Medlam?"

"No sir. The only reason I think he called us insolent scallywags was because I insisted that we take all the prisoners or none at all. We had murdered several soldiers and guards. If we had failed to get the prisoners home they would have received the death sentence. There was no way I was going to leave those men behind."

The officers looked at each other. Admiral Medlam had been hoping he would have the officers on his side, but Aaron appeared to be turning the tables on him.

"....Then sir, when we fired the barges the Admiral didn't like it one bit. I could understand that sir – after all our main job was to rescue the Admiral, but as the barges were *there*.... it was too good a chance to miss. I feel sure now, that their navy will be short of powder for some time to come." Another ripple of laughter echoed around the room.

There was a loud knock on the heavy oak doors. The Admiral of the board looked very annoyed that they were being interrupted at this critical moment. The door opened and a young naval officer stood to one side. A small, high ranking officer with an empty sleeve and a cunningly subtle patch over one eye, stepped inside. Everyone sprang to attention. Aaron, turning around in his chair saw a junior officer take the great man's cape and reveal a chest full of awards emblazoned on his coat. He removed his hat, and the patch revealing a badly damaged eye.

"Carry on gentlemen." He said in a rather gruff voice as if suffering from a bad cold.

"God it's Lord Nelson." Lieutenant Saunders whispered under his breath. Aaron sprang smartly from his chair.

"Ah, so these are the two rogues that raided that damn French town and released our men from that infernal prison then had the audacity to set the supply barges on fire. The whole town is talking about their exploits." He turned and addressed the board. "What is going on here?"

"Court of enquiry sir. Admiral Medlam has made a complaint about these two men my lord."

The small figure of Nelson seemed to rise another foot or so as he broadened his chest and walked directly towards Admiral Medlam, "Whatever can you mean Medlam – complaint – what is the nature of this complaint? From what I understand and there is great excitement in the streets about it, these two men put their lives at risk to release you and some of your crew from a French prison. I really would have thought you would assemble here to reward these men. This assembly will stand down 'til I get to the bottom of the matter."

The two officers that accompanied him stood by his side as he approached Aaron and Lieutenant Saunders, "I want to see you two men alone, please follow me. I shall hear your story from start to finish."

They followed him to a much larger room with great leather armchairs scattered about. A bright carpet on the floor contrasted oil paintings of Admirals and high ranking naval officers, many of them long since dead. A full length painting of Captain Cook dominated the fireplace where a blazing log fire roared wildly. Lord Nelson indicated to them to sit in chairs facing him as the other two naval officers took their place. The Captain, a tall man, was obviously Captain Hardy, his Lordship's constant companion. Comfortably seated and a glass of brandy brought in by a steward, placed at each elbow his Lordship said, "From the start tell me everything. You do realise of course that you are both celebrities in this town – what is more the news has reached London."

He listened intently without once interrupting them, at times shaking his head slowly from side to side.

"Well gentlemen – I am at a complete loss for words. What do you intend to do from here, it's men like you the navy needs badly."

"I am sorry sir," Lieutenant Saunders said, "but I mean to tender my resignation. I feel we have been so badly treated that it would be life to a service I no longer respect."

"Nonsense man! Never heard so much balderdash in my entire life. This navy cannot afford to lose men like you. You will be joining my ship H.M.S. *Victory* laying off Spithead in three days time with promotion. You Mr Jacobs, what are your intentions? Back to smuggling, no doubt. It is a pity. You would make a fine officer aboard one of H.M.'s Ships.

"No, my Lord. I regret to say my smuggling days are over. It is obvious that for anyone to break into that prison and successfully release those men, he would have to know every inch of the town. Even if no one recognised me I would be the prime suspect, for I was educated there. I practically grew up in that town."

"Ah that is a pity," There was a twinkle in the Admiral's remaining eye, "I understand your brandy is excellent."

Aaron correctly interpreted the twinkle, for everyone knew his Lordship's favourite tavern was the George Hotel in the High Street. It could be safely said that seventy five percent of brandy drunk in that hotel was brought in by Aaron. "No my Lord, I have sufficient funds to purchase my own ship and I intend to trade on the African coast."

"That's good Jacobs, I like a man with ambition. I hope it isn't slaving."

"Good heavens, no sir."

As his Lordship rose from his chair the junior officer rushed forward with his hat and silk lined cape. He shook hands in turn with each of them.

"What about the charges sir?" Aaron asked.

Nelson laughed, "What charges? Forget it, gentlemen. Charges? More like rewards. I am instructing the paymaster to reward you with a further two hundred guineas. You, Mr Saunders, I expect on my flagship in seventy-two hours time. Good luck to the both of you." With an abrupt movement he turned and made for the door, his aide rushing before him to open it.

After they left they both stared at the closed door for some moments.

"Well there goes my ambition of being your partner Aaron. It was a lovely dream for a few hours, but with Admiral Nelson as my patron, things just cannot go wrong. The news will spread around the fleet that his Lordship himself has ordered me to his ship. No doubt I will be the envy of every officer in the navy. Very sorry Aaron."

Aaron dismissed the apology with a wave of his hand, "To tell you the truth Mr Saunders, I wasn't that keen on having a working partner. However if you wish to indulge in a little investing – contact my lawyers in the High Street."

They were ushered back into the board room. The officers, with the exception of the two Admiral Medlams, were laughing and joking. The junior Medlam had a deep scowl on his face as the president of the board rose to his feet.

"You both have no case to answer. All that remains is for me to wish you both, and I think the whole of this board agrees with me, all the very best of luck for the future. You have shown both tenacity and bravery in this operation. Won't you please reconsider it Mr Jacobs and remain with us in His Majesty's Navy."

Aaron laughed, he could afford to be bolder knowing he had Lord Nelson on his side, "No thank you sir, that's the last thing I want."

Outside they both took a lungfull of fresh, crisp September air. The air of freedom – for Aaron had felt for the past few days that he was walking on a razor's edge, and that a century had passed since he was dragged from his lugger. He could hardly wait to return to the warmth of his own ship. It didn't compare in size to any man-o-war but it was his home. They shook hands warmly.

"Bye Saunders, and don't forget when you get your own ship treat your crew like men, not animals, you will find they respond."

"Bye Aaron, it has been a pleasure to be in your company."

Before he returned to his lugger Aaron had work to complete in the High Street. As he walked along the Hard and High Street, friends that knew him and some that didn't came out of the taverns to cheer him and slap his back.

"Well done Aaron." Some of those that could hardly afford to buy their own ale insisted on inviting him into the tavern to drink his health. Much to the relief of the majority, he thanked them but refused.

The lawyer's clerk saw him coming along the street and rushed to the door to let him in, bowing and scraping as Aaron entered and gave the clerk his hat.

"Captain Jacobs I am so glad to see you have arrived back and all in one piece." Etiquette was put aside, for no miserable lawyer's clerk should grasp the hand of his employer's client, pumping it up and down.

Aaron was shown into the inner sanctum and a leather chair pulled in front of the gigantic desk. The lawyer stood up and greeted him before once more Aaron had to recite the whole episode. By the time he had finished the lawyer was visibly shocked. He pulled out two glasses from a cupboard and a bottle of his finest port, kept solely for his most valued customers.

"Shall we get down to business now, sir?" Aaron drained his second glass congratulating the lawyer on his choice of port.

"The Admiralty are rewarding me a further two hundred guineas. With what you are holding and what I have from my previous activities I feel I have sufficient to buy my own ship and begin trading down the African coast."

"Slaving Mr Jacobs?"

"No, not slaving." Strange, thought Aaron, any mention of the African coast and immediately everyone takes it for granted that you intend to become a slaver, "that may be all most traders can think about, but there are other trades for a good merchant, other goods are in demand. I am aware you deal with ship owners and shipping in general, can you recommend a ship broker or builder?"

"I can do better than that. A friend of mine builds ships over in Bucklers Hard. Most of his ships are for the navy but sometimes he builds merchant ships. I know he does have a very nice ship, not too big, just over seventy feet long. It was built for a slaver, and is very fast. Better still, it is easily crewed. It's a beautiful ship with graceful lines – just three years old — and for the past six months it's been laid up."

He wrote a note and passed it to Aaron. "The builder is Mr Feltham. Just hand him this note and I am sure he will help you. Should you require an agent to handle this side of your business you can count on my services."

It was cold outside but the sun was bright, and where possible Aaron walked on the sunny side of the narrow streets. He was now eager to be safely back in his lugger with Polly and Willie.

He stood on the foreshore and gave the usual whistle. Willie, working on the deck, looked up and saw Aaron waving. Polly was soon on deck, still wearing a pair of Aaron's trousers cut down and a white shirt. She waved frantically and cursed Willie who was already in the lugger's

dinghy and rowing frantically towards the foreshore.
Willie jumped out of the small boat, as it crunched onto the
beach and wrapped his arms round Aaron.

"Pack it in Willie you will be bloody kissing me next."

They were back on the lugger in minutes. Polly, with the
coffee pot already on the boil, was crying and laughing at
the same time as she threw her arms around Aaron's
broad shoulders and repeatedly kissed him over his face
and neck.

"Calm down Polly, you're worse than Willie."

That night in the cosy glow of the small stove Aaron had,
yet again, to relate his story — he hoped for the last time.

Chapter Ten

"**P**repare to sail Willie." Aaron kicked the small sail locker where Willie slept when his skipper was entertaining Polly. It was uncomfortable in the extreme but now that Aaron was safely back on board the young crew member didn't have the slightest objection.

He crawled out on his hands and knees through the door to the locker, which was barely three feet high. He blinked, his eyes in the weak September sunlight and stretched.

"We aren't going smuggling are we Cap'n?" But he already knew this wasn't possible, for a smuggling trip always necessitated sailing under the cover of darkness. In any case the ripe time for smuggling had been a couple of days previous – when there had been no moon at all. Tonight there would be a new moon.

"No Willie, those days are well past. Today we are going over to Bucklers Hard – I hear there's a good vessel for sale and I'm taking you and Polly to inspect it."

Polly came on deck rubbing goose pimples from the tops of her folded arms. She yawned, "My God it's cold this morning Aaron," she watched Willie preparing the sails, "where are we off to ?"

"Wait and see Polly.... just you wait and see. Go below now and prepare breakfast."

Feeling the swell of the Solent once more, and in his own craft, sent Aaron's pulse racing. He faced the stubborn wind and made the ship tack incessantly towards the Southampton Water and his final destination Bucklers

Hard, an area he knew well. As a teenager his father had taken him to the shipbuilders while they had a new mast stepped, and seeing the great trees stretching almost to the water line he knew he was nearing his destination. They entered the Beaulieu River, hearing the activity of the noisy shipyard long before they reached it. Men crawled over half-finished ships, and wooden templates of ships' ribs littered the yard. A skeleton of one ship with its planking half completed stood on the stocks leading to the water, as did another ship almost finished with two masts stepped and another being manoeuvred into position. Skilled craftsmen, with sharp adzes, shaped the wooden ribs and iron bolts being driven home while men standing over saw pits sawed great trunks as blacksmiths' hammers working at the anvils in the open, resounded against the forest.

Willie rowed Aaron ashore on the small dinghy. As it crunched into the shingle Aaron jumped out and asked the first man he encountered where he could find Mr Feltham. The man touched his hat with his finger and pointed to a small wooden building. "He be there sir."

There was no door on the small wooden building and one wall was completely missing. A man, well into his forties and greying at the temples, was pouring over large plans.

"Mr Feltham?" The man looked round sharply.

"Yes?"

Aaron held out his hand, "My name is Jacobs, I was sent by my lawyer Mr Harris."

"Come in Mr Jacobs." He pushed forward a roughly made stool, the bark still on its legs, "What can I do for you?"

"Mr Harris said you may have a ship for sale."

He shook his head slowly, "Well Mr Jacobs I don't deal in merchant ships, at the moment my books are filled with the Admiralty. It's this war you know."

He went to the opening he called a door and looked out at the two ships on the slipway. He was a huge man that almost filled the frame of the open doorway.

"The Admiralty must have that one in two months' time. And the other, they want in two weeks. We are just stepping-in the masts. Where the hell they expect me to get the tradesmen from, God only knows. You can't get the men now Mr Jacobs, and I pay the best for miles around. My shipwrights get four pence an hour and some of them work up to seventy hours a week. They take home more pay than I do."

Aaron smiled to himself and thought, 'that'll be the day'. But Mr Feltham wasn't letting him off so easily, he went into a long tirade of how well he treated his men (they all looked half starved) and kept on and on as to the difficulties of procuring good tradesmen. In fact he touched on every subject except the business in hand. Aaron sat patiently listening, then was suddenly startled by the man shouting and thumping the table with his clenched fist. "Ah! Mr Harris. The lawyer man. A ship.... I know, it was old Captain Reeves.... I built it for him about three years ago. He wanted a fast ship for slaving. I don't hold with that myself but the plans he gave me were a challenge. Fast little ship, not too big. Designed it himself, you know. His wife went everywhere with him, she was the business woman, then she took sick and died off the African coast. He brought her body back to Portsmouth for a christian burial. It took the life out of him.... came ashore and bought a little house in the Forest then, would you believe it, he died a couple of months later. I think he just gave up the ghost.... his wife dying, then giving up the sea. He only has two nephews and I don't think he had much time for them. They gave Mr Harris instructions to dispose of the estate. The ship is the *Golden Falcon* and is laying in the Hamble. I often think old Captain Reeves has gone to join his wife in hell." He gave Aaron a bunch of keys. "Go and have a look at the ship, I think you will like her."

It didn't take Aaron long to find the ship, dropping anchor some hundred yards away. Willie rowed him and Polly to the ship in the small dinghy where they rounded the once bright stern decorated with gilt lettering and artistic scrolls, a large picture window at the stern. Aaron inspected the planking, taking out a knife and digging it in, the blade only penetrating the paint. He nodded his head in satisfaction. The bows were the most startling, the bowsprit stuck out for ten feet and the three of them held

81

their breath when they saw the figurehead, a large golden falcon with its wings outstretched and its beak open in a magnificent snarl.

Aaron climbed aboard and gave his hand to Polly in order to hoist her onto the deck. He looked around proudly, first going to the large cabin at the stern. No item of luxury had been spared and inside, below a large window that stretched the whole width of the ship was a seat covered in blue velvet with curtains to match. There was definitely a woman's touch to the furnishings. A highly polished table, now covered with a thin film of dust. A double bed in one corner and bookshelves filled with books, the Captain certainly had a variety of tastes. An ornate iron stove and two leather covered chairs. A huge triple brass lamp hung over the table and two oil lamps at the bed head. More oil lamps round the walls.

Polly gasped. "She is beautiful Aaron."

They inspected the rest of the ship. Like all sea going vessels the crews quarters were cramped. The small galley had two stoves enclosed in a brick walled section, the only other piece of furniture was a large table with several knives in a rack at the side.

At the stern stood two very large copper boilers on a solid brick fireplace. At first they were at a loss as to their function but Aaron soon realised, "It's for the slaves. Poor devils must have only ate when the weather was fine." He lifted the lid off one, it was filled with small metal bowls and crude wooden spoons. He pointed to the evil cooking arrangements, "That lot will be the first to go."

They lifted the cover of the first hold, the smell knocking them back. Polly hardly knew any other world but the stinking narrow streets of Portsmouth, but that smell was nothing compared to this. "My God Aaron, what is it?"

"Slaves Polly, slaves." They lifted the cover completely. Several rows of ringbolts were secured to the floor. A few feet above these a shelf, six feet wide, ran each side of the ship and at the edge another row of ring bolts. Barely four feet above this another shelf three feet wide with no room for a man nor child to sit. "This is where they kept the child slaves."

"They weren't they allowed on deck for fresh air?" The nauseating sight was affecting Polly, her eyes wet with emotion.

"That depended upon the whim of the Captain. Those dark stains you see all over the holds are where they did their business." Aaron pointed to a cannon mounted on the rails leading to the stern deck six feet above them, "That small brass cannon was loaded with grapeshot and trained on the slaves when they were allowed, a few only at a time, on deck. It is not unknown for a Captain to shoot a couple of slaves and throw the bodies overboard, just as a warning to the rest, the better looking of the women distributed amongst the crew. Once these poor people are captured they belong body and soul to whoever owns them at the time."

The second hold was an exact replica of the first – if anything in a much filthier condition. Polly not wanting to see any more of the slaves quarters, wandered back to the great cabin. After the hell she had just seen, she wondered how any man, never mind woman, could live alongside in such luxurious surroundings. There was a polished oak box against the wall, she hadn't noticed before. Lifting the lid and sliding out two brass fasteners from the front, it fell away and revealed a small organ. The top of the organ was filled with sheets of music and hymn books.

"Why the hypocritical old bastard...." Aaron crept up silently behind her and she jumped, her heart pounding inside her chest like a beating drum. Aaron picked up the heaviest of the books, it was a family bible. He slammed the covers together and tossed it onto the table echoing Polly's sentiment, "The hypocritical old bastard.... how could he justify reading the bible and at the same time trade in slaves. I hope he and that damn wife of his rot in hell."

As Aaron stood at the stern of his lugger watching the Golden Falcon fade into the distance, Polly came and put her arm round him. She knew him well enough by now, and when he made his mind up nothing would deter him. She knew that the ship already belonged to him.

As if talking from far away he said, "It will take some

time to clear out the ghosts and misery left behind in that ship Polly, beside the smell."

It was everything he had strived for – he had dreamed of such a ship – and he knew he wouldn't know happiness until he was striding the decks as its Captain.

Mr Feltham was on the foreshore ready to greet him as he stepped ashore from the dinghy, "Well Mr Jacobs, how did you find the *Golden Falcon*?"

Aaron hid his feelings with difficulty, "She certainly is a beautiful ship Mr Feltham but the stench stuck in my nostrils. I'm afraid Reeves was a bible-thumping old hypocrite and must be in hell right now. Is the ship haunted?"

Unconciously, Aaron's last question made Mr Feltham extemely uneasy. Several would-be buyers had turned down the ship for just this reason. One Captain going as far as to say, 'I wouldn't buy that damn ship if you asked five guineas for it.' He'd thought it must be haunted by the ghosts of slaves that had died crossing the Atlantic. The rumour had spread like wildfire – there was no one more superstitious than sailors.

"She's a fairly new ship Mr Jacobs. I built her myself and she's as solid as a rock." They were sat in front of a blazing fire of wood chips, cut from ships' timbers, "The cabin was designed by Mrs Reeves. It would be just right for you and that young lady wife of yours." He nodded towards the lugger where Polly was sitting on the cabin top wrapped in a blanket. Feltham poured out two glasses of strong sherry and passed one to Aaron, "She is going for a song..."

He studied Aaron's face as he sipped at his sherry. He didn't want to frighten him off, "....I am asking a rock bottom price – twelve hundred guineas."

Aaron laughed aloud, twelve hundred guineas would account for every penny he had, "Sorry Mr Feltham, that's right out of my league – I've wasted your time."

He was about to take his leave when Mr Feltham put a restraining hand on his arm. Aaron had been dealing with French traders since a child, and the gesture of Mr Feltham assured him the negotiations were far from over. "What price do you have in mind?"

Aaron quietly studied the ship builder's face. From his cautious tone he must have had the *Golden Falcon* on his hands quite a while.

"To be honest sir, my figure was five hundred guineas." The ship builder winced but didn't immediately reject the price, "....perhaps I could go to six hundred. I have to agree with you she is a beautiful ship. But that smell.... did Captain Reeves have trouble with his nasal organs? It's dreadful."

Mr Feltham was under no illusions. Previous potential customers had been put off buying for the same reason and he'd received orders from the old Captain's nephews that the ship must be sold at any cost to the next serious buyer, "Well perhaps, Mr Jacobs, we could compromise. Say eight hundred guineas and that old lugger of yours. It won't fetch a lot of money but if it fetched another hundred, it would make me feel I haven't been robbed."

Aaron stood up and held out his hand, "We can call it a deal Mr Feltham if you would get your painter to touch up the gold at the bows and stern. I will get some men over from Portsmouth to give the ship a good clean out, use lime on the inside, and get rid of the smell and finally remove all traces of the previous 'cargo'."

Two weeks later Aaron, with a new crew, stood at the bows of his ship, hands behind his back studying the coast line of the Solent and Hampshire as he took the *Golden Falcon* on its trials.

Chapter Eleven

A fair wind and a choppy sea lifted the sharp bows of the ship clear of the water. Aaron rolled confidently with the ship's movements hardly believing that he was the proud owner of such a fine vessel. His crew had worked hard scouring the decks and the holds of the ship to rid itself of the ghosts of the past. They scrubbed and holystoned both inside the holds and the decks themselves and only a slight odour remained as he passed the open holds. A few days at sea would reduce this smell further, but nothing would ever remove the dreadful human stains from the holds. All that remained now was to throw away those ghastly chains and ankle braces that had held the poor creatures locked to the decks. In mid channel he would stop the ship and ceremoniously throw the chains and the copper boilers overboard, laying any ghosts that would be lurking in the ship forever to rest.

Two days later they picked up with a naval frigate making its way towards Portsmouth, the frigates' crew lining the deck and watching the graceful ship pass. A young naval officer came to the ship's rail with his speaking trumpet, "Ahoy there Captain! Where bound?"

"Portsmouth sir."

"A graceful ship, sir, five golden guineas we race you to the Needles."

Aaron nodded his head and shouted, "Make it ten!"

They were within half a dozen fathoms of each other.

"Right!" shouted the officer, "Meet in the Dolphin tonight

at eight, winner takes all."

"Right lads, let's show what the *Golden Falcon* can do. We will teach these damn naval chaps what sailing is all about." At the same time he could hear from the frigate distinct orders and the sounds of the rope's end slicing through the air as instructions were shouted and men ran along the decks chased by petty officers.

For the first hour they raced neck and neck. The frigate jockeying for position and trying to come alongside the *Golden Falcon* and starve it of wind, but Aaron handled the ship as if it were a ballet dancer. Gradually, but surely, foot by foot, Aaron's ship nosed in front of the frigate, supposedly the fastest ship in the navy.

It was four hours before the Needles came into view and both ships were still racing neck and neck; *Golden Falcon* with her bows just a few feet in front. The frigate twice drew perilously close, with crews of both ships prepared to fend each other off constantly exchanging insults.

The excitement was growing, the naval ship's crew had been promised an extra tot of rum as a winning bonus, while Aaron's crew were hoping to build a reputation. Winning the race, of course, meant much more than ten guineas to Aaron. He needed to prove that the *Golden Falcon* was the fastest ship on the high seas.

Passing the Needles the *Golden Falcon* had stretched four lengths ahead of the navy ship and a cheer went up from its crew as they turned into the Southampton Water and anchored off Hamble. Polly ran up to Aaron and threw her arms round his neck, "That showed 'em Aaron; that showed them stuck up naval officers how to handle a ship."

After all the legal documents had been signed they took the ship round to Portsmouth and safely berthed at the Camber where it gathered a crowd of admiring sightseers. His old friends came down to congratulate him and were soon swigging his best brandy. But Aaron had little time for socialising and made his way to the office of his lawyer, who was now acting as his agent.

"Nice neat craft.... I watched you come into the harbour. She handles well I hope?"

"Perfect. In fact, far easier than I'd anticipated. We even raced a frigate to the Needles.... showed her a clean stern most of the way."

"I do have some cheerful news for you Mr Jacobs. I have managed a cargo for you to West Africa – a mixed cargo – and you know you can always pick up a cargo on the return from Madeira or the Canaries. Of course, there *is* still a fortune to be made in slaves."

"No thank you sir, that trade is the most repulsive on the high seas, to me it's worse than piracy. My men have worked for days scouring my ship and I still have the occasional smell assail my nostrils, I doubt if I will ever get rid of it."

Aaron was surprised that Mr Harris had brought the subject up. Had he got the cargo for west Africa purposely, to show him what a lucrative business slavery could be? A good slaver could make enough money on one trip to keep him in comfort for the rest of his life. All that was needed was good healthy slaves and to catch the market at the right moment. The West Indies was booming and the markets of New Orleans were demanding more and more slaves. At the same time the abolitionists in England were becoming more vocal and were gaining much public support. Traders knew it would soon be abolished and were replenishing their stocks as fast as possible.

Nothing would move Aaron. He took the papers from the lawyer and read the manifest, "I have to pick up the cargo at Plymouth and drop it at Lagos – I hear it is fever ridden down there Mr Harris."

"I believe so Mr Jacobs, so make sure you don't let your crew ashore." He stood up and leaned across his desk to shake hands, "Good luck Mr Jacobs."

Aaron assembled his crew amidships and addressed them.

"You know me men, I have at times drank with you. Well... aboard my ship I am your Captain and will be addressed as such," There was a slight murmuring amongst the crew and he let it die down, "There will be no rope's end of lash aboard my ship, any misdemeanours will be treated by fines stopped from your wages. Anything too severe and I can guarantee you this, the next sight of land

and the offender will be put ashore. I won't give a damn if it's inhabited or not, and fighting aboard this ship will warrant this punishment. I want no scurvy aboard this ship. It has been proved, without a doubt, that eating oranges and limes prevents this; so when we reach the Canaries we will take on fresh fruit and each man will be given an orange or a lime each day and he will eat it. Any man not eating his fruit will be fined heavily. There will be no drunkenness aboard. What you do ashore is your business, but aboard this ship I want a sober crew." The Captain searched their faces for any reaction, but they seemed in agreement, "Any questions?"

A hand shot up, and a toothless old man stepped forward, "Will Miss Polly be sailing with us Captain? It's unlucky to have a woman aboard a ship."

"Toothy Meadows. You stupid old bugger. Of course she will be sailing with us, she is part of the crew." One or two of the men laughed nervously and a couple shifted uneasily on their feet, "What damn nonsense is this? Don't act like of lot of stupid old women. The Captain who had this ship before me always sailed with his wife. Forty years I understand, until she died of fever caught from a slave. Now, come on.... any man that don't want to sail, go ashore."

Meadows sidled uncomfortably back into the crowd. No man made a move to go ashore.

Webber, an old merchant hand and a skilled cargo packer, was put in control of stowing the load, making sure that it wouldn't move in a high sea. He reported to Aaron, touching his forehead with the tips of his fingers, "All safely stored aboard, nothing will move that cargo sir. It's fitting as tightly in that hold as a fair maiden's glove."

"I trust you are right Webber, we will be passing through the Bay of Biscay in a few days time and you know the reputation of the bay."

"Aye, I do that sir, I have sailed through there many a time sir, and that's a test for any man's seamanship." He threw a glance over Aaron's shoulder towards Polly who was making herself useful in the great cabin. At the same time Webber cast an envious eye around the graceful surroundings, far different from the crews' quarters. Nevertheless he had been at sea for many years and his berth was luxury compared to some ships he had sailed on.

Willie tapped on the cabin door and entered, touching his forehead with his knuckles, "We are prepared to sail sir. The men are at their stations."

Aaron stood at the ship's wheel. This was the great day he had dreamed of all his life, and he felt a lump come up in his throat. Every man's eye would be upon him, and a small crowd had gathered at the dockside, including some of the crews' wives and families dabbing their eyes, as the gap between ship and quay widened.

A slight breeze filled the few sails needed to manoeuvre. Orders were shouted and the men responded, as they drifted towards the middle of the harbour from where the tide would pull them around and they would head towards the entrance.

The ship responded well to Aaron's touch. Several men-o-war were anchored in the roads and the crews were all looking towards the *Golden Falcon*, a pretty sight as she cut through the water. They passed the frigate they had raced a few days previously and several signal flags were hoisted. Aaron wasn't acquainted with them but Jenson an ex-navy man smiled and shouted to Aaron, "They wish you good luck and God speed, Captain!" He dipped his red ensign in recognition and one or two of the crew raised their hats and cheered.

They were soon out in the open sea but clung to the coast as much as possible; for the country was still at war with the French and Spanish, and the *Golden Falcon* would make a valuable prize. Yet Aaron was so confident in his ship that he felt he could outrun any enemy ship – French or Spanish. By nightfall they passed Land's End and were out into the open Atlantic, the ship cutting through the waves, sails filling and billowing out, bows lifting and coming down with a smack. Willie had taken the wheel and Aaron was sitting in his cabin polishing off a meal of fresh beef and vegetables washed down with a tankard of fine ale.

"Pass me the cheese, Polly." He looked up at her and in

the flickering pale light from the oil lamps Aaron noticed that she hadn't touched anything on her plate, "Not feeling well Polly?" He stared closely at her face, even in the pale light he could see she had changed colour, her face like a waxen mask, and her lips, usually full and rosy red, had retreated back into her face. What he could see of them were an ashen grey. As her hand stretched out and pushed the cheese dish towards him, she shook her head.

"Better eat something Polly – try a bit of bread and some water – if you *are* sea sick it won't be so bad if you have something to come up."

Suddenly Polly snapped back at him, "Shut up Aaron!"

She raced for the cabin door and he followed her up on deck, his mouth still full of cheese and bread, and the tankard of ale in his hand. Polly was hanging over the ship's rail, retching violently. He gently put his arm round her, "Don't worry Polly, the first few days are the worst."

She pushed him away, "I wish I were dead Aaron, I feel so dreadful."

He led her gently back to the cabin and placed her on the bed. Knowing it would get a lot worse, Aaron worked the sheets into a wide strap and secured her to the bed. He tied a bucket to the bed and, holding her up in his arms, forced her to drink a glass or water. It stayed down for less than a minute, but made the retching easier. He sat beside her mopping her sweating forehead with a damp cloth. Polly was set to spend the most miserable night of her life, "Now take is easy Polly. Keep sipping this water and if you can, eat some dry bread."

Aaron returned to the deck and looked around. There was no sight of land and he took out his telescope to study the horizon for a few minutes before snapping it shut. The clouds hung heavy, "We are in for a real blow today Willie, but we are making good time." He leaned over the side of the ship and watched the bows slicing through the water, feeling proud of the way she confidently cut through the waves, "If the wind gets stronger we had better shorten sail, we don't want them blowing away."

The words were hardly out of his mouth when a gigantic wave lifted the bows clear of the water and the hull fell crashing back with a mighty roar as it met the water. Again 'shorten sail' orders were shouted and the crew already at their stations acted quickly as the ship, tossed and turned, heeled over on its side, righted and shook herself like a small terrier dog after a swim.

"I hope you are right Webber about that cargo – this will prove it." Webber grinned and stuck his thumb up.

For three days the storm was at its most fierce. Then when they thought it was all over, the ship was caught in the vortex of a gigantic whirlpool, and raced round and around in diminishing circles, as if a destructive young child was playing with a sail boat in a pool of water. The vortex at its outermost rim was easily three miles in circumference. The more the ship was spun around the smaller became the vortex until they felt they were locked in a tight bottle. Several of the men crossed themselves, as Aaron attempted to lash himself to the ship's wheel. But to no avail, he had lost complete control, and it spun endlessly. Desperately, he tried to hold on until it seemed it would break his arm. Not given ordinarily to religion, he felt it was about time he should give it a try and sent up a silent prayer as daylight turned to night in the swell of the gigantic cavern.

Just as everyone had given up hope, the swirling ceased as suddenly as it had started and instead of heading downwards the vessel began spinning up and up until they reached the top and shot out of the water like a suddenly released cork. They returned to the sea with an almighty crash that reverberated through the entire ship, the waves still mountainous.

"Soon as you can Webber, get down in the holds and see if any of the timbers have sprung."

In the forecastle that night every man agreed that they had never experienced anything like it in their lives. Poor old Meadows retreated to a corner of the mess shaking his greying head, "I *told* thee so.... ne'er have a woman aboard ship.... they *do* bring bad luck."

"Bad luck? You silly old bugger, we're still alive ain't we? She brung us good luck, I should think.... or we should all be in Davy's locker by now – shark meat I can tell 'ee."

One day later and the sea was as calm as a mill pond. They carried out a thorough inspection of the ship, there was some slight damage to the starboard rail but the timbers below were in perfect condition. Aaron was pleased with himself and confident he could sail the ship around the world if he had to.

Chapter Twelve

With just enough wind astern to drive them along at six to eight knots, there was not the slightest trace of the catastrophic whirlpool and storm they had left behind in their wake. The crew were old hands at sea and it became the topical talking point for weeks – everyone, without exception, claiming they had never encountered anything like it.

"I went round the Horn on a three decker once. The waves were higher than the masts and the ship tossed and turned. We'd all given up hope of ever seeing dry land again, but it was nothing compared with that whirlpool." The old sailor shook his head and repeated, "I ain't never seen nothing like that."

The heavy clouds that had been with them since they entered the Bay, began to disperse allowing the sun to turn the blue calm sea into a brilliant golden haze. Bedraggled, her blonde hair hanging round her shoulders like knotted ropes, Polly staggered on deck with a blanket round her shoulders. As Willie ran towards her, she looked terribly unsteady on her feet and he spread the blanket out on her usual position on deck, "Feel any better Polly?"

She shook her head, "I think I died in that cabin Willie." She shaded her eyes from the brilliant sunlight, "Get me something to eat will you?" He knew then she was over the worse.

As the sun grew warmer Polly took advantage of it. The crew no longer took notice of her laying on deck with a pair of Aaron's trousers cut down to fit her and a white shirt tied at the waste. She lay there trying to make out the words in a book Aaron had loaned her. At times Willie or Aaron would come to her aid and help her out, but it was surprising how quickly she learned to read. At other times she would watch the antics of the dolphins racing and somersaulting around the ship and be amused at these displays of water acrobatics which, to Polly, were a show for her benefit. Racing in front of the ship and darting away at the last moment to avoid coming into contact with the sharp bows, these great sea mammals were playing and frolicking in a wonderland along with the greatest variety of rainbow coloured fishes Polly had ever seen. Whenever possible she would lean over the ship's rail and watch the flying fish playing a most prominent part, skimming and skipping across the waves.

Willie came and stood beside her leaning on the rail, "It's strange Willie, a few nights ago when we were in that violent storm I wished I were dead, but look at this around you, the beautiful sunshine, a clear blue sea and the sky coming together on the horizon. Doesn't it make you feel so happy to be alive? It's such a far cry from the dirty old streets of Portsmouth. You don't know how happy I am Willie, to have left that all behind me."

The young man placed a consoling hand on her shoulder, "It was worse for me Polly, at least you had a roof over your head. Me.... I had to sleep where I could find a hole to creep in. Sometimes, I went without food for days."

They hadn't realised just how long they had stood there until Menzies filled the air with a fast-moving shanty on his fiddle. Darkness fell with a suddenness only found in the tropics, and they laughed together as some of the crew danced a jig on the deck. Polly seized Willie's hand and pulled him towards the dancers, "Come on Willie! You will have me crying if we stay here wallowing in our own self pity."

It was midnight before she joined Aaron in the great cabin. She awakened early next morning to the shout of 'Land dead ahead!' and the crew running about on the deck above. As excited as the rest of the crew she jumped into her trousers and shirt and ran barefoot to the deck. All she could see was a white crested mountain top poking through the sea mist.

"That's Tenneriffe!" a crew member shouted, "I would recognise that mountain anytime."

It was another three hours before they could see the land mass that was the Canaries.

A balding man with a large round pot belly stood at the quayside waiting to greet Aaron and Polly, as Willie and another crew member rowed them ashore in the ship's small dinghy. Polly listened closely as Aaron related warnings he had been given concerning the man on the quay, "He'll get half of what he asks. He is an agent and will relieve you of the last penny."

Polly was still dressed in trousers and shirt, opened slightly at the neck to show a cleavage exciting enough to set a man's pulse racing. The agent licked his greasy lips and stood dangerously at the edge of the shaky wooden quay in an effort to get a better view down her shirt, a sickly grin on his face, "Señor, señor, you want supplies? You tell me. I get a good price for you." He took a lump of chalk from his pocket and waved a piece of slate above his head. "Water señor, I have nice sweet water."

Aaron had prepared a list and handed it to the man. "Oranges, lemons, limes, bananas, fresh vegetables, potatoes, tobacco and wine."

"Señor.... that is very good."

He started to do his calculations and wrote a few figures down, then handed Aaron the slate board. Aaron was perfect in French and although he had a smattering of Spanish, it still left a lot to be desired. He made a pretence of reading it then shook his head, "No señor, these prices are far too high. We can get these stores in Madeira at half this price. I understand there is an agent over there – an Englishman – a very honest man. The water is a quarter of this price." He tapped the slate with his hand and shaking his head whistled through his teeth, "Look at the price of this fruit, it is scandalous. I would do better dealing with the growers." He drew a line across the bananas, "Far too many, they will rot even if I were to give the crew bananas for breakfast, dinner and tea."

"I am an honest man señor." His face took on a pitying look like a man grossly insulted but didn't want to retaliate. A sale was imminent and the English always paid in gold, business hadn't been too good what with the war and siding with Napoleon, so he tried a softer approach. "Señor our water is very soft and sweet, Madeira water is hard." He spat on the ground to emphasise his contempt for Madeira water. Aaron made out he wasn't interested in what the agent had to say, while Polly turned her interest to the locals selling fruit and wares on the quayside.

The agent grabbed Aaron's arm, "All right señor," and making out he was revising the list, he rubbed the slate clean with his elbow and rewrote the bill. Aaron took the board, read it with a look of disgust, then halved the original price and handed it back. The agent slapped the flat of his hand against his forehead, then pulled out an enormous handkerchief. Polly thought he was going to burst into tears. He dabbed his sweat soaked forehead and neck, blew his nose furiously then clasping his hands together as if in prayer, he waved them up and down imploring "But señor, I have a wife and ten children.... I have my men to pay. Señor.... I cannot do it at this price."

Aaron lifted his shoulders with complete indifference and turned to walk away, but again the agent put a restraining hand on his arm and again broke into a nervous sweat, sensing a deal slipping away, "All right! You pay me now?"

"When I see those stores and water aboard my ship, you will be paid in gold." He shook the man's clammy hand, feeling that under any circumstances he wasn't to be trusted. He sent word to Wilson, the next in charge, to check every item as they arrived on board, then headed for the small town, Polly, with her long golden hair tied behind her neck walking between Aaron and Willie. Her skin, bronzed by the sun, caused many heads to turn.

Several small boats were surrounding the ship, all busy loading her with stores when they returned from town. Wilson was anxiously waiting for them as they stepped on deck. "Had a couple of Spaniards here Cap'n." He touched his forehead, "Bit hot under the collar, waving their arms about and shouting. I hadn't the slightest idea what they were talking about, you know what these foreigners are like, but they seemed upset, I think they wanted to know what we are doing here. I told them to sling their hooks."

Aaron never discovered what the two men wanted or who they were. The agent had the labourers working non stop with the crew, agitated until every item was aboard. Just after midnight the work was completed. The agent, hat in hand stepped aboard. "It is all aboard Captain." He handed Aaron the slate with every item checked and signed by Wilson. Aaron counted out the gold coins and prepared to sail. The tide and wind was in their favour and they headed out to sea and the African coast.

To celebrate their escape from what the crew had thought was certain death and to celebrate their first landfall on foreign land Aaron ordered that each man should be issued with a bottle of Spanish wine. With a fair wind the ship glided towards the African coast. The old fiddler was still protesting how unlucky it was to have a woman on board, but now not so loudly. The wine soon took affect and half way down the bottle the old man took out his fiddle, soon the whole crew were singing and dancing. Polly came on deck and stood by the ship's rail her long blonde hair blowing in the breeze, now turned a silver colour with a bright moon behind her. She leaned over the rail watching the phosphorous blue sea being pushed away by the bows of the ship. For the first time in her life she was beginning to realise she was completely free. As she turned and waved to Aaron at the ship's wheel, his temples throbbed; he realised just how beautiful she was. Deep in thought he bit through the stem of his clay pipe, the bowl fell to the deck smashing into a dozen parts, spreading hot tobacco ash across the deck. She put her hand to her mouth and suppressed a laugh.

Chapter Thirteen

Dawn was just casting its golden glow over the calm sea as the sun slowly skirted the horizon, heralding another hot day, such as it had been for the past week. A shout from the mast head brought the ship to life, 'Land dead ahead'. Those on deck jumped to various vantage spots, but it was another two hours before anyone could make out the land shrouded in an early morning mist.

Aaron, his hands behind his back, walked towards the bows. A few minutes later Polly silently walked up behind him and slipped her arm through his, he nodded towards the shore, fully satisfied with his navigation, "There you are Polly, your first glimpse of Africa, not very impressive is it?"

Polly didn't answer but stared blankly at the jut of land where silver sand stretched from the tree line and the sea gently lapped against the shore. The few palm trees bent slightly against the off shore breeze.

Aaron turned towards the masthead, Gibbons who always boasted he had the best eyesight afloat shaded his eyes at the glare of the sun on the white sand.

"Masthead there!" shouted Aaron, "What do you make of it?"

"Not a lot to see sir, looks deserted, plenty of undergrowth further up the beach, could hide a tribe of cannibals sir."

This was said for Polly's entertainment – she shuddered.

Gibbons knew being an old seafarer that cannibals were

few and far between on the coast and never this far North. It did the trick, Polly turned her attention from the shoreline and went below to prepare breakfast for Aaron. Cold meat, hard biscuits and cheese washed down with a quart of ale.

Returning to the deck Aaron could see the shore more clearly now. He gave Willie orders to follow the coast line and ordered Newton to take a regular sounding. They rounded the jut of land and headed south.

Next morning the shore line had changed tremendously. Willie had altered course, taking the ship further out to sea; the sea having turned slightly boisterous. Aaron studied the shore through his telescope. White crested waves crashed against the silver sand, thick vegetation ran almost to the waters edge and monolithic trees of bent and twisted palms rose from the dense undergrowth. He turned his attention towards Willie, who was certainly shaping up to deep sea life, handling the ship's wheel as well as his skipper, "Keep her on that course Willie and don't take her too far into shore."

Newton was taking soundings and constantly shouted out the depth; they were quite safe with a steady twelve fathoms beneath them. Most of the crew watched the shore silently slipping by, the only sounds to be heard coming from the sea as it slapped against the creaking hull.

Silently a brig had stolen up from behind and the crew caught unaware before one of them shouted, "Sail coming up from astern sir!"

The shore forgotten, the men rushed to their action stations. Pirates still abounded in this area. Two men rushed to the small brass cannon. Aaron issued what muskets he had aboard – those without he issued cutlasses.

"Keep your arms out of sight 'til we know his business."

They didn't have to wait long, it was a fast craft, "*Golden Falcon*, is Captain Reeves aboard?"

The voice was loud and clear. He seemed to know the ship and the old Captain but was he friendly? Aaron thought hard as he picked up his speaking trumpet, "Captain Reeves and his wife are dead. I am the new owner, Captain Jacobs."

"Doing a bit of slaving Jacobs? Some prime niggers just north of Freetown – two Arab brothers just brought some in from the interior, but watch the bastards, they would sell their own grandmothers if they could find a customer. They only handle the best, but take care. They are rogues, especially if you are new to the game. We just took a few to Morocco including three fair skinned Spanish girls we picked up in the Canaries.The Arabs love the fair skinned girls, you should get yourself a few, fetch three or four times what niggers fetch – the fairer the better. Captain Williams in the brig *Carib* – he has the right idea – gets blonde girls from Europe. They fetch a king's ransom, the younger the better."

If the ship had been any closer, the contempt on Aaron's face would have been obvious. He could hardly contain the hatred in his voice as he shouted back, "No, we have a cargo for Freetown, then back to England."

"That's your fault Captain Jacobs, you won't get very rich that way." The ship turned in the opposite direction.

"I've been told about this white slaving. They play on the girls' naivete; fill them up with ideas that they will live like princesses so that very often they go willingly. They are treated well on the voyage out so they look their best when they arrive. Immediately, they are sold into servitude and in days become sex slaves. Once inside the seraglio they never step outside again. After a few years they lose their beauty and girlish looks and become household slaves. If they try to escape they are tied into sacks, weighted down with heavy stones and dropped into the sea." Aaron stared hard at the stern of the departing ship and cursed him aloud. "I hope the bastard sinks!"

The *Golden Falcon* tacked towards the shore and a wide estuary. A silver stream of clear water wove its way through the dense bushes, looking especially cool and inviting, the barrels aboard ship already tasting brackish.

Gibbons approached and touched his cap and nodded towards the shore, " There's fresh water here Captain. We need it sir – our water is low and don't taste so good."

Aaron studied the shore – his arms folded – stroking his chin deep in thought, "I dunno Gibbons, I'm not familiar with this coast. It looks deserted but those bushes could conceal an army. From what I have heard the natives here think every white man's ship is a slaver."

Cautiously he took out his telescope and studied the shore. There was neither signs of habitation nor footprints on the shore line. He ordered the watch to drop anchor and the ship's long boat to be lowered. Several casks were lowered into the boat. "Take two men with muskets Gibbons, and four men to fill the casks. The men with the muskets will remain with the boat and are to push off at the first sign of danger. Any sign of trouble – drop the casks and get back here as fast as possible and in one piece."

He studied the shore again, "There doesn't appear to be any signs of life but all the same, be bloody careful."

"I want to go ashore Cap'n," Willie touched his forelock, "I can handle a musket....." Aaron looked doubtful, the crew were watching him keenly, they knew the bond between their Captain and Willie.

He hated the idea of letting him go but was in a tight spot. If he refused they would think it favouritism – nothing would be said – but there would be muttering in the crews' quarters if anything went wrong. Reluctantly he agreed but with a further warning, "Be very careful Willie."

All eyes watched from the ship as the long boat, heading to shore, was lifted high on the crest of a wave and rushing at a tremendous speed before being flung far up on the beach. The men scrambled ashore carrying the casks and cautiously walking towards the stream, some flinging themselves into the clear crystal water and drinking until they thought their stomachs could take no more. Willie placed himself between the stream and the ship's long boat, his finger on the trigger of his musket, intently watching the dense scrub. So far so good – they filled the casks and returned to the long boat.

Gibbons keen eye had spotted a narrow path leading through the undergrowth, "Be careful lads, someone does live around here."

He reported his findings to Aaron, who tasted the water, "Nice and clear Willie. What do you think?"

"Well.... apart from the path Gibbons spotted, it looks

alright – he said the path hadn't been used very much. We could risk another go Cap'n."

Four casks were already filled and they were halfway through the final two when a blood curdling yell rented the air, followed by loud swishes as broad bladed spears embedded themselves in the sand around them. One smashed into the fleshy part of Evans' leg. He ran for a few paces before falling flat. Willie, who was nearest to him, grabbed the shank of the spear and pulled it free as Evans screamed with pain. Musket in one hand he dragged the casualty to the long boat, where the remainder of the crew helped drag him aboard, blood gushing from the open wound. Dozens of half-naked black warriors poured from the undergrowth as Willie lifted his musket and fired high over the heads of the yelling mob. They paused for a brief moment giving enough time for the remainder of the men to push the boat into the surf. A spear embedded itself as far as the transom where Aaron was sitting. Struggling against the surf, they felt as if it was throwing them back onto the beach as they pulled the oars with all their strength. The boat battled defiantly against the incoming waves before edging gradually into deeper water.

"Where the hell is Barber?"

Willie counted the boat's crew, "Anyone see Barber? Did the natives get him?"

"I don't know Willie, the last I saw of him he was filling his cask. He dropped it and did a header into the scrub."

"Did the natives see him?"

The men looked at each other. If the natives had spotted him there would have been more blood curdling yells, and they would certainly have dragged the body into the open to show the ship's crew that they were unwelcome.

Aaron was very disappointed to think he had lost a crew member. Everyone had been kept alive so far, and he had every intention of keeping it that way, "He must still be alive – I will go and parley with them."

"I know a few words of Arabic sir, shall I come with you?"

"Don't be a damn fool Gibbons, it's the Arabs they hate. They are the slavers – if they hear their language it would be the end of us."

Polly was plainly terrified as Aaron jumped into the long-boat, and pleaded with him to stop.

"We can't leave him here Polly, if he's still alive."

The men rested on their oars safe outside spear throwing distance as Aaron tried to signal to the natives that they wanted only fresh water. He stood up, showing them his musket in his hands, before throwing it to the bottom of the boat. Cupping his hands he started to make believe he was drinking,

"Water!" he shouted.

The natives shook their heads from side to side. He picked up the musket and then laid it down again, holding up his hands in a peaceful gesture.

"Right, ship oars, go no further."

He took off his coat and headed into the water rejecting the protests from the boat's crew. The men picked up their muskets and shouted warnings, "Don't do it Cap'n they will murder you."

Aaron struck out strongly for the shore, into the deep surf where he was picked up and thrown unceremoniously several yards up the beach deposited at the feet of one of the natives brandishing a spear a few inches above his head. Other natives quickly surrounded him. Trying to conceal his nervousness he stood up, pointing towards the stream and making gestures that he wanted to drink. He kept hearing the word slaver, a word which apparently struck fear into them. Aaron shook his head and stated clearly, "No slaver." Then, pointing to himself again and then towards the clear stream, "Water".

It was then that he realised his one big mistake – he had failed to bring any goods with which to barter. He stood at the foreshore and shouted to the boat's crew, "Go and get something to barter with; knives and a couple of hatchets."

It was half an hour before the boat returned running straight up onto the beach. He took the knives and handed one to a native who looked like the Chief, then gave him the small hatchet. The Chief started to laugh and, pointing to the stream, nodded his head as the natives started to laugh and jump about like small children.

Aaron looked over their shoulders and saw Barber peering from the undergrowth, his face bleeding and badly scratched, "Come on Barber! They seem friendly enough."

As he crashed through the undergrowth the natives continued to laugh, taking the casks from the men and filling them, carrying them to the boat and helping them to launch it through the surf.

If Aaron thought his troubles were over, he was rather mistaken. Polly, who had witnessed every move he made ashore through his telescope, had been absolutely terrified and it was obvious she had been crying. As he stepped triumphantly over the ship's rail she rushed at him, thumping his chest with her clenched fists, "That was the most stupid thing I ever saw..... those heathens could very well have killed you.... then what would have happened to us? And what about the ship?"

Aaron threw back his head and roared with laughter, "They wouldn't have killed me Polly. I would be too tough for them to make a good meal. You weren't really worried about me – you were thinking of yourself and this ship."

Polly knew she would never get any sense out of him. As he watched the natives walking along the shore following the ship as it set sail and waving their spears in a friendly farewell, Aaron laughed again, "We got our fresh water didn't we?"

Chapter Fourteen

For the next few days Polly gave Aaron the angry silence, speaking only when spoken to, and only answering in the briefest of words. The ship sailed smoothly down the West African coast with the sun at its most fierce and the crew constantly saturating the decks with salt water to prevent the tar between the deck planking from melting. Aaron kept as close to the shore as possible, and once ventured the ship so close that they could smell the pungent odours from native fires but without any sign of the inhabitants – although there was every sign of life. Canoes were drawn up on the beaches; fishnets hung over poles to dry; and smoke rose from the deserted villages. Everything there showed the signs of a prosperous village without the evidence of human habitation. No children played on the sands, nor where there any women standing over the fires preparing meals, and no men worked the nets or fished in the sleek canoes.

For the first time in two days Polly spoke, "Where are all the people Aaron?"

"No doubt using their common sense Polly. This coast is notorious for slavers and at the first sighting of our sails they will have vanished into the bush. A white man's ship means fear to these people – to them it means a slaver and I would bet that this ship above all, for it was notorious. They trust no white man and who can blame them."

Aaron had the uncomfortable feeling that dozens of pairs of eyes were peering at them from the thick undergrowth.

Polly stretched out on deck on her blanket, wondering if this was all a dream, the filthy streets of Portsmouth half a world away. The smoke filled taverns; the selling of her body to prevent starvation was forced into her subconscious to rear its ugly head as during a bad dream. It had never happened. She was free, and for the first time in her short life she was happy. The crew who, when she first came aboard had tried to ignore her had finally, if reluctantly accepted her as one of them. Occasionally she helped out by cooking for them, but her priority was looking after the welfare of Aaron, the man she adored. After her duties were completed she loved to stretch out on her blanket on the deck and just lie there turning a golden brown, her hair bleaching in the sun turning to platinum. But her greatest satisfaction had been in the improvement of her reading under Aaron's tuition. Like Willie she was a fast learner and had already read several books chosen from Aaron's classic collection. She could hardly wait until they reached civilisation to replenish the bookshelves.

A true romantic at heart she loved the nights when the moon cast a shimmering silver path across the black sea, and would stand at the ship's rail staring into the distance. The fiddler, a man of many moods she was sure, could read her thoughts and reaching for his fiddle would often play sentimental ballads. When the crew heard the fiddle they would wander on to the deck and the ballads would turn into rollicking sea shanties and the occasional bawdy song in which Polly would joyfully join.

Paralysed by these idyllic surroundings the days and evenings quickly passed, sometimes she hated the idea that one day they would reach their final destination and would have to turn around for the voyage home.

"I wish this could last forever Aaron." She was leaning over the ship's rail staring into the sea, completely void of other ships. They were alone on the vast ocean. Aaron put his arm around her tiny waste and gave her a comforting squeeze.

"Only one ship has ever managed that state, Polly, and that's the *Flying Dutchman*." As he told her of the ghostly ship that forever sails the mighty oceans, she shuddered.

The *Golden Falcon* rounded a headland and for the first time they saw a populated community – a community that by African standards could be described as a small town. Several mud huts and one or two brick buildings and a larger building like a fort stood prominent on the headland jutting out to sea. Natives were going about their daily business.

Aaron turned a telescope onto the land and gasped.

The beach was littered with row upon row of natives tied together. Rough wooden yokes around their necks had been tightly secured with strands of palm fibre. All of the natives stared back dejectedly at the ship which they believed would be taking them to a destination far away from the homeland they were so familiar with. Men and women, some clinging to small children, others with babies at their shrunken breasts, and young girls showing their first sign of puberty, all with the same dark eyes filled with fear. The sight held a grim fascination for Aaron. From this distance he could experience the agony they were going through, the rough tree yokes chaffing their necks and every muscle in their bodies aching after the long trek from the interior with just enough food to sustain life and the constant threat of the overseer's whip if they failed to maintain a steady progress. Stopping only when the slavers themselves needed a rest.

He silently handed the telescope to Polly and pointed towards the shore. She caught her breath and sobbed – tears immediately and uncontrollably rolling down her cheeks. She never spoke but hurriedly turned away, Aaron attempting to console her by putting his arm around her heaving shoulders. Still, she must know the truth.

"These people have no future Polly, and have no idea what is in store for them. They will be taken either to New Orleans in America, or to an island in the West Indies and sold to the highest bidder. The babies will be parted from their mothers and it has been known for a ship's Captain to throw one or two overboard just as a warning to the other slaves to obey. If a slave looks ill he too will be thrown overboard just in case he carries some infection. They have no say in their lives from this moment on."

Two majestic looking Arabs stood over the slaves. They were dressed completely in white from head to toe, in clothes which Polly later graphically described as white sheets with a dishrag around their heads. Over six feet in height with diamond-encrusted curved daggers thrust into their belts, they held rhino bull whips in their hands.

Polly, now recovered from her initial shock was again handed the telescope.

"That is what you call the true blue Arab trader Polly, all fully trained in hell itself. They are without doubt the most evil of the lot, no feelings whatsoever for their fellow man and their excuse is – 'It's the will of Allah'."

As Aaron spoke one of the slavers uncoiled his whip and flashed it wickedly across the backs of the line of slaves who recoiled in agony and terror.

Several canoes were drawn up on the shore and two men lifted each of the Arab slavers into the largest canoe, before four powerful negroes began paddling furiously towards the *Golden Falcon*. The sweat saturated muscles of the oarsmen rippled and gleamed in the bright sunlight.

"Looks like we have company Polly. Ugly looking bastards ain't they?"

But they were far from ugly. As they drew nearer Polly grudgingly admired their physique and aquiline features. Sitting calmly in the canoe, they were haughtily contemptuous of the natives who inwardly cursed them and prayed silently that the craft would overturn, drowning them both. There was little doubt that the Arabs were brothers – both from the same cabbage patch, as Polly intuitively put it – albeit with the devil's wife for a mother.

The canoe came alongside and both Arabs were lifted by their negro attendants onto the ship. The slightly taller of the two looked suspiciously around the decks, which were familiar to him, and doubt lines folded his forehead. He neither recognised the Captain nor any crew member – they were faces he had never seen before.

Still looking perplexed, he said in perfect English with a very slight accent, "Surely this is Captain Reeves' ship?"

"No sir, this is my ship. It *was* Captain Reeves' ship, but he is now dead and no doubt sipping wine with the devil himself. Without doubt so is his harlot of a wife."

"It is the will of Allah Captain." As he said this, he placed
two fingers to his forehead and bowed slightly with a stoop
of his shoulders in a begrudging way.

The silent Arab never took his eyes from Polly for one second. After speaking quietly to his brother they both stared
at Polly and laughed slyly.

"I think one has taken a fancy to you Polly," a member of
the crew said. The men had gathered protectively around
their Captain and Polly, for not one of them trusted the
Arabs with their wicked looking curved knives and their
false humility.

Polly resorted to her Portsea slang to emphasise the general distrust, "I don't trust either of them. And I don't
fancy 'em mauling me around." She took a couple of steps
backwards into the safety of the crew.

Franklin, an old sea dog, had served with the Med-
iterranean fleet for a great number of years where he had
picked up a smattering of Arabic said, patting Polly's
shoulder, "You'll be alright there Polly, they are very rich.
He has just told the other Arab to ask the Captain how
much he will take for you and whatever it is, he will double it if you're still a virgin." The whole crew burst out
laughing, well aware of her past life. But Polly didn't
laugh. That was the part of her past life she was trying to
block out of her mind.

Because of the many tales Aaron had heard about Arabs
talking on any subject (but the business in hand) for hours
on end, he was surprised to find that these two were an
exception.

"Your ship was spotted several days ago Captain, we came
overland to reach you here. We trust you have taken over
Captain Reeves' business. Our reputation for dealing only
in prime stock is well known. We bring them from the best
interior lands, big strong field specimens – they will fetch
a good price across the sea Captain, and will give you no
trouble. If we were to take them further down the coast we
could get double and be paid in gold."

He turned and shouted to the negroes in the canoe, who
without question or looking at him, paddled furiously for

110

the shore. While they waited for the canoe to return the Arab asked, "This beautiful *woman* Captain – she is your *wife?*"

"No sir, she is not."

The Arab turned to his brother with a perverted gleam in his eye and they talked in excited, urgent mutterings for several minutes. The second Arab, his arms as well as his mouth, shouting and gesticulating furiously like an over enthusiastic orchestra conductor, stopped only briefly now and again to look at Polly, constantly licking his lips.

Polly shook with fear as the taller Arab stepped forward and let her long blonde hair slide through his fingers, the colour fascinating him. Polly's jaw had dropped with startled fright before Franklin stepped forward and caught the slavers' wrist in a vice-like grip and spoke menacingly in Arabic. The wildness in Franklin's eyes stopped the Arab in his tracks, and his hand fell to his dagger. No man before had dared lay a hand on him and certainly not in the defence of a woman. His country and his customs decreed that women were subservient chattels. Angrily he turned to his brother and a furious argument broke out, it was obvious to any man watching, that whatever the expense the brother wanted Polly. Again he started bargaining with Aaron, "The *woman* is not your *wife*. My brother wants her and will give you a good price, paying in English guineas."

Aaron, a wide grin on his face, turned to Polly, "How much do *you* think you're worth Polly?"

"Don't joke about things like that Aaron, I hate you when you talk like that. I wouldn't sleep with that monster if you gave me a king's ransom."

"Sorry mister, no deal. In fact she hates the sight of both of you."

The Arab's nostrils flared and his faced turned to a crumpled snarl. The argument would have continued but was interrupted by the return of the canoe banging against the ship's side. There were half a dozen slaves aboard yoked together making it difficult for them to clamber aboard. This was not helped by the negro overseer beating them from below with a heavy stick, as both Arab slavers on

111

deck took turns to smash them viciously with the butts of
their bull whips. Polly turned away, her clenched fist in
her mouth preventing her from crying out.

"These are very healthy slaves Captain." The taller Arab
dragged the first one forward still yoked to the others
causing them to stumble. This inspired the younger slaver
to lay into them with his whip, no doubt trying to impress
Polly. He pinched the arms and legs of the slave and with
admiration said, "Please look at these muscles Captain.
What splendid field hands they would make. At auction in
Orleans Captain they will fetch a good price."

Aaron snatched the knife from the Arab's belt and cut a
slave free, turning him several times to examine him.

"What about this one? The whip marks and sores on his
neck where the yoke has chaffed? When this sore heals it
will leave him scarred for life. You know as well as I do
that black men and women that have whip marks or scars
fetch less money. Plantation owners believe they must be
trouble makers."

Aaron was talking like a seasoned slave trader leaving the
crew with doubts about their Captain. Polly too was having doubts, he looked and sounded quite business like.
The crew wanted nothing to do with the filthy business
and shuffled uneasily on their feet, muttering amongst
themselves. But they knew they could do nothing about it,
aboard ship there was no one above the Captain. Only the
Almighty himself. Surprised too, for Aaron had always
spoken out against slavery and slavers and had been bitter
in his condemnation. It had also been fairly said that he
hated the Royal Navy for the way the men were treated,
little better than slaves. When men preferred to rot in
prison rather than serve in one of His Majesty's ships
there was something radically wrong with the system. At
least in prison men did have a reasonable chance of survival whereas at sea there was the hidden terrors of ship
life. Being smashed to pieces by enemy guns; sailing often
in ships barely seaworthy and even then at the mercy of a
Captain who held the balance of life or death in his sadistic hands. Drowning was a constant fear for a pressed man
– forced up a rigging when on land he had climbed no

higher than his house stairs.

The Arab slaver however, was not taken in by Aaron's false expertise. He had dealt with hard-bitten slave dealers all his life and was starting to look worried. He had spotted the ship a few days previous and stopping here to meet it had seemed a good idea, saving them another two hundred miles to the slave stockade.

Recognising the *Golden Falcon* he was under the impression that Captain Reeves was still in command. The old Captain had always been on the lookout for good quality slaves. Trying hard to convince Aaron he pulled the slave closer, "These marks are nothing Captain. By the time you reach the islands they will have disappeared – a few buckets of salt water down the hold every day will soon dispose of them."

He shouted orders to the crew in the canoe and a moments later a man appeared with a clay bowl and a piece of filthy rag. Forcing the slave to his knees, he scoured the man's neck. The slave squealed with pain but he continued to rub harshly, his brother dancing with delight and laughing hysterically, "They don't feel pain Captain, that is just for show, they always react like that hoping to receive some sympathy."

"Well that surprises me, I mean just look at the blood pouring from his neck where you rubbed it so hard. Surely if they bleed like us, they must feel pain."

The slaver sensing things were not going his way, spread his hands forward, "Oh no Captain! I feel pain.... then you see.... I am not a slave."

He threw a look at the slave, who cowering before his gaze, had been touching the blood as it trickled from his neck. The look from the Arab said, 'Just wait until I get you ashore – you will pay for that show of cowardice', but the slaver changed the subject, "They are all prime stock Captain, no coastal blacks. Bad slaves are coastal blacks, having been under the influence of your Christian people. These slaves make good slaves, Captain, and at the price I am asking, you will think 'Allah has furnished me with the brain of an idiot'."

"How many do you have?" Again the crew looked at each

other.

"Two hundred Captain, that's how many Captain Reeves liked to take. Thirty women of child bearing age, two sucking babies and nine with children; twenty young virgins and forty boys. The young girls are just right to be house trained. The rest are field hands.

While the slaver was absorbed in singing the praises of his slaves Aaron slid unobtrusively over towards his crew and whispered to Gibbons, "Slip into the galley and bring me a red hot poker or a knife, but don't let this animal see you passing it to me."

Chapter Fifteen

Any doubts that lingered among the crew concerning their Captain's intention of taking up the slaving trade were soon dispersed when they saw Gibbons return with a red hot poker concealed behind his back. He surged his way through the crew, before discreetly handing it to Aaron. The slavers, meanwhile, obliviously continued to profess the gory virtues and insensibility to pain of their prime stock.

Aaron showed the poker to the taller Arab, at the same time wetting the tip of a finger and thumb causing a loud hiss and cloud of steam, "Do you mean to tell me if I put this across a slave's face he would never feel it?"

The slaver thought this a great joke, "That would not be very prudent Captain. As you just remarked, a slave with burns or scars does not always fetch the best price."

"Well all I wanted to do was try it out – like this!" Aaron plunged forward and drew the poker across the slavers' face avoiding his left eye by only a fraction of an inch. The piercing scream reached the foretops, and the faces of the slaves changed in expression from incredulity to nervous grins before quickly returning to feigned apathy to avoid the notice of the second slaver. He, though, was busy backing away from Aaron and covering his face with his forearm, as his brother rolled about the deck in agony, screaming.

"I am no slave Captain! I am *no* slave...."

In agony, the wounded Arab reached down for the curved

knife in his belt, but Aaron was faster and kicked his arm sending the bejewelled knife skidding across the deck to land at the feet of a crew member.

The crew responded by surrounding the other slaver and disarming him, while the black overseer stood apart, his eyes staring bewildered – he had never seen anything like this – his Arab masters humiliated in front of the slaves. Trembling, like a man in a fit, he dropped his wooden stave.

Aaron spoke to him, in a soft tone assuring him he would not suffer, "Do you speak English?"

The man, wondering what this may lead to, nodded in the affirmative and softly answered in an almost inaudible voice, "Yes."

"Well I trust you also speak the native tongue. Tell these people they are no longer slaves. Tell them to return to their homes."

The overseer talked to them for a few minutes pointing shorewards. They looked more scared and suspicious than ever, gesticulating and shouting in a dialect that Aaron nor his crew could understand.

"What is the matter with them man, don't they want to return home?"

"No sir," replied the overseer, "they cannot go ashore here. The minute they are released from their yokes they will be captured by other slavers. This place is a clearing house. The Portuguese are the main slave traders in this area – see that castle there? That is where the slave pens are...."

He had pointed to a far promontory, and now paused to wipe the sweat from his forehead before continuing, "Normally we would have continued along the coast.... maybe two hundred miles from here, but when they saw your ship, they believed you were Captain Reeves. They hoped to save time and a long march."

"What if I send some of my crew fully armed to protect them, and went inland for a few miles?"

Knowing that he had found a white man he could trust the face of the overseer turned to an infectious smile, revealing two rows of extremely white teeth, accentuated more so by the black background of his face, "Captain you

116

do not know what you are saying. You can not know this place. Slavery is money here and for such a valuable string of slaves as these, the Portuguese would kill their own mothers. Those ashore would think of nothing of murdering you. They are very wicked men."

This gave Aaron troubled thoughts – if he took these slaves ashore and released them they would be rounded up. They would fail even to get off the beach. Two hundred slaves? What could he do with two hundred slaves?

But he was beyond the point of no return. The two Arab slavers were crouched on deck, the taller one still groaning in agony from the burn which had left an inch wide weal across this face that was already blistering. He crept towards Aaron and wrapped his arms around his legs and wept.

"Effendi! Effendi!" he whimpered, "You take my slaves.... they are yours." Aaron lifted his foot, trying to kick him away, "....they are good slaves.... they will make you very rich. You must put me ashore Captain."

"You evil bastard. The only way you will reach the shore is by swimming to it." He tried to drag himself away, the slaver's arms still wrapped limpet-like around his legs.

"Look! Effendi, I have money," he slid out a leather pouch from inside his robe and emptied a large amount of gold coins on to the deck, "you take me ashore and like the slaves, these will be yours. You take us ashore effendi and they are all yours."

"Pick up those coins Willie and get two strong men..." he paused, "Hang on.... cut those slaves free. Let *them* have the pleasure of slinging him over the side. The snivelling pig is staining my deck."

Calling a man a pig was the biggest insult a Muslim could receive. He clung tighter to Aaron's legs, "But effendi I will give you more." He took out another soft leather bag and tipped out several stones. One, extra large, was the size of a pigeon's egg.

"What the hell do I want with these dirty stones? You stupid bastard."

The man cowered back fearing he had lost his battle for freedom, "They are not pebbles Captain – they are dia-

monds. Rare blue diamonds.... as blue as the sea and sky.
An English woman would sell her soul just for one small
blue diamond.... very few people know where they come
from."

Aaron picked up the largest one and held it to the light,
but it made very little impression on him. He tried to
scrape off the dirt but nothing happened and picking up
the rest of the stones he returned them to the soft leather
pouch, and headed for his cabin. Alone, he could think better and sort out the corner he had led himself into. He
threw the pouch into a drawer and sat at the table, his fingers drumming out an incessant rhythm. It was twenty
minutes before he believed he had the problem solved.

Returning to deck Aaron summoned his crew.

"Right lads, I believe I have a solution. First of all yoke
the two slavers together and let them taste a bit of their
own treatment. Polly, tend to the sores on the slaves necks
and any other injuries. I see you have given them water, go
and see if you can find any hard biscuits.

He turned to the black overseer, "It's your job to get the
rest of the slaves aboard and as soon as they arrive make
them squat on the deck. Take those damn yokes off and
make sure they cannot be seen from shore."

The man pointed to a large negro, well over six and a half
feet tall. "That man sir, he was a chief in his own village,
they will take orders from him. We must tell him what you
intend to do."

"Call him over."

He stood in front of Aaron towering head and shoulders
above him, his head looking straight forward and his eyes
appearing to penetrate Aaron's soul. He had an enormous
chest and striking features, wide nostrils and thick lips.

"Ask him what is he doing here and how such a man was
caught and made into a slave?"

The overseer talked to the man for some time, the crew
staring at him open mouthed, as he hardly moved a muscle. Then looking directly at Aaron, the large negro started
jabbering away as the overseer translated sentence by sentence.

"He was the chief's son and had claim to be chief. When

the old man died, his half brother was very jealous and wanted to be chief. He was the son of his father's second wife and had the village witch doctor on his side. Between them they intended to kill him, but the Arabs were in the neighbourhood so they drugged and bound him and sold him into slavery with his two sons and wives."

"Well he is a slave no longer, his wives and children will soon be aboard and we will release them all further down the coast, maybe in two or three days time when we see a good landing place. Tell him we wish to get started straight away and have wasted enough time here."

Using the two canoes and the ship's long boat they soon had all the slaves aboard. Releasing them from their yokes and making them squat on deck left just enough room for the crew to go about their work. Bags of mealie, the natives' staple diet, had been stacked on the shore ready to feed the slaves and was brought aboard. As it was impossible to cook, Polly did the next best thing and found as many buckets as possible which she filled with water and soaked the mealie, smashing in bananas and other soft fruits. The slaves were half starved and ate the food with relish.

Aaron then called the overseer to his cabin, "Right Sam, they are all safely aboard, your job is done and you can go ashore. I trust you are in a hurry to return to your family."

Fear gripped the overseer, Aaron could have sworn his skin turned grey, "No Captain! I can not go ashore.... they will kill me when they know what has happened. I must come with you Captain. I will scrub decks, and I will learn to sail. I am no slaver sir, I knew what would happen to me, in a few years they would sell me. I speak English, I speak French.... and Portuguese, and many native languages. I must stay aboard Captain." A desperate gleam came into his eyes, "I will kill the two slavers for you."

"No, there will be no killings. Just reassure these unfortunate people that they are no longer slaves."

Aaron called Willie down, "We will be a bit crowded for a couple of days — maybe three — and I don't want these slaves messing up the deck. Get the carpenter to make up some toilets on the side of the decks, not the stern — I don't want it putting me and Miss Polly off our food. Go ashore, take a couple of men with you, and see if you can get some milk for the small children."

Returning to the deck Aaron looked over the side and could see that the ship was overloaded. He now had two hundred passengers excluding the smaller children, and many large bags of mealie had filled the hold. It was late when they set sail and headed south and for the first time the exhausted Captain felt a surge of relief pass through his body. He returned to his cabin and Polly poured him a large glass of brandy, which he half-drank. Placing his head on his arm across the table he was snoring deeply within a minute.

When he awoke Aaron felt the surge of the water under the hull. He sat up and stretched, the smell of cooking filled the cabin, and he drained what was left of the brandy in the glass before going on deck to stretch his cramped legs. Gibbons and several of the crew were waiting and approached him silently.

Gibbons touched his forehead, "Captain – we honestly thought you were about to take up slaving. Some of the men were on the point of mutiny and we would like to say we are sorry."

"Nothing to be sorry for Gibbons. I couldn't have taken the slaves – my holds were full." Aaron smiled.

"No Captain. When those slavers came aboard we really thought you had brought us out here on a fool's errand and had the intention of slaving. But when the Arabs started bartering and you slashed the tall one with the red hot poker we realised our mistake. We *are* very sorry for doubting you."

"Alright lads, you know my feelings about slavery and you can all rest assured there is no chance of us ever joining that abominable trade. We will set the Arabs ashore tomorrow but I am afraid the other people will be staying for a day or two. Go about your business and tell the fiddler to start tuning up – we will try and cheer these unfortunate people up a bit." The crew delayed, unsteady on their feet as if something was on their minds.

"Come on Gibbons, spit it out man, what's on your mind?"

120

"Well it's like this sir, setting the slaves free is one thing and every man aboard is going along with that, but this man Sam – we understand that you are keeping him on as a crew member. Does he share the fo'csle with us?"

Aaron looked him squarely in the face, "I am sorry to hear you talk like that Gibbons. Do all the men feel the same?"

The men failed to look directly at Aaron and kept their heads slightly downcast. Gibbons who seemed to be doing all the talking said quietly, "Not all the men sir."

"Well to tell the truth, I hadn't quite made up my mind but seeing you lot shaking like leaves in the wind has made it up for me. Sam was doing a job he hated, no wages, more like a slave himself and he knew what his fate would be when they finished with him – he would be sold. Twice a year, sometimes three, he was forced to trek through the jungle with these men. No boots – his feet like tanned leather, he had to martial the slaves and yoke them together. He speaks several languages and native dialects and is a very intelligent man. What he did is the same as you or I would do, otherwise he would have been killed or sold straight away into slavery. Self preservation they call it. So I will tell you what I intend to do. He will be signed up as a crew member straight away and any man that doesn't like sharing with this man can sign off at Freetown, paid in full, plus a share in the gold sovereigns we took from the slavers. Good day gentlemen."

He turned his back on them, the matter was closed.

Chapter Sixteen

"Get those two Arab slavers ready Willie, the next convenient cove we see we will stop and let them off. Strip them and make sure they have no more money or valuables salted away between the folds of their robes."

The taller Arab, still moaning about the pain inflicted on his face by Aaron, squirmed along the deck, "But Captain you cannot put us ashore on this hostile coast. With nothing to defend ourselves, not even our knives, it will be like murder – you would condemn us to our deaths."

Aaron lifted his foot to kick the slaver, who cowered, covering his face with his arms and rolling himself into a bundle, no doubt learning this lesson from the slaves he had tortured over the years.

Aaron's foot landed harmlessly, "Don't you tell me of murder and condemning people to death. These people you condemned to a living death, you sadistic bastard. You can thank your lucky stars you have survived this long, if I had listened to my crew you would have been thrown overboard during the night, you *and* that evil brother of yours. Believe me the time is up for you and this evil trade. Important voices are being raised in protest in the British Parliament; influential voices. You have a fifty-fifty chance of surviving ashore, if the wild animals don't get you the natives you have been preying on might; but at least you have a better chance than these poor people had."

With a look of contempt Aaron handed him a handful of

hardtack and a bucket of water. Both brothers scrambled on their hands and knees, fighting to be the first to the bucket of water, much to the amusement of the ex-slaves who roared with laughter.

"There is one thing in your favour, if the wild animals get you they might reject your stinking flesh."

It was late afternoon when they discovered a quiet little cove with a stream leading down to the beach, over which played a very slight surf. The two slavers made a last desperate plea to Aaron, throwing themselves flat on the deck. It took four of the heftiest crew to lift each man and throw them into the bottom of the ship's long boat.

Aaron looked down upon them, "You know what your people say – 'It is the will of Allah' – just let us hope that you are in favour with him for one thing is certain, you will not get my blessing. I would advise you to find a stout stick, using one won't be too hard for you, you have had plenty of practice."

All the ex-slaves watched as the small boat pulled for the shore, but it wasn't quite over for the slavers. There was a further humiliation, the crew made them fill the water barrels and carry them back to the boat. No doubt it was the hardest day's work they had ever done in their lives. To make matters worse the crew encouraged the overseer to stand over them with the rhino bull whip in his hand with instructions to use it if they slackened.

Afterwards Aaron asked Sam if he thought the Arabs stood any chance of survival.

He shrugged his shoulders and smiled, the two rows of white teeth illuminating his black skin, " I do not like their chances Captain. As you have said they must put their faith in Allah. There are very few animals that come this close to the shore, what they do have to worry about is seeking help from the villagers. Once they know they are Arabs and unarmed, well.... I would sooner have faced the wild animals. The heat too, that is ferocious."

Aaron turned his head and smiled, for Sam was not only intelligent but had a sense of humour that ran parallel to his own. There was little doubt they would get on fine and he would soon mix with the crew.

As the ship sailed comfortably along Aaron and Polly were studying the ex-slaves. "They are a real handsome bunch Aaron." She turned to Sam, "Where do these people come from Sam?"

"They come from the interior Miss Polly, three full moons away. They haven't seen many white people and never one with golden hair like yours, that is why they are so curious and keep pointing at you. See the very tall lady over there, leaning against the rails?" Polly looked to where he was pointing, she would have stood out in any crowd, her skin was like ebony, deep penetrating brown eyes, "Her husband sold her, just as he sold four more of his wives for failing to bear him any children. It was the husband who was impotent – he couldn't lose face."

"Tell them we will be putting them ashore tomorrow," interceded Aaron, "and will need a good night's rest. They will have to make their way back to the villages themselves. We will fill sacks and they can take as much mealie as they can carry. They can have two machetes and two knives – I am sorry we cannot give them more."

"Don't worry about that sir, they will get along fine. The chief will take charge, these are bush natives and although they don't all come from the same tribe or village they will fight together. The chief will return to his own village, he says he will kill his brother and the witch doctor."

But it was another two days before they found a satisfactory landing place, dropping anchor at the mouth of a small river. The chief supervised the landing from the ship and, the last to leave, he went down on his hands and knees and wrapped his arms round Aaron's legs, kissing both feet and jabbering in his native tongue. Aaron helped him to his feet and gestured towards the shore, but the chief continued to speak rapidly in his own native tongue.

"What is he saying Sam?" Aaron asked, an uncomfortable smile on his face.

"I told you Captain, he is a chief of paramount importance and has paid you the greatest of honours. It is the lowest of the low that usually kisses the chief's feet. He says you will be treated as a great chief if you ever visit the interior. He says that one day you must follow the great river until you arrive at the lake. Cross the lake in a canoe and continue one more day's walk. When you visit him you can have many more of the stones the Arab gave you."

Aaron, tears clouding his eyes, ran his hand through the chief's tight curly hair.

With all passengers safely ashore Aaron gave orders to crowd on as much sail as would take the ship to its destination. The negroes stood on the shore waving frantically at their benefactors until the ship was out of sight.

Sam stood at the ship's rail, a grim look on his face, his eyes following the coast line. He wondered if he was seeing his homeland for the last time and what the future held in store for him. Of one thing he was certain. This good Captain and his fine lady had treated him like a human being and would never sell him into slavery. He had no need to worry, Sam soon became extremely popular with his shipmates.

"What do you think will happen to them, Sam?" Polly asked him.

"They will survive Miss Polly, they will make spears with the knives and machetes. The chief will take some of the women as wives. They are bush natives and will find food where a white man would starve." He threw a mischievous glance at Ernshaw and Gibbons sitting on the top of number one hold, a mocking twinkle in his eye.

The crew were happy; they could really get some speed on the ship again and that night they found out that amongst Sam's many talents he had a most powerful baritone voice and soon picked up the words of songs making the crew laugh the way he sometimes pronounced them and often adding words of his own native tongue.

Polly watched keenly, her arm through Aaron's. "What a fine man he is, just look at those muscles." Aaron smiled and patted her hand, but she continued, laughing as Sam awkwardly attempted to do a jig with some of the crew, "What will you do with him Aaron? Will you be keeping him on?"

"What else can I do, in a few days time we will be at Freetown and he certainly can't go ashore there."

Sam's laugh dominated the singing and dancing, two rows

of white teeth splitting his shining face in two. Aaron doubted if the man had ever been so happy in his life. these were his first days of real freedom and, it could be said – the first days of his life. A new life, something he had never known, "I suppose we will just have to take him back to London and sign him on as a permanent member of the crew. By the sound of him he should work out fine."

They sighted many vessels throughout the next week, most of them flying the white ensign and plenty of vessels from the East India Company. The native villagers on shore no longer fled when they saw their sails, but canoes, going about their daily business, waved gaily at them.

"Definitely not slaving country, Polly."

They arrived at Freetown their ship no longer conspicuous among the forest of masts, including several naval vessels, that crowded the harbour. They dropped anchor and Aaron was rowed ashore to seek out the ship's agents. The smell from the anchorage was bad enough but the moment he stepped ashore it became intolerable. The first thing to greet him was the open sewer, kept at a high temperature by the blazing heat of the sun, which turned it into a steaming cesspit that ran the whole length of the road. Three feet wide, and impossible to tell how deep, it was full to the brim with every kind of human waste floating on top. Ramshackle wooden bridges every few yards lead to a footpath the other side.

The streets were as crowded as those of central London. There were fruit and spice sellers with their wares spread out on blankets and women with colourful billowing dresses, shouting and screaming their wares; very fat women with babies strapped to their backs, great brown eyes staring over their mother's shoulder in bewilderment wondering at the chaotic scene around them. Other women, backs as straight as ramrods, balanced large bundles or clay gourds of water on their heads and never spilled a drop. No one talked normally, every one appeared to shout. The noise was incredible, rising and falling in waves.

Aaron held a handkerchief to his nose as he crossed a rickety bridge outside a large imposing red brick building. A white man lurched out, and Aaron showed him the piece of paper on which was written the agent's address. The man swayed and held the paper at arms length trying to focus his bloodshot eyes. As he swayed to and fro, Aaron put out his hand to stop him falling, and the man continued to stare. The stench from his gin sodden breath forced Aaron to turn away his head. The man was dressed in thin and threadbare cotton clothes with a hat perched askew on the side of his head. Sweat stained, he could not have bathed for some time, the smears beneath his arms turning black. He turned the paper several times, and Aaron was ready to grab it from him twice, as he came near to falling into the open sewer. But each time the drunk managed to catch hold of the building and stop himself.

"You won't get any sense out of him my friend, he hasn't been sober these last ten months. What are you looking for?" A passer by had stopped to watch the comic scene.

Aaron snatched the paper from the man, who continued to stare at him, his eyes crossed before carrying on along the path beside the open sewer, supporting himself occasionally against the wall of the buildings.

The passer-by pointed towards a large building, "You will find the agent there. Just walk straight in, he never gets drunk before sundown so at this time you will get at least some sense out of him."

Aaron nodded his thanks and, carefully negotiating the rickety old bridge, once more kept to the middle of the dusty road until he came abreast of the agent's office. Up three wide stone steps and into a red quarry stone passage, he sighed with relief, it was cooler than he dared to hope, his own shirt now clinging to him with sweat. He knocked at the first door.

"Come in."

"Mister Townsend?" The man was sitting with his back to him staring through the open window, a bottle of gin at his elbow. Strange Aaron thought, he had been told the agent never got drunk before sundown, and here he was sitting with a bottle half-full of gin and a glass beside him. He was soon to learn, like most white men in this town, the agent drank gin all day, every day – but it never had any affect on him.

127

That is, apart from his breath.

As he turned Aaron caught a whiff of the most foul breath he had ever encountered. The agent gave a slight smile and revealed two rows of stained and irregular teeth, before opening a drawer and taking out another dirty glass. He offered the glass and the bottle to Aaron, who declined. With a shrug of his shoulders the agent filled his own glass with gin and knocked it back in one go.

"So you have brought out a cargo from England, the boss will be pleased. What kind of trip did you have?"

The agent obviously wasn't interested. He couldn't have cared less if the ship had sunk, it was just a case of being polite and making small talk, "I will try and get you unloaded as soon as possible. Try not to stay too long Captain, this town is not called the 'White man's grave' for nothing. Don't allow any of your men ashore if you can possibly help it, half of them will go down with fever before you are two days out. We have everything here Captain, you name it, we have it. Malaria; yellow fever; dysentery; beriberi; cholera. Then we have to put up with poisonous snakes, spiders and believe it or not we have crocodiles which come down the street in the rainy season. It has been known for the odd lion to come to town. Don't eat the fruit until it has been thoroughly washed and for heaven's sake don't let them drink the local brew. Unless, of course, they wish to go blind."

He lifted the bottle of gin and pointed to the label, "Make sure this comes from England."

With all these horrors, Aaron wondered why the hell the man stayed here. As if Mr Townsend had read his thoughts he looked questioningly at Aaron, "Why do I stay in this God forsaken hole? A good question. I have nowhere else to go, Captain Jacobs. I was told of this job in England, where I worked for the same shipping line in London. Five times my normal salary – yes, five times. That should have told me there was a catch, especially when they told me I would have my own house and servants. Of course, I had not seen the house then. When I reached here it turned out to be a flea bitten pit, with hardly any furniture. What furniture there was, was eaten

128

away with wood worm and other parasites, the bed was
bug ridden and the first night I slept with a bloody great
snake curled up on a pillow. The servants were an old
couple eaten with arthritis and though I couldn't swear to
it – I believe the old lady was a leper, half her foot was
eaten away. I knew nothing of this when I left England nor
was I told that out of the last five agents three never completed their five year contract. They died. The other two
returned physical wrecks. I have two more years to go
before my contract finishes, that's if I make it. There
comes a time in one's life when the thought of death holds
no more terrors.

I drink two bottles of gin a day, and after sunset I begin
a quart bottle of brandy. I can tell you Captain when a
mosquito or a fly bites me it drops dead with alcoholic poi-
soning." He poured himself another glass and pushed the
bottle towards Aaron, who again declined.

"Wise man Captain; very wise man."

The agent read the manifesto and nodded his head, Aaron
hadn't any idea how much the man had drunk that day
but when he stood up he steady on his feet and quite capable of carrying out his duties, "All intact I suppose
Captain?"

"Right down to the last package. When can we start
unloading Mr Townsend, I would like to return as soon as
possible."

"No time like the present Captain." He rang a small brass
bell on his desk and two black youths almost fell into the
office. They had been standing by the door, "Right Mackie,
and you John, get a dozen lads down to the docks. I want
the Captain's ship unloaded. No time wasters or lazy buggers they will get a shilling a day and I want it unloaded
in two days, if they get it finished in a day they will still
get the two days wages." The two youths grinned widely
and dashed from the office.

"By the way Captain, do you want a cargo for Cape Town?
We had a Dutch ship arrive two or three weeks back, the
Captain was talked into slaving – was promised he would
be rich in a couple of trips, so he dumped the cargo here.
It was his very first trip to Cape Town, a young man like

yourself. He dumped his cargo in our warehouse, take it on to the Cape and you will get paid for the whole trip from Holland, less our storage."

He handed Aaron the ship's manifest.

Stepping out into the brilliant sunshine Aaron and the agent were forced to shield their eyes, the sun had become hotter and it was difficult to look towards the cloudless sky. The sweat circles beneath Aaron's armpits were spreading over his shirt and darkening the edges. The trees which lined the dusty street drooped lazily, offering no shade to the tormented inhabitants.

"God man, how do you survive the heat, and this smell?"

The agent answered, his brows risen, and sweat running down his face, "You tell *me*...."

Aaron was relieved to see his ship anchored out, at least it should be cooler there

"I will let you know about that cargo for the Cape as soon as we unload Mr Townsend." He was in a hurry to return to his ship, the walk from the agent's office having sapped his strength.

Chapter Seventeen

For the full fee from Holland to Cape Town, Aaron had agreed to carry the cargo. Within two days his own cargo from London had been unloaded and the new cargo was safely in the holds.

The weather had remained fine with a fresh wind blowing uninterrupted from the Arctic until it pounded on the surf against the African coast.

There had been no further complaints about Sam messing in with the rest of the crew, and Aaron never brought the subject up again. He had a crew he trusted and they trusted him. Every man knew what was expected of him – Sam soon became familiar with the rigging. As if in response to the devotion of the crew Willie followed his Captain like a faithful dog follows its master – the old days when he was the only crew member leaving a small ship together with Aaron to visit the taverns of Portsea, were now gone. Occasionally after a smuggling trip Polly may have came aboard for a few days, and Willie would retreat to his cubby hole where the spare sails were stored, and this he'd accepted, but now there was a crew of experienced sailors and Polly a permanent member of the crew.

Aaron had realised what was going through the lad's mind and during a quiet spell, called him into his cabin for a friendly chat.

"One day Willie, who knows, you could have a ship of your own.... we never know what is waiting for us round the corner."

This did little to improve his self confidence, a gutter urchin from the slums of Portsea, he shrugged his shoulders , "Not for me Captain, I'm happy just as I am."

"You will learn Willie. When you first came to me you knew nothing. I had to tell you then to wipe your nose or to take a bath and you couldn't tell a good brandy from a cheap wine. Now you could join the ranks of connoisseurs. You could neither read nor write, now you borrow all my books and I never get them back." Willie looked sheepishly at him, as a smile curled Aaron's lips, "There is very little you don't know about ships, Willie. Never put yourself down – you are a clever lad. When I see all those other urchins running round the streets of Portsea it makes me wonder how much talent is wasted. If only the City fathers took more interest in them and gave them an education it would benefit everyone.

"Look at my father Willie, a smuggler all his life just like his father before him and both very successful – a pain in the arse to the revenue men – and yet only once in his lifetime of smuggling did he have to jettison a cargo. He was a forward looking man, self educated but he made sure I had a good education and what is more, when I was very young he left me with a French family 'til I learned to speak the language like a native. But I didn't want to be a smuggler all my life. I wanted a ship, my very own ship that I could take round the world if I had to. So – rescuing old Medlam didn't make me favourable with the lower deck, aye, and a good few officers – but it enabled me to buy this ship, and here we are Willie, a couple of years have passed. If anyone told me I would be navigating my own ship down the African coast I would have told them they were out of their minds. Never put yourself down, Willie. Never."

During the long nights at sea Willie, under the pale light from the oil lamps in the main cabin would sit for hours trying to improve his reading and arithmetic and, when Polly would join him the cabin resembled a classroom. His duties complete Aaron joined too, with a bottle of his finest brandy sitting and discussing old times, until Willie rose unsteady on his feet and made his way to his own cabin.

Once, they were woken during the night feeling the ship being tossed around like a cork. Aaron dressed quickly and rushed to the deck, rain like glass rods tearing at his exposed face and hands. The crew were untangling the sail shrouds cursing and shouting above the noise of the rain and heavy waves that thudded against the sides of the ship. The night turned into a nightmare with the wind unable to make up its mind and constantly changing in all directions. Polly soon succumbed to sea sickness, and though not as bad as when they crossed the notorious Bay of Biscay, it was still sufficient to make her wish that she wouldn't wake in the morning. The storm didn't last long, and by mid-day it had abated sufficiently to let Polly out of the cabin and on to the deck, taking in great lung fulls of the fresh sea flavoured air. By late afternoon the sea turned and in a couple of hours resembled a sheet of glass. Polly sat in her usual place, a glass of brandy watered down by her elbow.

The weather remained calm with a steady wind behind them pushing the ship along at eight knots. Aaron took a sighting and, marked his position on the chart, "If this keeps up we should be at the Cape in a few days Willie."

They sighted several sails as they neared the Cape but most days they were completely alone on the vast ocean, it appeared as if the whole world had deserted them. But Aaron was feeling master of the whole world and was over-joyed when the lookout sighted land, his navigation proving spot on and almost to the time and date expected. A dark smudge at first, as it neared Polly gasped and pointed, "My God Aaron what is that?"

But it was Gibbons that answered, he was quite familiar with this area and had voyaged several times to the Cape.

"Why that's Table Mountain, Polly. It overlooks Cape Town – most days it has a large white cloud over it. The locals call it a table cloth."

The crew clung to every vantage place in order to view the great mountain. They were anxious to visit ashore – their first since the Canaries, since Aaron had refused them at Freetown. They had grumbled at first, but when Aaron had recited the grim story of the agent, their enthusiasm had waned. "Wait 'til Cape Town, it's a little more civilised there," he'd told them, "the heat is not so oppressive, though you still have to be careful, it's colonised by both the Dutch *and* the English. There's no love lost – as you can imagine."

The ship had sailed past the headland and well out to sea again, before a favourable wind was found to carry them into the safe haven of Cape Town harbour. They safely anchored amongst a dozen other ships of every nation, waiting their turn to tie up at the inadequate dockside.

The town itself was a hive of activity, the quayside piled with crates and bales of every size and shape. Strong natives, stripped to their waists, toiled amongst the stacks of goods, their black muscular bodies glistening with sweat. Along the streets negroes were selling every known variety of fruit and vegetables and many unknown specimens heaped high on barrows or on colourful blankets spread on the ground. It was a busy and thriving town, the position on the map making itself the half way point between the Dutch and British Eastern Empires. But it was its fine brick and stone buildings that lent the town a final air of prosperity, contrasting as they did starkly, against the wooden shacks.

But both silent and noisy resentment was building up. The Dutch and the British were jealous of each other; the blacks hated the Indians; and everyone hated the coloureds – the people of mixed races – and the Dutch had developed their very own language, Afrikaans.

"Better get me ashore Willie, I have to go and sort out this agent."

" I shouldn't bother if I were you Captain. I think we have a visitor." Willie nodded towards a small boat moving swiftly across the water towards them, two sweating muscular negroes bent over the oars and a white man sitting snugly on the stern. He fanned himself with a straw hat, dressed in what was once white clothing but now dark grey with sweat, he was puffing on a large cigar. The small boat vanished under the stern of the *Golden Falcon* and reappeared on the lee side with a thump. The two negroes held the small boat against the hull while the white man negotiated the rope ladder that Willie and a crew member had lowered down. Once aboard, he bellowed a few instructions to the two negroes, speaking to them in their own language. He didn't bother to take Aaron's proffered hand nor raise his hat, giving Aaron the message that he was neither wanted nor needed in the port.

"What are you carrying Captain?" His voice was hard and guttural, the vowels rubbing against his larynx.

Aaron liked to get to know a man before he made up his mind, but in this case he made an exception. He disliked this man intensely. Aaron didn't answer but handed the man the manifesto given to him by the agent in Freetown.

The man, while studying the papers, eyed Aaron up and down with deep suspicion, "You have nothing else aboard?" The words were spat out.

Aaron shook his head but knew an explanation was necessary. The cargo *had* originated in Holland, "The Dutch Captain abandoned this cargo at Freetown. He found it more lucrative to take on a cargo of slaves for shipment to America."

If he thought this would move the man, Aaron was mistaken, instead he took out a soiled handkerchief and wiping the sweat from his forehead and neck, answered in his absurd guttural voice, "Good luck to the man. I wish he *had* come here, we would like to get rid of a few. It's all these blacks are fit for. They have neither sense nor feeling. At least as slaves they get fed and clothed. The owners pay good money for them – it stands to reason they will get looked after."

Aaron felt the hairs on the back of his neck rise. The small scar on his face reddened, a certain sign he was losing his temper. He had recently scarred a man for life for saying those very same words, but restraining his temper he said, "Slaving won't be with us for very long. Mr Wilberforce is getting very strong backing from influential persons. I can assure you that, soon, the *stinking* trade of slaving will be completely banned. "

The man stared acidly at Aaron and raised his voice, "That is typical of you English. Damn interfering busybodies. Don't you understand? These people are much better off as slaves. Instead of having to live in the jungle or on the open veldt, they are looked after and fed well. None of you people want to believe that out here this is the way they live – like wild animals."

"It is not only the English," answered Aaron, "The Scottish, Welsh and Irish too, influence the laws of our country. When these four countries get together the rest of the world will sit up and take notice."

The man dismissed the conversation with a wave of his hand, "I told you Captain, go back to England and take your countrymen with you. Let us get on with running this country – and tell those damn *influential* people to keep their noses out of our business."

Aaron was about to say something he may later have regretted but was cut short by the Dutchman turning his back on him and pointing towards the town.

"You will find your agent there at the large red brick building, you cannot miss it, it's the largest in town." He handed the manifest back to Aaron and stepped over the ship's rail. Aaron sent up a silent prayer hoping he would slip and break his neck. The man hesitated as he caught sight of Polly, dressed in her white shirt and cut down trousers.

Pointing at her with a shaking finger, his eyes widened with disgust, "Who is that woman Captain?" His words hard and offensive, he broke into another sweat.

"What the hell does that have to do with you? Get off my ship. As far as I'm concerned my business with you is finished."

The man turned towards Aaron with a glare, again shaking a finger pointing at Polly his face showing signs of apoplexy, his voice affected, "Don't dare to come ashore dressed like that, you brazen hussy. Make sure you dress like a respectable Boer woman or I will have you locked up for indecency. No decent white woman would go about like that, showing off her body – we leave that to the Kaffir women."

Polly glared back.

"And I suppose you can't keep your perverted eyes off them. I wouldn't want to come ashore, you short arsed bastard. You are a damn hypocrite."

Polly nodded towards the shore in the direction of several women with long black dresses and poke bonnets that almost covered their faces, and brushed a large blue fly from her face. He stared at her unbelievingly. No woman had *ever* dared to speak to him in this fashion.

She turned away from him. In spite of his words, she knew he was mentally undressing her with his eyes, for she was a very attractive woman. Polly walked deliberately away, wiggling her bottom with exaggerated movements and swept the deck, much to the amusement of the crew.

But she desperately *did* want to go ashore – it had been months since she had trod firm ground. She had no idea what influence this man had ashore.

Chapter Eighteen

Within minutes of the Boer official leaving the ship Polly regretted her words. She had been aboard the ship for so long the thing she most wanted was to go ashore and take a long walk along a firm piece of ground that didn't heave under her feet. The smell of Freetown lingered in her mind – at least Cape Town showed some kind of civilisation. She stared longingly shorewards watching the population going about their business, and looked wistfully as the first part of the crew were rowed ashore.

Aaron thoughtfully consoled her by putting his arm around her shoulder and she soon came into her own again, "Sod him Aaron, he's a bloody old hypocrite, I'll *go* ashore – dressed as a cabin boy. I'll sweep my hair up; bind my tits and walk ashore with some of the crew. Being stuck on this ship for months on end is not very funny Aaron – so stop smiling."

"I wasn't smiling at that Polly, you haven't been swearing for months and as for dressing as a boy, that is nothing fresh, you've been wearing my trousers and shirts ever since we left England."

Aaron detested that damn Boer, or Dutchman, or whatever he liked to call himself and enjoyed the thought that he may be putting one over on him. Back in the cabin Polly stripped and Aaron trimmed her hair without it losing its femininity, Polly sweeping the rest on top of her head and forcing a hat over. She regretted losing some of her hair

138

but knew that by the time she reached England it would have grown again. Aaron ripped an old sheet into broad lengths and bound her breasts tightly, polly gasping for air with a little moan, then padding her waistline getting rid of her feminine shape.

"Just keep that bloody trap shut Polly." He warned her as they stepped into the ship's long boat with four crew members. At the same time he warned everyone of them not to lose sight of her and keep close. "I shall attend to my business with the agent."

The pleasant smell of the fresh fruit was overwhelming, for the main street was littered with piles of every description laid out on colourful blankets each side of the busy street. Polly tasted everything in sight, and sucked at a fresh mango for the first time in her life, the juices running down in streams over her chin from the succulent fruit – passion fruits, fresh figs and dates, oranges the size of cannon balls, and rosy red apples that looked as if they had been polished in wax. Bunches of grapes so large it took two hands to lift a bunch. She grew so excited at such an abundance that she almost gave the game away with a shrill laugh. A black lady in a colourful dress looked at her with a wrinkled brow. Polly winked and the large black lady letting out the loudest guffaw she'd ever heard, shaking her head from side to side, and wagging her finger at the girl,who took an instant liking to her and made arrangements for a delivery of a large quantity of fresh fruit to the dockside. It was probably the largest order the woman had ever received from one customer and she was more than willing to oblige.

Polly had got away with it, nobody recognising her as a female – apart from the black lady, who on their return was waiting patiently at the quayside with the fruit. When she saw Polly her shiny black face beamed, revealing two rows of pearly white teeth. It took two trips in the ship's boat to get them all safely aboard.

At the same time Aaron was making arrangements at the agent's office to get the cargo unloaded and receive his payment.

"Damn funny affair this cargo," commented the agent,

"the Captain dumping it at Freetown and then taking up slaving. It should have been here months ago, most of it's farming equipment for the Boers who are trekking up to the Orange River country. Mind you, they won't find the natives there are quite so docile – Matabele country up there – we don't see that tribe down here. You see them in Natal and not many whites venture into their country. Big proud fellows they are, their king is not known to be very fond of the white man – not as I blame him."

He swivelled his chair round and stared through the open window and pointed to a small group of natives with their backs to the wall of a derelict house, some fast asleep though it was only midday, dressed in rags and waiting for any kind of work, never mind how menial.

"Damn missionaries!" The agent spat the words out. "They go into the open veldt and spread the word and get their claws into the poor wretches, trying to teach them to read and write.... they finish up here handling any kind of dirty, degrading job for a mere pittance just to keep body and soul together. Those damn bible thumpers have taught them the fear of God and terrified them. Well it's too late now, there's no going back. Believe me Captain I know these natives, I have travelled up country, and they are happy go lucky – until they reach civilisation – then they change. In a few years time they'll start looking round and seeing the great divide between black and white and say 'here – what's going on? I want some of this good life myself'. Believe me Captain when that happens I want to be a couple of continents away. Three more years here and it's back to Dorset for me. A small house with half a dozen acres and I'll live in comfort for the rest of my life. That is if the damn fever doesn't get me."

Aaron laughed, "That's funny, the agent in Freetown said the same words."

"I am not surprised Captain, that is white man's hell up there, you are lucky if you survive five years. It's not quite that bad here but it's every British man's dream to serve his time and get back to Britain. Not so the Boers, their sole ambition is to make this a white man's paradise and every native a slave. Damn hypocrites, I see them setting off to church with a prayer book under their arms, then returning home to thrash their native servants."

The agent took out two glasses from a drawer in his desk, wiping them with a dry cloth before passing one to Aaron and filling it with a fiery liquid, "I suppose you *do* drink brandy Captain?"

Aaron nodded and took a sip and his face twisted in agony. The agent saw the look on his face and burst out laughing, "Bloody disgraceful isn't it Captain? Local stuff, cheap and nasty – you have to acquire a taste for it. It's what the locals call 'Dop' – more like 'Dope'. Since the war in Europe we haven't seen a decent drop of brandy."

Not wanting to upset his host, Aaron held his breath and downed the drink in one gulp, shuddering as the fiery liquid scorched the inside of his throat, "I see what you mean," he gasped, "damn potent stuff – send an honest drinking man out of his mind." He held the glass towards the light, took another sniff and shuddered.

"You will be returning to England now I suppose? asked the agent, "If you hang around for a few days I'll try and find a cargo for you."

Aaron took out a chamois bag, selected the largest stone and threw it on the desk. "What do you make of that? Hold it to the light, it looks pretty."

The agents studied the stone for a few minutes then casually threw it back on the desk. "What is it supposed to be?"

"They are supposed to be diamonds. You could say I took them as part payment further up the coast."

"Part payment," laughed the man, "You've been done. I know of no-one finding diamonds in Africa. There are rumours that someone discovered them in the interior further up the coast – but in this country there are always rumours. Two Arab slavers – tall chaps, brothers, are supposed to have discovered their source but as no-one can say they've actually *seen* any diamonds....well. Mind you I wouldn't like to tangle with those two bastards, they would slit your throat just for looking at them – reckoned to be the best and hardest slavers on the west coast."

Aaron thought it wise to keep quiet about his brush with the two Arab slavers. He returned his leather bag to his pocket and the agent, muttering to himself 'Diamonds', gave a little laugh and sat down – again replenishing his glass.

He called his native servant, "Go the rounds Charlie and see if we can get a cargo for England."

Polly, back on deck, was dressed in her usual gear. The shirt, already stained with sweat, clung to her skin, making her breasts now released from the stranglehold stand out neatly, "It was damn hot tied up in that sheeting Aaron. We passed the old Dutchman, he looked straight at me but didn't recognise me."

She pulled the top of the shirt away from her breasts and blew down the front to cool them, "God, was I glad to get aboard and into some decent clothes on again." She pointed to the baskets on deck "Bought quite a bit of fruit and vegetables ....."

Aaron threw a casual glance at the purchases – he knew he could trust her. She had proved her capabilities on the outward voyage and apart from a few bouts of sea sickness, had taken to it like a seasoned sailor.

"When do we unload and make our way home Aaron?"

"Start unloading tomorrow, the agent is looking around for a cargo for England. He is also arranging to have our water casks filled."

A full week passed before the agent had found a small cargo and loaded it ready for the homeward journey. Polly had shown little interest in going ashore again. She knew the Dutchman had put a watch on her to make sure she was decently dressed. Several natives had watched the ship each and every day.

Sam had taken to sea life and became a firm favourite with the crew, settling down to the day-to-day routine; always laughing and flashing two rows of white teeth. Having witnessed the way the blacks were treated ashore he had no ambition to explore this strange port. He sat on deck watching the black stevedores being mistreated by the white men and their black overseers, shaking his head in despair. He was delighted when the ship put to sea again, his show of excitement infecting the crew.

Polly was looking forward to seeing England once again, it

felt like they had been away for years instead of months and by the time they reached it, it would be Summer. But as Polly thought of England the memories started flooding back – memories she would sooner forget.

She stood at the stern of the ship, a full moon casting a wide silver path from the far horizon. Aaron came and stood beside her, and she slid her arm between his, "Can I sail with you again Aaron, on another trip?" She looked directly into his eyes, a sincere pleading on her face.

Aaron loved teasing her and answered "I don't know Polly.... that sea sickness of yours.... it really puts me off my duties."

"But I ain't sea sick now Aaron, it was only that damn Bay of Biscay." They both stared at the moon. Polly knew it was the time to have asked him, in this romantic atmosphere she knew she could ask for anything.

Still it was several tantalising minutes before he slowly answered. "We'll see Polly, wait until we get back."

He gently patted her hand, and looked towards Willie at the wheel, "It's a fine night Willie, we have a fair wind, if this keeps up we should make excellent time." He winked his eye at Willie and with his arm round Polly's slim waist vanished into the cabin.

They called once more into the Canaries. With plenty of space in the hold, there was no reason why they shouldn't take a cargo of wine back home, he had plenty of connections in that trade. If possible he would get a couple of barrels of decent brandy. The same agent was at the quayside in exactly the same spot to greet them. Polly thought he had taken up residence. He salaamed several times almost to a point of embarrassment, and when he straightened he again couldn't take his eyes off Polly's cleavage.

"You had a good voyage Captain?" He wasn't really interested, as far as he was concerned Aaron was just another potential customer.

Aaron just nodded his head and Polly said to the agent, handing him the list "None of your fancy prices."

The agent licked his full blown greasy lips, "No lady."

Three weeks later they were anchored off Dungerness waiting for a favourable tide.

Chapter Nineteen

The crew were paid off in London. Polly was overwhelmed with the amount of money she was paid and subconsciously totted up how long she would have to work in the taverns to pick up so much. She shuddered and quickly dispensed with such nightmarish thoughts. She was Aaron's now, and only Aaron's, but at the back of her mind she knew they would never marry. She would remain his mistress for as long as she possibly could, just living from day to day. In all her life she had never been happier, her main dread was waking and finding it was all a dream. Aboard she was treated the same as the crew and hadn't been left out when the money they took from the slaver was shared. Having been paid the five gold guineas, along with her wages, her purse was the heaviest it had ever been.

She now had the freedom to do exactly as she wished and her first destination was the dressmakers. Not one of the ordinary, run of the mill dressmakers but the finest in town. For too long she had dressed as a common sailor in Aaron's trousers and shirt, so comfortable at sea, but so plainly unsuitable here in London. She wanted Aaron to see her in the fine delicate dresses she had so much admired on the ladies of Portsea – the Naval and Army officers' wives – when they attended the great Balls, promenading on the Governor's Green, and the Garrison Church. When they visited the hotels along the High Street, they had looked down at her, noses held high as if she had been a bad smell. Now with money she could, and would, compete.

At the first salon she entered, the madam and her assistants were reluctant to serve her. Polly felt the silk gowns running the fine material through her fingers as, behind her back, the two assistants put their hands in front of their mouths and suppressed giggles. Even Madam was dubious and went to reprimand her, "May I be of assistance?"

"Yes.... this dress.... how much is it and may I try it on?"

"Well, I am afraid it is very expensive. I have some cheaper cotton dresses over here." She pointed to the rear of the shop.

"I wouldn't have asked you about this dress if I had wanted a cheaper one." Polly put her weighted purse on a small table, it was obvious by the sound it made that it was full of coins and any reluctance on the owner's part turned to overpowering attendance as she beckoned her two assistants over.

"Try this madam," she draped a fine silk dress over Polly's arm, "with that beautiful hair and that golden hue to your skin I don't think madam could choose more wisely. Madam will be a sensation at the Opera and be the cause of many a twinkle in a gentleman's eye."

Polly's mind was not on any Opera. She felt like saying, 'Bugger the Opera' but looking at the full length mirror she saw for herself the transformation. From a deck hand to a beautiful lady. Now she could prove it to Aaron. She could *be* someone.... someone he could be proud of.... and not the picture of a Portsea whore, rushing about the deck in cut down trousers and one of his shirts. She finally settled on three dresses each a different colour, and tipping the gold coins onto the table, counted out the exact price. The two assistants stifled a slight cry, for they had never seen so much money, the usual clientele would charge it and take months to settle the account.

Aaron spent the afternoon with his agent and solicitor and managed to find a cargo for South Africa. It was late afternoon when he returned to his ship and the sun still warm, he settled on deck with a glass of brandy. Most of the crew were ashore and there was little else to do.

Dozing off he was awakened by the sound of iron rims rattling over the uneven cobblestones on the quayside and was surprised to see the carriage stop at the gangway and a beautiful young lady alight, her face partly covered by a wide brimmed hat. She was halfway up the gang plank before he realised it was Polly and almost choked on a mouthful of brandy.

"Heavens Polly, whatever have you done with yourself? What has happened to my crew member, has she jumped ship?" She took his hand as she stepped on to the deck, twirling around so Aaron could fully appreciate the beauty of the dress.

"Do you like it Aaron?"

"But I'm almost speechless Polly – You look absolutely gorgeous." The two ship's crew remaining on deck, standing with their mouths open, obviously agreed with him.

"Alright men, you can close your mouths now, it's only Polly." They moved away shaking their heads.

"If there was a great Ball I would be pleased to have the honour of conducting you there. But never mind Polly, I will take you to the Opera instead.... just to show you off. We'll show the 'oitey toitey' lot that we can mix with the best, and I will go in my new Captain's uniform."

He stood up and, inspecting her more closely, sighed, "I knew one day I would make some kind of a lady out of you Polly."

Aaron's mind flashed back to the days when Polly had worked in the taverns – her battle cry, "Drop my kecks for sixpence sailor." Now all that was in the past, she had been and saw places only dreamed about; places she had only heard sailors talk about. She now had money in her purse she had earned honestly, and could spend on her slightest whim.

Polly was in a world of her own just as Aaron was.

Aaron was not only pleased with a very profitable and successful voyage, but he had achieved something not many other ship's Captains had achieved. Through rough and foul weather, windless days when they were becalmed, he had lost not one man. Not through accident nor through disease. He'd turned out to be a Captain a hundred years ahead of his time with a happy crew that would have followed him to hell and back without the fear of the rope's end or the cat. Some of the crew, at first, had baulked at the idea of eating an orange or a lime every day but he had proved to one and all that it kept the dreaded scurvy away. He paid them well and he fed them well, fresh food when available, and the promise that every man would get his full pay at the end of the voyage. If any crew member had died, his next of kin would receive his full pay. Best of all he instilled confidence in his crew.

"We sail in two weeks time for Cape Town Polly, so we will make the best of it. I am going down to Portsmouth tomorrow, do you want to come with me?" A twinkle appeared in his eye and a note of defiance. "I think we might just stay at The George Hotel. The boss always made me use the back entrance when we delivered the brandy there, I will enjoy walking in through the front door."

"Me too Aaron. I used to watch those high ranking Naval and Army officers hand in hand with their wives or mistresses going in and out, looking down their snooty noses at me. One day I was looking through the open doors and the manager came out and politely told me to piss off."

She was determined she would go back to her old childhood neighbourhood and show off her fine clothes. It would to be her crowning accomplishment – she could be a real lady accompanied by her black servant, "Can we take Sam with us Aaron, you could go and buy him some finery."

"That's a good idea.... poor bugger won't go ashore on his own. He still doesn't trust the white man. He went on the dockside today, to stretch his legs and all the local urchins kept shouting after him, 'Where's your tail Blackie?' The local dockies were shouting and encouraging the kids. Sam ran back to the ship scared to death. I will take him ashore first thing and get him fixed up with breeches and a nice coloured jacket – he loves bright clothes."

By noon, Polly was dressed in her finery and Aaron in his new Captain's uniform, with Sam in bright blue breeches and a yellow jacket with shiny leather shoes and large silver buckles that made him limp like he had received a full blast of buckshot in his bottom. A chaise arrived at the gang plank pulled by a pair of magnificent white horses. Sam sat up proudly next to the hostler, his white eyes wide with wonder as they started through the great city bustling with life, hawkers shouting their wares, street musicians practising their arts. Business men bustling about and street urchins chasing after them begging for money or trying to jump on the back for a free lift. The driver turning round and shouting and threatening with his whip, only to receive a mouthful of abuse.

"Don't do that, my man." Aaron scolded the driver. He reached for his purse and threw out a handful of copper coins. Sam laughed as he watched the urchins scramble across the road, fighting for them.

As the crowded city gave way to the countryside Sam was quite overcome. During the night it had rained and the aroma of the fresh countryside was overwhelming. Sam kept raising his head to breathe, taking in great lung fulls of the sweet air.

"Very nice Captain," was all he could say, repeating it every ten minutes.

After what seemed like the thousandth time Polly said, "For heaven's sake Sam, give it a rest."

They pulled up at the George Hotel in the High Street and several flunkies failing to recognise Polly, rushed to her assistance. Soon the couple were alone in one of the hotel's best rooms and Polly threw herself on the large four poster bed, her wide brimmed hat sat comfortably on a side table. It had been a long hard trip down from London.

"Those snooty buggers – I reckon if they had recognised me they would have thrown us out."

"Not likely Polly, a full purse breaks down all social barriers. In any case, someone did recognise me. Do you remember that Admiral I rescued, he was sitting downstairs in one of the large leather armchairs – I saw his eyebrows shoot up when he looked at me."

They had their meal served in their bedroom, and Aaron quietly sipped his brandy, "It's not like that marvellous brandy you used to serve here my man," he said to the waiter who was serving them.

He winked his eye at Polly who joined in, "Yes my dear, one place you could always get a decent brandy was at The George. They had a wonderful reputation."

"Yes sir, we always served the very best, we had a reputation second to none. Alas it isn't available any more, our supplier has completely vanished. He knew just where to buy it. One minute he was here the next he was gone."

Polly, trying to hide her smiles and putting on a phoney accent said to Aaron, "I know you always enjoy a good brandy dear, we should have gone to the Dolphin Hotel, their brandy is splendid."

"Not any more madam, I believe they had the same source, there isn't that class of brandy to be had anywhere in the City." He bowed slightly to Polly, "Madam" and backed away towards the door but Aaron held him up.

"Tell me waiter, is that Admiral Medlam sitting downstairs, his face looked familiar to me. I thought he was captured by the French?"

The man's attitude changed almost to a point of malice, and he stepped quickly back towards the table. "It is sir, he was captured by the French but one of our local men, a well known smuggler and a very brave man, almost single handedly rescued him from the prison." He lowered his voice as if he was taking Aaron into is confidence. "He was also the man that kept the hotels supplied with brandy, always the best, we certainly miss him."

The door closed behind him and Polly, unable to hold out any longer, burst into laughter "You really had me going Aaron, I don't know how I kept a straight face."

Next day, Polly did a tour round her old haunts. Stepping out of the hotel, two flunkies opened the doors for her but no-one recognised her, partly because of the clothes she wore and the wide brimmed hat covering half her face. With her darkened skin and sun-bleached hair, however, it was doubtful if her own mother would have recognised her.

Aaron was stopped by the Admiral just as he was about to step out into the open, "Aren't you that fellow that rescued me from that French prison?"

Aaron pushed past him, "No sir, I am not, and if you

should speak otherwise would you please speak more quietly. Half the Navy from here to the Nore would willingly slit my throat if they should hear you. Good day sir."

"Damned impudent fellow – it *was* him, I should have had him flogged." He muttered towards Aaron's back.

Aaron had an appointment with his local lawyers. The clerk who forever seemed to be sitting at the window saw him coming and rushed to the door to meet him, bowing and touching his forelock. Aaron was his hero, and the type of man he would have emulated had his father not insisted upon his becoming a clerk, an occupation he would probably endure for life.

"Good morning Captain, did you have a good voyage?"

"Yes, very good." Aaron was led down the dark passage by the clerk, to the inner sanctum where he knocked and waited for the word.

"Come!"

He opened the door and stood aside to let Aaron pass. Closing the door after him, the clerk didn't move but kept his ear flat against the door hoping to hear of any further adventure, he wasn't to be disappointed. The lawyer, sat in the same leather chair just as if he hadn't moved an inch since the day Aaron left him, poured out two glasses of Port and passed one to Aaron.

The Captain gave a detailed report on the voyage, before concluding, "I will be returning to the Cape in two weeks time, with a full cargo. Please make all arrangements with Lloyds."

As they had talked, Mr Harris had poured over the ship's papers, and now brought items he considered untenable to Aaron's notice.

"You seem to have paid rather high wages Captain.... and look at these food bills. Rather extravagant aren't they? These bills from the Canaries to the Cape seem very high to me. These are luxuries that sailors could surely do without."

"I don't agree with you Mr Harris, break it down and it works out for food about two pennies a day for each man. I never lost a man through accident or disease, and I keep a very happy and contented ship."

This argument made little impression on Mr Harris, to whom a sailor represented the lowest form of human life. All he was interested in was how much profit he had made. Giving the crew fresh fruit and vegetables made him almost foam at the mouth – it was unheard of on the lower deck, where crews were used to eating mushy peas and salt beef and pork. He began to voice his thoughts to Aaron but had hardly managed a couple of words when Aaron raised his hand.

"No, Mr Harris.... I realise you do have a small share in my ship, but your profits have been pretty good. If you don't like the way I am running the business I will buy your share out today."

"There is no need for that Captain." He had already worked out his share for the small sum he had invested and wished he had invested more, for it showed a clear twelve per cent profit even after taking into account Aaron's generous pay-out to the crew.

Polly had not realised the power of being well dressed and what it could do for a woman. Those that did recognise her found it hard to talk and when they did the talk was stunted in the mistaken idea she had become a lady. But none of her old friends welcomed her with open arms as they had in the old days. She was hurt – hurt deeply – and was greatly relieved when Aaron began to prepare for the return trip.

As they were leaving the dockside area Polly saw a bundle of rags sitting in a corner and she stopped the chaise, "Just a few minutes Aaron." She alighted and went over to the bundle of rags and touched it. A female head slowly raised and gave a toothless grin, revealing a misshapen row of discoloured teeth and a smell of gin sodden breath. She raised a half-filled bottle of gin and in a blurred voice offered, "Have a sip my lady?"

"It's you mom! What are you doing here?"

"Mom.... she answered in a slurred voice. Why do you call me mom? My gal Polly.... she's dead... I think. Go away lady, and leave me alone." She took another swig of her bottle, "My gal Polly she's dead.... nobody wants me now."

Polly turned to the chaise, with tears in her eyes, "I can't leave her like this Aaron. Just look at her, she's wet through and smells terrible.... I don't think she's eaten for a week.... she's all skin and bone. I'll have to do something for her."

They returned to the tavern and Polly explained the situation to her old boss.

"Look, she's old and she's frail. She looks to me like she is dying, you've a spare room down in your cellar – take her in, clean her up and give her two square meals a day. Give her a bottle of gin a day, some clean clothes, and make sure she takes a bath. Here are twenty golden guineas, I will pay you a golden guinea every week to look after her, and will pay you in full when we return. If she has improved by then and looks good you will be well rewarded."

She called two street women over, filled their glasses with gin and told them where they could find her mother.

"Bring her here, clean her up and there's a golden guinea for each of you."

"Yes Miss Polly, just leave it to us, we'll clean her and see that the landlord looks after her."

"You are a kind hearted woman Polly," Aaron said to her when she returned to the chaise. "Your mother threw you on the streets when you were a kid, and didn't give a damn if you lived or died. Anyone could have murdered you for all she cared." He shrugged his shoulders. "Still.... she *is* your mother I suppose."

They stopped only one more time, at the top of the Portsdown Hill that overlooked the great harbour. Polly alighted from the carriage and with Aaron's arm round her shoulders looked over the old City and harbour.

"Nobody seemed to want to know me Aaron, I have lost all my old friends."

"Never you mind Polly, it was a life you were lucky to leave behind. When you return to the ship this will all be a bad memory."

Stripped of her finery and back to wearing trousers and open necked shirt Polly once more began to enjoy the shipboard life again. She stood at the forepeak and allowed the brisk wind to brush her hair – as if it were brushing away her past life. Only the memory of her down and out mother continued to cast a shadow over her new found happiness. She knew that if she had kept up her old lifestyle – then she would have ended up exactly as her mother had. She shuddered at the thought.

In a few days they would be at sea once again.

Chapter Twenty

The cabin was empty, and Aaron sighed deeply. It could mean only two things – Polly had gone shopping again, and he could count on her buying even more of those damn dresses. There was nowhere to put the damn things of course – but no doubt she would find room even if it meant hooking some of his clothes out of the cupboard.

Polly was obsessed with dresses, but he really couldn't complain. She worked hard aboard and it was her own money, perhaps the only real money she'd ever had that she could call her own and insome small way maybe it made up for those younger years when she'd been forced to walk the streets around the docks in Portsmouth.

Nevertheless, the cabin was fast becoming more like a high class dress shop.

There was a soft tap and the door opened. Willie, never waiting for an invitation, doffed his cap and smiled, "Seen you come aboard Captain, any cargo?"

The lad no longer enjoyed the days in port, and was always anxious to be off on another adventure.

"Aye Willie, we have another cargo for the Cape – sail Monday week. That gives us ten days to unload the cargo and get some of those jobs done around the ship, revictualling and taking on plenty of water."

"Yes Captain. I take it you haven't read my report yet. That man Young, he's been with us since the first day, he should have been on watch, and was drunk. I confronted him, and he stalked off the ship to the nearest tavern.

There were three bottles of wine in his diddy box. You must talk to him Captain."

Aaron sighed deeply, "I suppose he's still at the tavern. Get his gear together and put it at the top of the gang plank, but bring him to me the minute he steps aboard."

He sat down heavily as Willie left the cabin. This was the first time, since taking over the ship, that he had needed to punish a member of his crew. He had to show the others that he meant business. Aaron refused to consider corporal punishment but neither could he allow Young to get away scot-free.

While Aaron was swilling away his disappointment with a bottle of brandy, Polly entered the cabin negotiating the narrow doorway with a large box. Not many years ago this manoeuvre would have been accompanied by mouthfuls of bad language, but recently Polly had curbed it for Aaron's sake.

"Not more dresses Polly.... where do you intend to store them all, for heaven's sake?"

"Don't be such a grumpy old miser Aaron. You want me to look nice don't you?"

"No! I mean ....Yes! I wouldn't mind if we could store them properly.... Why don't you buy something that is useful aboard ship, instead of cutting down my trousers and using my shirts?"

Polly gave her girlish laugh – the one that always ended with a teenager's giggle – and spulled out three pairs of trousers all in the most brilliant and amazing colours. One pair a brilliant red; another a bright yellow; and the third pair a very pale blue, along with six shirts also of very bright colours. She held the shirts in turn against her body and swung around, "Do you like them Aaron?"

"Yes....very nice Polly. I bet they cost a fortune."

"So? It's my money." She started to strip off her shore-going clothes and change into her new trousers and shirt, "What colour do you prefer Aaron?"

Although Aaron didn't really care what Polly wore, he would never dream of hurting her feelings, and lifted each shirt in turn making believe he was giving the question his full consideration.

"I think maybe the yellow ones Polly.... although I do think you could have chosen more practical colours, dark blue or black, these will get filthy in no time."

A subdued Young climbed the gangway. His shipmates had informed him in the tavern that the Captain wanted to see him when he came aboard and seeing his kit stacked on deck by the gang plank confirmed his worst fears.

Willie was there to greet him, "Young, you are to come with me to the Captain's cabin."

Willie turned his face away from Young's breath which tainted the air with the smell of strong liquor and tobacco. He tapped lightly on the cabin door and this time waited a few minutes – for he knew that Polly was now aboard.

"Come...." Aaron's voice was soft. Willie told Young to stay outside and entered the cabin, trying to hide a smile when he saw Polly in her bright yellow fancy pants.

"I have Young outside, Captain."

Aaron turned to Polly, "Leave us for a few minutes Polly, this won't take very long. Show him in Willie."

Young stood dejectedly across the table from Aaron, shifting uneasily on his feet and they stared in silence at each other for a several moments.

"Young, I know you like your drink – who doesn't – but there is a right time, and a right place. You have committed two of the most serious crimes aboard my ship. Two crimes which, if you had committed aboard one of H.M. ships, you would possibly have ended up on the end of a rope. At the least your back would have been stripped down to the spine.

"If this had happened at sea I would have put ashore at the first landfall, inhabited or not. You can thank your lucky stars that aboard this ship we resort neither to floggings nor to capital punishment. I should take you to the local magistrates where, for certain, you would be sentenced transportation to the Colonies.

"Instead.... you are finished on this ship. Your belongings are on deck." Aaron took out a small leather bag and, spilling golden coins on to the polished table, counted several and pushed them towards Young, "Here is your pay right up to the minute – you were caught drunk and incapable of watch."

Young tried to protest, "I know I had too much to drink Captain and I am sorry for that. But the wine, I bought in Madeira, and I have never broached the cargo. That wine was paid for in Madeira."

Aaron looked at the man with contempt and shook his head, "Now Young.... you are a drunkard and a thief. Please do not make yourself a liar too. I know every single item that was brought aboard this ship while we were in port. You know the orders, everything has to be declared when you step aboard. Neither you nor any member of this crew bought wine." He pointed to the three bottles on the table, "That wine was part of the cargo. Now go ashore quietly before I change my mind and have you thrown into the local prison and see what the magistrate has to say about it." He pointed his finger towards the door, "Out of my sight Young."

Aaron swung his chair around to face the stern window. Young didn't argue any more, but shuffled from the cabin stifling back his tears, realising he had just lost the best job he'd ever had at sea. Aaron too was sorry to lose him, Young had been a very good sailor and could have had a very good future before him.

As if he were in another world Aaron sat up straight in his chair, his hands together and his two fingers on his lips, he wasn't worried about replacing Young, there were dozens of good seamen waiting for a berth on the ship – his name had spread like wildfire. He was a good and considerate Captain, but one of his trusted, and what he thought was a loyal seaman, had let him down. He stared at the large East India merchantman tied up behind him, there was little doubt that Young would have been swinging from the yard arm if he had committed such a crime aboard there.

Dusk was falling by the time Aaron went on deck. He lit his favourite short stemmed clay pipe and leaned on the stern rail watching the East India man preparing for sea. It was a warm night, the sky clear and the stars taking up position for their lonely vigil over the old town. Everywhere there was hustle and bustle, barges and lightermen going about their business shouting and cursing; ferry men waited to take passengers across the murky river. Willie approached him quietly, he knew his Captain didn't like being disturbed when he was in his melancholy moods, quietly he asked, "Any orders Captain?"

"We will be taking on the cargo for Cape Town in the morning Willie, go ashore and get a replacement for Young. A couple of decent looking seamen were enquiring when I came aboard – choose one." He handed Willie the manifesto, "Let Carter know what we will be loading."

At first light the ship and quayside came to life. All night long carts drawn by horses had rattled over the cobbled quayside, now each dray-man was expecting to be unloaded first. Carter was down the hold while Willie was supervising and helping to lower the cargo. Sam worked like two men his black body drenched with sweat.

The new man was already aboard helping witht the cargo. Willie had selected wisely, he stood well over six feet with a chest like a beer barrel, stripped to his waist, he worked with a will. If he wanted to make an impression on Aaron he had certainly succeeded. Aaron ordered him to his cabin. "How long have you been at sea?"

"Almost thirty years Captain, man and boy. I was a powder monkey first, then an able seaman. I served with Nelson aboard the *Victory* at Trafalgar – I helped to carry his body down to the sick bay Captain."

There was a note of pride in his voice as he mentioned the great man's name. Aaron smiled to himself, this must be the hundredth time he'd heard men speak of having had that distinct honour and thought to himself, "God Nelson must have had a load of lead in him, when I saw him he could have weighed only eight stone and yet it took about a hundred men to carry him below."

He poured himself a drink and listened to the man's story. "After I left the Navy sir I worked coasters and colliers on the East coast, a dirty job and the food was terrible, but I stuck it out for three years. Then I signed on an East India man."

"Take your shirt off and turn around."

The man looked surprised but obeyed. Aaron looked closely at the man's back for any signs of whip marks, it was
clear apart from a few freckles.

"Right, put it back on – your name?"

"Peters, sir" he answered clearly.

"Are you married?"

Peters shook his head, "No sir, no close relatives apart
from a sister who lives on the south coast, I haven't seen
her for years."

"Well Peters, when you sign on this ship you sign for the
return voyage. If anything happens to you your next of kin
will get the full pay. Do you know your sister's address."

Peters shrugged his shoulders, "Don't know where she is
Captain, even if there *was* any money coming from me I
doubt she would bother. She married well I believe."

"This is a happy ship, Peters, and we intend to keep it
that way. The food is as good as we can make it – in return
we expect your full cooperation, no slacking and no drunkenness aboard. What you do ashore is your business but
aboard this ship it's my business – sign here."

Aaron pushed the ship's book across to the man and
expected the usual cross – instead his signature was in
perfect copperplate writing.

"We should finish loading sometime tomorrow and will
sail within a couple of days, if you have anything to bring
aboard go and get it now."

By evening the next day the ship was fully loaded and
prepared for its long voyage to the Cape. Aaron was
pleased with Willie's choice and when work stopped the
festivities began. Every man was issued with a quart of ale
and much to the surprise of the crew, when Menzies took
out his fiddle Peters produced a concertina and joined in.

Chapter Twenty-one

The Bay of Biscay greeted Polly with its usual turbulence, and using every ounce of strength, with a spirit of defiance she tried to combat it. But on the third day she finally succumbed and rushed to the cabin with her hand firmly over her mouth. Aaron followed her as she flung herself across the bed, and lifting her legs, made her as comfortable as he possibly could.

"You did very well Polly, three days, and the old Bay was certainly kicking up rough."

"Go away, Aaron, please.... just leave me alone.... I am about to die anyway and I want to die alone. But promise me you won't put me in the water amongst the sharks.... take me home and let me be buried on dry land."

Aaron laughed, "You are not going to die. And if you did, do you think I would keep your stinking body aboard here for months? Pull yourself together – you *were* starting to get used to it.... and anyway, what the hell am I going to do with those dresses filling my cupboard? None of the men will wear them, they don't fit."

This brought a smile to the corners of Polly's mouth.

"Now pull yourself together – eat some dry bread and water – otherwise I will slap your arse."

"Wait 'til I am well again Aaron.... I will look forward to it." The words faded on her lips as she fell into a deep sleep.

Two days later they left the turbulent Bay and sailed into smoother waters, Polly's sea sickness soon forgotten. She rushed on deck with a plate of food and a blanket and stretched out in her usual place, "How far are we from the Canaries Aaron? I'd give a king's ransom to put my feet on dry land again."

She turned her face towards the wind and allowed it to fan her, once more breathing in deeply, "Why can't the sea be like this always Aaron?"

He shook his head and lit his favourite short stemmed pipe, "I promise you Polly, when we hit dry land we will take a nice long walk together."

"Say that again and try to convince me.... I tell you what Aaron, I bet when we reach the Canaries that old grease ball will be on the quayside wringing his hands and pleading poverty."

As predicted, the fat greasy Spaniard was at the quayside, sweating profusely, far more than usual, constantly wiped his forehead with a piece of cloth. He had spotted the ship the night before, making towards the island, and was waiting at the crack of dawn for its arrival. He had known the Captain was a keen business man – that he could put nothing over *him* – but he was in for a bigger shock when Polly approached him with the list of required stores, she was an even harder nut to crack. Aaron had admired the way she'd purchased the fruit in South Africa – it had lifted another burden from his shoulders. When she had finished and paid for the goods the Spaniard asked to see the Captain. Aaron kept him waiting.

"Captain, I have two crates to go to Freetown. They are very important and must go without any delay."

"Sorry Alphonse, both holds are full and there is no way that I can take on extra cargo. In any case, I am not heading for Freetown"

Alphonse became extremely agitated, sweat oozing from every pore as he anxiously bit his bottom lip, "But it is *so* important Captain the man will pay fifty golden guineas." He took out a leather purse and spilt some gold coins into his hand hoping the sight of the money would influence Aaron, "You say you are bound for Cape Town Captain, Freetown is maybe two, three days out of your way. What do you say.... seventy-five guineas?" He rattled his purse in front of Aaron's face.

"I have no more space Alphonse.... can't you get it into your head? *I have no more room!*" His voice could almost be heard on top of the volcanic mountain that dominated the island. But he had to give Alphonse credit for his perseverance.

"Please Captain.... you have plenty of room on deck, take them as deck cargo... look these crates are barely two metres high – a metre each side – they will take up very little room."

"Alphonse.... I do not like deck cargo it impedes the crew going about their duties."

Alphonse fell to his knees and held his hands together as if in prayer, pushing them up and down, tears forming in his eyes.

"Alright Alphonse I will take them. But it will cost you a hundred guineas."

Life crept back into the agent's face as a huge smile spread across his greasy features, "A hundred guineas Captain, my poor family will have to go without food and clothes." Nevertheless, he counted out the money.

"Exactly one hundred guineas."

Aaron thought a final tear fell on the last coin.

"Alphonse," he smiled, "you were told to pay me a hundred guineas in the first place you cheating old rogue. I will bring my ship alongside this afternoon, I want to be out of here on the first convenient tide."

He took the list from Polly and the order was fulfilled with very little arguing. It seemed as if the Spaniard wanted them away as much as Aaron.

As soon as the ship came alongside the stores were hauled aboard and the two crates loaded. The agent came aboard making sure they were secured to his satisfaction, Aaron having the satisfaction of paying for the stores with some of the gold he had been paid to ship the two crates.

Two days out from the island they became becalmed, the wind dropping completely. Not a whisper of air. Looking over the side they could see an image of the ship mirrored in the clear water, the slightest sound carrying from the stern and heard clearly at the bows. The sails hung limply like a curtain at the theatre. It had an affect on the crew, and they slouched around fanning themselves and talking in hushed tones. The decks were constantly doused down in sea water preventing the tar between the planking from melting and the sails were tacked constantly in the hope of catching the slightest breeze.

Aaron ordered a barrel of water placed on deck, shielded from the sun with a wooden cover on it; the whole covered with a wet blanket to try and keep it cool. The blanket had to be dipped in the sea frequently, and dried out in minutes. Bottles of wine bought in the Canaries were kept cool in the sea tied with lengths of twine. Everything remained ghostly quiet. Several men baited hooks and dropped their lines in the clear water, while shoals of fish played around them but failed to bite.

Polly sat with her back against the crates sipping water laced with brandy, "Christ it's hot!"

Willie paused in mid-answer as Polly's smile suddenly turned to a puzzled frown, "Sssshh Willie." She placed her head flat against the packing case, "I'm sure I heard something ...."

Willie gave his usual raucous laugh, "It's the heat Polly, it's getting to you. I once heard an old sailor talking in a tavern, he said he knew of people going mad with this heat.... it kind of curdles the brain. Take it easy Polly – go and sit in the cabin and take the sun off your brain box."

Two members of the crew standing near became a little curious and moved nearer, "What is it Polly?"

"I thought I heard a slight movement in this crate." They both put their ears to the crate, and one of them looked strangely at Polly.

"Watch it Polly.... do as Willie said and don't let the sun get at you." They both burst out laughing and walked away.

The ship's carpenter passing by came nearer to see what what all the fuss was about and examined the crates closer sliding his fingers along the joints.

His brow creased to a frown. "Get the Captain, Willie."

Quite a crowd had gathered as the carpenter said to Aaron, "See anything strange about this crate Captain?"

Aaron did exactly as the carpenter had done, but noticed nothing strange about the two crates apart from the fine workmanship, which was rather unusual for such crates carrying cargo. He shook his head, "Looks alright to me."

"Well Captain, it's nailed permanently on three sides.... but just look at this edge...." the carpenter ran a hammer along the fourth side, "....and yet it feels very secure. It can mean only one thing – it must be secured from the inside."

Curiosity overcame him, and he jumped on top of the crates, loosening off a plank. As he bent to peer inside he jerked his head back, "Bloody hell Captain, I don't know what's inside but whatever it is – it's gone rotten."

Aaron swiftly joined the carpenter on top of the crate but pulled his head back as the smell hit him. The interior was too dark to reveal the nature of its stinking contents, "Put the plank back and seal it as quickly as possible. Something has really gone off in there."

Still becalmed the next day all hands were wetting down the decks with sea water when a crew member, passing the crates, noticed a thick green slime escaping. Dipping in his finger, the sailor smelled it and recoiled, "My God! What the hell is it?"

The Captain was again called to the crates and immediately ordered the carpenter to open it up completely, doing as little damage as possible. After several blows the first plank was removed and in the still hot air the smell from the interior forced the onlookers to scatter in all directions. Inside, the four walls of the crate were padded with a kind of coconut fibre with a couple of feet of straw on the floor. It was several minutes before anyone noticed a tall black figure coiled up in the straw. Two men grabbed him by his ankles and dragged him away from the crate. The man was filthy, and covered in human excreta.

"Drag him into the shade and douse him with buckets of sea water. Then give him something to drink.... fresh water, not too much or he might choke. The poor bugger is hardly breathing." Aaron lifted the man's limp wrist and felt the pulse, it was very slight. They threw several buckets of sea water over the still form but it was minutes before there was a slight flicker in his eyes.

A further inspection was made of the coffin like crate. The straw stank to high heaven, and a bucket in one corner was overflowing with the human waste. Another bucket in the far corner, now empty, had once been filled with water. Aaron sat on the ship's rail staring at the opened crate and its contents before making up his mind and violently smashing it to pieces. Several crew members heaved it overboard, while Aaron ordered the remaining crate to be opened. Inside they found a fast decomposing body, once very black but now turned a ghastly grey. In one corner of the crate lay several wicked looking knives and a machete.

"Wrap the corpse in a sheet of canvas," ordered Aaron, "we will give him a decent send off."

The first man, now struggling to sit up was held down by several eager hands, his eyes staring with fright at the people standing around him.

Sam seemed to have taken charge. "He's an Ashanti man Captain.... see his tribal scars. They are great warriors and slavers. They will take anyone for slaves, often raiding the coastal villages, and selling their captives to the Arab slavers. Some they keep as slaves for themselves. They are a very wicked people Captain, their king is very powerful and sits on a golden stool. No-one has ever conquered them." Sam put his ear to the man's chest, "He is very ill Captain, I will see to him." He gently slapped the man's face until he stirred once more, his eyes wide open with fright. Sam spoke to him in his own language and there was another flicker in his eye. He sat with the man throughout the night who by morning was sufficiently awake to start answering questions.

Aaron, after breakfast, came on deck where several of the crew were gathered around the sick man. Sam was speaking to him in his own language, the man blurting out unintelligible sentence then clamping his lips together.

"He is very scared Captain."

"He will have something to be scared about if he doesn't give me a good explanation. I want to know why him and the dead man were nailed up in crates and armed to the teeth. Tell him Sam, if he doesn't answer your questions he will be thrown overboard to the sharks."

At this point two large sharks were circling the ship and two crew members lifted the man up so he could see the two large fins breaking through the mirror like ocean. His eyes bulged out in fright and he pulled away from the two men, stammering something to Sam.

Sam looked at Aaron and translated, "The two Arab slavers Captain.... they have put a price on your head.... a hundred golden guineas. They want you dead or alive. Those two crates were bolted from the inside, and during the night they were supposed to burst out and stab you to death before returning to their crates. The slavers said that your crew would be blamed. They were ordered by their Chief to obey. If they failed they would be tortured to death by bamboo."

"Bamboo Sam?" Aaron stared in disbelief, "How in hell do they do that?"

"Well Captain.... by using a bamboo shoot that's still growing. They are forced to sit on it after the end has been sharpened. Bamboo grows very quickly but not swift enough to let them die fast.... Three or four days, sometimes as long as a week, out in the open and given enough water to keep them alive. It is very wicked Captain. Sometimes if they are married or have a family they are tied sitting up facing them. And if their family tries to comfort them, or kill them to stop their suffering, they die by the same method."

"No wonder the poor sod is terrified.... better he was fed to the sharks. But did they actually think they could have murdered me in my bed?"

Sam shrugged his shoulders, "The Ashanti could walk within a foot of you Captain and you wouldn't know they were there. They didn't realise it would be so hot in the crates Captain, and it seems they were not getting enough fresh air. Then, when we became becalmed, they ran out of water."

There was a slight rustle and the sails flapped noisily. Aaron looked up just as the sails began to fill. Within half an hour they were speeding down the west coast of Africa.

Chapter Twenty-two

The *Golden Falcon* was gaining a reputation as the fastest ship afloat. Anchored beside an East Indian merchant man she looked small and insignificant with the capacity of her holds only a fraction of that of the larger ships. What she lacked in size, however, she certainly made up for in speed. A heavier merchant man setting sail at the same time as the *Golden Falcon* would be soon left well behind.

"Have you any idea what I can do with an Ashanti I have aboard my ship?"

The Cape Town agent looked puzzled. It was an unusual question, "Ashanti? Where in hell did you pick up an Ashanti? I've never seen them *this* far south."

The agent poured out two glasses of the gut rot he had the audacity to call brandy, and indicated a chair across the other side of the desk. Aaron took a seat and carefully related the whole story, interrupted only occasionally by the agent whistling through his teeth at the hair-raising bits.

"So you're the bugger that robbed the two arab slavers. Are you in trouble! There's a large reward on your head, Captain Jacobs, from here to Morocco. They are the most dangerous men in Africa." Aaron sipped reluctantly at the dreadful brandy, as the agent continued, "I bet the whole slaving fraternity are after your guts – they all want to curry favour with those two. Pity really I had a nice cargo

167

for Freetown but if I were you I would give it a very wide berth."

Aaron nodded his head in an off-handed manner, "Get me unloaded and the new cargo aboard. No-one is going to interrupt my trading."

The agent was quickly putting one and two together and coming up with the right answer. It had been rumoured that it was the Arab slavers who knew the source of the legendary blue diamonds. Hadn't Captain Jacobs asked him questions, last trip, on just that subject?

Casually he asked, "By the way Captain, do you still have those stones with you?"

"I think so, they are laying around in my cabin."

"I will come aboard later and take another look."

"Please yourself.... in the meantime secure that cargo for me."

Later that afternoon the agent came aboard and sat in the great cabin. Aaron filled his glass with real brandy, and as the agent sipped it, his face beamed with pleasure.

"Good stuff Captain."

Aaron had been scrambling through the drawers and now stood up clutching the soft leather pouch containing the precious stones. He handed it to the agent who examined the contents, this time more closely.

"I dunno, they look pretty useless." But he knew the rumours were strong about the rare blue diamonds and Aaron *had* been in touch with them, perhaps it was worth a gamble, "Tell you what Captain, I will give you a hundred pounds and chance being robbed."

Although Aaron could no longer be classed as poor the money still sounded a lot. Still, he thought it better and wiser to forestall, "I'll hang on to them for a while longer – after all they cost me nothing. If I do decide to sell them you will have the first refusal."

In two days they were ready for the sea once more. An idea struck Aaron, and he called the carpenter, Willie and Gibbons to his cabin, "The crates we were *supposed* to deliver to Freetown – well, I have decided that we *will* deliver them." To the carpenter he said, "Make me two identical crates, go ashore and get the timber, by the time we reach Freetown I want them completed." He counted out several gold coins.

"That will be easy Captain, they will never know the difference." The men, though, were puzzled to know what Aaron intended to do with the crates. In fact, all Aaron knew was that the two Arab slavers were at war with him and that he could never peacefully sail these waters with such a threat hanging over his head. It was either the Arabs or Aaron. And Aaron felt too young to die.

Nearing Freetown he called a council of war – and Polly was included, "The slavers desperately want me dead. So, we will give them some of their own medicine. When the carpenter makes up those crates, this is what I want doing. Willie will go ashore and let it be known that the Captain was murdered in his bed by one of the crew. Get whoever wishes to open the crates to come aboard the ship – I have a feeling it will be the two Arabs – when they do Gibbons and I will emerge from inside. We will finish them off with their own knives. Ironic isn't it?"

Everyone laughed nervously at this idea, for they all knew that while those two disciples of the devil were still alive they would never be free to trade.

Aaron had taken the wheel as they neared Freetown when Sam came rushing up to him, "Captain! Captain! The Ashanti has dived overboard and is swimming for dear life towards the coast."

He handed the wheel to Willie and walked to the stern of the ship. The Ashanti was by now three to four hundred yards away and striking furiously for the shore. Aaron shook his head, "He may make it if the sharks don't get him. But what will he do? He certainly can't go back to his tribe."

Nearing the port Aaron kept out of sight and gave Willie his final instructions, "You must get the two slavers aboard Willie. Say one of the crew murdered your Captain in his sleep and you now want to trade in slaves. Tell them you have always known it was more lucrative. But first tell the men ashore you have a cargo to unload. Remember It is imperative you get those two devils aboard this ship."

Every crew member fell in with the operation. Willie even

started wearing the Captain's coat, much to the delight of
Polly, "Just because you are wearing his coat, Willie, don't
mean I have to sleep with you ."

Willie and Menzies were a long time ashore and Aaron
was worried. Had those two devils captured them? Aaron
and Gibbons were not allowed on deck, and the heat in the
cabin was stifling. But they could see the ship's long boat
pulled up on the shore.

Suddenly there was movement on the dockside, and Polly
shouted, "They are on their way back Aaron, but they don't
have the slavers with them."

Willie dashed to the cabin. "The slavers are further down
the coast Captain and are due here in about three hours.
A fast runner has been sent to let them know that the ship
has arrived and you have been murdered. I was given an
instruction to send the crates ashore, which meant we
would never get the slavers onto the ship. I'd remembered
how the second slaver had taken a shine to Polly, so I sent
a message that we have decided to sell her if the price is
right."

"Why Willie! I thought you were my friend.... you wouldn't
sell me would you?"

"Don't be silly Polly, when they heard for sure that the
Captain was dead they wouldn't give a damn about the
crates. There is only one thing guaranteed to get them
aboard this ship – and that is the chance of buying you.
Anyway.....he'll make you a lovely husband Polly." Willie
burst out laughing.

"That was a bright idea Willie," said Aaron, turning to
Polly and smiling, "It looks like you have your uses after
all."

"They will be here in the morning Captain, and we ought
have Polly all trussed up. I've set the price at one hundred
guineas and no questions asked."

That evening Polly, Aaron and Willie sat down to a meal
of roast chicken, cold beef and onions washed down with
ale. They tried to play cards but neither of them could concentrate. Apart from Admiral Medlam there was no-one
Aaron had ever really hated – until he met the two Arabs.
Now the two slavers had overtaken the Admiral in his

170

most wanted list. He knew while they remained alive no port in the whole of Africa would be safe for him – their shadows would forever haunt him. The news of Aaron's death had restored the faith that the natives had lost in the two slavers. Once more the Arabs could hold their heads up with pride and as an added bonus they would let it be known that they had purchased the Captain's woman – the one with the golden hair.

They retired to bed but sleep did not come easy. Aaron was tense – waiting for the morning – and the heat did not help. At first light Aaron was out of bed and sitting on the long settee beneath the huge window. He had helped himself to a large glass of undiluted brandy to try and enforce sleep but now it just forced more sweat from his body. He watched the glorious sunshine illuminate the sea and land, turning it into a kaleidoscope of fascinating colour. But of the slavers there was neither sight nor sound. He ate breakfast and changed his sweat sodden clothes for the third time.

When the alarm was given, the excitement conjured muscle movement inside Aaron's stomach – the slavers had just left the beach. Unseen from the shore he made his way to the first crate while Gibbons took up his position in the second, locking himself in from the inside. Polly, sat forlornly at the edge of the ship's hold with her wrists and feet tightly secured, was crying floods of crocodile tears as the two Arab slavers boarded the ship.

"Come on woman, let these nice gentlemen see what they are getting for their hundred guineas."

Willie dragged Polly across the deck and a sinister glint flashed through the eyes of the second slaver as he focused on her body. He licked his lips lecherously as he ran his fingers through her blonde hair, and felt all over her unblemished body. Polly shuddered. He was sizing her up as he would a slave and she tried to back away, but Willie pushed her forward.

"Go on Polly, give the nice gentleman a kiss. Now the Captain is dead we have no need of you. We never wanted you on this ship in the first place."

"A hundred guineas," the slaver hesitated, "she is no virgin." He tried to pull her trousers down for a closer inspection, but she pulled away and lashed out with her two hands tied together. The slaver retaliated by swinging his hand across her face and a trickle of blood ran down the corner of Polly's mouth. Willie clenched and unclenched his hands. Next to Aaron, the girl was his best friend and he hadn't expected to see her treated so badly. He stepped forward and caught the slaver's arm as he drew it back to hit her again.

"Hang on mate, she ain't yours yet."

The slaver threw the leather pouch to Willie's feet. The lad glared at the slaver as he picked it up and began to count it.

"It's all there!" The slaver sneered.

"It had better be. These men don't like being cheated, one of them has already killed their Captain, and none of them would hesitate to kill you."

The taller Arab suddenly gave a sinister laugh and kicked the first crate.

"You stupid fools! It wasn't one of your men that killed your Captain – it was this man!"

With a loud laugh he kicked the side of the crate. The whole front fell away and out rushed Aaron with the diamond studded knife held low in his hand. As it entered the man's stomach it made an upward sweep and the man's intestines became visible. Like a burst balloon, blood gushed from several arteries. The second slaver stood rigidly still, his mouth agape as he watched his brother sink to his knees clutching his abdomen, bright red blood spurting out and staining the deck. Paralysis had set in and the brother was transfixed to the deck staring in disbelief. He looked around, expecting no mercy and sank to the deck on his knees. Willie lashed out with his foot which landed squarely between the man's legs. This was followed by a tremendous kick to the jaw and the man's head snapped back as he pitched forward onto the deck – dead with a broken neck.

Aaron began to shout orders, "Wrap them up and put them out of sight....then strip them and start searching their clothes, make sure they have nothing left of value when we tip them over the side. And let's get unloaded and on our way to Madeira....Scrub the decks straight away.... if the blood soaks in under this heat we will never get the stain out. "

No-one from the shore had witnessed the events unfold aboard the ship. For the first time Sam showed himself on deck – he'd had no desire to be confronted by the slavers. Aaron smiled at him as he stood agape, hardly believing that this could be the forms of the slavers under the blankets, "You can have the pleasure of slinging them overboard tonight Sam."

Sam backed away, his eyes wide with fear. "No, no Captain. I don't want to touch them, they are wicked men."

"They are dead men Sam – they can't touch you."

That night was a moonless night, and no-one felt in the mood for singing. Aaron refused to say a few words over the dead bodies, as the crew prepared them for a sea burial.

"Every man is entitled to a few words and a decent burial Captain." Collins was inclined to be a bit religious, never drinking nor swearing.

"Well you say a few words Collins, if it makes you happy. The only words I wish to say is 'may you spend eternity in hell'." Aaron walked away as the splash of the two bodies indicated their journey to a watery grave.

A fair wind took them to Madeira without further incident. They loaded with fine wines and a couple of days later set sail back to the Canaries. Nearing the harbour, Aaron took himself to his cabin. The agent, who never seemed to sleep, was parading up and down the quay and puffing away at a freshly lit cigar. Every few minutes he stopped and monitored the ship's progress, sighing with relief when they finally dropped anchor. The agent didn't wait for the ship's boat to come ashore but jumped into a smaller craft tied up at the jetty and two sturdy men rowed him out. Willie and Gibbons helped him aboard – none too gently – while Polly did her famous sobbing act on top of the ship's hold. The agent glanced around the ship trying to look casual, and when he saw Polly his face lit up. Casually he asked about the whereabouts of the good Captain, which brought on another sobbing act from Polly.

Trying to sound sympathetic, the Spaniard asked, "How is the Captain?"

Aaron burst out of the cabin. "I'm fine.... you fat, greasy, bastard! Alive and well– no thanks to you." He stopped directly in front of the agent, their faces just inches apart. "How much did those slavers pay you to get those crates on my ship? You surely didn't think for one moment you would get away with it, did you?"

The agent's jaw sagged and the fat cigar fell from his mouth, rolling along the deck and landing in the scuppers.

"I did not know what was in those crates Captain. I was only told to get them to Freetown as soon as possible."

Aaron brought his hand vioently across the agent's face, as he cowered against the ship's rail.

"I tell you Captain I knew nothing about the two black men...." As soon as the words had left his mouth he realised his mistake and turned himself into a tiny ball covering his head with his arms.

Aaron looked at Polly, then at his crew who had gathered to see what was going on, "Who mentioned anything about black men, you lying bastard? Of course you knew what was in those crates. It was you that made all the arrangements, padded those crates and furnished them with straw and provisions. Did you actually think those poor devils could survive out there in that heat? One man died, but the other lived and told us the whole story." Aaron pointed to Sam, "He speaks their language – he told us everything.... now, how much did they pay you?"

The agent saw the determination in Aaron's face, and realised he was quite capable of having him thrown overboard. It was a long way to the shore and he was in no fit state to swim that far. Foam ran from the corners of his mouth.

"Two hundred guineas Captain."

"You are an evil devil like most of the traders in Africa." He held out his hand, "Well you failed to do the job, so I consider that I am entitled to the money."

The fat man hesitated before counting out the money.

"And another hundred for my trouble."

His jaw dropped and he stared blankly, "But Captain, I am a poor man. I have a wife and children. Please Captain...."

"Please Captain...." Aaron mocked him, "You are lucky I am not feeding you to the fishes, you deceitful bastard. We come here regularly and trade with good money and you sell us to the highest bidder. You will pay up, and for every minute I am kept waiting it will be another golden guinea."

The agent in his excitement to get the money out spilt it all over the deck and the crew helped themselves scrambling with the agent on all fours.

"Look at it this way," Aaron put his foot up the agent's backside, "you no longer have to worry about the Arabs. They're both dead, and have most likely joined Captain Reeves and his witch of a wife in hell."

"Dead Captain?" He had been shocked to see Aaron alive and kicking after he came on deck, but now he was reduced to a blubbering mess, "They can't be....they owe me ...." He cut himself short.

Aaron let out a throaty laugh, "Well it's for sure you won't be getting any money from them now – and if I thought for one minute that it was you who supplied them and other slavers with fair skinned girls, you would be joining them in hell. Sooner than you think."

The man crossed himself several times and shook his head violently, "Not me Captain, I do not trade in fair skinned girls – I don't trade in slaves at all."

He quickly jumped down into the small boat, and as it slewed away from the side of the ship, he did a stationary dance with flaying arms, lost his balance completely and plunged into the sea. The ship's crew lined the rails laughing and jeering as the fat greasy agent huffed and puffed in an effort to scramble back aboard his dinghy.

Chapter Twenty-three

After an uneventful voyage they dropped anchor in Table Bay, Aaron congratulating himself on a safe and record-breaking passage. The Harbour Master, the same short Boer they saw on their first voyage came aboard and studied the manifest. Polly saw him crossing the harbour in his small boat being pulled by two strapping negroes, and immediately went to her cabin and changed into her most revealing clothing – the skin-tight red trousers and loose blouse, revealing every sinew and muscle in her body. Her blouse plunged at the neckline leaving nothing to the imagination.

As the Boer stepped over the ship's rail Polly rolled past with an exaggerated sway, her buttocks and breasts swinging in unison, and winking at him as he caught her eye. He stared at her, words failing him; his jaws clamping up and down without a sound.

Stamping his foot, he approached Aaron, "Do you allow that hussy to roam around your ship like that, hardly dressed?"

A humorous glint came into Aaron's eye. "No, sometimes she wears nothing at all – it depends on how the mood takes her."

The man turned his attention back to Polly who was leaning over the ship's rails with her bottom well stuck out.

"My God," he spluttered, "you hussy! Don't you dare come ashore dressed like that or you will be thrown into jail."

Polly reverted to her Portsea tavern language, "Shut up

176

you silly old bugger.... I don't want to visit your damn hypocritical town."

Red with rage, his hand shaking like a leaf in a storm, he
handed Aaron his manifesto, "Get unloaded as fast as possible Captain and out of this port. And take that damn
wench with you – this is a respectable town." He flounced
off the ship with all the crew laughing at him.

The agent was waiting for him in exactly the same position he left him a few months previously. He didn't bother
to turn round when Aaron knocked – he had watched the
ship approach.

"You made very good time Captain, it is certainly is a very
fine vessel you own. It also seems you have made a couple
of very bad enemies. You have upset two of the most dangerous men in Africa. The two Arab slavers I am talking
about. Disreputable brothers, they have influence from
Morocco to the Cape and no doubt back up again from the
Cape to Cairo. The word has gone around that you robbed
them and set their slaves free.... now they have placed a
reward on your head – a reward that would make some
white men skin their own mothers. Just imagine what a
black man would do for that kind of money. My advice to
you Captain, while you are on the African coast, is to stay
aboard and even then don't allow anyone on your ship."

The agent swung round to face Aaron and gave a benign
and sympathetic smile, "Very dangerous men Captain. I
advise you not to put into any port on the West coast. Me, I
would sooner take my chances with a couple of mating
black mambas – extremely poisonous snakes – in my bed."

"There is no need for either of us to worry about those two
evil bastards. They are both dead, very dead indeed. I was
born a smuggler like my father before me, and his father
before him. We traded along the French coast smuggling
brandy and wine, and have spent my life dodging the
Revenue men. I've learnt the art of self preservation from
the age of sixteen when I took over from my father, so I
learnt from a very early age to look after myself."

The agent seemed to be absorbed in Aaron's first sentence,
and stared at him open mouthed with a glass of the deadly
brandy half way to his lips.

Almost inaudibly he gasped, "Dead? You mean...." He pointed hesitatingly towards Aaron, "....you mean to say you killed them?"

Aaron nodded, a sickly grin on his face accentuating the vivid scar on his upper lip, "Yes they are both dead."

Aaron went on to relate the story from the time he took on the two crates in the Canaries. When he'd finished the agent replenished the two glasses and proposed a toast.

"Well Captain, you are a brave and lucky man. Enemies did I say.... well there are also plenty of men who will shake you warmly by the hand. A lot of people will be glad to see them dead."

They drank steadily for the next half hour making idle chit-chat. The brandy was strong and unpalatable but Aaron was starting to get used to it.

"Down to business Captain. Do you fancy a trip to the new penal colony in Australia?" He waited for a few moments to let the question sink in, "I have two men very anxious to get there. They have two convict servants with them and a dozen sheep – a new strain they are trying out, and want to breed out there."

Aaron laughed, sipped his brandy and shaking his head answered, "I do not carry passengers. I am a cargo ship, not a very big one at that, and I certainly have neither the room nor the facilities to carry sheep."

"Captain.... you could be on a very good thing here, it seems this man is not short of cash – in fact the 'sky is the limit'. I've been giving it some thought since they approached me and I guessed you would be here soon. A conversion could easily be managed. One hold into two separate cabins and cooking facilities and the other hold could take the sheep together with the food they require. The two servants could sleep on the sheep's bedding and they will carry their own water. They will pay for all the work required and when you arrive in the colony they will see that you get your ship back in its original state. They are very eager to get away and when I mentioned your ship and how fast it was they seemed very enthusiastic."

Aaron looked doubtful and slowly shook his head, "I don't know.... passengers, sheep, convicts. It's something I have never considered. Let me think it over."

"The two gents are staying at the local hotel. Let's make arrangements for a meeting in this office at ten thirty tomorrow, it may lead to a new opening with an expanding route for you. I tell you Captain, Australia will be a great country one day, those that get in first will be the winners. I understand they are already sending wool back to the old country. If I were twenty years younger that is where I would be heading for – a new country, a new start. Believe me the Boers will totally take over this country."

That night around the dinner table Aaron discussed it with Polly and Willie.

"How long will it take?" Polly asked.

"A couple of months or so, depending upon the weather, if we hit no snags."

Aaron turned to Willie, "What do you think Willie?"

Willie shrugged his shoulders, "You're the Captain. It's all the same to me, this ship is my home so I go where the ship goes."

The two men were waiting at the office when Aaron returned the next day, sipping the customary white man's drink – gin, having politely declined the awful gut rot the agent drank. They stood, as the agent introduced them, weighing Aaron up. Aaron returned the compliment. The man who appeared to be in charge was extra tall, some six feet six inches but rather thin, with a long face that sported a droopy moustache, had a straight aquiline nose, and deep brown eyes that seemed to penetrate Aaron's brain. His clothing was immaculate and a diamond pin held a cravat in place, dressed like that he would have gone unnoticed walking down the Strand in London. The other man was dressed just as well, not so tall but quite thick set, a full set of whiskers neatly trimmed and from his stature it was easy to guess he had been a military man. He held a thick malacca cane topped with a silver ball, and when he sat down, placed the cane on the floor and gripped the silver knob resting it between his knees. Pleasantries were exchanged.

"Well gentleman I must tell you that first and foremost I

am a cargo ship not equipped to take passengers or live
stock. There is no way I can give you my crew's quarters."

"That is alright Captain, we are aware of your ship. The
agent here has told me that it can be converted," he hurriedly added, "at our expense of course. It is imperative
that we get back to the colony as fast as possible. One of
our two convicts is extremely handy with tools and an
expert carpenter.... no doubt you have your own carpenter
aboard so converting one of the holds into two cabins
should not be too difficult. With our own cooking facilities,
we will be entirely independent of your crew. The other
hold can be converted to take the sheep and they will be
looked after by the convicts, who will also sleep and live in
that hold. We will take on our own water which we can
replenish when we reach Ceylon."

"We must get those sheep to Australia as fast as possible.
They are an extraordinary breed of sheep – but I won't
bore you with the details."

"Well gentlemen," answered Aaron, "so long as I am not
involved in any expense for these conversions. I am not
only the Captain, I also own this vessel. Our present cargo
will be unloaded by noon tomorrow, when you can inspect
the ship for yourself. But I must warn you now, it will not
be a very comfortable voyage."

"It is not comfort we are looking for Captain, it's speed
and the sooner we start the better."

One thing that could be said for the two intended passengers – they were very punctual. The sun was dead above
their heads when they arrived at the *Golden Falcon* next
day.

Aaron consulted his time-piece and welcomed them
aboard, "Dead on noon gentlemen, you certainly don't
waste time."

The taller of the men answered with a nod of his head and
began inspecting the ship from fore to aft. The shorter
man turned to Aaron, "A fine craft Captain, is she really as
fast as they say?"

"Yes sir, she is the fastest ship afloat." There was pride
etched on Aaron's face as he answered.

"Well, I am satisfied." The taller man spoke for the first time since arriving at the ship, "The Major here will supervise the conversion, my two convict servants will arrive first thing in the morning. At the moment one of them is locked up in the local jail. The other convict is tending the sheep. They will be kept chained while they are aboard Captain." A smile flickered across his face, "You will have no trouble with them, they are both harmless."

The slight smile on his face quickly vanished when Aaron answered sharply, "On my ship nobody will be chained. This is not a convict ship, it is a happy ship and it will stay that way. If they are harmless, I see no reason to keep them in chains. And one more thing gentlemen – we do not use the rope's end nor the cat, on this ship."

"But discipline Captain.... How do you maintain order? You can not run a ship without discipline. My convicts *must* be kept chained. One has already attempted escape, which is why he is being kept in the local jail."

"If you treat men like animals you must expect them to behave like animals. My men know how far they can go. Any misdemeanour and they are put down at the first sight of land, inhabited or not. I have had only one case of indiscipline. Fortunately for him we were docked in London at the time. But he knew the rules, and I wouldn't give a damn where it was, he would have been put ashore. I have been running this ship for some time with several trips to West and South Africa and I have never lost a man through accident or fever. I intend to keep it that way. When, and if, your two convicts board this ship you will make sure that there are no shackles or ropes on them. If that does not suit you, then you must go and find yourself another ship. I do hope, Mr. Mackie, that I have made myself quite plain."

Mackie didn't take too kindly to Aaron's attitude. Like his partner, the Major, most people appeared to cow down to him. It seemed that he had a lot of influence, both in Australia and back home in England, and came from a very influential family. In the event, he held his tongue. Aaron docking in Cape Town had been extremely fortuitous, being both Captain and owner he was able to make instant decisions, and Mackie had already spent far too long in this God forsaken country where the ignorant Boers seemed to have power even over the British.

Later that day the first convict arrived with the Major.

"This *convict* is Davies, Captain." It wasn't an introduction, and appeared only to serve in distinguishing the man from the other convict, "Brownlow will arrive just before we sail. Mr Mackie did not like the idea of him coming aboard while we are in the harbour."

With a shrug of his shoulders Aaron answered, "Please yourselves Major. I don't give a damn what he does so long as he wears no leg irons. Leave them either at the jail or on the quayside." He turned to the convict and pointed to the holds, "Alright Mr Davies, get on with your work, you will find the timber aboard and all the tools you need."

For a few seconds the convict seemed hardly able to move. This was the first time for many years that anyone had addressed him as 'Mister' or spoke civilly to him.

For the next week the crew took on the role of shipbuilders with the sawing and hammering reverberating throughout the ship. Black men, temporarily brought aboard as helpers, singing all the time in rhythm to the blows of the hammers. The first hold was soon completed, and resembled part of a passenger ship. Two cabins complete with a wardrobe, a small built in dressing table and wooden bed. In the far corner was a brick built kitchen. It was not only Brownlow's job to tend the sheep but also to do the cooking for the two gentlemen and Davies; but his first concern was the sheep. Davies also tended the sheep and waited on the two men.

Two cane tables were brought aboard, a cane chair, and a small chair, as well as expensive bedding. It was the first time the crew had seen Mr Mackie since he first inspected the ship. He supervised the loading of his precious sheep, whom he considered more valuable than the two convicts. Several tons of fodder and barrels of water; a couple of crates of chickens and food for the passengers; together with several cases of wine, were brought aboard. As the wine was loaded Mr Mackie counted every bottle, taking out first a bottle of white wine and holding it up to the strong sunlight, before nodding his satisfaction and replacing it in the crate. He leaned over the ship's rail and shouted below to two native policemen with a white policeman in charge, "Alright get those irons off that man and bring him aboard."

Brownlow heaved himself over the ship's rails, his legs bearing the red marks where the leg irons had held him. The crew were staring at this poor wretch as he clambered over.

"He don't look very dangerous to me Aaron." The man was stood on the deck his head bowed, Polly smiling at him.

"Right Brownlow, you are aboard now but let me warn you, make any attempt to jump overboard while we are here and I will blow your bloody brains out." Mackie patted the pistol tucked into his belt. Aaron was to learn later they were a matching pair of dual pistols and that Mr Mackie was a champion marksman.

Brownlow's eyes were riveted on the deck, his hands dangling by his sides. "I won't try that Mr Mackie."

Patting the pistol again and a glint in his eyesMackie warned, "I will make sure of that Brownlow. You are in enough trouble already for doing a runner while we were here – so don't go making it worse for yourself."

"I don't like that man Aaron," stated Polly, in a voice which must have been overheard by the two men, "make sure you don't invite him to dinner too many times." She was in one of her rare tempers.

"I doubt if he would accept," whispered Aaron in reply, "his sort never do. They've brought enough food to feed a regiment and enough furniture to fill a decent sized house. They will keep to themselves. The Major doesn't seem too bad, but he seems to 'kow tow' to everything Mr. Mackie says and does."

It was late afternoon when the hustle and bustle of the ship preparing to depart died down, the ship finally departing on a favourable tide and the crew back into the day to day routine of running a ship.

Chapter Twenty-four

It promised to be a long and laborious voyage and starting at the end of the first week the ship ran into a violent and tropical storm.

"Batten down those hatches Willie. Tell Mr Mackie and the Major they can come and share with the crew or they must remain down in the hold. Whatever they choose they must make it quick." And as if nature was sending a priority warning a great wave washed the ship from stem to stern. A few minutes later Aaron watched Willie and two crew members batten down the hatches and wasn't surprised to hear that both passengers had chosen an honourable death rather than share the humble crew's quarters, "Bugger them Willie, if that's where they want to stay."

The wind reached such ferocity that Aaron thought they would never make it, although in spite of this a smile spread across his face when he saw Polly dash across the open deck towards the main cabin. He handed the wheel to Willie and followed her. She was stretched out on the bed groaning, and he secured her tightly with another blanket wrapping it around and tying her in.

The sea was in torment with waves crashing against the hull in every direction and giant swells crashing over the ship's decks. The crew stood by, occasionally losing their footing and grabbing blindly to the ship's rails and rigging. Every man knew his duty in these circumstances and no orders were shouted, it was a frantic struggle to keep the

ship on an even keel. Night fell, with the men still standing at their stations, the moonless night making the grey
sea and foam even darker. It continued for three days and
nights without let up, no hot food and only hard tack to
nibble at, the men's stomachs groaned with hunger and
they tightened their belts. Slowly the sea receded – only to
be followed by a belting, heavy rain. Some of the sturdier
men took advantage of the heavy rain and stripped to their
waists allowing the stinging rain to batter their bare
chests and backs, it was heavy warm rain. With the coming of dawn nothing had changed, the ship bucked up and
down as it chased down one steep valley after another, rising and curtseying, the masts circling in figures of eight.
Polly staggered from the ship's cabin and rushed to the
ship's rail hanging her head over the side and vomiting
violently.

"Are you alright Polly?" Aaron asked, trying his best to
suppress a smile. "The worse is over now Polly, by midday
the sea will have calmed down."

By noon it was sufficiently calm to issue a hot meal to the
crew. For almost three days Aaron had hardly moved from
the wheel, "Better see how our two intrepid passengers
are, Willie."

Cautiously and reluctantly Willie and a crew member lifted the cover from the hold. Life had been relatively easy
for the two convicts; although both had been violently sea-
sick for a few days, at least they hadn't been waiting hand
and foot on their two masters, at their every beck and call.

Within a couple of hours on going on deck Mackie and the
Major visited the second hold to see how the sheep had
fared, never bothering to ask how the convicts had taken
the battering. Mackie inspected the sheep carefully, "This
one doesn't look too good Davies, is she going to be
alright?"

"I should think so sir, I suppose they must be as prone to
seasickness as any human being." He would have liked to
have said, 'They took it better than you, you rotten bastard,' but that would have meant more trouble when they
reached Australia.

"Don't think about it man, either she is going to make it or

he isn't, though for your sakes, both of you, she'd better."
He threw a glance, his cold steel eyes boring into the convict Brownlow, "Pull yourself together man, you look
dreadful. Get on to deck and get some fresh air into you –
come on get up and get out of it."

Brownlow, who was far worse than anyone and still suffering from seasickness rose unsteadily to his feet and
staggered over to the wooden ladder that would have
taken him to the deck.

"And take these two cane chairs with you I want them on
deck, then you can bring my drinks."

Brownlow could hardly pull himself up the ladder and
catching hold of the chair, he dragged it along by its back
legs.

"Watch it man – handle it more carefully." Davies ran forward to help Brownlow, "Damn you Davies! Look after
that sheep."

He pushed Davies back violently, but fortunately he fell
against the fodder, hatred filling his eyes as he stared at
Mackie's back.

"You look after that sheep! If anything happens to it I will
hold you entirely responsible – don't you know its value?"

That apparently, summed up his colonial outlook on life.
Sheep were more valuable than convicts – the latter could
be replaced for free but sheep cost money.

"I can't be responsible for the weather Mr Mackie, that's
in the good Lord's hands."

"Don't you dare answer me back you swine." He lifted his
arm and swished it across Davies' face. As a trickle of
blood ran from the corner of his mouth and down his chin,
Davies wiped it away slowly, with the back of his hand.

"I'm sorry Mr Mackie," which, of course, was just what
Mackie wanted – the convict pleading with him.

Mackie and the Major strutted up and down the deck with
their hands behind their backs while Brownlow struggled
with the two lounge bamboo chairs. Willie saw the man
and as he ran to his assistance, Mackie intercepted him,
"Don't bother with that convict, he needs no help, he is just
shamming. He is well over his seasickness by now."

But Willie only had one master aboard this ship and let

fly at Mackie, "You miserable bastard.... when you were almost unconscious down there, you looked half dead.... can't you see this man is sick?"

"It is of no concern to me. He is here to do a job and by God he will do it or I will want to know why."

"Well you *do* know why don't you, you stupid bastard."

He went to lift his hand to Willie, who sneered at him. "Just try it Mackie, and I will have you over the side of the ship in a moment, and if I can't do it there are plenty of men standing around who will gladly assist me."

"Don't you dare speak to me like that you dockside trash. God, if you were one of my convicts I would have your back stripped bare for speaking to me in that fashion. I know your Captain will not allow me to use a rope's end or cat but believe me when these two men step ashore and are safely back at my farm they will pay for all this insubordination."

Willie looked at Brownlow whose eyes pleaded with him not to provoke Mackie any more, he knew he would suffer once they landed. It wasn't over yet, Davies struggled on deck with the heavy weight of the sheep, now a dead carcass. He carried it on deck and laid it before Mr Mackie, whose evil temper knew no bounds. Looking at the body of the sheep, he almost foamed at the mouth.

"Why you incompetent swine, you have let the beast die!" He kicked out at Davies, the toe of his boot landing between the man's legs. The convict bent over double with pain, and as Mackie brought his clenched fist down hard on the back of his head, the man fell forward before rolling over on his back groaning in pain. Mackie was about to lift his foot again when Aaron, who had been watching the incident from the steering wheel ran forward and tripped Mackie's foot.

"Don't you dare use violence on this ship. That man was not responsible for the death of your sheep. It just couldn't take the violent sea. We should make the best of it man." He turned to the crew, "Fancy a bit of lamb for dinner lads?"

The new man Peters stepped forward, "I can butcher it Captain."

"Right that's settled it then. Lamb for dinner lads!"

"I paid good money for that sheep, Captain."

"Well, it's dead meat now – worth I should think about two sovereigns." He took two coins from his pocket and handed them to Mackie.

In the tropical warmth the meat would not last any more than two days. So the crew made the best of it.

After the terrible storm the sea calmed down, steam rising from the decks and rigging covering the ship like a white shroud. The crew's clothing and bedding festooned the decks and ship's rails. Brownlow was sent below to clear out his two masters' cabins, Mackie deciding that while the sea and weather were favourable he and the Major would sleep on deck.

Brownlow was sat on the rail at the stern of the ship, as far away from Mackie as circumstances would allow. Aaron was pacing the deck and saw the forlorn figure sitting there and staring into space. As he approached Brownlow started to rise and Aaron waved him down, "Don't bother Brownlow." It was one of the few moments the man had to himself from the day he'd boarded the ship, as he'd been at the two men's beck and call day and night. Gibbons was in earshot, and Aaron called him over, "Get me a bottle of wine and two glasses from my cabin – Polly will be there."

On Gibbons' return Aaron poured out two glasses and handed one to Brownlow, his look of instant surprise turning to curiosity when Aaron sat on the ship's rail beside him.

"How did you get into this situation Brownlow?"

The man just shrugged his shoulders with indifference. It took two more glasses of the rich red Madeira wine to loosen his tongue.

"What brings a lot of the people out here Captain – minor crimes, pick-pocketing, poaching, you name it. Me, it was different. Back home I was a shepherd and worked for one of Mackie's relations – an uncle of his was the local magistrate. They'd heard of all the land out in Australia up for grabs and were almost first in the queue. I don't know

188

why.... they own great tracts of land on the south coast of England and on the Scottish borders. Well Mackie was sent out to size up the situation, and seeing it looked good and its potential was soon granted thousands of acres of land by Governor Phillips and as much free labour as he wanted. That, of course, wasn't enough for him – he wanted an experienced shepherd. I don't boast when I tell you there isn't a thing about sheep I don't know.... rearing them.... breeding them..... whatever. At first they wanted me to come out voluntarily and did everything to try and coax me. But I wouldn't come, it was very stupid of me.... I knew by fair means or foul they would eventually get me. First they accused me of stealing their sheep, which was ridiculous Captain, I was quite happy and contented – I had my wife, my two kids, and a little cottage, money was of no great interest to me. Then one night they came and dragged me out of bed and the next morning I was brought up before the magistrate. I don't think I need tell you who the magistrate was – it had all been arranged... in minutes I was sentenced to seven years transportation and imprisoned in the hulks of Portsmouth Harbour. But not for long, soon I was given top priority and was in the first transport to leave for the colonies. Guess who was waiting for me when we landed – yes, Mr Mackie. Before the remainder had disembarked, I was already on my way to his farm twenty miles out from the town."

Brownlow, having been carried away with his story, paused to look around and see if Mackie had left his chair, "It had all been a set up, I found out that one of the farm hands back home had sworn that I had sold him the sheep. Then, when I had been out here for nearly six years and was looking forward to soon going home, Mackie held a dinner party at his home and one of the guests suggested he should get a better strain for his sheep. Quite honestly Captain, they *were* a pathetic lot – what Mackie knows about sheep wouldn't buy me a shirt button. Anyhow.... he immediately sends one of his house-convicts to fetch me from the sheds. I was brought over and stood before the dinner party – dirty and shackled in chains. About a dozen women were sat around the table eating an enormous meal and drinking wine, and there was I looking like a specimen from the cesspits, my stomach sick with hunger. One of them asked my opinion on the possibility of finding a good strain for him in South Africa – I believed we could.

When we arrived at the Cape I managed to find a good strain for him and the Boer that sold them said I knew my job and would I go and work for him. I would be a free man – but I soon realised it was a put up job.

"Mackie knew I had only just over one year to go, but the offer was very tempting especially when the Boer said I would be able to send for my wife and children. He hid me for three days... but of course – inevitably – the soldiers came for me. They knew exactly where to find me, hiding in the Boer's barn. God! What a put up plot.... as I left the Boer's Farm he just stood looking at me and laughing. When we arrive at the colony I will be up before the magistrates, and will get a flogging and another seven years. Maybe even ten. I could even be hanged for trying to escape – but I'm far too valuable to Mackie."

The man was without hope and Aaron rightly thought he may even throw himself over the side. The convict was only prevented from doing so by the sight of the sharks' fins slicing through the clear water.

Aaron stood up and patted Brownlow on the shoulder, "Never mind mate, something may turn up.... who knows? Mackie may slip....fall overboard."

"Don't tempt me Captain. Believe me, if I wasn't a God fearing man I would have gladly given him a good push, but who knows, maybe perhaps, someone will do it for me. I'm afraid I could not take a man's life."

Aaron dropped the unfinished bottle of wine into Brownlow's lap, "At least you had the pleasure of seeing him laid low by that violent storm, bedridden with seasickness."

For the first time Brownlow's face smiled, "Alas Captain, so was I.... so was I." He shook his head sorrowfully.

"Land dead ahead!" The shout from the masthead brought the ship to life. The crew off duty sprang for the shrouds and any vantage point above the deck. Aaron took out his powerful telescope and trained it on the smudge of land on the far horizon as Mackie got up from his seat and looked towards landward without much interest.

"Let me know when we can see it better."

In fact it was four more hours before they could distinguish anything – and only then a few palm trees waving indifferently in the light wind. Two more hours and they dropped anchor just outside Colombo.

Aaron had been warned about the violence in Ceylon and took two of his heaviest and tallest crew with him when he left the ship. A large group of children soon began to follow them, all begging for pennies.

The town was smelling of rotting garbage and unwashed bodies. The sweat began to run down Aaron's face, chest and back, his clothes sticking to him. His mouth felt dry, and, with some relief he eventually arrived at a large important-looking brick building. Stepping inside, the coolness after the heat took his breath away – he felt he were standing in a cold bath of water – as the sweat on his clothing turned ice cold.

The stone flagged floor, the whitewashed walls and the overhead fans gave the building a comfortable coolness. He smiled at an Indian sitting in the corner of the room, a long piece of cord attached to his big toe, pushing a fan to and fro on the ceiling of the building, looking as if he were fast asleep. A small Indian, in western dress, approached Aaron bowing and scraping – he noticed that Aaron looked hypnotised at the man pulling the fan, "Punka Wallahs Sahib." He rubbed his hands together and asked in a refined voice, "May I be of assistance to you Sahib?"

"Yes, we have just dropped anchor outside the harbour and need fresh fruit, vegetables, and plenty of fresh water. We are in transit to Australia – carrying a valuable cargo of sheep so make sure there is plenty of water."

The native led them through a labyrinth of dark but cool corridors, stopped at a door and knocked, someone answering from inside, "Enter!"

The native opened the door for him and he stepped inside. The room like the rest of the building was cool and airy as another Punka Wallah was sitting in the corner with the light cord tied around his big toe. A man, sitting at his desk with his back to them stood up and turned around. He was a contradiction – with a face as brown as a berry and as wrinkled as a prune he could easily have been mistaken for a native but as soon as he opened his mouth it was obvious that he was from the remotest part of the Scottish Highlands.

Aaron handed him the list, "I need these stores."

The Scotsman studied the list, "No problem.... Captain." He looked up at a large fly pitted clock, the face of which was the same colour and texture of the Scotsman's skin. "At seven in the morning Captain, for I am in no doubt you are in a hurry to get away from this God forsaken hole."

He took a half-bottle of Scotch Whisky from a drawer in his desk and wiped the inside of two glasses with his fingers before filling them, "I usually wait 'til sundown Captain.... but this is a special case."

'And no doubt,' Aaron thought, 'any case was a special case – and a good excuse for a daytime drink.'

"You are not alone are you Captain?"

Aaron shook his head. "No...I was aware of the reputation of this place and brought two of the biggest members of my crew – they can deal with most situations."

"Quite right Captain. The children that roam these streets begging.... for heaven's sake don't give any of them a penny ....you will be mobbed to death or even start a civil war. My advice to anyone fresh to this town is – 'Do your business and get back to your ship'."

The Scot slipped the list of stores into his pocket, "Leave it to me. I will see you get everything." They shook hands, "Good luck Captain – watch your back 'til you get aboard."

The streets became more crowded as the day wore on – every dark face carried what Aaron thought was a sinister look – as they made their way back to the ship. Captain .Jacobs couldn't take his eyes away from the pathetic creatures that roamed the streets. Women with tiny children strapped to their backs; crippled beggars holding out scrawny hands, looking as if they'd eaten nothing for days; swollen tummies and bulging eyes. Yellow robed men walking in lines and holding out begging bowls, snake charmers and street hawkers, everything added to the deafening sounds. The smell had increased with the heat and it became unbearable, the sun now directly overhead. Aaron stepped up his pace pushing his way through the crowded street.

It was Gibbons who first spotted a man edging his way in front of them and creeping from doorway to doorway, occasionally nodding signals to another man across the street, both men dirtier and scruffier than most. When they reached the next corner the men made their move, each slipping a razor sharp and slightly curved knife from their belts. Gibbons closed in on Aaron, crying a warning as the man lunged forward his knife raised above his head and about to strike, and smashed downwards on the native's hand. The man immediately dropped the knife, a look of surprise on his face as Gibbons followed with a hefty kick to his crutch. Sinking to his knees his face distorted with pain, he quickly received follow-up kick to the jaw, and landed on his back spread-eagled on the hot pavement. Gibbons – fourteen stone – jumped and landed on the man's arm, the breaking of which could be heard above the din of the street. It was all over in less than thirty seconds. The other native witnessing the fate of his companion took quickly to his heels.

"Leave him lads.... he's not worth it." said Aaron breathless with excitement. The ship's long boat was still tied up to the quay steps and Aaron jumped in quickly followed by the other two crew members, Gibbons stopping momentarily to look around. They rowed like demented men, all pleased to see the back of the city, the oars spreading the filth floating on the water.

"That was too damned close for comfort Gibbons." Aaron said laughing and wiping the sweat from his forehead. In twenty minutes they were safely aboard their own ship and Aaron related his experiences to Polly.

She shuddered, "Don't you go ashore again Aaron."

In turn Gibbons related his story to the rest of the crew and anyone that had been interested in going ashore soon abandoned the idea.

Chapter Twenty-five

Pleased to see the back of the filth ridden city the crew, after loading supplies, worked with a will to get away from the harbour but it seemed as if nature itself was against them. The ship fell straight into a dead calm with just the slightest offshore wind and after twenty four hours the harbour they had left could still be seen. What little wind there was drifted them slowly along, hugging the shoreline. Hearing Aaron's experiences had dispersed any ideas Mackie and the Major had for going ashore and they were content to wait until they reached their next and final destination. The crew too seemed in a happy mood, the sea rising and falling in smooth swells. As the sun strengthened, the mist from the shore shrouded the ship in a blanket of silence. It was mid morning before the mist cleared, the shores on both sides plainly visible, as they sailed between the main island of Ceylon and one of the islands that dotted the area.

"A sail to starboard Cap'n!" The shout came from the mast head.

Aaron studied the small native craft through his glass, "Looks as if he is in trouble, the sails are flapping and the man at the tiller looks as if he is either dead or unconscious." Aaron turned his ship towards the craft.

"I should take it easy if I were you Captain, the crew may have gone down with some kind of fever." The Major was speaking a lot of sense, he had been stationed in India for some while and was well aware of the unexplained fevers

that riddled the continent of India and Ceylon, "Yes,
Captain, and they may be pirates trying to lure you within
boarding distance – this coast is notorious for pirates.
They sham all kinds of tricks to get near you and before
you realise what is happening they are swarming all over
the ship."

"Still.... if a ship is in distress we must go and see. We will
take all necessary precautions." He ordered the small
brass cannon to be primed and loaded with scatter shot
and as many men as possible armed – those without guns
were handed cutlasses including the two convicts. Mackie
protested but Aaron said, "It was the Major's suggestion
we take precautions and they won't get very far with all
these armed men around, don't be so worried." Mackie
and the Major armed themselves with duelling pistols,
sports guns and a cutlass, it was as if the major was wishing for a fight.

The gaps between the two ships narrowed, everyone stood
by breathing slowly. Gibbons, always itching for a good
fight preferred a cutlass, his sweaty hand gripping it tightly, his throat was dry and he could feel his pulse throbbing
in his temples. "Bring the black bastards closer." His cutlass moved up and down.

Suddenly the air was rented with blood curdling screams
as dozens of grappling irons came flying through the air.

"What did I tell you Captain, the damn rascals are
pirates." The Major was the first to move. With his cutlass
raised he went along the rail slashing the grappling ropes,
but as fast as he slashed them more rained down on the
ship and the first native came swinging aboard. Followed
by several more brown skinned men as agile as monkeys.
The first native fell back blinded as the Major slashed
across his face, and dropped into the sea screaming. The
brass cannon exploded sending several natives flying from
their ropes, but there seemed to be no end of attackers
renting the air with terrifying screams. As Aaron wondered where they had all been hiding in such a small craft
two natives rushed towards the Captain's cabin and
stopped dead as they were confronted by Polly standing in
the doorway, a pistol in one hand and a cutlass in the

other. The gun exploded and a native fell to the deck blood pumping from a great chest wound, and as the other man hesitated she lunged at him with the cutlass, penetrating his bowls – a woman was the last thing they expected to see facing them and the hesitation had cost them their lives. Aaron lashed out at a native as he tried to scramble aboard and severed his head with one mighty sweep. Davies, the convict, had charged another native with his cutlass and a curved sword crashed to the deck. But still they came on, one running along the ship's rail like an experienced tight rope walker, sword in his hand. Brownlow rushed up as the pirate held the sword high above his head ready to crash down on Mr Mackie, and took a glancing blow on his shoulder which sliced the muscle on his lower arm as if a butcher had cut a steak. Brownlow recovered and thrust with his cutlass, the native recoiling and falling into the red stained sea.

Still they came on, Mackie picking up a wine bottle from his table and smashing it against the ship sending the sharp pieces of glass flying along the deck scattering in all directions, followed by two more bottles. The natives came to a halt – where guns and cutlasses had failed, broken bottles succeeded. Most of the natives stopped dead in their tracks, those that failed to screamed as blood began to ooze from their feet staining the decks red. Polly, seeing the devastation the broken glass had caused dashed into the cabin and gathered all the bottles she could find, proceeding to smash them across the deck, which took on the scene of a slaughter house with the natives hopping around like demented dervishes, and swinging back to their ship cursing and swearing. The brass cannon fired a parting shot into the mass of retreating natives.

Ten pirates were left dead and two badly wounded. Without ceremony all twelve were heaved overboard, the two wounded screaming for mercy. One crew member had been very seriously wounded and Brownlow, the convict, had a great lump of flesh sliced from his lower arm. While the remainder of the crew prepared to set sail, Polly attended to the two wounded men. The broken glass was swept up and thrown overboard and the decks scrubbed down in a vain attempt to remove the spreading patches of red stain.

"I would say Mr Brownlow saved your life Mr Mackie. Great presence of mind *and* bravery don't you think?" Asked Aaron, studying the colonialist for any signs of gratitude or compassion, "So I suppose it will make a difference to the charge hanging over his head," continued Aaron insistently, " attempting to escape I mean – I suppose you could forget that, at least. As a kind of reward.... don't you think?"

"It will all be taken into consideration at his trial Captain. Attempting to escape is a very serious business and can carry a death sentence. I suppose I can assure you it will never go that far.... Brownlow will probably get off with a few years added to his sentence. It still must serve as a lesson to the other prisoners – let one off too lightly and the others start taking liberties."

"But the man saved your *life* Mackie. If it hadn't been for his swift action we would be wrapping you up in an old sheet and pitching you overboard. Good God man, have you no heart?"

Mackie sat down, picked up his book, and continued to read trying to ignore Aaron and his pleading, "As I have said sir – it will be taken into consideration at his trial."

Aaron felt his temperature rising. There could be no compromise with this man, Brownlows, as a human being, meant nothing to him. In a way it was a pity the convict stopped the native. The only consolation was Aaron's insistence that Brownlow be kept from waiting on Mackie hand and foot – this despite protestations that he was well able to return to his duties.

"The man is *not* fit to work, Mackie. I am the Captain of this ship and will decide when a man is able and when he is not."

They headed directly out to sea, putting Ceylon and the islands as far behind them as possible. Aaron swung his telescope around to check there was no sign of any craft, taking a last lingering look at Ceylon and hoping he would never see it again.

"I will be in my cabin, Willie." He handed the ship's wheel

over to him, "If anything untoward happens let me know." The remainder of the voyage was uneventful and they settled down to the usual ship's routine.

It was a great relief one morning, at first light, that a shout was heard from the mast head – "Land, dead ahead, Captain!" Aaron jumped into the rigging and looked towards where the man had pointed. The land was closer than expected and by late afternoon they were passing through the heads saluting the man on one of the points and entering one of the most magnificent harbours in the world. The sea, mirror-like, was reflecting the few powder puff clouds scurrying across the azure blue sky. Slight waves lapped against a silver white sand and green trees and bush bordered the shore, while flimsy native canoes were drawn up on the sand. Black children, devoid of clothing, unashamedly played in the shallow waters. Several native men, some holding long slender spears and elbow shaped instruments, watched the lazy progress of the ship as it made its way towards its anchorage, .

"Why Aaron, you would think it was paradise itself. The natives don't seem to have a care in the world."

This, from Polly, was overheard by Mr Mackie and he smiled – a very rare occurrence – "Don't let that fool you Miss, they are nothing but thieves and robbers, untrustworthy. They would steal the clothes off your back if you didn't watch their every move."

"Well it looks to me as if they don't need clothes. They seem content and happy without them."

"Filthy creatures Miss!" The Major joined in the conversation, coughing, "No sense of decency. Beat their wives unmercifully."

"Well it smells better than London or Portsmouth and as for decency – back home the girls are forced to sell their bodies for a few coppers and the men treat them like dirt. So where is the difference? As far as I can see, they look happier and more carefree than your prisoners."

The conversation came to an abrupt end as the activity around the ship increased.

Mackie had plenty of influence in the colony, for the next morning they were ordered to take the ship to the quay, taking precedence over other ships waiting to discharge their cargo. The sheep were carefully run down the ramp that had been prepared overnight, followed by the two convicts who, as soon as they reached firm ground were shackled.

The crew followed them down, Polly kissing both men in turn and Aaron shaking their hands warmly, "Goodbye Brownlow, I will see if I can't have a word with someone in authority about this. I will most certainly leave an affidavit with the magistrate. We must be able get a good solicitor to act for you."

"I shouldn't worry if I were you Captain. It's all a set up and you would struggle find any solicitor to act against Mr Mackie. I have no doubt they will give me another seven years – but thank you all the same. If it is at all possible Captain, I would be grateful if you could get word to my wife and let her know I am fit and well. Tell her she is not to wait for me."

A trooper mounted on a horse came between Aaron and the two convicts, "Would you mind not getting near those two convicts Captain – one of them is very dangerous."

Aaron laughed out loud, "Dangerous! They don't look very dangerous to me. Not with those heavy chains around their ankles. These two men here are my friends. They maybe Mr Mackies' slaves but they are still my friends."

"Slaves Captain? There are no slaves in this colony. These men are convicts serving time here because the gaols back home are overflowing."

The last anyone saw of the two convicts, they were trudging after the sheep, their movements painfully impaired by the chains. Polly felt her insides churning for she had grown very fond of both men – especially Brownlow who had borne his wound without compaint.

They turned towards the ship to see a lady in a fine carriage surrounded by a crowd.

"My, madam, what a pretty dress," the lady in the carriage addressed Polly over the heads of the milling crowd. She was about forty. It was easy to see she had been a beauty in her youth, but in Australia the sun had taken its toll. Her dark, almost jet black hair, was streaked with silver, and lines had appeared by the side of her eyes, but as the crowd parted and she held her hand out to Polly her finger nails were seen to be immaculately manicured, "It's so nice to see beautiful clothes again. I think that must be what we miss in the colony – keeping up with the London fashion houses." The women, gathered around the carriage, nodded their heads in agreement.

Polly for her first taste of Australia, had donned her finest silk dress and as she moved, the sun picked up the folds which came alive in the bright sunlight. The women were starved for fashion – though no doubt by the time the *Golden Falcon* reached England again Polly's dresses would be 'old hat'. This gave Polly a smart idea.

"I have plenty more on ship ladies.... would you like to come aboard and see them?" There was an enthusiastic chorus of agreement and they followed her up the narrow gangway and into the great cabin, all looking at the double bed and exchanging knowing winks. This, of course, did not go unnoticed by Polly.

"Do you always go to sea with your husband Miss Polly?"

"Oh... he's *not* my husband. Perhaps one day.... but we are great friends and at the moment we just want it to stay that way. Captain Jacobs is a very fine man – the *Golden Falcon* is his own ship and his men are devoted to him. No whips or rope's end on this ship – do you know we have been to sea for several years and have never lost a man with scurvy or disease once. The Captain has had the need only to punish one man, and that was for being drunk and stealing the cargo."

This made the women very curious. "Well if he refuses to use the rope's end , how would he punish anybody?"

"The rule is we set them on the first land we sight. Fortunately for the man concerned, we happened to be docked in London. No.... we have no trouble on this ship. The men love their Captain and would follow him to hell and back."

Polly pointed to some convicts being helped along by a red jacketed trooper, a long bamboo cane in his hand which he used freely, "That is absolutely unnecessary."

She laid out her collection of dresses on the ship's rails, as the women went into raptures, picking them up and holding them against their bodies. One young girl selected a white silk dress and held it against her body, tears forming in her eyes as she exclaimed in a broken voice choked with emotion, "My God Polly this is so beautiful.... may I try it on?" Polly nodded and the girl vanished into the cabin. When she reappeared the fashion-starved women stared blankly at her, one gasping, "Oh my word Miss Hattie, you look so beautiful."

Polly sat her on a chair and combed the girl's hair until it hung in brown folds resting on her shoulders, "This dress was made for you Miss Hattie."

She held the largest mirror she could find on the ship and stood back until Hattie could see most of her own body in the mirror and the tears started to flow, "I haven't seen anything like this since I came to the colony with my father ten years ago. Would you sell me this dress Miss Polly? I will give you anything you ask."

Polly, normally such a soft touch, instantly knew she could count on a very good profit from the fashion starved women. And after all, she only wore trousers and shirt aboard ship and could easily replace the dresses when they arrived back home. Still, she hesitated, "I don't know Miss Hattie, I have only worn the dress once and that was to try it on at the dressmakers in London. It's my favourite and I was saving it for a special occasion."

But the girl was adamant. It was easy to see she had been doted on by her father, "I must have it Polly. Whatever you paid, I will give you double."

Polly shook her head, "....I'm sorry Miss Hattie."

"Please, Polly.... I will give you *three* times what you paid for it."

"But it cost me twenty guineas, Miss Hattie." This was not enough to put the young lady off.

"Alright then! I will give you sixty guineas."

"Well, If you want it that much.... I can always get another when we arrive back in London."

"I will be back in the morning Miss Polly. Don't you dare sell it to anyone else." Miss Hattie removed the dress and held it to her face, "Oh thank you Miss Polly... thank you."

This began a minor stampede as the other women all selected dresses and began bartering and forcing money upon Polly.

Aaron entered the cabin and watched the women with amused astonishment, "Have you offered your guests a drink, Polly?"

Aaron selected a bottle of his best Madeira red and several Waterford glasses. Pouring each guest in turn a drink, he held it to the light, – "Your health ladies."

"Mmmm, what beautiful wine Captain, wherever did you buy it?"

"Madeira, madam, the finest on the Island." In minutes the ladies were begging him to sell them a bottle.

Triumphantly, if unsteadily, they left the ship – most of them with at least one bottle of wine, and a London dress folded over their arms. Polly sat down, shaken, and looked at Aaron across the table, "To think Aaron, they were begging *me* for those dresses and *you* for that wine. Back home not one of them would have looked at me twice."

Chapter Twenty-six

The cabin was hot and close but it wasn't the weather that was keeping Aaron awake. It was what had happened during the day and since the ship had docked at this faraway harbour, the other side of the world. Crowds had gathered around the ship as soon as it tied up at the wharf, crying out for news of the homeland and wanting to discover what kind of cargo they were carrying. When Polly introduced them to her dresses the women had been beside themselves. Polly stirred, as Aaron, looking up at the ceiling said, "Do you know what Polly?"

He waited, until she drowsily answered, "What Aaron?"

There was enthusiasm in his voice, "If we ever come to this country again we could make a fortune. The inhabitants crowd round the docks whenever a ship arrives just to see what cargo it is carrying.... those women almost mobbed you when you showed them your dresses."

Polly was wide awake in seconds and sat up smartly, "Strange you should say that Aaron, I was thinking it myself. I made up to five times what I paid for some of those dresses. Should we come again I'll bring plenty more, you should see the long list of goods they want."

Although they were only covered with a thin sheet Aaron rose from the bed sweating. He poured out two glasses of brandy hoping it would induce sleep and passed one to Polly. They talked until the early hours, but in spite of two more glasses of brandy sleep just would not come. Aaron was relieved when dawn came flashing through the stern window, the rising sun casting a golden path across the great harbour. It looked so serene he felt he was intruding.

"God, Polly, this looks so peaceful you just can't imagine the misery that's going on here. Ashore I mean – those poor convicts, it must be hell."

Polly just grunted. Sleep had finally overtaken her.

He had been staring out of the stern window when several feet came pounding across the deck, and Willie could be heard talking. Aaron couldn't make out the words, it was just a rumble, but he could tell that voice anywhere. He dressed and took a slow walk on deck, Willie was in conversation with two men by the gangway. Gibbons was testing the lines to the shore, "Morning Gibbons."

Gibbons touched his cap, "Morning sir."

At the sound of Aaron's voice Willie turned around, "Morning Captain, two gentlemen to see you sir."

While they waited Aaron asked Willie if he had been ashore yet.

"No Captain. But I could see plenty of drunks passing by during the night – it's worse than round the docks in Portsea."

Aaron turned to the two visitors and shook hands. Both men were six feet tall, one shabbily dressed, the other almost as shabby but very clean. It was the better dressed man that spoke first, pointing to the other man, "My friend here Captain, he wishes to return to England."

"Sorry gents, we don't carry passengers. We are not equipped for it. I have just brought two passengers here and to be honest, it's put me off paying passengers for good."

"Arrr, I suppose you mean Mackie and his number one. I know what you mean Captain, but to be very honest we really can't pay much – my friend here is willing to work his passage home. Of course he won't expect paying, and the little we *can* afford would barely pay for his food. I can tell you Captain he is a very hard worker – not a sailor – but I know he will pick up his duties very quickly. He is willing to do anything."

"I am from Government House. This man was sent out

here seven years ago on a diamond theft charge but was completely blameless. The guilty man was charged with another misdemeanour and was due to be hanged when he confessed. At first no one would believe him but by chance this man's lawyer overheard the confession. He finally got someone to listen."

This man can go home on the first available ship that will take him. He is a good, reliable man Captain, and has been working at Government House for the last four years. Naturally the governor and I are very anxious to put right any damaging wrong that's been done to this man." As he put his hand on the man's shoulder, it was plain to see he thought well of him.

"What's your name?" Aaron looked at the man, a bit taller than himself with deep blue eyes and blonde hair, he had a straight honest face with a strong jaw line. Aaron liked what he saw.

"Hargreaves, Captain. I am sorry I have no sea experience sir, but I'm very willing to do anything to get back to see my wife and son. It's been almost nine years since I was last home. They kept me in the old ship's hulks on the river for two years and as you know my sentence didn't start 'til I reached this port. Please Captain – I will do anything to get home." His eyes pleaded with Aaron.

Aaron hated paperwork and felt this may be a chance to get it off his hands, "Can you read and write?"

This question was put direct to Hargreaves but before he could answer the other man gave a slight chuckle, "Read and write?" Hope shone in the man's eyes, "Mr Hargreaves has the finest copper plate writing in the colony. He has practically run the clerk's office since he came here to Government House. I can honestly vouch for this man's conduct, we will be losing a great clerk – whoever takes him on in that line of work will be the winner."

"Right Mr Hargreaves, you have a berth if you wish. From this day on you manage the ship's books. It will be a bit of a crush in the fo'c'sle but on fine nights the men sleep on deck. I do have to tell you we have a black man aboard, who is treated exactly like everyone else and is a valuable member of the crew."

"Why should I mind Captain? This is my ticket to freedom and if I had to, I would sup with the devil to return home. There is nothing wrong with blacks Captain, we have our fair share here."

"You don't seem to bare any ill feelings towards your fellow countrymen for being holed up here and separated your family. I know exactly how I would feel, I would curse them to eternity and that's a fact."

Hargreaves shrugged his shoulders, "How can I blame them Captain? I looked the guilty one. I had the diamonds in my charge. I'd left my bench for just a few minutes, when I returned the diamonds were gone. I was the only one in the workshop, and naturally I looked guilty. I still don't know the culprit or how he came to be in the workshop without my knowing. What else can I say? It's all over now."

"Right, Hargreaves, get what clothes and kit you have and report back here by noon. I am trying to find a cargo but this place doesn't look tremendously prosperous at the moment, though I understand some farmers may be shipping wool back home."

"My luggage is at the bottom of the gangway Captain – if you can *call* it luggage." He pointed to a pathetic bundle on the quayside.

Hargreaves took his leave from his companion and it was plain to see they were great friends, "Now don't forget Hargreaves if you decide to return with your family I will see that you get a good occupation in Government House. We will all miss you. Why not think it over – you could return with your wife and son – the opportunities here are enormous. It's a new country, and one day it will be a great nation, you will be in almost at the start and apart from your work in Government House the governor will grant you a few acres of land."

Hargreaves shook his head, "Thank you Mr Palmer, but this country has too many bad memories for me. To be honest with you I don't know if my wife will have waited for me all these years. I couldn't blame her if she hasn't."

They shook hands warmly, Palmer putting his arms round Hargreaves' shoulders, "Good bye Hargreaves and I wish you all the luck in the world."

After two days Aaron had found only half a cargo of wool
and a few botanical specimens for a naturalist back home.
He looked rather disappointed when he arrived back at his
ship but was greatly surprised to see Mackie and his constant companion waiting for him on deck.

"Ah Captain, I hear you are looking for a cargo to return
home. I want these four packing cases to go to London, for
my brother."

Mackie pointed to four large packing cases on the quay.
Aaron frowned, they looked more like cages, closed in on
three sides but the fronts open and barred. It was difficult
to see inside. Each had a couple of feet of straw at the bottom and what looked like two furry lumps sticking up in
the centre.

"What the hell are they? No thank you Mackie – no more
livestock."

"These are no trouble Captain, they are kangaroos. When
I was last in England I told my brother about these
strange animals he was very anxious to get hold of some.
He will pay you very well."

"No doubt he will pay me well for my services just as you
and your brother did for Brownlow. You got him out here
on a trumped up charge so that he could teach you all
about sheep breeding. Now it's another trumped up charge
by which you intend to keep the poor man here."

"Brownlow is a thief Captain. A sheep stealer – a crime
that carries the death sentence. My brother saved him
from the hangman's noose."

"You and I both know that is rubbish. Brownlow is a God
fearing and loyal man. When those pirates tried to kill
you, he saved your life. He could easily have let you die,
and for a reward you will testify to yet another trumped up
charge against him in order that he can fulfil your selfish
needs. You are a rat sir! And as for your brother's kangaroos, if for one minute I thought they were man eaters I
would gladly take them home for nothing – if only in the
hope that eventually they would bite his damn head off.
Good day sir."

With that Aaron turned his back on the two men. Mackie

was seething with rage while the Major was contemplating offering a dual to the Captain. The Captain had taken no more than a dozen steps when he stopped abruptly. A thought had suddenly struck him and he returned to the two men, both red faced with anger, "One minute Mackie – when is Brownlow due in Court?"

"Friday. But I fail to see why that should be any of your business. At the moment he is in the town jail waiting his trial. I want to get it over quickly, so he can return to his work."

Aaron laughed, "I see you still have plenty of influence here Mackie. Drop the charges against him, and I will take your kangaroos back to England for nothing. No charge whatsoever."

Mackie pondered the situation for a few minutes and shook his head slowly. "Attempting to escape is a very serious crime Captain....."

"Rubbish Mackie, you know damn well he didn't try and escape – it was a put up job between you and your Boer friend. Tell the magistrate about Brownlow saving your life and that you have reconsidered the charge. You will be a hero amongst your own crowd and gain far more respect from your convicts. Let Brownlow finish his time and return to his family. He can teach other men his job, such as Davies."

Mackie didn't give him a straight answer but instead, hesitated and said, "I will give it some thought Captain."

The time passed slowly, Aaron wanting to get away as fast as possible yet also wanting to observe the case against Brownlow as it progressed.

He was the first person into the Court on the Friday. If things went wrong Aaron intended to intercede on the man's behalf. Brownlow was called into the dock, heavily chained with two guards, one on each side. The magistrate looked him up and down for a few moments before the indictment was read out.

"This is a very serious charge, prisoner, very serious indeed. Out of the kindness of his heart Mr Mackie, a very eminent man in this community, took you – on your honour – to Cape Town, and allowed you freedom of movement. How did you repay him? You attempted to escape. Do you have anything to say to this court?"

Brownlow looked downcast. Whatever he said would be twisted around. He had known before he'd stepped into the dock that he would receive at least a few years added to his sentence. All thoughts of being reunited with his family had vanished – he just shook his head.

Mr Mackie was called to the stand and as he turned to face the court, was surprised to see Captain Jacobs sitting in the public gallery. Aaron stared squarely back at Mackie as if to say, 'Charge him, and you can say goodbye to having your bloody kangaroos shipped to that devoted brother of yours.'

Mackie paused and licked his lips, "Well sir.... as you may have heard our ship was attacked near Ceylon by pirates. Brownlow was very brave and indirectly saved my life. As a reward I would ask that this charge be dropped."

"But Mr Mackie, escaping is an extremely serious offence, often carrying the death sentence. This is a very generous gesture by you. However, we cannot allow him to get away with the charge scot free. I must sentence him to twenty lashes. In addition, he must not leave your land at any time without your written permission until his current penal servitude has ran its course."

Brownlow could hardly believe his ears and stood open mouthed in the dock. Looking around the Court astonished he saw Captain Jacobs sitting there. Aaron subtly winked his eye.

Mackie's brother wielded the big stick in the family – he wanted the kangaroos, and would have them – Mackie was doing nothing from the goodness of his heart. As Brownlow witnessed the slight smile on Aaron's face, matched by the scowl on Mackie's, he needed no further explanation.

The kangaroos were soon hoisted aboard, much to the amusement of the crew and onlookers, with plenty of fodder for the long journey home.

"There you are Hargreaves, besides your clerical work these animals will be your responsibility. You can sleep alongside them, down in hold number two, or you can suffer overcrowding in the foc's'le along with the crew. Which reminds me – how are you getting along on with them, Sam in particular?"

"Fine Captain, and Sam seems a nice chap. I only wish he wouldn't keep calling me sir."

Aaron laughed. "He calls everyone sir."

Chapter Twenty-seven

Several days out from the colony and the men were in groups on deck talking amongst themselves, Hargreaves included.

Aaron smiled to himself. The man had settled down well, and the Captain's judgement had been proved correct. The man was an admirable clerk. He stopped short as if suddenly remembering something, "Hargreaves if you have a few minutes to spare, would you follow me to my cabin?"

Hargreaves' forehead creased into a frown as he entered the Captain's cabin, surely he hadn't done anything wrong. He watched Aaron rummage through the large chest before finally finding what he was looking for – the small leather bag. He pulled out the largest stone, "I understand you were in the diamond trade Hargreaves, what exactly did you do?"

"I cut the diamonds and polished them, and then valued them. I believe I have as good a knowledge of diamonds as anyone Captain."

Aaron handed over the large stone. Open mouthed, the sweat gathering on his forehead, like the morning dew on a rose petal, Hargreaves held the diamond up to the light and slowly turned it around, before whistling through his clenched teeth, "Captain, if this stone is not flawed it will be worth a king's ransom. At the moment I cannot be certain, but it is probably a rare blue diamond. I have worked with some of the rarest stones in the world, but never anything like this." He sat down on a chair and with his elbows on the table, again looked at the diamond as the light streamed in from the stern window. He stopped dead as Aaron emptied the leather pouch onto the table. One by one Hargreaves picked up the stones and examined each in turn as if he were in a trance.

"Let me polish one for you Captain. I haven't the right tools, but I may get a bit of a sparkle on one to test it further. If they really are blue diamonds and not flawed, you will be the richest Captain on the ocean waves. I just cannot believe it, all the years that I worked in the trade and I have never seen anything so beautiful." His hand trembled as one by one he returned them to the leather pouch, "A woman would sell her soul for a necklace made from just one of these, sir."

Aaron laughed, "That's strange, the man I got them from said exactly those words."

For the first time since he relieved the slaver of the diamonds Aaron took a serious interest in them, "Tell me Hargreaves just how much are they worth? They look like a heap of dirty stones to me, I almost threw them overboard until the agent in Cape Town offered me a hundred pounds. After that I guessed they must be worth something."

"Overboard? A hundred pounds? Good God!" Hargreaves was almost hysterical, "If this one isn't flawed, it would fetch sufficient money for you to retire immediately." He held it up to the light as if in a dream. Then emptying the leather bag again on the table, using the largest one as a focal point, he laid them out gradually in the form of a necklace. He picked one up and went to the window then gradually drew it along the glass. It left a tell tale serrated cut, "They are definitely diamonds.... Let me just clean this one up a bit."

"All right Hargreaves see what you can do with it."

Instead of just slipping it into his pocket, Hargreaves picked it up and carefully wrapped it in a piece of cotton cloth. Willie let him have a piece of holystone that he had been using to clean the bloodstains from the deck after the encounter with the pirates and Hargreaves sat in a shaded corner of the deck, continually rubbing it up and down,

wetting the holystone occasionally, much to the amusement of Polly and the rest of the crew.

After three days he tapped on the Captain's cabin door.
"Come."

Hargreaves could hardly contain his excitement, "I told
you Captain! Just hold this stone up to the light and see
that beautiful colour." He handed the stone to Aaron, who
casually held it up and looked at it.

"It's very nice Hargreaves."

Hargreaves gulped and swallowed hard, his face changing
as if he'd been grossly insulted, "Nice, Captain? Why it's
the most beautiful stone, I've ever had the privilege to
work on. Put it away safe Captain. Put it somewhere very
safe. And for heaven's sakes don't let the crew know its
value."

"But my crew are trustworthy Hargreaves. In them I have
every confidence."

"Sir, I once knew of a man who killed his own brother in a
dispute over a diamond necklace that wasn't a fraction of
the value of any of these diamonds. I implore you to be
very careful."

Realising at last that he had something of extreme value
Aaron removed the bottom drawer of his chest and carefully put the bag underneath. They was to be no more mention of the diamonds until they reached London.

At Table Bay the little Boer came aboard and took the
manifesto from Aaron, scrutinising it carefully. Polly, who
had seen him coming and quickly changed into her tightest fitting trousers and open necked blouse, undone
enough buttons to reveal where her breasts parted. She
then walked past the Boer with an exaggerated wiggle of
her bottom, flickering her eyebrows at him as she passed.
The Boer tutted loudly, trying to avert his eyes.

"What on earth are those animals, Captain?" He pointed
to the crates and went down the hold to get a closer look,
"Giant rats?"

"No, they are kangaroos and come from Australia. I
believe they have evolved from a long line of Dutchmen,
whose ship was wrecked off the Australian coast. Some
Aborigines found them, looked after them, and eventually

they intermarried. I must admit they do look queer."

"We Dutch do not intermarry with blacks Captain."

The words were spat out before the little man realised that Aaron had been winding him up. Staring at Aaron, his eyeballs popping from his head, he muttered something unintelligible, stamped his feet and went straight to where the rope ladder hung over the rails – and giving Polly a withering look he made his way to the dinghy. She returned him a wide grin and wished the bloody dinghy would sink before it reached the quay.

The crew picked up a small amount of cargo for delivery to London and the next day the *Golden Falcon* was on its way. A few weeks later, following a brief stop at Madeira in order to pick up wine and fresh fruit, they were sailing up the Thames. Aaron's agent had been notified immediately they had sailed into the estuary and was waiting at the dockside.

As he read the manifesto, his eyes widened, "What the hell are these Captain?" He pointed to the crates on the list.

"Kangaroos – I want them unloaded straight away, poor things have been in the hold for weeks."

After three days, Mackie's brother came striding into the docks and made his way through a vast crowd that were constantly gathered around the crates. He stared at the beasts and gave a loud cry of astonishment when a baby kangaroo poked its head up from his mother's pouch. Aaron walked over from his ship and held out his hand, which the man completely ignored. Immediately Aaron took a dislike to him – there was obviously little to choose, in the matter of manners, between the two brothers.

"I take it these are my goods?"

"Yes. We did have four to start with but it looks like there has been an addition to the family."

"You are not going to charge me extra, are you?"

Aaron laughed, "You are in luck Mackie. Due to a private arrangement I have made with your brother, I am not going to charge you anything. However, Hargreaves here has been in sole charge of them throughout the voyage, I think you should thank him and reward him."

"Thank him? Reward him? Good God man he has only carried out his duties. I will remove these beasts to my estate
– when I am good and ready."

"That is entirely up to you Mackie, but you will have to
make your own arrangements for their safety."

The man was unused to people speaking to him in such a
manner and showed his resentment, "How dare you speak
to me like that my man. You will keep watch over these
animals until I have made suitable arrangements."

"I am *not* your man. I am the Captain and the owner of
this ship. Our responsibility is to deliver these crates to
this dock. My job is now over."

Mackie went red in the face as if he were just about to
throw an epileptic fit, and twiddled his riding crop as if he
was about to raise it and bring it down across Aaron's
shoulders. As quick as a flash the Captain caught him by
the wrist, twisting and wrenching until it fell to the floor.

"Put that riding crop on my person Mackie and as sure as
hell I will kill you."

He turned abruptly and returned to his ship. Mackie
stared at his back unable to believe his own ears. The
crowd that had gathered to see the kangaroos had enjoyed
an added attraction and many were openly laughing,
"Don't 'e mess with Captain Jacobs sir..... if *he* don't kill
you, one of his crew will."

Mackie was foaming at the mouth as he pushed his way
through the guffawing bystanders, "Out of my way you
cursed lot." This brought a louder burst of laughter from
the jovial crowd.

Polly spent the first two days ashore replenishing her
stocks of the latest fashion in dresses. Having plenty of
money to spare, she hired a coach to ride around the great
city and with Sam dressed in his finery, standing at the
back of the carriage, she felt a real lady. Sam stared in
wonder at all the buildings – but to him the greatest of all
was St. Paul's cathedral which stood out like a sentinel
over London, proud to be the last resting place of the
nation's greatest Admiral. It was also the one place – apart
from business – that Aaron intended to visit.

"Hargreaves – what do you suggest I now do with these

diamonds?"

"Well Captain.... I have given it a lot of thought and there
is only one man that can handle this sort of diamond. A
Dutch Jew, who came to London from Amsterdam many
years ago. You must go and see him and ask his advice."

"And where will I find this man?"

"I'll take you there Captain, but I won't come inside. You
are aware of what happened to me – I may be innocent but
mud sticks."

The building was shabby and in need of a clean down and
a coat of paint. It resembled anything other than a place
that dealt in thousands of pounds worth of precious stones.
Aaron had left Hargreaves at the end of the street, climbed
three stone stairs, from which years of footsteps had worn
away the centre, and now stood at the entrance. He pulled
a rusting iron chain at the side of the flaking door and a
loud clanging echoed from the interior. It was some time
before there was any response and a panel six inches
square in the centre of the door slid open to reveal the face
of a wizened old man with a pointed white beard squinting
through.

"What is it?" The words rolled around his tongue.

"A colleague has advised me to contact you. I have
brought something to show you. He said you may be interested." Aaron held up one of the smaller diamonds in his
hand and the face in the open panel lit up. A yard away
he immediately recognised what it was.

"A blue diamond – where did you get this?"

Aaron waited patiently as many iron bolts were pulled
back. He was led into the premises and down a bare passage to a room that was sparsely furnished with a table in
need of a good scrub, and two chairs. The old man gestured, "Sit down Mister." The chair was hard, and the
faint glow of a fire burnt in the grate, "Let me see that
stone again, Mister?" It sounded like a question.

"My name is Captain Jacobs." Aaron pulled out the stone
and handed it to the Jew, who brought out a square of
green velvet placed the diamond carefully upon it. Aaron,
in turn, emptied the remains of the soft leather bag onto

the velvet cloth and the old man's jaw dropped. His eyes widened and his chair, sliding back, almost tipped him to the floor.

"My God... my great God... wherever did you get these Captain?"

"West Africa – they were taken in part payment from two Arab traders."

"*Part* payment! That is incredible... how much more do they have to pay you? Why these stones here could buy half of England."

He picked up the largest stone and took it to the window holding it up to the watery autumn sun. He was positively drooling, "I must let my sons see these stones Captain." He placed the largest stone back on the cloth.

The old man went out and a few minutes later returned with his two sons. One man, over six feet tall, broad shouldered and thick set, was a handsome man in his early thirties. The other was a dwarf – the smallest man Aaron had ever seen – who, with a little difficulty, jumped onto the chair and gasped, picking out the largest stone and examining it closely.

In a squeaky voice he said, "Father if there are no flaws in these stones, they will be the rarest we have ever seen or ever handled." With this he jumped from his chair and without a word to Aaron or his father, beckoned to his brother and left the room.

"My son is one of the world's leading authorities on diamonds, Captain Jacobs. He has devoted his life to them. You see... being the size he is most, people laugh and stare at him, so he hardly leaves this building. He lives here night and day. Some nights when it is dark he walks across the road and stares into the muddy water of the Thames... people can be very cruel Captain."

"I know sir, I have just returned from one of the cruellest places on God's good earth, where vicious atrocities are carried out in the name of so-called justice. Also, sir, if you wish to see cruelty at work try and get a glance inside one of His Majesty's ships – it is a wonder there is not mass mutiny."

They sat at the table again, and the old man poured out

two glasses of port. As he passed one to Aaron, who sipped it and smacked his lips with satisfaction. It was a good port.

"Now Captain, tell me what you would like me to do with these magnificent diamonds. There are several options open to you – I could polish them and sell them on the open market; or I could make them all into one of *the* most beautiful necklaces in the world and sell it to the highest bidder. I know of gentlemen who would willingly pay a fortune for such a necklace."

There was a tap on the door and the dwarf entered again. Without a word – just a nod to Aaron – he handed his father a sheet of paper, who in turn handed it to Aaron as his son quietly left the room.

"My other son, the tall one, is a designer. He has drawn a rough sketch of how your diamonds would look made into a necklace."

It was Aaron's turn to gasp,"He did this drawing in just a few minutes. Both your sons are very talented sir."

Two hours later, after having made short work of a bottle of port, it was finally agreed that the diamonds would be turned into a necklace, set in gold.

"I will charge you five percent for making the necklace, the value of the gold, and another five percent for selling it – even then Captain, you will be a very wealthy man."

They shook hands to conclude the deal, and as Aaron turned to the door a thought stuck him, "After you have made the necklace – is it possible that I could have a copy of the drawing?"

The little Jew's face turned into a wide grin, "Don't worry Captain, you are not the first to ask. When some lord or landed gentry has one made it is almost certain he will ask for a copy of the drawing. I often wonder who receives the copy – his wife or his mistress." He opened the door and was still chuckling as Aaron left.

Chapter Twenty-eight

Hargreaves spent his first week ashore seeking out his wife and child. Although signed off the ship's crew, Aaron had felt obliged to allow him to use the ship as a base. The man soon became very despondent.

"No luck Hargreaves?" Aaron asked him when he returned on the fifth day.

He shook his head sorrowfully, "No Captain – I asked around the place where we last lived but my wife seems to have vanished without trace. I did meet a man I worked with in my last place of employment who said the last he'd heard of her she was living near Blackheath, but she could now be anywhere. He will ask around."

"If you don't find them... will you go back to Australia?"

"No sir if I don't find my family before you set sail I would like to sign on again. I really did enjoy the life aboard."

"There will always be a berth here for you Hargreaves. You took a lot of the clerical work off me and you certainly fell into the job."

Two weeks after docking, the *Golden Falcon* was preparing to set sail from Wapping and Hargreaves had found no luck in locating his family, "Well I didn't expect any woman to wait ten years for me Captain." He fell into a silence and watched the shore as the tide carried them down the estuary.

"I mentioned your predicament to my agent." Replied Aaron, "He is a man about town, and knows a lot of useful people. He will make some enquiries. I gave him your

wife's last known address and he will take it from there.
So settle down Hargreaves, all is not lost you know."

Their final destination on this trip was Australia and
every man had loaded up with anything that could be sold
at a profit when they arrived. Aaron smiled to himself,
seeing them struggle aboard, wondering how they would
fit it all in to their already cramped quarters. His own
cabin was no better – there were dresses, coats and hats in
every available space.

"I'm pleased you left a space for me to get into bed Polly.
Just look at this pile of news sheets, what on earth do you
want them for?"

"They're starved for information Aaron – it might be stale
to you, but it's new to them."

Aaron sat down perplexed, "The next thing we know you
will be opening up a shop out there."

Little did the Captain know, that the same thing had been
going through Polly's mind. A shop just for ladies. It would
be the first of its kind in that place and the colony would
be growing fast. The land, with its ideal climate, was good
for growing crops and raising stock, and needed people to
work it. The land was going for nothing, so many poor
farmers were volunteering to go out to the colony, and the
idea of opening the first ladies' shop kept racing through
Polly's mind, keeping her well-occupied.

She didn't bother, when they reached Cape Town, teasing
the little Boer when he came aboard. When he gave her
the usual look of disdain she didn't react, but instead
stared vacantly at the shore, watching the badly dressed
Boer women going about their business with long black
dresses that scraped the ground and poke bonnets covering half their faces. Still in dreamland, Polly let Willie and
two crew members row her ashore while the ship took on
fresh water and supplies for the last leg to the colony, and
ordered her fruit and vegetables from the same black lady
she had met before. They greeted each other like old
friends as Polly removed the wrappings from a parcel she
had carried from the ship.

"Here you are Peggy, I have brought this for you." It was a
large wide brimmed hat that Polly had owned for some

while and like most women, had tired of it.

Peggy's eyes were almost popping out of her head, as Polly adjusted the hat to fit her.

"Oh, you look so beautiful Peggy, it suits that lovely round face, and you can tell your friends that it came all the way from England."

The poor lady was speechless, for the only headdress she had ever worn was a coloured turban-like kerchief. She finally stammered, "Is it for me lady?" Large tears ran down her black shiny face.

Polly put her arm around the woman's shoulders, "Come on sweetheart, you look beautiful." It was a while before they could get down to the business of supplies for the ship.

Aaron, calling into the agents hoping for a cargo on his return visit, was offered the usual glass of terrible brandy. He held his breath, not to offend the agent, and gulped it down in one go, shuddering involuntary and returning the glass to the desk.

The agent laughed and was about to offer a refill when Aaron quickly put his hand over his glass to prevent further torture, "I would rather not if you don't mind."

"It's like everything Captain, you get used to it if you have to."

"Yes, but you could go blind in the process. I suppose it does eventually destroy the taste buds and you don't notice the damn stuff – like smoking, it becomes a habit."

As if to agree the agent lit up a foul smelling hand made cigar. It filled the office with a nauseating stench, defying the air that was coming through the open window. Aaron waved his hand across his face, "Your cigars are almost as bad as your brandy."

"Well, it keeps the flies away. But come along Captain, we are not here to discuss the merits or demerits of our cigars and brandy. Let us get down to business. Have you made up your mind what you want to do with those stones?" He tried to hide a sarcastic smirk, "I mean, of course, blue diamonds. I have a client that is interested and has told me to offer you one thousand pounds sight unseen. He will risk their being genuine or not."

News, like disease, travels fast in Africa. It had soon got around that the two fanatical slavers had been murdered and possibly robbed. It was also heavily rumoured that the two slavers had known the source of the finest blue diamonds in Africa, and the agent had put two and two together. Aaron, too, could add up and was nobody's fool, though what the agent failed to realise was that when he had first offered a hundred pounds Aaron had been tempted – if he had gone to five hundred he would be the owner of them already.

"I should think you *would* offer me a thousand. I'm afraid I have had them valued – by England's foremost diamond expert. He could not even put a price on them." To rub it in Aaron withdrew a sheet of paper from his pocket, "This is a drawing of what the diamonds will look like when they are made into a necklace. They *are* real blue diamonds."

"They are beautiful Captain." The agent did not seem over bothered that he had just missed out on a deal which would have settled him for life. From the first he had realised that the Captain was no idiot, "I suppose you are off to Botany Bay. We had a large convict convoy pass through here two days ago, they must be emptying all the prisons back home. Some of those ships are dreadful, almost as bad as the slavers that operate up along the west coast."

The agent rummaged through several sheaves of paper and pulled out a couple of sheets, "I will have a cargo for you on your return." They stood up and shook hands.

"Thanks a lot, we hope to make a fast voyage, and won't bother calling in at Colombo – not after our first taste of the place..." The agent laughed and slapped Aaron on the back.

It was an uneventful passage, very hot most of the way but a fair wind that drove them steadily along at eight to ten knots. Still, it was a great relief when the masthead shouted, "Land dead ahead Captain!"

The crew jumped about like agile monkeys in an attempt to get a better view of dry land. Sam, since joining the ship had only ever been ashore a couple of times – and that was to escort Miss Polly. Willie hardly ever went ashore, regarding the ship as his true home. Some of the crew would pay a visit to their wives and families when in England, but overall were content to stay aboard during most ports of call. However, when land was sighted after long and sometimes weary voyages, it raised their spirits and they felt a kind of exhilaration.

The *Golden Falcon* passed through the heads, a lookout at his post signalling to the town that a ship was arriving while on the other shore a lone Aborigine stood moodily on one leg, the other hooked around a tall spear – a silent sentry.

The anchorage was crowded with ships and they dropped anchor fifty yards from shore. Polly made out several of the faces standing at the quay and held up a broadsheet – the news they were hungry for. They pulled up alongside the dock later that day and the gangplank was hardly down when the women swarmed aboard. Polly, ready for them, had the dresses and hats for show already laid out along the decks.

Aaron passed them smiling and shaking his head, marvelling over the change that had come over Polly since the day he bought her aboard before he was shanghaied into carrying out the rescue mission for HM navy. He handed his manifest to the agent who, after much scrutiny, nodded his head in satisfaction, "I see you have brought seed potatoes and picks and shovels." He handed the list back to Aaron, "I have a few bails of wool for you Captain – fine wool at that – they will prove to be the lifeline of this country.... Oh, and a few barrels of salted mutton for your crew – my compliments."

"Most kind..." replied Aaron, "While we are here, we will want to buy fresh beef.... I hear there are beef breeders here now."

"No problem, Captain. Mackie has been breeding the best beef in the colony. The man will own half the damn colony before very long. It seems even the governor has to jump at his bidding... and he's got the New South Wales Corps in the palm of his hand. There will be big trouble in the colony before very long... corruption. Let's face it the legal tender is rum. It's a pity Captain, a beautiful country and

once a route is found over the Blue Mountains there will
be plenty for everyone."

Within two hours Polly had sold every piece of clothing
she had with her. Hats, shoes, and dresses – and to every
purchaser she gave a broadsheet. Her investment had
returned her a threefold profit.

Mrs Turner, her favourite customer, invited her out for a
drive, and once away from the bustle of the crowded town
and into the open countryside the horses settled down to a
steady canter.

"It's so beautiful out here Mrs Turner." Polly sighed as she
settled back into the soft cushions of the carriage. They
drove along for miles towards a large brick built house
that the lady assured Polly was as solid and impressive as
anything built in the old country.

"Mrs Pilgrim will be most pleased to meet you, she gets
few visitors out here, let alone someone fresh from
England." She lowered her voice and tapped Polly's knee,
confidentially whispering, "She comes from one of
Britain's oldest families you know... married beneath herself and so her family settled a large amount of money on
the couple and sent them here. A little bribery in London
and the next thing you know they are granted a large tract
of land... it prospered well. Her husband is quite charming
really, 'though middle class.... his father owns a couple of
mills in Yorkshire."

"I would hardly say that a man who owns a couple of mills
in the north of England is exactly destitute."

Mrs Turner screwed up her nose as if the subject was too
tasteless to discuss. As far as she was concerned being rich
did not make a gentleman. Polly inwardly chuckled to herself and wondered what Mrs Turner would have to say if
she knew she was sharing her carriage with a one-time
dockyard prostitute. But Mrs Turner had no need to worry,
her husband too, had been given great tracts of land, some
of the best in the colony – and all with free labour – by a
grateful government ambitious to see the far flung colony
self supporting. Of course being related to one of the earlier governors of the colony had a lot to do with securing this
prize parcel. Polly was gradually changing her mind about

224

Mrs Turner, she may be a good customer but alone on this bumpy road she was showing her true colours.

They turned up a wide dusty drive lined with poplars that Mr Pilgrim had arranged to be sent out from England. A convict was lovingly attending them and touched his forelock as they passed – a gesture which Mrs Turner begrudgingly acknowledged with the slightest nod of her head. He was a very young man, scarcely eighteen and Polly smiled down at him.

"He is such a young boy Mrs Turner and so far away from England and his parents."

"He is a rascal, believe me Miss Polly don't bother your pretty little head about these rogues. This is very likely the best place for him – he probably comes from some vermin ridden house in a dreary back street. Here he has plenty of sunshine and I know for certain that Mr and Mrs Pilgrim feed him very well, better than he deserves if you ask me."

The carriage stopped and an old ex-convict ran from the side of the house and caught the horses' bridle, then touching his forelock he opened the door of the carriage.

"Hello Tom," Mrs Turner said with a snobbish sneer in her voice.

Tom nodded his head, "Morning ma'am."

"He is a good example Polly, finished his seven-year term long ago and decided to stay." She said this as if the convict wasn't there. Polly assumed he must have decided to stay because he had no family left back home. Polly could understand this – staying here at least meant that he had a roof over his head and decent food.

Her first contact with Mrs Pilgrim proved to be a pleasant one. Polly could see she was a lady, her smile lighting up the verandah. Petite, with an hour-glass figure, deep brown eyes and flaming red hair that hung over her shoulders in well-kept waves, she held out a tiny hand, "Miss Polly, I have heard so much about you and the beautiful dresses you bring over – but they failed to tell me how beautiful *you* are. I understand you travel all the time with your husband. It must be very nice being permanently aboard a ship. It certainly hasn't damaged your complexion. But do be seated, I am starved of company so you must excuse me if I tend to gabble on. Sorry you cannot meet my husband, he will be away from here for a few days – he has to meet that horrible man, Mr Mackie."

Polly gave her usual giggle, "I know exactly what you mean, we had him aboard our ship for several weeks, him and the major."

"Ah, the major – we call him Mackie's shadow – he can't move without him. I really don't know what to make of the man, he acts like a real gentleman and yet follows Mackie around like a faithful lap dog."

Mrs. Pilgrim rang a tiny brass bell and a small aborigine girl, dressed in a white frock that reached just below her knees, came running in. She carried a glass jug full of fresh lemonade and covered with a lace cover weighted down with glass beads round the edges. Mrs Pilgrim put her arm around the girl's tiny waist affectionately, "Ju-Ju is my little friend, she doesn't speak much, thank God." She smiled and so did Ju-Ju, revealing perfectly white teeth, "When she does speak she swears terribly, she hangs around the convicts' quarters and I suppose they think it's very funny when she repeats it."

"Why don't you keep her away from them Bess..." interrupted Mrs. Turner, "it's not very nice hearing her use that filthy language."

"I would stand more chance of turning the Hawksbury river uphill. These native girls mature very quickly and the convicts are the only men around here. I have tried everything – locking her in her room, making her miss her dinner. I have even taken her frock away and when I do that she starts her native dancing. I tell you, she is a problem. Sometimes she vanishes for weeks on end. My native boy tells me she goes walkabout with her tribe. It's as if by some strange instinct she knows when her tribe is near here. We can always tell when she has gone, she leaves her dress over the verandah."

"Why in heavens' name do you keep her?"

"I don't know... she goes away, then one morning, perhaps months later, we find her asleep on the floor of her room and she starts work the next morning as if nothing has happened. And when I scold her she just laughs and says one or two swear words. I know I shouldn't... but she has such an innocent face."

Polly was learning a lot about the native mind and admired them and Ju-Ju for their spirit of freedom. For a native she was very pretty, without the thick lips associated with African blacks, her hair a mass of open curls, but her eyes were her most enduring feature. Like large brown saucers with a glint of a paramount smile dancing in them, her figure would be the envy of any London society and when she walked there was a slight spring in her step like a young ballerina.

It was a reluctant goodbye when they finally took their leave, "I do hope you will come again Miss Polly, I am afraid this time I did all the talking. Perhaps next time you will tell us of some of your adventures aboard the *Golden Falcon*. I am sure you must have dozens of stories to keep us occupied for quite a few days." She blushed deeply and lowered her voice to jst above a whisper, "Do you not get frightened being the only woman aboard ship with all those men?"

Polly laughed, "Those men, believe me Mrs Pilgrim, are like baby kittens."

Mrs Pilgrim put her arm around Polly and kissed her with affection on her cheeks. Polly detected a tear in her eye when she said, "To think in a few months time you will be back in dear old England. I miss those dear old bleak Yorkshire moors more than people imagine."

She was still holding Polly's hand as she stepped aboard the carriage, reluctant to let her go. As the carriage reached the bottom of the dusty path Mrs Pilgrim was still standing there, a tiny handkerchief in her hand and dabbing her eyes as she waved.

Chapter Twenty-nine

On their return to England there was momentous news for Hargreaves. His wife and family had been located living within walking distance of the docks. Overjoyed with the news, he had set out to contact her, only to arrive back at the ship crest-fallen, as dusk approached.

He knocked on Aaron's door.

"Come."

Hargreaves walked in and stood before the desk, the same desk at which he had often sat, poring over the ship's accounts during the long voyage to Australia, "With your permission Captain, I will be signing on again."

Aaron looked up in surprise, "Didn't you find your wife then, Hargreaves?"

He lowered his head, "Yes Captain, I found her..." He was fighting back the tears, "... living with a man. She seems to be very happy. I waited across the street from where she lives and she came out with my son..." Hargreaves' disposition lightened as he mentioned the boy, "... big strapping lad, much bigger than his mother. You just never realise they grow so much – when I left he was such a tiny boy."

"Did you speak to her?"

"No sir, to be quite frank she looked so happy – a man came to the door with her and waved as she left. It breaks my heart, but I cannot blame her Captain. It is over ten years since I left and I have to admit she looks fine – well dressed – she hardly looks half starved, and so long as he treats her well Captain, why should I intervene? She didn't see me, so I won't bother her any more. But that boy of mine.... he does look great. A big strapping lad." He went to the door, hesitated and turned, "It *will* be alright to sign on again Captain?"

"Of course Hargreaves. I will be glad to have you aboard. I was not looking forward to this damn clerical work." No more was said of Hargreaves' encounter with his wife. Aaron told Polly, but didn't dwell too much on it. They had known how much Hargreaves had wanted to be united with his family.

Next morning Aaron ordered transport and gave the hostler two addresses on paper, "Do you know these two addresses?"

"Yes sir."

"Then take me to the jewellers first and hurry."

Aaron knocked on the old jeweller's door and waited a few minutes before the door panel slid open. The familiar face of the old jeweller appeared, and seeing Aaron standing there the old face split into a thousand wrinkles and the door bolts slid open.

"Come in Captain, come in." He held out his arms as if greeting a long lost friend, but instead Aaron seized his hand and shook it warmly. He was shown into the room he had entered before but this time a great fire was blazing away.

"Sit down Captain," The old man drew a chair closer to the table and spread out his piece of blue velvet. He vanished quickly into a back room and returned a few minutes later escorted by his two sons. The dwarf hoisted himself onto the chair and his father handed him a velvet box about a foot square which he opened as if it were a delicate piece of fine glassware. As he did so Aaron gasped. The dwarf laid the necklace on to the blue velvet cover, his hands trembling.

"My God it is beautiful."

The Captain felt afraid to touch it as the jeweller and his two sons watched his face, letting him savour the beautiful necklace. The dwarf told him it was his masterpiece, "I have always wanted to create such a necklace as this. All we require now are your instructions. What shall we do with it, Captain?"

"Well first, I would like to bring someone else to see this beautiful necklace. Did you make a replica?"

The three of them exchanged glances. How many times had they heard this same request before. The taller son left the room, returning after a few moments with an identical velvet box and opening it. He took out a similar necklace and laid it beside the original – only an expert would be able to tell the difference.

"You see Captain, what did I tell you."

Aaron stared at it for a few moments, before smiling, "You certainly *did* tell me, sir." He stood up to take his leave, "Obviously I would like you to sell it to the highest bidder. I must congratulate you and your two sons sir, it is a work of art."

The old man followed him to the front door, "We have sent an artist's impression of the necklace to all potential buyers – any person that can afford it that is."

They shook hands and Aaron seemed to float down the three worn steps to where the carriage was still waiting.

"Right, straight to the other address I gave you, and wait for me."

It was almost dark when he returned to his ship. He paid off the hostler and gave him a generous tip.

"Thank 'ee Captain," and touched his forelock, "you are a real gentleman sir – God be with 'ee."

"Great news Polly. I have found Hargreaves' wife and she will be here first thing in the morning. It looks as if we may be losing Hargreaves after all. She is a fine woman Polly, and that son of hers is all muscle but he has a brain to go with it."

"But what about the man she is supposed to be living with. Didn't he have much to say?"

"Not really, he is her brother. Ten years makes a difference to any man and that is why Hargreaves failed to recognise him. Splendid chap actually – made something of himself in the City and when he found Hargreaves' wife more or less destitute, he took her and the boy in, and gave

230

the lad a decent education. The wife took care of him and managed the house. She wanted to return with me tonight but I thought it best to wait until morning. Of course, I am sorry to lose Hargreaves." As an afterthought Aaron said, "By the way the jeweller has finished the necklace. You can come with me and see it in the morning."

"My God Aaron, you are a tease with women, making poor Mrs Hargreaves wait until the morning and now making me wait to see the necklace. You will never understand women Aaron, they are impetuous."

"My Polly, that's a big word for you. Have you been reading my books again?" They both laughed.

Aaron was out of bed and on deck at first light. Mrs Hargreaves and her son were standing on the quayside. Polly was right, Aaron did not understand women. He brought the woman on deck, "Why Mrs Hargreaves, whatever are you doing here this early in the morning? It's very cold, come into my cabin please you will find it much warmer. I will bring your husband in shortly."

Polly welcomed the woman and made her some coffee, but the poor woman's hands were shaking so much that she had difficulty in holding the cup. Aaron returned to the deck and found Hargreaves.

"Go to my cabin Hargreaves, Polly wishes to see you about some supplies."

"Aye, aye Captain." The man touched his cap and wrapped his heavy coat around his body, "It's Bloody cold this morning Captain, I'll be glad to get back to the tropics... never thought I would ever want to see Australia again but that is about the only thing I miss – the beautiful hot weather."

He tapped on the cabin door and heard the familiar voice of Polly bidding him to enter. He stopped dead in his tracks as he opened the door and saw his wife and son standing at the opposite end of the cabin. She rushed to his arms and smothered his face in kisses as the boy hovered to one side with tears in his eyes, catching hold of his father's hand. Polly beat a hasty retreat.

An hour passed before they re-entered the cabin, where it looked as if the three of them had been crying.

"You will have to excuse us Hargreaves," said Aaron, rather embarrassed, "but we must get ready to go out. I am afraid business still has to go on... stay here as long as you wish. Polly has to go and see those damn dressmakers and I must see my agent. We will be away for a few hours so you are welcome to make yourselves at home." He winked his eye at Polly, "Look Hargreaves, I need an escort to carry something very valuable. Would you mind if I took your son along with me, he looks as if he can look after himself." He put his hand on the boy's shoulder, "They call you Nelson, don't they son?"

"Yes sir, sorry... it's a very common name now, everybody seems to name their son after the Admiral."

"Yes I met him you know. I once did a little job for the Navy. I can tell you he was a very decent fellow..." Aaron had his arm around the boy's shoulders as they left the cabin and he nodded to Polly as if to say, 'Hurry and leave them alone.'

Hargreaves followed his son and Aaron on deck while Polly got changed.

"Why does it always take so long for a woman to get ready to go out Hargreaves?"

"I don't know Captain, I haven't had much experience for the past ten years." They both laughed as Polly came out of the cabin.

"Right Hargreaves," said Aaron, "I'm sure you and your wife have plenty to talk over and I doubt if we will be back much before nightfall – there are two bolts on the door."

He gave a knowing smile, "Thank you Captain."

Aaron chose the same carriage he had the previous day, "To the jewellers my man."

The man stopped at the door which had now became familiar to Aaron, "Wait here lad, keep the man company."

"What is this place Aaron?" Polly asked as he knocked on the shabby door. "It don't look much to me."

"Wait until you get inside."

The panel slid back and the old man beamed as he recognised Aaron. He slid open the bolts and held the door while they entered, Polly whispering, "It don't look that good inside neither."

"Shush Polly! Just wait and see. I will show you the most beautiful thing you have ever seen in your life."

She giggled, "I've seen it many times Aaron."

He smiled and slapped her wrist, "Behave yourself Polly or I will make you wait outside."

The room was very warm and the fire roared up the chimney as the old man drew up two chairs and poured out three glasses of port, "Your good health lady, and you too Captain."

His two sons entered the room, each with a velvet box in their hands. Polly could hardly take her eyes off the dwarf as he climbed on to the chair, Aaron kicking her under the table in warning; but the dwarf was used to being humiliated, "Don't worry Captain, I'm sure the lovely lady does not mean to be rude. There are not many men of my size and when I do venture out, which is very rare, people stare at me. I am quite used to it."

But Polly had taken a liking to the man and stammered out her apologies. He held up his hand and opened the first box. She gasped, almost swooned, and it was a few moments before she found her voice, "They are so beautiful sir... my God." She took a large sip of her port, her throat dry, and her hand shaking as she lowered the glass from her lips, "Don't tell me these are thee rough stones we had on the ship, Aaron?"

"Actually... no Miss. These are." The dwarf opened the other box and laid it down beside the necklace Polly had just inspected. It would have taken a real expert to tell the difference. The light from the fire reflected on to the diamonds bringing them to life with vivid colour. He closed both boxes and, after lowering them to his lap and shuffling them about, he placed them back on the table, "Now Miss... you tell me which are the real diamonds."

He began a little squeaky laugh that infected everyone in the room. Polly hesitated and coughed to control her laughter, then after sucking her index finger pointed bravely to one of the boxes, "This one – I think."

The little man gave another squeaky laugh, and shook his head.

"Sorry Miss – you have just chosen the glass duplicate."

233

He closed the box with a snap and opened the second box. "You now see Miss... the great difference, so if any gentleman gives you a cheap diamond you will know."

Aaron took the genuine necklace and hung it around Polly's neck, she fondled it carefully and a fly pitted mirror was brought in for her to look at.

"Oh Aaron, it is so beautiful." He went to take it away but she held his hand, "Let me wear it for a few minutes. please..." She twisted her neck to various positions, studying the necklace from each angle

"Well Captain, we need definite instructions. We believe we will soon have a potential buyer. A client with a very young wife – her heart is set on it. He is a Duke – that is all we can say, except that he has a brother-in-law, another Duke, and they are bitter rivals." He giggled like a schoolboy, "I have also sent the brother-in-law a copy of the picture – soon they will be bidding against each other and as usual it will probably end up with a dual." The three jewellers thought this very funny and the room rang with laughter.

Regrettably Aaron removed the diamonds from Polly's neck and replaced them with the replica, "Sorry Polly, I am afraid this one is for you."

Polly bent down and kissed the cheek of the dwarf then kissed his brother and father in turn, "It was nice meeting you gentlemen. I am sorry I couldn't have the real thing."

"Madam nothing could enhance that beautiful face of yours. The Captain is a very lucky man."

The carriage was still waiting for them. Nelson was sat patiently in his seat and brightened up when he saw them. Polly gave the driver orders to drop her at the dressmakers, while Aaron visited his agents.

It was quite dark by the time they returned to the ship, and Aaron knocked politely at the cabin door, hearing quick movements inside before Hargreaves undid the bolts, both him and his wife looking flushed.

"Very warm in here I see, Hargreaves."

A few minutes later Polly arrived at the cabin, along with the carriage driver and Nelson both fully loaded with several large parcels with which they had struggled up the gangway.

"The boy is good company Hargreaves and as I don't suppose you wish to sign on now, how would you mind my taking him on? He is a very clever boy. We had a great day out and went to a coffee house for dinner – he can certainly eat."

"Well Captain, my wife and I have been talking about this, and we do not wish to make any decisions either way just yet concerning our son. However I have decided, if you are agreeable, that I *will* sign on for another trip, my wife has been alone for so long she is almost used to it. Her brother has been very good to her and I intend to talk with him in the morning. I would then like to spend a few days with my family. If that is alright with you."

"Don't worry Hargreaves spend as much time as you like, we won't be sailing for at least three weeks. We have a cargo for Australia again, so it will be a long voyage – think hard on it."

Three days later Aaron received an urgent message from the jeweller to see him at once. The old man was waiting just inside the door when Aaron arrived for as soon as he did he heard the bolts slide open, "Good news Captain. The Duke I told you about – him and his brother-in-law were at loggerheads here yesterday, I really thought they would kill one another. My son managed to get the Duke up to thirty thousand pounds before his brother-in-law shot out of here in huff."

"Thirty thousand!" Aaron sat down hardly daring to believe it. This time the jeweller gave him a glass of brandy.

"Of course there is my commission and the cost of manufacture... but we did have a few chippings left and my son made this ring for your fair lady. This time you can tell her it's the real thing." He handed over a most beautiful ring.

"That is very kind of you sir, but how do you know it will fit her, she has a very tiny hand."

"Oh, it will fit her alright – you have no need to worry about that. My small son... he never took his eyes off her hand and I will tell you what I will do Captain; If that ring does not fit her precisely I will reduce my commission by one per cent."

Of course the ring fitted perfectly and filled Polly with pride, "Look Aaron I bought this beautiful dress today, I think it will go perfectly with my necklace."

"Yes Polly and you look a real lady, so tonight I will take you to the Opera and you can mix with the so called real ladies. Mind, not one of them can hold a candle to you."

At the opera that evening several ladies stared at the imitation necklace almost to the point of rudeness, but not one of them considered that it may have been an imitation. Aaron had ordered a private box overlooking the stage, and with her beautiful tan and blonde hair all eyes were upon Polly. However bored she may be, more used to the bawdy songs in the taverns and boisterous dancing than she was to the opera, Polly still enjoyed the attention she was given. Aaron was soon wishing it was all over, and almost fell asleep during the second act. Crowds had gathered in the foyer and as Polly gracefully came down the wide staircase all eyes were turned in her direction.

A Naval Officer came over to Aaron and held out his hand, "Aaron my dear friend how the devil are you, it's been a long time dear chap."

Aaron's forehead creased into a frown as he struggled to recognise the man, and there was an awkward pause before he realised who it was, "My God, Mr Saunders, how are you?"

Soon they were talking of old times totally forgetting their women friends, "So, Mr Saunders, how did things turn out?"

"I was with Nelson at Trafalgar. Hardy was with him when he died just after we had heard the great news that victory was ours. The casualties were dreadful, a real gory mess."

"But I see you are a Captain now, that was a quick step up the ladder wasn't it?"

"Yes, after Nelson died I thought that would be the end of my career, but my exploits on that French trip with you was all around the Navy and I soon got another ship *and* promotion. I think the fact that we had lost so many officers at Trafalgar had a bearing upon the situation. It meant rapid promotion," he modestly said.

It was then that they remembered their women friends, and Captain Saunders called his lady over, one of the most beautiful women Aaron had ever seen.

"Captain Jacobs... I would like you to meet my sister, Elizabeth."

Aaron was transfixed by her beauty, deep brown eyes that contrasted with a mass of red hair falling in waves and surrounding her small face, tiny nose and mouth.

"Elizabeth... this is Captain Jacobs. I have told you many times about him and our raid into France. The men in the lower deck never forgave him for rescuing Admiral Medlam, but he would not leave France without the rest of the prisoners, even though we were threatened with being put into chains."

Aaron took the outstretched tiny hand and kissed it gently, "Don't believe all he says Miss Elizabeth, your brother is one for spouting a good yarn."

Polly touched Aaron on the back and he turned, "Oh Miss Elizabeth... this is my friend Polly. Polly... this is Elizabeth and her brother Captain Saunders, we are old friends."

They walked outside together and stood talking, "You must come down home one weekend Aaron and stay with us, bring your friend Polly. You must meet my wife, she couldn't come tonight as we are expecting a new arrival. "

While Polly and Elizabeth walked behind together, Aaron was making up for lost time with Saunders, "My sister is a widow Aaron, her husband died in the West Indies from fever. He had a Frigate down there but the whole ship was ravaged with fever." He lowered his voice, "Mind you Aaron, he was a bit of a snob and I can't say I miss him that much – my sister is well off without him. My wife is staying down at Esher, my family have a large estate there, nice and comfortable and some good shooting. I like to get down there as often as possible. Why not pop down there?"

"I would love to but I have to prepare for a long run out to Australia in a few weeks time, perhaps the next time I land. It would be nice to have a decent chin wag again. I have my own ship now and about to purchase a second. "

"I knew you would do well Aaron, and I'm pleased to hear it; just sorry that we couldn't have kept together, perhaps when I finish with the Navy you will find me a berth. Who knows you may have a fleet of ships by then."

They took their leave at the corner of the street with Aaron promising to visit their country home the next time they were in England.

It was a cold and crispy evening. Aaron and Polly decided to walk back to the ship.

"What's the matter Aaron, you are very quiet. I think you have taken a fancy to the Captain's red-headed sister. She was very beautiful wasn't she, you would never dream she had a six year old son." Polly made a point of emphasising the last remark, and Aaron sensed that a tinge of jealousy had crept in.

He tried to pass it off with a laugh, "Don't talk so stupid Polly. Even if I did, do you think the likes of her would ever give me a second glance?"

But Aaron was not very convincing. He never spoke again until they reached the ship and helped a silent Polly up the narrow gangway.

Chapter Thirty

With a fortune in the bank Aaron set about finding another ship. A larger one than the *Golden Falcon* that could take a large cargo to anywhere in the world.

The driver of the carriage had been constantly in attendance at the quayside since they docked – Polly and the Captain were very good customers and always paid well with a good tip. He was there waiting patiently early one bright morning when Aaron strode purposefully down the gangplank and hailed him.

"Right my man I want you to take me to a shipbuilders' yard further down the river, do you know the one I mean?"

The man touched his cap, "Well sir, they're three further up river, all building large ships. Which one do 'ee mean?"

"First one we come to. But you wait for me outside, I will be wanting you all day today." This brought a rare smile to the weather beaten face of the hostler.

The first yard was rather quiet, which suited Aaron, he knew since the great victory at Trafalgar that the Navy had cut its ship building programme. The yard would be very keen to build a ship for Captain Jacobs.

The gates were wide open and as the carriage drew up Aaron jumped out and walked to the office.

A tubby little man rolled up and greeted him, "Morning sir."

Aaron acknowledged this, "Bit quiet aren't we Mister err.....?" As he hesitated, the man interceded, "Walker, sir."

"Ah! Walker... yes... I hear you build good ships here is that right?"

"The best sir! Most of the Naval ships are built here. Of course now the French are settled, not so many now. At the moment we have one for the East India company on our books and a small collier, but as a rule our slipways are full."

Aaron had a rough drawing of the ship he wanted built. He drew it from the inside of his coat and placed it on the office table, "Can you tell me approximately what a ship like this would cost?" And added quickly, "Of course I am only shopping around at this moment."

The tubby man studied the rough sketch, "Using it for slaving Captain?" he asked, giving Aaron a knowing wink.

"No I damn well am not! It's mainly for the Australia run; for cargo and for fare paying passengers."

The builder became agitated, fearing he had upset Aaron. Work was hard to find and he had already laid off half his workforce, "I meant no offence Captain. It's just that I want to know exactly what it will be used for, so I can draw up plans and build it to your satisfaction."

"Right then Mr Walker, draw up the plans and I will meet you again in three days time. If I am satisfied we will discuss a contract."

Aaron did not visit the other shipyards he was quite satisfied with what Mr Walker had to offer, he looked very competent.

He had given Mr Walker only three days to draw up plans and was pleasantly surprised when he returned to find the completed drawings of a very fine ship.

"You are surprised to see the plans ready Captain. To be honest with you – we need the work and we already had plans from ships we have built over the years so it didn't take my designers long to modify one to your requirements." He rolled out one drawing, a side view of the ship.

"Here you see, Captain... the cargo holds. Above and on the sides, cabins for passengers. We reckon you could carry about one hundred passengers in comfort – crowding them in a bit, maybe you could double that. Port side could be partitioned to take the more expensive, higher-paying passengers in self-contained cabins."

"Excellent Mr Walker, providing the price is right I would like contracts drawn up and delivered to my ship the *Golden Falcon* tomorrow in the afternoon. Mind, I don't want any work skimped."

"It won't be sir, we only do first class jobs."

The next day the contracts were signed.

"We should be returning from Australia in about six to seven months time, MrWalker – I have arranged through my bankers to pay the deposit required so there is no reason why you should not commence building immediately."

The shipbuilder nodded agreement and paused, "By the way Captain, have you a name for your new ship?"

"Yes Mr Walker, we will name it the *Golden Eagle*."

That evening, after dinner Aaron casually asked Polly, "I have to return to Portsmouth again in the morning, would you like to accompany me? I have to see my agent and lawyer. Also I need extra crew – old Harry at the tavern can usually find me some decent men."

"I don't think I want to go down there again Aaron, it only revives old memories and to see my old friends still working as prostitutes upsets me. You go down there Aaron, I have some shopping to do here."

"Well don't forget to leave enough room in the cabin for me to get into bed... when I get my new ship Polly you will be able to take as much clothing as you wish."

The coach which left the Seven Bells in Chelsea at seven every morning, was considered one of the fastest coaches in the land. Aaron was the first at the tavern, his idea being to make sure he had the most comfortable seat in the coach. Unfortunately the coach was draughty, the seats hard, and the roads themselves left a lot to be desired. Occasionally after managing to doze off, he would be rudely awakened by the large ditches that the coachman had failed to negotiate. At times, it felt to the Captain rougher than the worst storm at sea. They made several stops to change horses and partake of a meal but overall it was a long and dreary trip.

Aaron was somewhat relieved when the coach rose to the summit of Portsdown Hill overlooking the grand harbour and its many inlets. Ships lay at anchor, their masts like a forest of trees. The coach crested the hill for a few moments before making its descent into the great port. The old fortress at the far end of the harbour stood out plainly. It had been there since the Norman Conquest and in an ironic twist of fate had recently held French prisoners of war.

The streets of the old port were just the same as he had left them years before. They still smelt of rotting sewage – the occasional corpse of a dead dog or cat alive with fat and bloated rats feeding on them. Urchins with dripping noses, holding out filthy hands ran excitedly after the coach. It was hard to distinguish between girls and boys. Aaron had known what to expect and had a handful of coppers ready to throw out. Opposition to this from the rest of the passengers was totally ignored by Aaron as he sent the coppers scattering across the road with the dozens of scruffy and dirty children chasing after them, shouting and swearing at each other.

He walked into his special tavern, the one in which he had always met Polly, and at first the owner failed to recognise him. That is, until he ordered his usual brandy, "And none of that usual gut rot you serve up, my man."

"Sorry sir, we we haven't been able to get any really good stuff for some years now...." The words faltered in his mouth as recognition suddenly dawned on him, "Aaron bloody Jacobs – you swine... what the hell are you doing back here, someone told us you'd settled in Botany Bay, you *and* Polly."

"Come on mine host! Settle in Botany Bay... the only settling I do is on my own ship and that takes me all over the world. Botany Bay, yes, we go down there very often, that's why I've called to see you. I'm having a second ship built and will soon be needing another good crew. You know all the best seamen around here, keep your eyes open. I'll be back here in less than twelve months and will be signing them on."

Aaron spelt out the rules of the ship to the tavern owner, "I don't mind if a man likes a drink – I enjoy one myself. But I don't allow drunkenness on watch."

"Yes Aaron, it's all about how well you keep your ship and I doubt if getting a crew for you will be a problem. I will hand pick them myself."

Aaron's next port of call was to his lawyer and agent and he received the usual warm welcome from the clerk, " It is so nice to see you again Captain, I trust you are keeping well."

Before Aaron could answer the clerk had ran to the lawyer's office and tapping gently on the door, was greeted by a gruff voice shouting, "Enter."

He vanished inside and a few moments later showed Aaron into the office, holding open the door as he did so.

Mr Harris came round his enormous desk in greeting, "Captain Jacobs. So nice to see you."

The efficient clerk knew exactly what would be required and returned with a large folder, placing it before the lawyer who undid the ribbon holding it together. He studied the papers and looked directly at Aaron, " It seems we have had a very profitable year Captain, though it could have been better if you hadn't overpaid your crew. Look at these food bills – rather extravagant... fresh fruit, there seems enough here to feed all of Portsmouth."

"I beg to differ sir. So far I haven't lost one man through the dreaded scurvy or any other disease. Sure I pay them well but they would work twenty four hours a day if I asked them and they would follow me to the ends of the earth. No – what I have paid them has been returned tenfold and best of all I have a very happy ship. In all these years I have only had to put one man ashore."

"Yes, and you should have had that man up before a magistrate and imprisoned. Broaching the cargo – that's a hanging offence."

"Wrong again sir. Treat the men like animals and they behave as such. Now you handle my shore affairs and let me handle the ship – we have all made a good profit, yes all of us, and you haven't had to move from this desk. Incidentally – I am having a new ship built."

At this the lawyer looked up straight.

"Oh don't be alarmed," continued Aaron, "I am using my own money. It won't affect your profit."

"But this is a bit of a bombshell Captain, to say the least. As a small shareholder I would like to be kept informed."

"Well I'm informing you now. I am actively looking for cargo and paying passengers for the Colony of Australia. It's now October and with a bit of luck I will be ready for September or October next year. I would like you to carry out the advertising for me."

The Captain returned to the tavern for a night's bed following a rousing farewell celebration. All drinks had been on Aaron and the next morning a crowd much the worse for drink, were waiting at the coach house to give him a traditional Portsea send off.

Back in London, Webber the handler, was busy taking on cargo and laying in stores. Several cart loads of goods were waiting to be unloaded but Webber knew his job; it wasn't a case of first arrival to be the first unloaded – he studied each cart-load in detail so it could be displaced in the most efficient manner.

There were plenty of seamen crowding around the ship hoping for a berth. The news had spread of the humane way Aaron treated his crew, but his regular crew had all signed on again and Willie came to meet Aaron as he climbed the gangway.

"I'm a shade worried about old Walters, Captain. He is getting past it, coughing and wheezing like an old church organ, and some of the crew are complaining that they are carrying him."

"Are they now? You listen to me, we all have to get old Willie, that is the way of life and we have be tolerant. If anyone else complains send them to see me. At the end of next trip I will take him down to Portsmouth to Mrs Willis. She has a house down in Portsea, and for a few shillings a week she will look after him. Better sign on another man, nevertheless, but put old Walters on keeping the deck clean – let him take it easy this trip."

Adverse winds and some violent storms stretched the voyage out and it was eight months before they reached Sydney Cove. The ship was sighted at the heads leading into the great harbour and, the news soon spreading around the town, a large crowd of mostly women gathered at the quayside. They waved at Polly who was standing at the stern and the gangplank was hardly in place when the women, all dignity gone by the wind, rushed on deck chattering away like a waggon-load of monkeys. Polly brought out the consignment of dresses and laid them on the ship's rail for inspection. The women could hardly contain themselves as they fought for the dresses.

"Ladies, ladies, please!" Polly held up her hand, "Don't damage the goods, there are plenty for all of you and a news sheet for every buyer – the latest news when we left London."

Aaron could hardly hide his smile as he stepped down the gangplank and threw a glance in Polly's direction shaking his head slowly. How she had changed. She certainly had the women under her thumb and within a half hour she had completely sold out except for one dress which she kept by especially for Mrs Pilgrim.

Aaron called two men up from the wharf and asked them to carry a large timber board for him wrapped in canvas, as he made his way to see his agent. The agent gave him a warm handshake and removed the canvas wrapping to reveal in bold Old English writing :

Aaron Jacobs – Importer of Quality Goods

The agent smiled, "This must be the fanciest sign in the Colony, Captain."

Two days later the ship was ready to sail with a new cargo, so negligible it was hardly worth the time and effort to carry. Yet, it had still proved a profitable trip for Aaron and an exceedingly profitable trip for Polly. She now had a list of goods-required a mile long.

"I have been invited to spend a couple of days with Mrs Pilgrim,Aaron. Do you mind?"

"Well, we won't actually be sailing for a few days yet Polly. I intend to look around for some more return orders."

Aaron was saved the job when he saw Mr Mackie and his shadow striding up the gangplank. He didn't demean himself by shaking his hand, "Ah Captain. You will be returning to the Colony, on another trip?" Before Aaron could answer he thrust a long list of goods he required into his hand, "This is a list of my needs."

Aaron handed the list straight back to Mr Mackie and in a brusque manner informed him, "I have an agent to deal with these matters Mr Mackie." He pointed towards the warehouse, "See my agent," and abruptly turned his back on the man.

"I never deal with Jews Captain. I always go straight to the top man."

"Nothing at all wrong with Jews, Mackie. So called Christians could learn a thing or two from them." Aaron, by this time had dropped the 'Mister' bit, "I no longer deal with the general public; if you need goods, see my agent." The Captain, in no mood for an argument, headed straight to his cabin.

No love lost between the two men, Mackie followed him to the cabin protesting all the while, "Look I must have these goods.... else I will tell you this Captain! I will tell you that you.... will have difficulties. You will have trouble ever getting into this port again."

"Blackmail Mr Mackie. Influence have we? Now let me tell you something! I hate damn snobs! And I hate slavers! You are both Mackie. A snob and a slaver!"

"Slaver Captain? How do you make that out?" Mackie was flabbergasted.

"Did you, or did you not attempt to ensure that Brownlow received a further sentence of imprisonment on this colony. You accused him of escaping, when you know it was a put up job. The man even saved your life and you wouldn't see him free. You contented yourself with a whipping for the poor man. Free labour. Do you not call that slavery, or worse than slavery. If one of your men dies or is worked to death, you simply get another – free of charge. A slave owner has to pay for his slaves so it's in his best interest to at least feed them. Now get off my ship! "

Aaron's permanent smile turned into a burst of laughter, "Ask your wife what she will then do without her fancy dresses. It will be the last you get of you-know-what, from her."

"You disgusting animal...."spluttered Mackie, "...I won't be spoken to in this way..." He had always thought of himself as the most important man in the Colony.

Later that day Polly came into the cabin. Aaron was asleep on top of the bed, and she pushed his legs until he opened his eyes.

"Aaron, just take a look at this." She held out a bag and tipped the coins onto the table, most of them golden sovereigns. He sat up and rested on one elbow, blinking several times, "You certainly made it this time Polly, how much is there?"

"I made a profit of 300 pounds and I have a list here for double that amount. I have this idea Aaron; the agent said he could build me a shop next door to his warehouse. He did these drawings for me, won't that be nice Aaron?"

"Yes. But who will run it for you? You can't do that and all the buying in England."

"I've thought of that. Remember when we were in Portsmouth the trip before last? One of the girls in the tavern wants to get away from that life, she's a great seamstress and hates what she has to do to live. The agent gave me a list of items we will need for the shop; glass for the windows, heavy brass lamps... Do you realise Aaron this would be the first shop dealing entirely in women's clothes. It has to be a success, you only have to see how they react when they know our ship is about to dock."

"Well Polly, I have to hand it to you. Do what you like, you have my full support. When we have the other ship trading you will be in a position to bring in more stock."

Their conversation was interrupted when Jamieson and Hargreaves came down and knocked on the cabin door, "Captain, sir."

"What is it?" Aaron patted Polly's head and went to the door.

"I think you had better come on deck there are a couple of unhealthy looking men taking a keen interest in the ship. They have questioned one or two of the crew, asking when we are sailing, what the Captain is like and other questions."

Aaron went on deck and Hargreaves nodded to two men who were loitering around several bales of goods. As he looked at them they turned away, "Shouldn't worry too much, men, all the convicts here take a look at the ships, after all we will soon be sailing for England. Those poor bastards don't know when they will be returning. Just keep alert – Polly here is going up country for a couple of days."

Chapter Thirty-one

Mrs Pilgrim was waiting outside the homestead, news had reached her that a carriage was on its way and impatiently she tapped her feet as it came closer to the house. Visitors were few and far between out here in the bush and anyone was welcome, she was starved of news. Her face brightened when she saw it was Polly, she waved and Polly waved back and as she alighted Mrs Pilgrim put her arms round her.

"Well, Mrs Pilgrim, I have taken you at your word and have come to spend a couple of days with you."

"Oh Polly, that is wonderful." Tears of joy gathered in the corner of the woman's eyes, "You are as welcome as the flowers in May. My husband will be here shortly, he is out on the land at the moment. But I am so pleased to see you; before he returns let us get down to some real women's talk. Tell me, how is London looking? And tell me all about your experiences aboard ship."

"Hold on a minute Mrs Pilgrim... I've just arrived and I'm staying for two days. We will have plenty of time for talking."

"Oh I do beg your pardon Miss Polly. You see I am so lonely here with no-one to talk to, even my little Ju-Ju has gone walkabout. I haven't seen her for over a week and I think she is with child. I keep telling her to keep away from those convict huts."

Polly shrugged her shoulders. She had a wealth of experience concerning men; drunks and seamen who hadn't been ashore for years on end. Men cheating on their wives. No, there was very little Polly didn't know about that side of life, but she dare not let Mrs. Pilrim know. Their was only one man in her life and that was Aaron, even if her instincts told her it would not be forever. There had been a subtle change in him since being introduced to the red headed beauty. Aaron knew of Polly's past – as did some of the crew – and she felt deep within her a certainty that she and Aaron would never grow old together.

It was nightfall before Mrs. Pilgrim's husband returned and he was just as pleased to see Polly as his wife had been, "Stay as long as you like Miss Polly, we get so few visitors."

"Not if you keep calling me Miss Polly. Please call me Polly, I do hate these formalities."

Mrs Pilgrim left the room and returned a few minutes later wearing the dress that Polly had brought her, "What do you think of this Andrew, just fresh over from England, it's the latest fashion back home."

His eyes shone with pride as he stood up to take a closer look, "Bye... but it makes you look more beautiful than ever Beatrice; like the old times when we went to the Opera." He took her in his arms and oblivious to Polly sitting there, gave his wife a most passionate kiss. Polly smiled, she knew now why Mrs Pilgrim stuck to such a lonely life – they were still passionately in love.

Andrew filled a glass with brandy, "I will make my way to bed now Beatrice." He nodded to Polly, "I will leave you two alone, I know Beatrice is starved for women's company and you can talk as long as you like."

"Before you go Andrew, I was thinking of asking the Gilberts over tomorrow – we haven't seen them for over two months and I would like the opportunity of showing off my beautiful dress."

"Anything you say dear." He kissed her again, "Goodnight dear."

The Gilberts lived over twenty miles away and Andrew set off on horseback early the next morning. They arrived early afternoon and Polly was struck by the lonely life these settlers led, to see a new face was a pleasure that they seldom enjoyed. The Gilberts made a fuss of her and bombarded her with questions about London. Had she been to the Cotswolds? Mrs Gilbert talked about the old country trying to control the homesick tears welling up in her eyes, "Oh, I should love to see those dear Cotswold hills once more."

Her husband, a man in his early fifties and balding fast, just shook his head with indifference. Her children a daughter of seventeen with a face full of freckles, tutted and said, "If I had been born in a cooler climate, I wouldn't be disfigured with these damn freckles... just look at them Miss Polly, I am a freak."

"Oh no you are not, you know, they are quite charming. You will turn the boys' heads anywhere. The climate makes no difference – I have seen the prettiest girls back home and with a sight more freckles than you."

An elder brother, Samuel, who was about twenty, and six feet tall with a mass of curly blonde hair and piercing blue eyes, had never seen another seventeen year old girl – freckles or not. His shoulders were very broad and he looked like a man that could look after himself. He was reaping the benefit of the new country, holding a contract with the government for cutting timber which he sent down to Sydney Cove. He had also made several attempts to cross the Blue Mountains and was reputed to hold the record of penetrating that formidable barrier – further than any white man. During dinner his father, Andrew, had chided him on his attempts and said, "Those mountains will never be conquered."

"Oh yes they will Father, I reckon some of those Abbos know a route but won't let on. There's a fortune waiting for the first white man that does it and stakes a claim. I bet if someone started a rumour there was gold over there, the mountains would be conquered within days."

A joke nearer to the truth than he realised.

The dinner party went off well and the guests were left speechless when Beatrice changed and appeared in her new dress. When Mrs Gilbert and her daughter saw it they went into raptures and demanded that Polly, on her next trip, would bring them such a beautiful dress each.

"I will do better than that ladies, I am thinking seriously of opening a dress shop and milliners exclusively for ladies. The Captain is having a larger ship built and is making a permanent run to the Colony – bringing paying passengers. I am falling in love with this country – Although I doubt that I could ever stand the loneliness of country life."

The men retired to the next room while the women remained in the dining room. Mrs Pilgrim put her finger to her lips and brought out a bottle of port and four glasses, the four of them giggling like school girls, "You shouldn't Beatrice," Mrs Gilbert mockingly scolded her but didn't refuse a full glass. By the time they had finished talking and it was time for the Gilberts to return home the bottle was empty and the daughter was slightly the worse for drink – fast asleep on the sofa.

"Leave her here Mrs Gilbert. Andrew will bring her over in the morning. She likes that little mare we have, she can ride that."

Mrs Gilbert said to her husband, "Polly has been relating some of the experiences she has had on the ship... did you know the ship was attacked by pirates?" She was still chattering away when they boarded their carriage.

Polly and Beatrice stood waving to them from the drive, "Smell that fresh earth Polly, isn't it beautiful. In this bright moonlight you can see for miles."

Polly took her tearful farewell of the Pilgrims the following day and promised them she would visit again on the next trip, "It really has been a very pleasant time Beatrice. Believe me I will never forget your kindness." She made the man drive slowly back to the ship, "It's so pleasant here," she told him.

Later that afternoon she arrived back at the ship. The town seemed dustier than ever and rowdy. Convicts kept the streets clear of rubbish and builders and labourers were noisily about their business. Men touched their foreheads to her as she stepped daintily through the dockside trying to avoid piles of baggage and goods waiting either to be collected or shipped. She climbed the narrow gangplank and Gibbons and another seaman Fielding stood guard on

252

deck. "Expecting trouble Gibbons?"

"Not really Miss Polly, but you have to take precautions here." He smoothed the pick axe handle through his hands. "The Captain is in his cabin Miss Polly, he told me to tell you to go there as soon as you arrived. We hope to get away tonight."

Aaron was laying down fast asleep on the bed. As Polly entered the cabin, he sat up sharply, "Have a good time Polly?"

"It was beautiful Aaron, Mrs Pilgrim is such a lovely lady and last night she invited her neighbours round for dinner. It was fantastic, but they are very lonely people out there Aaron, and I don't think I could stand it for too long. They took me all over their land – you should hear those Kookaburras, laughing their damned heads off. There were all kinds of animals, big birds like ostriches, and some little cuddly animals they call koalas, as well as kangaroos. Mr Pilgrim reckons *they're* a pest. It was a very nice experience and I have promised to go again when we return."

"You had better go on deck Polly, we will be sailing in a couple of hours time. God it is damn warm today..." He strode on deck, where all the crew were at their posts. They had been away a long time, for longer than normal due to the difficulties of the outward bound voyage. By nightfall they were ready to sail.

"Prepare to sail Willie! We have a fair offshore breeze."

Slowly the gap between ship and shore widened, a small crowd had gathered at the quayside. *The Golden Falcon* was hardly three feet from the shore when there was a mad scramble as men rushed from behind crates and bales, violently pushing their way through the crowd. The ship's agent was knocked to the ground sending his steel rimmed spectacles flying across the quayside, stopping just at the edge, a foot from the water. Men jumped from the quay grabbing hold of the ship's rails, quickly scrambled on deck, some holding wicked looking knives in their mouths, others carrying man-made cudgels. The leader carried a hand gun in his belt, this he quickly brandished in Aaron's face, "Quickly now, Captain, get this ship as far away as possible or I will blow your brains out." He spoke with a refined Irish accent.

Aaron remained calm, "I can only go as fast as the wind can carry me, although I could do better if you took your damn arm from around my throat and that gun from my temple."

A shot rang out from the shore. It was all happening so fast, the ship now only ten feet from the shore. A man who had been clinging to the ship's rail, trying to get a foothold screamed out, threw up his arms and fell into the sea. A red patch spreading on the back of his shirt. The trooper who had fired the fatal shot was trying to reload when another trooper rode up and fired; another man clutched his arm and shouted to the Irishman holding the gun to Aaron's temple, "Shoot the bastard Riley."

The ship picked up an offshore breeze and began to move swiftly, in minutes they would be out of range.

"You have gathered that we are escaped convicts Captain. I want you to take this ship to the mouth of the Hawkesbury, from there we will pick up six more convicts then we will make our way to the Irish coast."

"I can't do that. Firstly I have no charts for the Irish coast and we only carry enough food supplies to take us to the Cape – we replenish there."

"My understanding is that you do have enough food and water. All you have to do is get us within a mile or so of the Irish coast. I suppose you do know where Ireland is. Get us there and I promise you no harm will come to you or any of your crew."

"But even if we could spread out the stores we don't carry enough water for such a long trip even for the crew, let alone extra men."

"Well let us pray for rain and when it does make sure you collect as much as you can. Ration it now – my men won't care about shortages, we are used to going around with empty bellies, nothing can equal the torture and abuse we have survived in this hell hole."

"But you are asking the impossible. There's not only the food and water, we must take into consideration the weather. A few days calm or a great storm could jeopardise the whole voyage. On occasions we have lain becalmed for days, aye and weeks, with the sea like a millpond."

"We'll take our chances Captain. From what we have gathered from around the docks you have the fastest ship afloat – if you can't get us there no-one will." He turned to one of his men, "How many made it Cooper?"

"Six sir, two were shot by the troopers."

"Right, search the ship and see if you can find any weapons, they must have some aboard."

The man returned a few minutes later roughly handling Polly, "Found ourselves a nice wench Riley, my God she is something."

Aaron pushed the gun away that Riley was holding to his temple, "Take your filthy hands away from my wife."

The man laughed and caught Polly round the waist, pulling her closer to him. But he hadn't reckoned without Polly's spirit – she was quite used to handling drunks and louts. She had momentarily stopped struggling and when Cooper thought he had her at his will she brought her knee up sharply between his legs. As he curled up in pain she belted him across the back of his neck with the side of her hand. The crew and convicts alike burst out laughing.

Aaron put his arm around her to comfort her, "Are you alright Polly?" For an answer she turned and kicked the man again.

Riley walked over to the man, caught him by his collar and lifting him to his feet he pushed him against the ship's rail with his head bent over facing the water, "Cooper you are an ignorant man. How do you expect the co-operation of these men if you show no respect? See this water below?" He forced the man's head over the rail, "If you dare touch this lady again or fail to act in a civil manner towards the Captain and the crew you will be going over the side to feed the fishes. Is that understood?"

Cooper muttered something inaudible and Riley shook his head, "Say it louder so that everyone can hear, and apologise to the lady and her husband the Captain." He shook the man's head, "Louder!"

"I am sorry lady and you Captain. It won't happen again,"

"Right. Branagan, search the Captain's cabin and see if

you can find the guns."

But Aaron interrupted him, "There are two, I will get
them for you. I don't want my cabin ransacked."

Branagan was ordered to accompany the Captain to the
cabin and returned carrying the two guns, one of which he
handed over to Mitchell another of the escaped convicts.

"From now on Captain your wife will be treated as a lady
and no harm will come to her." Riley turned to Polly, "I,
too, am very sorry for what has happened madam, you
may rest assured there will be no recurrence."

They were passing between the heads and out into the
open sea, the ship was picked up on the surf, and a couple
of convicts lost their foothold as the ship bucked and
rolled. Riley looked around to make sure no-one had followed them. As the ship picked up speed, Riley looked
pleased, "It would seem we chose the right ship Captain,
her reputation for speed is well founded."

"You don't stand much chance of getting away with it
Riley, as soon as they recover and realise what has happened they will send the Royal Navy after us. I noticed
there were three or four Naval vessels anchored in the
harbour."

"We must take what chances we have Captain." He looked
at the ship's wake stirring into a white foam, "I doubt if
the Navy has a ship afloat that can catch this vessel." He
said it with a satisfied smile on his face and looked around
the faces of his fellow convicts, "It looks like Butler was a
casualty. Pity, he was the only one that knew anything
about navigation. Still, if the Captain does everything
expected of him we have nothing to worry about."

Aaron's mind had not been entirely idle. If the dead man
Butler had been the only convict with a knowledge of navigation, and they happened to run into a violent storm it
could disable the convicts with sea sickness. Also – on such
a long voyage – there would be moments when they would
become reckless. Better to play along and try the soft soap,
he was good at that.

Riley sat on an upturned box next to the wheel. Aaron had
to raise his voice to be heard above the noise of the sea and
brisk wind, "Of course Mr Riley you do realise I suppose

that boarding a ship makes you pirates and they hang you
for piracy."

"Far better to be hanged than to live an existence as a
slave in that hell hole. Eight long years have been torn
from my life and they expected me to die there. Frankly
Captain I would much *rather* be dead. I have been planning this since the day I arrived... chained like a dog,
kicked and humiliated, fed on stale bread and water. No
Captain death holds no terrors for me. Tell me, do you
believe in heaven and hell?" Aaron nodded, "Well I have
just passed through hell so I only have heaven to look forward to. It is worse than slavery here. Slaves cost money
– convicts cost nothing... you die, they replace you the next
day. You work from sun up until sun down, and like a dog
you are chained to the wall in some damp stinking hole.
Then there are poisonous spiders and snakes and every
vermin under the sun. My boss, he had a fine house built
with the cells below – all built with convict labour. When
he had guests he brought them down to the cells to watch
us chained to the walls. If he happened to be the worse for
drink he would show off, kicking and beating us until the
blood ran, and him a Catholic like myself and a fellow
Irishman. Can you believe it Captain? A Catholic treating
another Catholic like that, then the man had the audacity
to attend Mass every Sunday and ask for the forgiveness of
his sins. From the day of my first flogging I became a fully
fledged Atheist. Six of my fellow convicts escaped and
became bush-rangers, they have a high price on their
heads, having killed two troopers. They will be waiting at
the Hawkesbury for us."

Aaron let the man do most of the talking, by the sound of
his voice it was easy to tell he had been well educated. He
agreed with him on every point – he must at all costs gain
the man's confidence. But life in the Colony must have
been hell for a man of his upbringing, "What I don't understand Mr Riley, is what a man with your apparent fine
background can have done to get sent to a place like this?"

Riley laughed, "To tell the whole story Captain would
stretch the length of this voyage. I am not making excuses,
I killed a man. Frankly I should have been rewarded, he

was a brute – a filthy drunken brute, my stepfather. My own father died when I was quite young. He owned a stud farm in Southern Ireland and when I was eight years old my mother married again. For the first few years everything went well, he ran the farm, made a fuss of me... that was, until he realised that when I became of age the farm would revert to me. From then on he started on my mother trying to persuade her to make everything over to him. She refused, and the more she refused the more violent he became. Then one day he struck my mother in front of me, I was almost twenty at the time and in another year the farm would be mine. One of our servants told me he gave my mother regular beatings."

"He was in the stable one day, and I told him to his face that if ever he struck my mother again I would kill him. He was a very big man much taller than me, and he laughed in my face. I just hit him as hard as I could, he staggered backwards and fell into the straw, unfortunately – or fortunately – there was a large pitchfork just below the surface of the straw. He fell back on it and I saw the prongs come out of his chest. I was arrested and taken before the magistrates – I explained I didn't intend to kill him, but one of the stable lads had heard me threaten to kill him. There was still an element of doubt so they reduced the charge to manslaughter, but that didn't stop them from giving me hard labour for the rest of my natural life. It would have been more humane if they had hanged me."

"My first few years out here I was sent out on the road gangs, breaking stones in the quarry – that is no fun Captain, when you have heavy chains around your ankles." Riley lifted his trouser leg to reveal a red band two inches wide and scarred from the continual chaffing, "Then they asked if anyone had knowledge of horse breeding. Believe me I stepped out of the pot and into the fire, stone breaking was a picnic compared to what was in store for me. The man I was sent to was illiterate and when he realised I was educated he took the greatest delight in humiliating me in front of his so-called friends. What needled him was that he had never been really accepted by

258

the social climbers. Social climbers! That's a laugh, most of them would never have got through my front door back in Ireland. Anyhow... for what it's worth Captain, that is my story in a nut shell. I must warn you, by fair means or foul – I intend to get away from this place."

259

Chapter Thirty-two

The *Golden Falcon* hugged the coast as close as Aaron dared, and they could hear the surf pounding the shore. Riley sitting next to the Captain, and never leaving the wheel once.

"You had better put one of your men at the stern, Mr. Riley," said Aaron, "I have no doubt that the alarm has been sounded and they will be chasing after us. I believe your story and you have my deepest sympathy, but taking my ship from me is nothing short of piracy and they won't give up the chase. You know they are still searching for the *Bounty* mutineers and have scoured the Pacific."

"I will try and get you to Ireland but it will be a long and tough voyage. But you must control your men – if any of them should lay a finger on Polly or harm any of my crew I will personally kill them with my bare hands."

Aaron looked Riley straight in the eyes. The scar on his face became livid, standing out prominently on his weather beaten face.

"You have had my word Captain. If any of my men dare to touch or interfere with your crew or your wife, I myself will kill them."

Aaron examined the crude chart that Riley had given him and posted several men to look out for the estuary. Hargreaves, who had lived in the Colony for years, had some idea of its whereabouts and was the first to spot it. He pointed, "There she is Captain."

Aaron was forced to tack several times until he came

within hailing distance and dropped anchor, "It would be suicide to try and get closer Riley, not only will the ship be in danger but so will every soul aboard."

"Well in that case Captain you will have to get the ship's boat out and row ashore."

"Sorry Mr Riley, none of my men will take that boat ashore, not in this surf. Your men will have to take it."

"They know nothing of boats Captain. Maybe Wells and Tomlinson know a little, but it will take more than two men."

"I will help to row them ashore Captain." Gibbons stepped forward followed by Menzies, "It's a bit tricky but we will do our best sir."

The ship's boat was lowered and the four men, two crew and two convicts manhandled the oars. Aaron watched through his glass as they negotiated the surf. A gigantic wave picked up the boat like a piece of flotsam as it slid out of view before reappearing a few minutes later, and everyone sighed with relief. This happened several times before the boat side-stepped the current from the river and ran up onto the sands.

"There is movement behind those tufts of scrub Mr Riley..." commented Aaron peering through his eye glass, "... there are nine men. Hang on there... one of them is a black fellow, an Aborigine."

"That's strange," Riley went to the ship's rail and studied the shore, "could be one of Oldfield's friends... he's very friendly with the natives and can speak a fair bit of their language."

The black fellow was left ashore and they watched with bated breath as the boat's crew fought again with the surf, making several efforts to beat the huge waves before finally shaking itself free and into calmer waters. It had been a hard, long row and the boat's crew had their backs to the ship. One of the convicts watching the progress of the boat which was now less than fifty yards away suddenly screamed out, "It's not them Riley!"

The words were hardly out of his mouth when a shot rang out and he screamed as his hands clawed the air. Another convict ran to his aid and several more shots rang out in quick succession. Two more convicts fell mortally wounded. Another convict raised his arms, "Don't shoot, don't shoot."

Aaron grabbed Riley and shoved him into the small wheelhouse. There were several pieces of old canvas kept there which he used for lashing around his back when the weather was bad, these he threw over Riley. The ship's boat banged against the hull, and Aaron welcomed aboard the leader, a Naval Lieutenant wearing a convict's coat over his shoulders in disguise.

"I am Lieutenant Chambers. Two of my men here are troopers the others are Naval. We have followed six convicts for several days to this point, using Aboriginal trackers. There are six more of my troopers ashore guarding the convicts." He looked round the ship's decks, "Where is Riley?"

"He dropped this gun," answered Aaron, handing the officer a service pistol, "before jumping over the side. He shouted that he would never return to Sydney alive. We did not see him surface again. Still, it will save you a trial, eh?" Aaron laughed to make the story more convincing.

"More likely he has been eaten by the sharks," commented Lieutenant Chambers, "the sea is infested hereabouts. You didn't see any signs of blood rising to the surface, I suppose."

"No, not a sign. He just vanished out of sight, hardly heard a splash when he hit the water, but I don't give much for his chances, we've sighted several sharks ourselves since leaving Sydney Harbour. I wouldn't like one of those buggers nosing around me in the water." He shuddered slightly.

The officer caught the remaining convict by his collar and hauled him against the ship's rails, "Get in that boat you bastard," he pushed the convict over, and his leg catching between ship and boat, he screamed in pain, "you will scream some more when they adjust the rope around your neck. We will make you regret you didn't receive the same fate as your associates." He kicked the first body, then ordered two of the troopers to throw them overboard, but Aaron stepped in.

"No, leave them, every man is entitled to a decent burial, I will bury them at sea and give them a Christian send off."

"Suit yourself Captain. I regret you will have to return to Sydney. We have to make statements for the enquiry and no doubt you will have to attend the trial. There will be a lot of questions asked about this. You had better send a couple of your men back with us to return your ship's boat." He shook hands with Aaron, "Good luck Captain, see you back in Sydney."

Polly came out on deck. She had locked herself in the cabin when she heard the shooting thinking the convicts had taken control of the ship, "What is it, Aaron?" She was happy to see him standing at the wheel, "Have the convicts left ?"

"Not all of them Polly, we have their leader hidden in the wheelhouse." He pulled the canvas away to reveal Riley hunched up in a ball, "Alright Mr Riley, you can come out now. I am sorry, but we have to return to Sydney. The officer appeared to be satisfied that you had drowned and become shark's meat. When we arrive in the harbour you must stay hidden and whatever you do, don't appear on deck. I will get two of my men to make some room for you in the hold, it will be hell down there, but we will try and make you as comfortable as possible. As soon as I have made a statement giving my side of the story we will make our way back to England. Now I can either put you ashore on the Cornish coast or you can come right round to London. Cornwall is usually alive with Revenue men so it may be advisable to return to London. Sorry about your men, we will bury them at sea later. Is the last man they took likely to say anything about your disappearance?"

"Not him Captain, he probably believed your story and will mourn my passing. Do you know, I almost believed it myself – I had to pinch myself to see if I was still alive."

That night Riley sat down to the best meal he had had for years, Willie joining them as he often did. The convict lay back in his chair as Aaron filled a clay pipe for him. He patted his stomach in contentment, "Ah yes Polly, that was the most beautiful meal I can remember in an age... something like I used to enjoy back in Ireland and have dreamed about since. In this God forsaken land, we most times ate kangaroos."

Polly pulled a face, "Oh those beastly animals, they look more like large jumping rats." Curiosity getting the best of her, she quietly asked, "What did they taste like?"

"Not too bad really, the meat is inclined to be a bit dry and lacking in fat. But the tails make pretty good soup – like everything else, alright once you get used to it. We did have mutton occasionally, if the boss found one of his sheep dead in the paddock. He would throw us the carcass ... heaven knows what they died of but it tasted very good."

They held a burial service for the two convicts and Aaron read the service, the bodies wrapped up in sailcloth and weighted down. Sharks had been following the ship all evening and throughout the night. The Captain sighed thinking it would not be very long before they ripped the canvas apart and tore at the bodies.

It was with relief that they sighted the heads and ran straight into the harbour dropping anchor a few yards from the quay. Aaron was rowed ashore and returned to the ship in a not very pleasant mood. Expecting to have signed an affidavit and hoping to get clearance, instead he was ordered to wait for the trial. If it was anything like the slow arm of the law back home and they could expect to be in Australia for months.

"Don't worry Captain, justice is swift here and there will be a great public hanging. There has to be a lesson to the other convicts, and we are already working on a multiple scaffold. It will be a show trial, and then they will hang." The officer of the Court made a gesture with his hands tying an imaginary rope around his neck and pulling it tight until he poked his tongue out and held his head to one side, his eyes opened wide.

"Well if it is cut and dried and the verdict already worked out, why the bloody hell do they want me to linger around for, I have a long voyage ahead of me."

"They have to make it look good and give a fair trial Captain, we can't have people going around saying we are barbaric." The officer looked around the clean office then poured himself another rum from a bottle on the table.

As predicted, by the end of the week Aaron was summoned to the Court to give his evidence. The dejected men answered their names in turn, well aware of the final outcome of the Court. The first six men had their charges read out 'that they did escape from lawful custody some six months previous with the intention of stealing a ship to return to their homelands. For six months they lived in the open bush as footpads and highway robbers, stole several horses and in their nefarious trade killed two troopers going about their lawful business. They then connived with Riley, now deceased, to escape from the Colony.'

The convict who had been left aboard and the two who were captured when they rowed ashore were now charged with piracy. Aaron was called to the witness stand to give his account of the crime.

"When the prisoners boarded were you already at sea?"

"Only just sir, I suppose at the most we were about three feet away, it was all over so very quickly. The first I really knew about it was when I heard a shot ring out and one of the convicts squealed. Before I could take any action we were overpowered. I was alone with just one member of the crew, the others were at their posts preparing to leave the quay."

The Judge turned to the Naval adviser sitting next to him and held a whispered conversation.

"And the convict Riley, Captain. You say, in your statement, that he jumped overboard when the troopers boarded your ship. Yet Sullivan, another convict, never heard a splash nor did he see him jump."

"I don't doubt that, sir. When Sullivan heard the first shout from the small boat he began shivering with fright. I doubt if he heard a word being said, he was more concerned with his own life as no doubt, if I were in that position, I would be scared." A ripple of laughter went round the small dark court room.

"What did Riley say as he jumped overboard? You claim he said he would rather die than return to Sydney."

"He made this statement more than once during the voyage down to Hawkesbury. I should say that the Irishman was at the end of his tether – what he said, he really meant. He was a well educated man and his imprisonment must have been a damn sight harder on him than an ordinary convict. Riley guessed his number was up and although he was handling a primed gun he made no attempt to fire on the oncoming boat."

"Are you absolutely certain that Riley could not have hidden himself aboard your ship, these are very cunning fellows Captain?"

Aaron's face twisted into a wide grin, "No sir, my ship is small as far as merchantmen go, there would be absolutely nowhere for him to hide. I heard a splash and ran to the rails but there was just a circle of white foam, he never surfaced. The officer that came aboard said he would probably be shark's meat, which strangely was another of Riley's sayings, 'I would sooner be shark's meat than return to that hell hole'."

"From what you tell me Captain you had many conversations with this man Riley. Tell me, how did you find him?"

"A very agreeable fellow, a good conversationalist, well read and very witty."

"He was also a murderer." The Judges eyes sparkled and he pointed his quill pen towards Aaron to ram the point home.

"So the law says – but I prefer to believe his story. No man, especially a gentleman like Riley, would stand aside and see his own mother beaten and abused by a drunken bully like his stepfather. I certainly would not and I am sure a gentleman like you sir would not."

"That is beside the point, we are not sitting here giving Riley a new trial, he was a murderer and judged so by a Jury of his own countrymen."

"There must have been some element of doubt or they would have hanged him there and then. As it was they brought in a verdict of manslaughter."

The Judge glared at Aaron, coughed and rather belligerently raised his voice not taking kindly to Aaron's inclination to defend the convict, "We have a case of piracy here Captain, and that is according to your own deposition. Thank you for your evidence, you may step down but your ship must remain in port until the case is completed."

Aaron guessed it wouldn't take long as the verdict was cut

and dried, a foregone conclusion. The Court was simply a showpiece – a lesson to other convicts in the Colony that it was stupid and foolish to try and escape. A week later the survivors of the failed coup were hanged in public.

Aaron was given clearance to put to sea, much to the relief of Polly and his crew. Everyone sympathised with the convicts, most of them realising, 'There but for the grace of God goes I'.

Chapter Thirty-three

Well clear of the harbour and safely out to sea Riley emerged from the hold and stared at the receding shore line, hardly daring to believe he was away from it.

"I sympathise with you Mr Riley," commented Aaron, "being stuck down that hold all this time. I once had a cubby hole in a tavern where I used to hide when the pressmen were active. If they had disbelieved my story and found you down there, I would have been hanged alongside of you."

Riley gave a throaty laugh, his Irish eyes sparkling, "To get away from that place I would have stayed in the hold for the remainder of the voyage to England."

"Right then, tonight you will dine with us in my cabin, and tomorrow you will join the crew. I'm afraid you are going to have to work your passage – in addition you will be paid the going rate."

Riley tried to protest but Aaron held up his hand, "This is not a slave ship Riley when you work for me you work for money but I have certain rules you must abide by."

He went through the rules in very fine detail, "The most important thing is every day you will eat an orange, a lime or a lemon. In all the years we have been at sea we have never lost a man through scurvy or fever. We always keep fresh fruit aboard, they are the first stores we buy when we reach a tropical port."

"Every night between five and eight we hold a school for

Willie and Hargreaves, they are studying navigation.
Hargreaves will be taking over this ship on its next voyage
as I am having a larger ship built which should be ready
when we get back in London."

"Your crew are very lucky, Captain." He held up his glass
and continued, "May I give a toast both to Willie and
Hargreaves, and to you Captain for giving me my life and
my liberty again."

There was no resentment shown in Willie's face knowing
that Hargreaves would take over the ship as he hoped to
be sailing with Aaron on the new ship. He still had a lot to
learn and was not so well educated as Hargreaves.

Riley settled down to shipboard life and didn't care what
he did to earn his passage home. The crew took to him
from the start and as he was scrubbing down the decks one
day under the sweltering heat he nodded to Willie, "It's a
pity Willie that the Captain intends to trade between
England and Australia, I could take to this life – especially
with a man like Captain Jacobs."

"I know what you mean Riley, I can understand what
Australia did to you. It's like Hargreaves, he never goes
ashore in Australia. Sometimes the men from Government
House come down to the ship to see him, but he will never
go ashore. The memories are too bad."

"I never knew that Hargreaves did time in the Colony. I
often speak to him in the crew's quarters but he never
mentions it."

"He wouldn't, he had only a couple of months to go to finish his time when someone in England confessed to the
crime and they released him. Mind you he will tell you he
had a cushy number out there – he was a clerk in
Government House, but it wasn't like freedom. One of the
Government chiefs came and asked Aaron to give him a
passage home, that's how he came aboard, but no, he never
goes ashore there. I don't think he likes to go on deck when
we arrive, he realises what some of those convicts go
through. As you know he has worked hard and studied
hard in order to take over this ship."

The *Golden Falcon* hit a violent storm in the Bay of
Biscay and it kept up all the way to the English Channel

only abating as they turned into the Thames Estuary. Polly had mastered her sea sickness and spent as much time as possible on deck standing at the forepeak allowing her blonde hair to blow back in the wind.

Before they docked Aaron called Riley into his cabin and took out his chamois leather bag, spilling gold coins on to the table. He counted out five and shoved them across to Riley, "This is your wages, Riley. I haven't worked out the bonus yet but I estimate it will be five guineas," he slid another five coins across the table.

Riley was deeply moved and tried to protest, "I can't take this Captain, I am happy to have my freedom."

"No-one works for nothing on my ships, you have worked very hard and you deserve this. I have discussed the matter with Willie and he said all the crew are in agreement with me, I don't want to hear any more about it. Now let's get our stories quite clear should you ever be recaptured – though heaven forbid that should ever happen. Your story must tally with mine or I might still end up dangling from the end of a rope. If you are ever found out, this is what you must say. You must tell them that when the troopers and sailors came aboard the *Golden Falcon* there was a lot of commotion. You dropped over the side and swam for shore. There you fell in with a black tribe who looked after you, until you saw an American whaler at sea and paddled after it in a native canoe. They took you aboard – make it convincing – say you had been living almost naked and the American crew thought you were a native until they heard you speak. Tell them most of the American crew were of Irish descent and when you told them your story they believed you and helped you to get completely away. You eventually arrived in Boston, before making your way into Canada. From there you worked your way back to England on a merchant ship. Do you agree that this sounds feasible?"

"Yes Captain, and you can be assured I will never, ever say that you conspired to help me."

"Now I want you to stay in the crew's quarters when we dock, and tonight after dark we will take you ashore. The men have collected some clothes for you, and Polly has prepared bread and cheese and a bottle of wine to see you on your way. I don't want to know where you are going, that is entirely up to you, but if you wish to see your mother do it straight away. They will not have heard of your escape as yet, that will take a couple of months. I doubt if I will have much time to say goodbye after this – it is always a very busy time when we reach port." He held out his hand, "Goodbye now, Riley and the very best of luck. You have been a very good crewman."

That night Riley was rowed ashore by Willie and another member of the crew and vanished in between the dark grey buildings, carrying his spare clothing and food in a bundle over his shoulder.

The next morning Aaron was greeted by his agent with the news that the *Golden Eagle* was ready, "It's the most magnificent thing you ever saw Captain. It looks like a triple decker warship but far more colourful, and the cabin for yourself and your good lady would grace any noble home with its own small galley, a table that will sit ten people and its own toilet facilities."

"We will be going down to see her tomorrow," answered Aaron matter-of-factly, handing the agent a long list, "In the meantime I require a cargo for the *Golden Falcon* we had a bit of a delay in Australia – make sure these supplies go aboard, they are for Polly's fine ladies. She takes dresses over there for them, 'though I can assure you there is no finesse about them when you see them squabbling for the dresses in my cabin."

Aaron and Polly wasted no time getting to the shipyard the next morning. The *Golden Eagle* was standing proudly in a very prominent part of the shipyard, at first glance Aaron held his breath and whistled through his teeth.

"Just look at her Polly, have you ever seen anything so magnificent?" As if in a dream he walked slowly towards it, as the builder came out of his office his hand stretched out in greeting.

"What do you think of her Captain?" But it was several moments before Aaron could answer, and even then only with a shake of his head and some unintelligible mutterings.

He scrambled aboard and looked from stem to stern, "It looks much larger than I imagined... I hardly expected to see it finished in time. You have done wonders Mr Walker."

"To be honest Captain, the hull was already completed at our other yard. It was meant for the Navy but after Trafalgar they cut down their ship building programme, so I converted it to your requirements. The interior design is exactly how you wanted it – the great cabin at the stern, which was intended for an Admiral, I have converted into spacious living quarters for you and the good lady, with its own small galley, pantry and toilet facilities."

He led them below the upper deck where partitions had created small cabins each no more than six feet square, with a middle sized bed that folded against the wall when not in use. The stern part of the deck was used as a dining and common room, the two lower decks were partitioned into several large dormitories.

"I have never fitted out a cargo passenger ship to such a high standard Captain. There will be no reason for anyone to complain about the conditions on this ship."

Aaron, of course, was years ahead of his time, the welfare of his crew and passengers was of paramount importance to him, "It's a very long voyage Mr Walker, and I have no doubt many of the passengers will be children. They will be paying good money and the least I can do is to treat them like human beings and not animals. I want it ready for its trials in two to three weeks time Mr Walker."

"That will be no trouble Captain, the sails are almost finished – just give me a couple of days warning."

And so Aaron's dream had finally come true, he could sail down the estuary with the knowledge that he owned a ship especially built for him, and above all it was paid for. He shook hands with Mr Walker and left to return to the *Golden Falcon*.

"Sit down Hargreaves." Aaron pulled out a decanter of brandy and filled both glasses, passing one to Hargreaves.

"Hargreaves, you have done incredibly well while you have been aboard. You have learned as much as I can teach you about how to run a ship and from today you will be the Captain of the *Golden Falcon*." Hargreaves stared at Aaron in disbelief.

"But Captain, what about Willie, he has been with you since he was a small boy. And the other members of the crew, besides all those sea faring men that are looking for work – there are ex-Naval officers on the beach, desperate for work."

"No Hargreaves I have talked this over with Willie. Firstly, he wants to come to the other ship with me and secondly, he is not quite ready for command. As for Naval officers, they only know how to run a ship using the rope's end and the cat. You know how I run a ship and I want it kept that way. We know your son now wishes to go to sea, and you may sign him on. You can also keep a few of the more experienced men. Gibbons is a good man, he has had plenty of sea time both Navy and Merchant. I will get you a replacement for Sam three more men." They shook hands.

Hargreaves went to the door and turned sharply, "My wife and I had not fully decided what I should do after this trip, Captain, she has waited so long..."

"I recommend you take her with you Hargreaves, I'm sure she won't mind." Aaron smiled and winked his eye, "After all, it's not much good letting a good bed go to waste."

Mrs Hargreaves was overwhelmed when she heard the news and hugged both her husband and her son, "So at last we will all be together once again. This is like a dream come true, I must go and tell my brother."

Next morning Aaron had business in Portsmouth and left early on horseback. It was going to be a long ride and he didn't like the idea of again travelling in an overcrowded coach. He stopped at a tavern at Esher for his lunch, remembering the open invitation he had to call on his old friend Lieutenant Saunders. He asked mine host where he could find the house – the family were rich landowners, well known in the area. Aaron was directed straight to Lieutenant Saunders' home, less than three miles from the tavern. The landlord held the horse's bridle while he mounted his horse, he touched his forehead, "Good luck to 'ee Cap'n, and watch out for highwaymen round here."

He found the path leading to the house, half-a-mile from

the main Portsmouth to London Road. He trotted around a
winding path and eventually entered a clearing. The house
stood aloof and directly in front of him, a pale sunshine
bouncing off the facade. It looked enormous. A young
woman and a child were playing on the lawn in front of the
house, where Aaron stopped. He hadn't realised that his
friend's family lived in such a palatial building, the
grounds stretching back for miles. The young boy looked at
him first and said something to the lady – she looked
round and waved at him. Aaron cantered slowly towards
her and touched his cap, "Morning madam, I was passing
and thought I would pay a courtesy call on your brother."

"I am so sorry Captain he was called to the Admiralty
only a few days ago, he has a command and will shortly be
off to South Africa and possibly on to Australia. But do
dismount, it strains my neck looking up at you."

"Very sorry Ma'am." Aaron dismounted and as he started
walking towards the house, a groom came running from
the side of the house and took the horse's bridle.

"Put this horse in the stable George." She ran her tiny
hand round the horse's withers, "We will give the Captain
a fresh horse for his return journey."

"That's very kind of you Ma'am... but do give me a gentle
horse I am afraid I am not a very experienced rider."

"For heaven's sake stop calling me Ma'am. You know my
name is Elizabeth and that's what I prefer. My brother will
be very sorry to have missed you, he is forever talking
about you and how you released those prisoners, refusing
to allow any to stay behind. How Admiral Medlam tried to
get you court-martialled because you refused. I know
Medlam and that ignorant son of his, we're related you
know – 'though not closely"

'Bloody hell,' Aaron thought, 'I've made made a mess of
this meeting.' But Elizabeth smiled, and Aaron tried to
blurt out some kind of an apology.

"Don't worry, the family hate them too. The young
Admiral has the most beautiful wife imaginable and he
treats her like dirt. I doubt if she will thank you for releasing him. During the time he was in captivity she was at
her happiest."

"It seems as if I have blundered all the way through. The officers I have spoken to all seemed to be in the same frame of mind."

"Do stay and have dinner Captain, it gets extremely lonely here – it would be nice to have company for a change. You can fill me in on some of your exploits, it must be nice to have such a beautiful companion travelling with you, she is a very lucky girl."

When he did manage to get a word in Aaron said, "I don't know about staying for dinner Elizabeth. You see I have to get to Portsmouth and to be honest I don't relish the idea of travelling in the dark. I wanted to get as far as Guildford tonight, or perhaps further."

"Don't worry about that Captain, we have fifteen spare rooms here. The least I can do is offer you accommodation for the night." She rang a bell and a few minutes later an elderly butler entered, "William, prepare a room for our guest, see that the fire is lit and a warming pan in the bed. It's very chilly at night, the Captain has just arrived from Australia and is sure to feel the cold. While you are here William, please draw that large chair up nearer the fire."

She started giggling, "I don't know what the neighbours will say, a young widow entertaining a man – and a seaman at that." The butler departed and a few minutes later a young girl came in and took the small child by his hand.

"Time for bed young man" she said, the boy kissed his mother then like a miniature gentleman shook hands with Aaron.

Aaron sat in the chair while Elizabeth poured out two glasses of sherry. They talked for two hours and Aaron related some of his exploits, she seemed absorbed when the butler returned, standing stiffly by the door.

"Dinner is served, madam." He led them to a long room adorned with paintings of all the Saunders' ancestors.

"Oh yes, Captain, those are all my ancestors – shifty looking lot aren't they? The one over the mantelpiece is my great, great... God I don't know how many greats, Grandfather. He was knighted by Queen Elizabeth, that's how I get my name. The eldest daughter in our family is always called Elizabeth. My brother always calls the house mine, but really it's his. He hates farming. Of course one day his portrait will hang on these walls. He also hates the idea of having to sit and have his portrait painted." Elizabeth gave a girlish giggle once more, and sipped at her sherry, "We had better take our seats else William will start sulking. Since my husband was killed he has kind of fathered me."

The dining table, made of highly polished oak could easily have seated twenty people. Elizabeth sat at the same end as Aaron, his chair next to hers.

While eating the sweet course her feet touched his and he quickly recoiled.

"I understand Captain in your smuggling days, that you imported a very fine brandy and are something of a connoisseur."

"Your brother must have been telling you a lot about me – please don't believe all you hear." Aaron took a sip of the brandy and nodded his head, "Well this is a nice soft brandy, French no doubt."

"Then you *are* a connoisseur, no-one else has ever told me that before. Yes, it is French, my brother knows a fisherman that brings it over."

Aaron felt a thrill go up his spine, her foot had made contact again, but this time higher up his leg, and he was about to move it when she looked directly at him. She turned to the butler, "You can go now William."

Elizabeth picked up the decanter of brandy, "Bring your glass with you Captain – or should I call you Aaron?"

"Please do, I hate being called Captain. It's nice when you are aboard ship but not very nice when you are in the company of a beautiful young lady."

She smiled as she leaned against his arm, "And a widow too Aaron. It is very lonely out here, I often wish I could settle in our home in London. There you have everything, theatre, riding in Hyde Park, a good social life and a round of Balls and parties. Alas I do have the farm to run, I only wish my brother could take more interest in it."

Aaron became increasingly aware of her close proximity and his pulse was racing. She wore a delicate perfume that aroused his feelings, and he soon discovered that she was a

very passionate woman. At first he thought it was the
brandy – she had drunk three glasses – but as she talked
he was aware that she was in possession of all her facul-
ties. She stood on her tip toes and kissed him, gently at
first but sufficient to arouse him. She was about to sit on
her chair, Aaron standing over her, when she pulled him
down – it was soon obvious that she had been starved of
affection and she kissed him again this time passionately.
Elizabeth was breathless as she stood up and catching his
hand she led him up the stairs and put her finger to her
lips. They began talking in whispers, his hand tightening
on her small hand. The bed was a heavily carved four
poster; quickly her dress dropped to the floor and her hungry lips found his again, her passion filling him with
undreamed of adventure. There could be no comparison
with Polly, who had been taught to make love from a profitable motive. Elizabeth was a willing partner and showed
him an experience that Polly could not dream of. They fell
asleep in each other's arms and when the watery sun fil-
tered through the large windows she shook him and whispered in his ear.

"You must return to your bedroom before the servants
rise." She giggled once more, "Did I disappoint you Aaron?"

"Good heavens no! It was a night I will never forget. A
most beautiful night."

"Well, Aaron, I hope it will not be be the last." She knelt
on the bed completely naked and again embraced him with
an undreamed of passion. Eventually he crept silently
along the carpeted passage and back to his room.

Elizabeth greeted him at breakfast and smiled, "I do hope
you had a good night Captain."

The butler looked sideways at them as Aaron answered,
"Very comfortable and warm. Unfortunately sleep did not
come too easily." While the butler's back was turned they
both laughed silently.

She then gave Aaron a conducted tour around the large
house stopping occasionally at the bedrooms – especially
the one in which they had spent the night. It was mid-
morning before he took a lingering departure. Elizabeth
had her own horse saddled and rode with him down the

long dirt road. Out of view of the house she leaned over
and again kissed him tenderly.

"We had better stop this Elizabeth," gasped Aaron, "before
I drag you off that horse and make love to you once more."

She answered with, "Promises, promises," and laughed
out loud.

"Will you call in on your way back Aaron? I think I may be
falling in love with you." She fingered the scar on his face
as he spoke to her in French, and answered fluently, "Well
Aaron if you really mean that, you will have to return
here."

He patted her knee and cantered away, turning again and
waving. Before he was out of sight, Elizabeth turned and
raced back to the house, to resume her lonely life.

Chapter Thirty-four

Aaron hardly noticed he had made it to Portsmouth, everything was obliterated from his mind except Elizabeth. He had stopped at no taverns and on seeing the great port laid out before him from the top of the hill he realised he hadn't eaten for several hours. He made for the George Hotel in the High Street and straight to the dining room where he ordered a plate of meat, thickly sliced, and a large tankard of ale.

Fed and washed, with a clean change of clothing he set about his business, making his way to his favourite tavern where he was warmly greeted by the proprietor. Aaron called over a street urchin, "Here boy, take the horse's bridle and when I come out I will give you a silver sixpence."

With a promise of a silver sixpence the boy would have been keen to commit anything short of murder, "That will be alright Captain, he won't get away from me." He gave a wide grin, hardly perceptible hidden as it was under a layer of dirt, and wiped his nose with the back of his hand.

Aaron walked inside the tavern with the landlord, "Did you manage to get me a good crew Harry? I only want the best."

"Surely Aaron, I could have gotten you half a dozen good crews and all very experienced. Once they knew it was you that wanted a crew I had no trouble at all."

"Right, I want them here first thing in the morning. I will need about thirty with several good top men amongst them and a couple of cooks. If you can find a couple who play musical instruments so much the better. Also a couple of men that can read and write, and if you know of any good officers that are on the beach, send them too."

"Don't worry Aaron, you will have the best and they will be here at eight in the morning. You can count on that." Aaron stood up to go back to his hotel but the tavern keeper put a restraining hand on his arm, "Take another drink before you go, won't you Aaron?"

He shook his head, "Sorry Harry I have been on the road for two days and hardly had any sleep and I'm about done in. So I will bid you good night, see you in the morning."

The little urchin was still holding the horse and Aaron sorted through his purse but couldn't find a sixpence, so he handed the boy a shilling.

"Hang on Mister I will go and get some change." Before Aaron could say anything the boy charged down the street clutching the shilling in his dirty hand and Aaron thought that would be the last he saw of him and started off to the George Hotel. He had just dismounted when the boy came running up out of breath and panting hard, "Here's your change mister," and held out the sixpence.

Aaron stared at it with disbelief. He knew what an extra sixpence could mean to these little urchins, a choice of a good meal or going hungry for another day.

"How old are you son?"

"Thirteen mister, well I think I'm thirteen." He drew the back of his hand across his nose, "And thanks for the sixpence sir."

He turned and was about to run off when Aaron caught hold of his arm, "Where do you live son?"

"Nowhere sir... well anywhere I can find a warm spot. Some days when I work in a tavern the boss lets me sleep in the cellar or in the bar and sometimes he gives me a meal or lets me eat the scraps. My mom threw me out when she found her new boyfriend."

How many times had Aaron heard the same story? It was just like Polly, and Willie, over and over again, "Have you ever been to sea boy?"

This seemed to frighten the boy and he tried to pull away. "No mister I always dodged the press gangs."

Aaron laughed and said, "I can understand that – just hang on here for a few minutes and hold my horse." He vanished into the hotel and returned a few minutes later, giving the boy two notes, "Here take this one to the little slop shop kept by the Jew in Queen Street – he is a great friend of mine, and this note give to the tavern keeper where you held my horse. I want you to get a good nights sleep. Tell them I will come and settle with them in the morning."

The boy turned and ran away shouting, "Thanks mister!"

In spite of taking several brandies and being absolutely worn out and tired, sleep would not come easy to Aaron. He lay awake thinking of Elizabeth and hardly daring to believe what had happened the previous night. He was sure he would wake up and find that it had all been a beautiful dream. And Polly, how would he break it to her? They had been together for so long now, he just could not imagine what life would be without her. Dawn was penetrating the room when he finally succumbed to sleep and it seemed an instant before the maid was knocking at the door, "It's seven o'clock, sir."

"Thank you." He washed and dressed quickly and went down stairs into the dining room to eat a hearty breakfast of thick slices of ham topped with several eggs and a large jug of coffee.

Along the old ramparts with the sea breeze refreshing him, Aaron walked to the tavern. A large crowd had gathered in front and he edged his way through, several of the men recognising him, "Morning Captain."

"Good morning men, I won't keep you waiting." The boy who had held his horse the day before was at the forefront of the crowd, all spruced up in new clothes, his face still sparkling from the cold water he had washed in at the back of the Jewish shopkeeper's yard. Aaron looked down at him, "I see you met my old Jewish friend then... gave you a good going over under the old water pump in his back yard did he?"

"Yes sir." The boy shuddered at the thought of the ice cold water.

"Well do you want to come and work on my ship then?"

The boy eagerly agreed, Aaron's friends had told him all about working on his ship and now it held no terrors for the boy.

"Well, get in the crowd with the rest of the men and take your turn." The tavern keeper had prepared a table and laid out a quill and ink and a large book.

"I will take them one at a time Harry," said Aaron, "send the first man in."

"Todd sir, fourteen years with the Navy sir as a top man." Aaron leaned back in his chair and studied him. He could usually learn a man's character by staring hard at him.

"Right take off your shirt and turn round." Apart from a small bruise and a birthmark the man's back was unmarked. "Can you read and write Todd?"

"Only a little sir," Aaron handed him a piece of paper and told him to read it, "These are my rules aboard ship, bide by them and you will return safe and sound. If you don't understand my rules completely, ask the landlord to read them out. If you are happy with them come and sign up."

There was hardly any need for the innkeeper to go into detail, everyone had heard how Captain Jacobs kept a good and happy ship. Each man in turn was told to become familiar with the rules and was told exactly what was expected of him. Some pulled a face when they learned they would be expected to eat an orange, lime or lemon each day and of the thirty that the innkeeper selected only one man was rejected – when told to strip and turn round, his back was a mass of criss-cross scars, evidence that he had been flogged on more than one occasion.

"Bit of a trouble maker are you Mr Weston?"

"No sir, not really. You know what those damn naval officers are like, you only have to look at them sideways and you can be flogged."

"Well I can understand that happening once Weston, but your back looks as if you've kissed the gunner's daughter on more than one occasion. Anyone who does that is a fool. I am sorry Weston I keep a happy ship and I want to keep it that way. Perhaps you can see me next time I am here."

"Sod you and your bloody job! You're no better than the navy rats."

Weston made a lunge at Aaron, who side-stepped and as the man stumbled across the table he bought the side of his hand down across his neck in a vicious chop.

"Don't bother to apply next time Weston." The tavern keeper and several men bundled Weston away.

The young boy was the last one in.

"What is your name, son?"

The boy gave a cheeky grin, "Tommy sir, Tommy Wright."

"Stand back son and let us get a good look at you. So, you think you fancy a job at sea... I will start you off as a cabin boy." Aaron turned to the tavern keeper, "I did ask for two boys Harry, do none of them of them fancy a job at sea?"

"After the horror stories these ex-sailors tell them and the way young powder-monkeys are treated, not many wants to go to sea."

Tommy' face broke into a broad grin, "My friend would like a job – he is not as big as me but he's strong and a hard worker."

"Right lad go and find him." The boy went to the door and poked his head out. He put two fingers in his mouth and let out a piercing, ear-splitting whistle. A few minutes later a bare footed boy came tumbling into the tavern breathless and panting like a dog. Aaron and the landlord both laughed, as they looked at the boy.

"You were not joking when you said he was small," commented Aaron, the boy stood there hardly daring to breath, his two bright eyes protruding through a freckled, unwashed face and a cheeky grin splitting his mouth.

"How old are you son?"

"Twelve sir." He gasped between pants.

"You look very small for twelve."

The boy shuffled on his feet and gasped out, "I am small sir, but I am very strong and I like work sir."

"Right, wipe your nose and let Tommy take you round to my Jewish friend. Make sure he gives you a good scrub down under his pump – and burn those bloody clothes! Tell him I will be down to settle with him this afternoon."

With that item settled he addressed the crew, "Does any man play a musical instrument?"

Three men stepped forward, one played a fiddle, the other

a concertina and the third a tin whistle, "Now all of you
have read my orders and know what I expect of you. My
ship is in London, you will be given two pounds for stage
fare and a months wages. How you spend it is your business, but be there in two weeks time."

Aaron walked round to the slop shop and watched his
Jewish friend performing with the small boy, every time he
pumped the freezing water up the boy slipped away,
"Captain Jacobs, he won't have you on his ship if you are
dirty boy."

Aaron walked into the yard and grabbed the boy, Tommy
enjoying the fun was bent up with laughter.

"Stop grinning boy. Grab the pump from Mr Goldman and
pump for all you are worth." A few minutes later the boy
looked a lot cleaner but resembled a boiled lobster, "Make
sure they are on the coach on Saturday."

Aaron informed them where the ship was berthed.

"Don't let me down you little buggers." He warned them.
Then Aaron shook hands, paid Mr Goldman and departed.

His next call was to his lawyers, the clerk saw him coming
and rushed to open the front door bowing and scraping,
"Mr Harris will see you straight away Captain." He
relieved Aaron of his overcoat, then tapped on the lawyer's
door.

"Come." A voice commanded from inside. The clerk put his
head inside the door.

"Captain Jacobs, sir." The lawyer, as usual was sitting at
the large desk.

"Well show him in man, don't stand there. Show him in!"
He raised his voice with every word until he was shouting.

Aaron eased himself between the half open door and the
clerk who was bowing subserviently to him. The clerk
closed the door behind him but didn't move away, putting
his ear close to the door. Aaron was his hero, the man he
would have liked to have been himself and he knew the
lawyer would want to learn every detail of action Aaron
had been through, but this time he was unlucky. Aaron's
mind was on his sweet Elizabeth and he wanted this meeting to be as short as possible.

"There isn't much to tell you Mr Harris, we take over the

new ship this week and it's already booked for passengers and a full cargo, we should sail in a month's time."

"That's very good Captain." He poured two glasses of his best sherry and slid one across to Aaron, "I do have two good paying passengers. Will you have a cabin for them?"

"I think so Mr Harris."

"What about the *Golden Falcon*? When is she due to sail again?"

"We are loading now, she will sail in about two weeks time for the colony. My agent out there gave me a list of requirements. The new Captain and his second in command are seeing to all of that that. I have just been down Broad Street to sign on my new crew, all have seen sea service."

"Let's hope you don't spoil them like the last lot." The lawyer looked down the list Aaron had given him, "Just look at this lot – oranges, limes, lemons. I've never heard anything like it in my life." He tossed the list onto the desk in disgust, "It's all very well Captain Jacobs, but these men are nothing at all like us. All seamen are the dregs of society. Start getting tough with them... show them who is Captain."

"Don't worry Mr Harris, they know who is the Captain. By the way I have a very old man aboard, he has been with me since I took over the *Golden Falcon*, he is old and sick. Now I want your clerk to collect him from the stage and take him to old Mrs Willis. want him to finish his days in comfort." He gave the lawyer the old man's name and the address of Mrs Willis. "Just see that he settles in."

"I hope this will be coming out of your pocket Captain because it isn't coming from the ship's profit. Don't forget I am still a share holder if only a minor one."

"Don't worry – just send me the bill." Aaron walked to the door, "Good day Mr Harris, I have a long way to go and I want to be there before it's dark." The clerk scuttled away from the door as soon as Aaron put his hand on the brass knob. He ran in front of Aaron down the passage and opened the main front door bowing and scraping in his usual manner. Aaron, who knew the man had been listening said, "Now don't forget, look after my man."

The clerk frowned and before he realised what he was saying he answered, "Why yes sir," then eyebrows raised, he put his hand to his mouth.

Aaron walked his horse up the steep hill that sheltered the great harbour of Portsmouth, remounted and cantered for the next few miles. Although he was in a hurry to meet Elizabeth again, he wanted to resist galloping the horse. Yet, no matter how he tried, he could not rid the woman from his mind and before he realised what he was doing the horse had broken into a gallop.

The horse was sweating and in a lather when he rode up the path leading to the great house. The front was gilded with the setting sun. She turned when she saw him and waved frantically, then lifting her dress just below her knees she ran towards him. He bent over and scooped her up in his arms. She held his face between her hands and smothered him in kisses, until with her mouth half open she planted a seductive and lingering kiss on his lips.

"Steady on Elizabeth, you will have us both off the horse."

But, tom-boyish she struggled up behind him and straddling the horse she put her arms round his waist and pressed her head against his broad shoulders.

"I have missed you so much my dear Aaron."

Chapter Thirty-five

Aaron didn't stay the one night as he anticipated – but for three nights. His new ship was ready and the *Golden Falcon* didn't sail for another two weeks. They spent the days riding and fishing for although it was late September they were enjoying an Indian Summer. They were sitting at the river bank, Elizabeth had her fishing pole in the water while Aaron lay down with his head in her lap, sucking the white part of a stem of grass, "It's like paradise here Elizabeth, if only it could last forever."

"It could if you would only let it darling. Why not give up the sea, stay here and help me to run this place? I promise you, you will never get bored."

He gazed into her eyes, "What do you see in me Elizabeth? You are so beautiful and could have the choice of any man in the county – rich men, titled men – men who could give you anything you wished for. Look at me, I'm not a pretty sight with this damn scar. A one time smuggler, and now a small time ship owner, with my income I could never keep you to this kind of life style, a large home and servants to satisfy your every whim."

Elizabeth burst out laughing, "Money isn't everything Aaron. You are brave, generous and you think of other people. From the moment you held my hand at the opera my heart stood still. You sent a thrill right up my spine. I knew then, you were the man for me. I tried to think of you as I lay in bed hoping that I would dream about you, and wondered every day if we would ever meet. Do you know I found out where your ship had docked when I was in London, and told the coachman to drive past there in the hope that I would see you. As for keeping me in comfort darling, there is no need to worry about that. My family made arrangements to keep me well provided." She lowered her head and kissed him passionately on the lips.

The days passed quickly and too soon he had to take his leave. Still reluctant to let him go Elizabeth gave the groom orders to saddle his horse and one for herself. She rode with him to the main London Portsmouth road, tears rolling down her face as they said their final farewells. She turned sharply and galloped away. Aaron stared at her back but she never turned and waved.

With a heavy heart he gave the horse his head and let him canter slowly along the rough road. His mind on Elizabeth, he very nearly relented and stopped; but the sea and his ambitions were a stronger pull. He was jolted back to reality when he heard someone shouting.

"Captain!"

He looked down to see the dirty faces of two small boys looking up at him, "What the hell are you doing here? I paid for a coach for the two of you and gave you money for food. And just take a look at yourselves, you have been sleeping rough in the new clothes I fixed you up with. Whatever happened?"

"Harry put us on the coach Captain and gave the driver instructions, but when we reached Petersfield two men wanted our seats and bribed the coachman, so he slung us off and gave us back our fare. We bought some bread and cheese at a tavern and somebody followed us. We hadn't gone half a mile when he jumps out from the bushes and starts hitting us with a big stick. He took what money we had, pinched what was left of our bread and cheese – so far we haven't had any food for two days. Last night we slept in a haystack."

"All right, climb aboard my horse, I'll take you to the next tavern." He gave them his hand and helped them up before setting off at a steady trot. They stopped at the next tavern and Aaron herded them inside, "Feed them mister," he addressed the innkeeper, "and give them as much as they can eat. I want them on the next coach to London."

"The next coach will be full Captain, there are only two go through here and one has already gone. We have three people waiting – It's always full. I can possibly get them on in the morning."

"That will do, but make sure they are well fed and cleaned up. I don't want them coming to my ship looking like street urchins."

Tommy tugged at the Captain's sleeve and nodded towards a man sitting on a bench alone, "Captain... Captain... that's the man that robbed us... That man there!"

The boy pointed to a man who was squinting back at them nervously. Realising he had been recognised, he made for the door. But Aaron was too quick for him and as he rushed past, he stuck out his foot. The man went crashing across the bar, his head coming into contact with the corner of a heavy thick pine table knocking him unconscious. Aaron picked up a leather purse tied to the man's wrist.

"How much did he rob you of lads?"

"Eight shillings Captain."

Aaron counted out eight shillings plus another two shillings and handed it to the boys, "Now look after it this time."

"What shall I do with this man, Captain?" The Innkeeper pointed to the prostrate man on the ground, "Shall I hand him over to the magistrates?"

"Do what you like with him. But when he comes round tell him if he ever touches any boy of mine again, I will kill him. Tell him in future, to stick to robbing adults."

Aaron arrived at the ship just as the sun was setting. Polly was already aboard ship and sitting amongst a huge pile of boxes in the cabin. The Captain's greeting was rather subdued and he didn't respond in his usual way when she kissed him.

"Had a bad trip Aaron?"

"Very tiring Polly. I doubt if I will be visiting Portsmouth very often. It's still the same old stinking town, full of

289

drunks and whores, pickpockets and thieves. Is it any
wonder we wanted to get away from it all?"

"Why the hell did you stay the week then Aaron?"

He was silent for a few moments. Polly was no fool and
she sensed there had been a change in his attitude. He had
always been so pleased to see her again whenever he had
been away.

"Well... actually I didn't stay in Portsmouth – I stayed at
Captain Saunders' house. I was invited there and couldn't
very well refuse; they treated me very well. Believe me
Polly there is nothing snobbish about them."

She turned her back on him and quietly asked, "The
Captain was at home, aaron – was he?"

"No, he wasn't... just his sister. You remember her, we met
at the opera."

Polly turned sharply towards him and stared blankly. She
knew something was wrong – he hadn't been the same
since he had first set eyes on her the night of the opera.

There was a deep silence, Polly knew she had no claims on
Aaron and avoided further questions. All along in her own
mind she had been certain that one day he would meet
someone special to him. If he hadn't met the woman of his
dreams he would have dedicated his life to ships and
realised his ambition of owning a fleet. She had been
devoted to him for years but in her own heart she knew
there would never be marriage at the end, no matter what
he had told her to comfort her. At the back of Aaron's
mind she would always be the small time prostitute that
worked the dockside taverns in Portsmouth.

She had spent many happy years with him and would
always be grateful. It was a lifestyle that many women
would have sold their soul for and now she was quite
wealthy by any standard – and it was all thanks to Aaron.
He was sitting on the edge of the bed. The bed in which
they had enjoyed so many happy hours and as she turned
towards him, she took his head in both hands and put her
face within a few inches of his, "Whatever happens Aaron,
let us always remain good friends, for without your friend-
ship I would rather die."

He gently pushed her away, "Whatever has brought this

on Polly?"

She shrugged her shoulders and went out on deck. Aaron was alone again with his thoughts and inwardly mused that he would never understand women. He rose from the bed and poured himself a brandy, rocking backwards and forwards and staring into space, trying not to think of Elizabeth for he had to prepare himself to hand over his precious ship and take over his new one. He didn't know how long he sat there although he managed to drink two glasses of brandy. He rose and strolled on deck.

Hargreaves had been very busy. The ship was spick and span and the cargo safely stowed away. It was going to be strange seeing the ship depart, but looking around he felt more comfortable realising that Hargreaves would make a more than competent Captain. Aaron looked over the side of the ship towards where Tommy and his friend were sitting on a couple of packets. He called Gibbons over and ordered him to fetch them aboard.

"You two boys! I hope you didn't get robbed by any highwaymen again – you had no difficulty finding the ship?"

"No sir." They answered in unison.

"Tommy, your duty will be to look after my cabin. You son, will help to look after the passengers. You won't be sailing on this ship, you are both coming on my new one. Don't be cheeky to the crew, be as pleasant as you can and you will find that sea service isn't as bad as people reckon it to be. You will see many new countries and some very warm countries. No doubt you will get sea sick some time, try and fight it – most people have trouble to start with."

He turned to Gibbons, "Take them to the galley Mr Gibbons and see that they get something to eat, poor little buggers look half starved – we will soon alter that aye? "

"We will that sir – a bit of nice sunshine and plenty of sea air and they will be as right as rain. Come along, lads."

"Another couple of protegees Aaron, my God you don't half find them. Where the hell did they come from?" asked Polly.

"Same place as Willie, they seem nice kids. That Tommy proved very honest. I offered him sixpence to hold my horse in Portsmouth and I only had a shilling. I thought I had seen the last of him but when I reached the hotel he was waiting there with the change."

"Well if they turn out as good as Willie you will be rewarded Aaron, but we will just have to wait and see."

Most of the crew signed up at Portsmouth were already on the new ship helping the builders to clean it up, ready to hand it over. That afternoon they warped it round to the quay. It was almost twice the size of the *Golden Falcon* and by the end of the week they sailed it up and down the channel on its trials. She was more sluggish but Aaron was pleasantly surprised at how well she handled. The top deck was made up into small cabins for the better paying passengers, approximately six feet by seven and much had gone into the design. The beds had stowing space below and the top moved up during the day. There was also storage space above. The double cabins, for married couples, were not that much bigger, just two feet wider.

The deck below was divided into two separate dormitories, the men to one side and the women and children the other. Aaron now had a full passenger list. It was all quiet, but in a few days when the passengers started to arrive the ship would echo to the sounds of excited children running about the decks.

By the end of the week the cargo started to arrive and Polly made sure there was room for her dresses and the usual ladies' refinements.

"You will shortly want a damn ship to yourself, Polly."

She laughed and said, "Oh do stop moaning Aaron, you are becoming real old fuss pot."

A regal looking carriage pulled up on the quayside with two footmen standing on the back, on the doors was a coat of arms. One of the footmen jumped down and held the door open as a well dressed gentleman stepped out and looked up at the ship. The passengers that had already arrived leaned over the ship's rail to see what was going on. The gentleman walked up the gangway and asked to see the Captain. Aaron, within earshot, walked over, "Can I be of assistance sir?"

"If you are the Captain, yes. I have an extra passenger for you sir."

"I am very sorry but we are completely full. I doubt if I could find room for a small rat, never mind a passenger."

The gentleman fiddled with the silver knob of his cane, "But Captain, it is imperative that this passenger goes straight away. There is no time to be lost. Whatever the passage money, I will treble it."

"But I can assure you sir, it is not a question of the money. I just can not take one more passenger, not under any circumstances."

Another passenger standing at the ship's rail, well dressed and smoking a cigar, pulled himself up to his full height of six feet four inches and held out his hand, "Ah, Lord Frampton, can I be of any assistance?"

Lord Frampton ignored the outstretched hand and gave the man a disdainful look, "Benton Beckondale – the family getting rid of you at last? I do not like you sir, you are a waster and a scoundrel. I very much doubt if the likes of you can do anything for me." He tried to dismiss the man by turning his back.

Benton touched Lord Frampton's shoulder with the tip of his cane, "Ah, but there you are wrong my Lord. You see I have a cabin aboard this ship which happens to be a double one. It may be a tight squeeze and the journey may be very long and dull but if, as I assume, the passenger in question is your son then he can crash in with me."

"What is the catch Beckondale? I have never seen nor heard of you doing anything for nothing." His Lordship's face was a brilliant red with temper as he poked Benton in the chest with the tip of his cane.

With a positive sneer on his face Benton answered, "Don't be like that your Lordship... your son and I are bosom pals."

"Bosom pals alright. Until you almost cleared him of his inheritance, sir. You are a no good scoundrel."

Benton Beckondale was a man who apparently accepted insults as easily as the proverbial water ran off a duck's back. He gave his Lordship a sickly grin, "But I am your salvation now my Lord. I am in a position to help rid you of that son of yours."

"How much is this going to cost me?"

Benton's sickly smile turned to one of arrogance. He knew he had a very powerful man under his thumb and played with him like an angler played with a fish, "Five hundred pounds."

"Five hundred pounds!" Lord Frampton exploded, "You must be completely mad sir!"

Benton craned his neck forward and the sickly smile disappeared. Becoming very serious, he whispered in his Lordship's ear, "But then again, your son could be hanging on the end of a silken rope."

His Lordship looked round to see if anyone had overhead the last remark, and called Aaron over, "Benton here has offered to share his cabin with my son, will that meet with your approval?"

"That is entirely up to Mr Benton, sir. He has paid for his passage to Sydney and what he does with it is his concern, although it may be a little crowded. It is a small cabin and I see Mr Benton is a very tall man."

"That is settled then. We will bring my son's baggage aboard. I assure you he will give you no trouble."

"Not so fast, my Lord. First the five hundred pounds please. And there is just one other thing, you have to clear my gambling debts at my club. Something in the order of a thousand pounds, which will also seal my mouth."

His Lordship's face became redder than an apple as he puffed and blew out his cheeks, "I will see you in hell first."

"Good my Lord! And I will have that son of yours to keep me company."

His Lordship thought for a few moments, slapping his silver mounted ebony cane in the palm of his hand. His eyes were ablaze with fury, "Alright Beckondale, I will cover your debts up to a thousand pounds. Not a penny more. Good day!" He turned to the two burly footmen and ordered them to bring his son aboard.

They staggered up the gangplank carrying a huge prostrate figure. Benton was tall, but this man could give him at least another two inches in height. They lay him on the deck as the other passengers gathered, gaping at him.

"Take him to my cabin, follow me." They managed to get

him to his feet and between them led him to the cabin.

"Not on my bed you damn idiots, put him on the floor over there."

"The floor sir?" One of the men questioned him.

"Yes, on the floor, you don't think I am sharing my bed with that drunken lout do you? Just look at him, he couldn't tell you the time of day."

Beckondale went back on deck and told Lord Frampton that his son was settled in. Not as though he could give a damn, he was glad to see the back of him.

"He has several crates of whisky aboard with him – which should keep him happy, and no doubt you will help him to dispose of them."

"Oh, no my Lord. I have many vices but drinking is not one of them. I drink only in moderation and when I do I have to confess it is only the common housewives' tipple – gin."

His lordship turned in a huff and hurried down the narrow gangplank without looking back. The iron rimmed wheels of his coach thundered away over the cobblestones as the two burly servants stood rigidly on the back.

Chapter Thirty-six

Compared to the *Golden Falcon* the new ship was sluggish, taking almost twice as long to complete the usual outward journey. With a decent wind behind her she could move satisfactorily, but with light winds she hardly moved at all, unlike the *Falcon* which Aaron reckoned could put on extra knots if someone coughed. However, she did have redeeming factors. There was plenty of room, including Aaron's own private cabin which could easily seat a dozen guests at dinner. A dinner that often stretched to first light and several bottles of cognac and Madeira wine, for over the years Aaron had accumulated what he liked to call a *decent* wine cellar.

He had kitted up his two urchins with splendid uniforms and had taught them, with the aid of his regular servant, to wait on table – a job they both thoroughly enjoyed, mainly because they could feast on the left-over food.

Several evenings he invited both The Honourable James Frampton, during his infrequent retirement from the bottle, and Benton Beckondale. But of the two, Benton was by far the most interesting guest. Both had been educated at top schools in the country, earning them along with their positions in society, a place in the country's famous regiments. Alas, James Frampton, better known to his intimate friends as 'Pissy-Arsed Jimmy', had soon succumbed to the bottle and when the regiment was ordered abroad he was found in a dockside shed two days after the troopship departed. His family connections saved him from being cashiered and a few days later he was forced to resign. On the other hand Benton had sailed with the ship and had covered himself with honours in India. But, alas, he worshipped cards and women; and very soon there was talk in the officers' mess. He was accused of cheating, something he vehemently denied, a duel was arranged and Benton instead of drawing blood to satisfy everyone killed his accuser. Of course everything was hushed up and after a few months he resigned. His father, himself an old soldier of the regiment cut his allowance and seldom spoke to him again. He subsidised his meagre allowance through gambling, at which he was no great shakes. One by one he was kicked out of the clubs and left to live by his wits – at this too he struggled.

Finally he was given a last chance, and was called to his father's country home where the old man sat on a deep leather chair while Benton stood facing him with his back to an enormous marble fireplace, in which a pine log some four feet long was burning.

"You stand there without a shadow of remorse looking down on me. I am not going to ask you why – I will never get the truth from you. You have enjoyed every privilege, fine schools, one of the best Regiments in the British Army and yet you have blown it all."

"Yes, father, I agree. But did you once ask me what I wanted? Everything in this family is done for you or for the sake of the blessed Regiment. You farm over thirty thousand acres here – and that is what I always wanted to do, farm the land. Whenever I voiced my opinion I was shouted down. The eldest son, I was supposed to enter the bloody army, the family Regiment."

"Well alright then. You want to farm – you bloody well shall. There are plenty of acres going in New South Wales. Your uncle is farming out there and has used his influence to acquire you a few acres. In two weeks time your ship will be sailing," he pushed across a small leather bag, "Get all the clothes you want, make a go of it, and I promise I will again allow you to claim your inheritance."

The old man, ready to bury the past, filled two large glasses of brandy and pushed one towards Benton.

"I am sorry father, but I don't drink."

"Well I suppose we must be thankful that drinking isn't one of your vices." He held out his hand as a token of semi forgiveness and they feebly shook hands. Benton knew he would never get the better of his father in an argument but in a way he was pleased with the outcome. He had heard quite a few stories about the colony and the idea that he could make a fresh start quite stirred him. A gambler and a womaniser he might be, but one thing he never lacked, was guts. He thrived on a challenge and going to the other side of the world to start afresh was something that did appeal to him.

The Hon. Frampton, who Polly disliked immensely, was another kettle of fish – a hopeless drunk. Benton would manage to keep him sober until the bottle was passed around but after that it would be hopeless. It was often Tommy's job to go around the table with the bottle topping up the glasses, and Frampton would set his eyes on him from the moment he picked up the first bottle. As soon as Tommy stopped at his chair he would grab the bottle and tip it quickly into his glass. The boy trying to retrieve it, as Frampton held on grimly, would appeal to the Captain who lifted his eyebrows as much as to say, 'Leave it alone'. With the next bottle Tommy would try and dodge past him unnoticed but he always lost. The boy had been brought up in the taverns that ringed Portsmouth dockyard, yet he had never seen a man drink so heavily as Frampton.

"So Benton, do you really think you will may make a go of it, farming out in the colony?" Aaron asked munching a great slice of cheese.

"Who knows, I shall take a look at the place. They tell me the women settlers look more like trained cows and that there are no big name gambling spots. So, yes... there may be a chance."

"Don't be fooled about the women Benton. Believe me there are some very pretty ladies. Just watch them as they crowd aboard trying to buy Polly's fine dresses. As for gambling, I really don't know – but where there is money someone will be trying their damnedest to relieve them of it. There is a lot of corruption unfortunately – the New

South Wales Regiment runs the place and they are the most foul-mouthed, corrupt, disgusting men you will ever see. You always sound as if you may enjoy a bit of adventure, Benton – when we land and you look directly westward there's a mountain range over which several adventurers have tried to find a passage. Believe me the man who discovers a route over them will make a fortune."

Aaron picked up his glass, "Well ladies and gentlemen, tonight there is a beautiful full moon and a very calm sea. I suggest we all go on deck and take full advantage of it."

The Captain was right – the ship was like a white ghost sailing down a silver road cast by the moon, with a gentle breeze causing the slightest ripple from the stern.

The poorer passengers were strolling about the decks and a complete silence shrouded the great ship.

"How much further have we to go now Captain?" one of the women timidly asked.

"Never ask how far we have to go ma'am, ask how far have we journeyed. We left Cape Town two weeks ago and I should say that the bulk of the journey is now over. This, you may say, is really the last lap. A long lap maybe, but just think how many miles we have made since leaving England. You will find it a lot warmer here and the changes they have made to the colony are unbelievable. They have brick houses now and some very large buildings. There are great opportunities for everyone – I have said this so often – people arriving here to settle are probably taking part in one of the greatest migrations in history."

"If the opportunities are so great as you say," asked Benton, mockingly, "and you look to me as if you are a man who would grasp at a golden opportunity – why don't you take part?"

Aaron, sitting on the stern rail and holding a glass of brandy looked at the men. He had been studying Benton and his companion since the day they had both set foot on the ship. Benton was a great conversationalist.

"But you see Benton, I have. The first day we arrived here on my ship the *Golden Falcon* I knew exactly what the colony wanted, a good link with the home country. So, I immediately made up my mind to buy a bigger and better ship and before very long I hope to own a fleet, with a regular line to Australia. When we advertised passages on this ship I could have filled her a dozen times. But I promised myself I would never carry convicts. That trade I consider as bad as slaving. But, mark my words, the people that have decided to stay here, and there are free convicts amongst them, will soon start kicking about Britain sending their convicts from the overcrowded prisons, they will want free men."

The conversation came to an abrupt halt when Frampton collapsed on the deck, dead drunk and with a glass still in his hand.

Aaron pointed to the prostrate figure. "Now there is a man who, unless he pulls himself together, will be dead within a year with the gut rot they sell out there, it's rum and usually serves a double purpose, stripping paint or inducing blindness." A couple of crew members came past and Aaron indicated the drunk, "Find a shaded spot and put this man to sleep – throw a blanket over him."

During the night the wind picked up and by first light it had turned into a gale, sufficient for Aaron to order shortened sail, "Let us hope this keeps up for a few days Willie, we are well over a month's sailing behind."

In fact the ideal sailing conditions kept up for all of three weeks and in that time they sighted three sails, "This route is starting to get very busy Willie."

They closed in on the third ship, a large East Indiaman bound for London, and Aaron had several letters for Elizabeth which he passed on. It was the last contact he made with any vessel for two months, after which they sighted the heads. There was great excitement when they passed into the great harbour, naked natives could still be seen on the North shore near the heads, causing much amusements among the children and scenes of modesty among the women. They struggled to find an anchorage near the shore amongst several other ships, merchant and naval, but as Polly had influential customers waiting they were soon accomodated at the ramshackle quay.

Chapter Thirty-seven

With the ship safely docked alongside the quay and the gangplank down, the horde of women that had congregated at the bottom rushed up the gangway like a herd of rutting deer. Dignity had completely disappeared for the women of the colony, all eager for news from home and to set their eyes on the latest creations of the fashion world. They crowded around Polly as she laid her dresses along the ship's rails.

Aaron nodded towards them and spoke to Benton standing near, "God Benton take a look at that."

"I am Captain, I am, and can hardly believe my eyes. What I have been told about the women out here is all lies. Some of them are the finest looking women I ever set eyes on."

He was wearing his brightest and best clothes, saved just for the disembarking and they caught the eye of several of the younger women. As Beckondale winked his eye at one beautiful blonde, he could have sworn blind she blushed but it was difficult to distinguish under her heavy tan. She smiled coyly and turned her head. Aaron couldn't fail to notice and said, "Well, Benton you certainly waste no time."

"Time sir, what is time? It is all in the mind, to me sir every minute in life is precious, that is one reason why I never sozzle my mind with drink. To me the most obnoxious sins in life are drink and gambling and I just cannot afford the both, so I make do with gambling and partake of a third sin – women. I always make sure she is a woman of means and can fully support herself. Just look at that idiot the Honourable Frampton down below, he has been drunk since we left England and hardly knows the time of day – he hasn't the slightest idea where he is."

Polly was going about her business and by nightfall half her stock was sold at an enormous profit and she was busy counting her gains when Aaron returned to the cabin, a broad smile spreading across his face when he saw that half her stock had gone and the cabin was almost back to normal. He never ceased to be amazed at the change that had came over her since she first joined the crew – from a small time prostitute to a wealthy and competent business woman. She no longer used the Portsea gutter language, Aaron had not heard one swear word from her the whole of the voyage which had been long and very tedious.

"I will be coming ashore with you in the morning Aaron, I have some arrangements to make with the agent about building my shop on the ground next to the warehouse. I want the finest and brightest shop in the colony – totally exclusive to women – all richly carpeted, with bright brass lamps and if possible a large glass chandelier like those toff ladies' shops in London. With seats all round for the customers to sit on, I hope it will become a meeting place for the better off."

"Now don't you tell me that you are becoming a snob. I wouldn't like that Polly."

"Don't be silly Aaron, I don't give a damn about the women – it's their money I am after and with such nice surroundings I intend to make them pay for the privilege."

That night Polly lay awake her mind continually on the project, the next morning she was up bright and early leaning over the ship's rails staring at the derelict land next to the warehouse and visualising her shop standing there.

A carriage drew up and the driver, a convict, came up the gangway, and handed Sam a letter, "I have come to pick up the Honourable Frampton."

"Wait here sir." The convict's eyes widened. No one had ever called him 'sir' since the day he was born.

Aaron came on deck reading the letter, "Have you anyone with you?"

"No sir, just me."

"Then you had better help him Sam. Do you have far to go?"

"No, not really sir, about fifteen miles ."

So the Honourable Frampton left the ship in the same condition he had arrived, prostrate down the gangway, carried by the convict and Sam. They made him as comfortable as possible and the last anyone saw of him he was riding away in the carriage. A few minutes later Aaron followed down the gangway to do business with his agent.

It was midday when Polly heard a cry from the quayside. Mrs Pilgrim was sitting in her carriage as Polly looked over the ship's rail and responded with a broad smile indicating for her to come aboard. They embraced, "It's so good to see you again Polly, did you have a pleasant voyage?"

She shrugged her shoulders, "Not really, just the usual, we had a mixed bag of weather, some days it was warm and some days we lay becalmed; other days it was wet and miserable with rough seas – it was very tedious."

Polly led Mrs. Pilgrim to the cabin and she gasped, "My God how beautiful and what a size."

This was the first time Polly was able to talk to someone sympathetic to her real feelings, and she poured her heart omitting nothing, "Things are not the same Mrs Pilgrim. It's Aaron you see, he has met another woman, he has been very moody and silent at times. Some evenings he sits at the stern of the ship, just staring into space."

"Oh no Polly, you must be mistaken, you have always struck me as the ideal couple. Are you sure you are not imagining it – this home of yours is so beautiful. You can not imagine how myself and many of the women here envy you and your way of life. It's so like a floating palace, and we always think of you as the most contented person alive."

"I thought so too until we arrived home last time. Aaron had business in Portsmouth and called in at an old friend's house – he wasn't at home, but his sister was. I'd met her some time ago, she is very beautiful with flaming red hair that flows past her shoulders, and deep penetrating brown eyes set in a childlike face – a young widow at that. She was married very young, sixteen I believe, but her husband a naval officer died of fever in the West Indies leaving her with a little boy. When Aaron arrived back from Portsmouth he was not the same."

"I am so sorry to hear it Polly... come and stay a few days with me, maybe it will be different on the voyage home I will throw a dinner party, it's been such a while since we had one."

"Well in that case you must wear the dress I have bought for you as a present. There are three on the bed, choose the one you want."

"Oh Polly," she picked up a white dress with a rather low cleavage, "this one is rather naughty..." They giggled like two young schoolgirls, "... but you must let me pay you for it."

"No thank you, I bought it especially for you, it's a gift."

Polly went to a drawer and, pulling out a square jewellery box, she lifted the lid. Mrs Pilgrim squealed and said, "Polly," in a long drawn out drawl, "it's the most gorgeous thing I have ever seen in my life, are they real?"

Polly shook her head and smiled, "No I am afraid not, the gold is genuine but the stones are replicas. I told you before about the run-in we had with the Arab slavers. Well, Aaron took the original stones from them, apparently they are extremely rare, and a Jewish diamond merchant had them made into a necklace. He sold them for an enormous sum, enough to enable Aaron to buy this ship."

"Well if this necklace is only a replica I would love to see the real thing. Did you see the original Polly?"

"Oh yes, they let me wear it for a few minutes. The man that created it was a dwarf and one of the nicest men I have ever met. He made this ring from the chippings of the real diamonds." She flashed her hand towards Mrs Pilgrim's.

"My God you are so lucky." She hesitated and said, "I wonder... Polly, will you bring the necklace with you, when we have the dinner party? And would you kindly let me wear it? I will surprise my husband – he will have a fit when he sees me wearing it. I will tell him they are real diamonds." So between them they conspired to give Mr. Pilgrim the shock of his life.

They met Aaron half way up the gangplank, "I will be gone for a couple of days Aaron, is that alright with you?"

"You don't have to ask me Polly, you are a big girl now. Go and enjoy yourself we won't be sailing for a few days, but be very careful." Aaron turned to Mrs Pilgrim and said, "Look after her dear." He then charged the rest of the way up the gangplank.

Polly was unusually quiet for the long ride back to the homestead. She was nothing like her old inquisitive self, hardly taking in her surroundings, and hardly jumping when a mob of large red kangaroos leapt up from the bush and startled her as they bounded alongside the carriage before springing away. To help cheer her up Mrs Pilgrim stopped the carriage near a large clump of gum trees.

"Come Polly, I have something to show you." She led her off the track to the trees. She stopped suddenly and held Polly back before creeping up slowly towards the trees, "Just take a look up there Polly." Pointing to a small bundle of fur, she picked up a twig and gently poked it. A head slowly turned round towards them and two large brown eyes separated by a button nose stared down at them, objecting to being disturbed from its sleep.

"Oh, how beautiful." Polly moved closer her arms outstretched to pick one from a lower fork, it hissed menacingly.

"Careful Polly, they are koalas and they can be very spiteful." She pointed to one further up the tree. "Look at that one Polly, it has a small baby on its back."

Watching the wild but cuddly creatures put Polly in a much better frame of mind and she was more chatty for the remainder of the journey, listening to Mrs Pilgrim's local gossip, and thankful that she had a friendly face to chat to.

"My little abbo has gone walkabout again Polly, she had a little baby you know... a light skinned little thing with a touch of ginger in its hair so it has to be one of the convicts but the baby is so cute especially when it looks at you with those large brown eyes. Ju-Ju vanished about a month ago – I walked onto the veranda one morning and her dress was hanging over the rails. She is such a strange, loveable creature... I have told her time and time again, no more babies, but all she does is burst out laughing and treats it as a huge joke. These convicts are teaching her all the usual swear words and the more I tell her not to use them, the more she does it. She doesn't have a care in the world and could teach us white brothers and sisters a thing or two. If we took a leaf out of her book, I suspect it would be a much happier and contented world. One day she is here all happy and contented the next day, like some phantom, she is gone. It really beats me how she knows her tribe are in this area, occasionally we see them but it is very rare. They are a very strange people Polly and certainly know more about life than we so-called civilised people."

"Looks like your husband is home, Mrs Pilgrim." Polly shaded her eyes against the bright sunlight and in the distance saw the homestead dancing on the heat haze and a tall man leaning against the veranda.

She laughed and answered, "That's not him Polly – it's Samual Gilbert, he has an uncanny knowledge when my husband is away. Makes the excuse that he has to keep an eye on me – doesn't like me to be alone with all these convicts and abbos around." Mrs. Pilgrim gave a wry smile, "Frankly I don't think his intentions are strictly honourable, there is a great shortage of women out here. My husband has gone off to those damn mountains again, he seems to be obsessed with them, he has been gone a few days. Like most of the men here, he seems to think there is prime land the other side of them."

Chapter Thirty-eight

Mrs Pilgrim stopped the carriage in front of the homestead and Samual helped them both from the carriage. First Mrs Pilgrim and then Polly, doffing his hat at the same time holding her hand held firmly in his grip and lingering much longer than he needed to help her down. She gave him a sweet smile.

A round cast iron table with four chairs were on the verandah and Mrs Pilgrim nodded towards them and vanished into the house. She returned a few minutes later with a large glass jug filled with lemonade and covered with a lace cloth with glass beads around the side to keep away the droves of flies. At her first sip Polly, marvelling at how cool the drink was in this heat, sank two full glasses, "However do you manage with this heat Mrs Pilgrim. The lemonade is so cool and the heat doesn't seem to bother you one bit."

"It's like everything else Polly, after a few months you get used to it and the best thing to do is keep on drinking as much fluid as possible or you can soon dry out."

"Yes that's what the convicts do," interrupted Samual, "deliberately dry out and become ill, then have a few days off. One of these days one of them is going to go too far and kill himself."

"You sound very arrogant Samual." Mrs Pilgrim admonished him.

"Don't you like the convicts then Samual?" Polly asked, already drinking her third glass of lemonade.

307

"It's the only labour we have out here and the lazy devils will get out of work if they can help it. We feed and clothe them and get nothing but trouble in return."

"I think I would be the same if I was in their place. From what I can see they look more like slaves..."

Samual poo-pooed this idea, "Damn convicts, all thieves and robbers the lot of them. I wouldn't trust them an inch. Because the prisons are full and overcrowded over in the old country, What do they do? Send them over here."

"Some of the crimes these people commit are hardly worth a kick up the rear – yet they get sent out here for seven years. Most of what they steal is usually to feed their families."

"If people can't feed their children, then why have them? Then they go and rob decent hard working people."

"Well, you will be pleased to know we had a ship of free settlers and some good people too – tradesmen and the like."

"Now that is good news Polly, really good news," said Samual without sounding too convincing, "It's what this colony needs, more law-abiding settlers."

"You know Samual, not all working class people are the morons you make them out to be. Take sailors for instance, Captain Jacobs never uses the whip or the rope's end and he cares very much for his men. He has them eat fresh fruit every day and has never lost a man with scurvy or fever. He pays them well and they always get shore leave, in return they would follow him to hell and back."

But Samual chose to remain unconvinced, "Well all I can say is, more fool him."

Mrs Pilgrim noticed Polly was becoming angry and quickly changed the subject, "Polly is opening a shop exclusively for women Samual. You should see the beautiful dress she has just brought over for me, I think we have a real business woman here." Her eyes were staring into space, "Just imagine it Samual, a shop exclusively for women – you should see some of those dresses. They remind me of when I went shopping in the old country. I doubt now that we will ever return to England, so we must make the best of it and with people like Polly I am sure this country will prosper."

Samual turned to Polly, a light in his eyes and a smile playing on his lips, "Does that mean you intend to settle here Miss Polly? It is people like you we want here."

"I doubt very much if it will be yet Samual. I have made arrangements for the shop to be built then I have to get a couple of girls to manage it and must make arrangements for my dresses to be made. Believe me, I have serious ambitions for this shop but I will be working for Captain Jacobs for some while yet. He has two ships now and will soon have another built. I reckon in ten years' time he will have a dozen ships on the Australia run. In the few years we have been coming here we have seen the enormous changes. Captain Jacobs says he wants his feet on the first rung of the ladder, there is great potential here."

"Then your Captain Jacobs is no fool Polly. I would like to meet him."

The conversation turned to the usual topic – the Blue Mountains. It seemed that people further out from the coast were obsessed with them, and from where they sat they could see the outline of the vast mountains in the distance, "One of these days Polly they will be conquered. I bet those damn abbos know their way over them. It just wants someone to start a rumour that gold has been discovered over there and everyone will be queuing to try their luck. They are just like a vast uncharted ocean."

"I would like to get a closer look at them Samual, I must admit they look magnificent from here."

"Well, if you would like a closer look we can ride a few miles nearer to them, the distance can be very deceiving... that is of course unless Mrs Pilgrim minds me taking you away for the day."

"No, not at all, in fact if my husband were here I may have joined you." But Mrs. Pilgrim's mind was more on matchmaking. Having watched them talking together they seemed an ideal couple. And after what she had heard about the Captain, she even considered the possibility of Polly becoming a neighbour. She knew that Samual had a roving eye for women and matching him with Polly might stop them from roaming.

"Can you ride a horse Polly?" This caused a roar of laughter from her and she shook her head.

"You must be joking, I am terrified of them, all I know about horses is they have a leg in each corner and a big head. When I was a small girl I saw one bolt down a street, it was dragging a large cart and it almost killed me. Ever since I have ben terrified of them."

"You won't be afraid of little Betsy, Polly. She is a fine young mare and has already been spoilt by my sister, anyone can ride her, she is as quiet as a pet rabbit. I will bring her around in the morning and let you see her; then if you think you can manage I will take you a little nearer to the mountains."

Next morning Polly was awoken by the hysterical laughing of a nearby kookaburra. She sat up sharply – it sounded as if it was in the house – and quickly jumped from her bed, staring through the window. Samual was outside mounted on a large chestnut mare and holding a younger horse by its reins.

She quickly threw on a pair of trousers and blouse, combed her hair and made her way outside. Samual had dismounted from his horse and seized a piece of twisted wire from a nail near the verandah. He lashed out with the wire for some minutes before bending over and picking up a large brown snake. He threw it into the paddock. Polly's face had turned a deep red and she trembled, it was several moments before she was able to talk and her first words were, "Was it poisonous Samual?"

"You could say that, but it's not poisonous any more."

"God," she sighed heavily, "and to think I actually walked over it. I saw that thick wire hanging there and wondered what it was for, now I know." She gave an involuntary shudder and noticed that Samual was staring at her, "What's the matter Samual does my dress shock you? I must say I haven't seen many women wearing trousers here."

"And you are not likely to. I keep telling my mother and sister to wear more casual clothing but I might just as well be talking to a brick wall. My mother won't allow it. My sister would probably like wear trousers, she is only just

310

seventeen.... But no, Polly, I assure you it's not the way you are dressed, it's the way you look. So beautiful with your golden hair hanging over your shoulders and the sun right behind – it looks more like a golden halo."

"Well come down to earth Samual you are not in heaven yet. Let me have a look at this horse and if I feel *it* doesn't like me or I don't like *it*, then that's your day's riding over."

He led her to the horse and instructed her to stroke its neck and whisper in its ear, "Now take it easy Polly, just a gentle stroke."

She whispered softly and the horse muzzled down to her shoulder.

"There you are Polly, she has fallen in love with you – as we all have."

After breakfast he helped her onto the horse. Polly put her foot in his cupped hands and he gently lifted her, adjusting the stirrups. At first Samual held the bridle and led the horse round the paddock, then without her noticing he took his hand away, "Keep your knees gripping the side of the horse Polly."

Convinced she could handle the timid animal she moved away. Mrs Pilgrim came outside the house to watch, "Very good Polly," and Polly feeling more confident put the horse into a slow canter.

"There you are Samual, I have packed a meal and a bottle of my lemonade. But let me see you back here before nightfall, Polly isn't used to this heat although I have to admit she looks very confident on that horse."

He rode with her away from the homestead and towards the mountains, Mrs Pilgrim waving to them as they vanished into the morning mist.

"This is very nice Samual, but I hope there aren't any more snakes where we are going. Are there?"

"I'm afraid there are Polly, but don't worry they wont attack you. I have to be honest with you, that snake I killed this morning must be the first snake I have seen in the last twelve months."

"They make me go cold. There are two things I can't stand – snakes and rats. I hate the damn things."

They stopped at midday for a picnic but the mountains

looked further away than ever and the whole ground danced on the heat haze. Suddenly Polly gave a little squeal and ran to her horse, "Quick Samual, there are some black people coming towards us, painted with white and carrying long spears and some bent things."

He burst into uncontrollable laughter, "They won't hurt you Polly, they are friendly. Look there, trailing behind." He pointed towards the rear of the column where the women struggled along with the children, the elders and the family goods, "There is Ju-Ju, Mrs Pilgrim's little abbo and she is carrying her new baby."

He stood up as the leader approached them and started speaking in a form of broken English. Polly could pick out a few words here and there. She walked towards Ju-Ju to see the new baby but as she approached, the girl shied away.

Samual shouted, "Steady Polly, she will show you the baby when she is good and ready. Right now she doesn't belong to Mrs Pilgrim, she is part of her own tribe." The leader was following every move Polly made.

"They will be gone in a few minutes Polly." He turned out his tobacco pouch and handed it to the leader, who in turn opened a woven rush bag hanging from the side of a woman and handed Samual a part of a snake.

"Fancy a piece of snake Polly?"

Her eyes widened, "Don't tell me you are going to eat that disgusting thing are you?"

"Well, I'm afraid I have to take a small bite or they will be offended."

Polly heaved at the thought of eating snake and made another move to get a closer look at the baby. This time Ju- Ju didn't object and proudly held the baby out towards her, "Beautiful, yes?"

"Very beautiful." Polly took the baby from Ju-Ju's arms, it stank terribly, "I don't think the baby has been changed Samual" and quickly handed it back.

The tribe moved away shaking hands violently with Samual, and Polly watched them vanish into the shimmering heat haze, "Why *do* they paint all that white stuff on their faces Samual?"

"They have been to a tribal meeting – what they call a cor-
roboree – and they always paint their faces and bodies. We
had better make our way back now Polly, it soon gets dark
out here, and we had better get a move on. Perhaps the
next time we can have a few days together, sleep out in the
open."

"What about the snakes and more abbos Samual?"

He gave his usual laugh, "Put it all down to experience
Polly. Now try and move a bit faster."

Chapter Thirty-nine

"**W**ell Polly, how did your first ride into the Australian bush go?" Mrs Pilgrim had seen them approaching from a distance made her way into the paddock to greet them. She patted the horse's neck.

"I will let you know as soon as I dismount," answered Polly, grinning, "my bottom is a bit sore and my knees – but I really did enjoy it. We met Ju-Ju out there, she is with her tribe. You could soon find out who the father is by eliminating those without red hair."

"I've already tried that Polly, and it leaves exactly five suspects and none of them will admit to fathering the child. They all think Ju-Ju is there for their amusement, not that she needs any encouragement."

She turned to Samual, "And as for you Samual – it will be very dark soon and I am expecting your family to dinner. I think you had better go out back and get cleaned up. My husband has only been back a couple of hours."

Polly went to the rear of the house and found Samual stripped to his waist and washing himself down in cold water, her heart seemed miss a beat and a lump the size of a duck egg filled her throat.

He stopped and turned to her, "I felt someone was watching me Polly, how long have you been standing there?"

"Oh, only a few seconds." She softly lied.

He threw a towel towards her, "While you are here you can make yourself useful and wipe my back, water has just

314

ran down it."

She wiped his back with the towel rotating it in small circles. Suddenly he turned round and held her tightly in his arms kissing her passionately, his mouth half open. She responded by putting her arms round him and her body close to his.

"Polly I love you." He whispered in her tiny ear.

"Samual, you know nothing about me... where I am from, my background, my association with Aaron. I am his mistress, Samual. Please... say no more because you will only be disappointed."

"I don't care where you come from Polly, or what you've done. All I know is I am madly in love with you and I want you to be my wife. Don't go back to England – stay here and we can be married within the month. You say you like it here, please stay."

"I'm sorry Samual, I like you too, and no doubt I could easily learn to love you, but please don't rush me. I have ambitions... my shop – I want it to be the best in the colony. I have to arrange for the dresses to come out from England and I have two girls to bring out. No I am sorry, I really am flattered... if I was to choose a husband, it would be you."

The conversation was cut short by the arrival of Mrs Pilgrim, a smile on her face as she saw them embraced, "Oh excuse me, I hope I am not interrupting anything."

They were sitting on the verandah when Samual's family arrived. His mother, a smartly dressed lady that held her head up high, was followed by her husband a barrel chested man with slightly balding fair hair. He wore a wide-brimmed straw hat, shirt and trousers. They were introduced to Polly in turn.

"You will have to excuse my husband Miss Polly, he *will* dress like a convict and cover his head in that filthy straw hat."

"But Agnes," he protested, "you know I have to keep my head covered in this damn heat, and I dress for comfort just like you should do. Those damn skirts dragging on the ground... damn corsets or whatever you call the damn things."

"Will you stop swearing Felix. Every other word is damn.
Damn this. Damn that. I am ashamed to take you out or to
have company."

The story was that she had met her husband while he was
employed by her father. Her parents never accepted it
although he had received a decent education. Felix was
dismissed on the spot but their love remained and they
continued to meet in secrecy. A hasty wedding took place
and they were shipped out to Australia, Samual being
born on the ship. With her father's influence they were
granted a strip of land, a prime plot that bordered on a
river, and it was highly successful. Two years later the
daughter arrived on the scene now seventeen and cursed
with the teenager's nightmare her face a mass of freckles
which she was ashamed of especially as her face was
framed with a mass of brown mousy coloured hair. But it
didn't detract from her rather beautiful face, a pretty nose
and cupid's bow shaped lips, she held her hand out to
Polly, "My, my, Miss Polly what a pretty dress. I suppose
they are all the rage in London?"

"Yes it is Kathleen, do you really like it?"

"Oh yes, it's beautiful and so are you, what lovely blonde
hair. Just look at mine and these freckles, how lucky you
are, you haven't one on your face and I am smothered in
them, I have tried everything to get rid of them."

"Whatever for? They are lovely, a girl back home would
give a king's ransom for freckles like that."

"That's what I keep telling mother. She should let me go
home for a few months I may get rid of them, it's this sun
Miss Polly. Who would want to get in bed with a girl
smothered in these damn spots?" But she was admonished
by her mother and laughed at by her father.

"Don't you start swearing like your father and don't talk
about going to bed with a man – a young woman in your
station of life does not say such things."

"Well it's true mother, even the convicts won't give me a
second look."

"How dare you talk like that Kathleen. I hope they don't
give you a second look or I would have them whipped.
Now less of this talk and I hope you don't go near those

convict sheds while my back is turned."

"Don't be silly mother."

The conversation was halted as Samual's mother gasped out loud, and they all turned to where Mrs Pilgrim was standing in the doorway. Kathleen's jaw dropped and even Felix and Samual gasped. She was wearing the off shoulder white dress that Polly had given her and around her neck she was wearing the necklace. Her hair had been brushed and combed by her convict woman servant. The blue replica diamonds stood out proudly on her bare flesh and her husband stood spellbound, his glass of brandy half way to his mouth.

"My God, Beatrice, you look so beautiful. And that necklace... wherever did it come from, it must be worth a fortune?" He looked suspiciously at Polly as much as to say, 'I hope you didn't sell it to her'. Polly laughed and Beatrice lifted her head.

"It would take my family's and your family's entire wealth to buy this necklace. But don't worry it's only borrowed and it isn't the real thing – this is a replica of the original. which is now is in a wealthy Duke's family. There is a story to this necklace Michael, a very long story and when we sit down to dinner Polly will relate it to you."

At that moment another female convict announced that dinner was ready. It was a large table that could seat ten people and was laid out with cut glass bowls, glassware and china with a small floral design.

They had hardly sat down when Felix said in rather a loud voice, "Come on then, Miss Polly, tell us all about those diamonds and how your ship's Captain came by them."

Polly was still telling them the story of the Arab slavers and the diamonds, when the men should have been retired to the verandah with brandy and cigars.

"Did the Captain actually kill the slavers himself Miss Polly?" Felix asked.

"Yes and helped to throw them overboard. Aaron hates slavery."

She flashed the ring the jeweller had made for her.

"These are the actual diamonds. See how blue they are?

317

This was made from the chippings when they cut a diamond to shape. The one diamond these came from would have fetched thousands."

"You must lead a very adventurous life aboard that ship Miss Polly." Kathleen said.

"Believe me, she does," Mrs Pilgrim answered, "perhaps next time we will get to ask her to relate how they were boarded by pirates off Ceylon. I think when Polly does settle ashore it will be very difficult for her after leading such an adventurous life."

Samual suggested to Polly that they go for a walk under the moonlit sky and she readily accepted.

"Don't go too far," Beatrice said, "it's near midnight now, and I have promised Polly an early start tomorrow. She wants to go across the fields and down to the river's edge."

Polly and Samual stopped under a gum tree and with with her back to it, he placed his arm over her shoulder, "Why don't you stay Polly. The life you lead is dangerous and if anything happened to you, I think I would kill myself."

"Don't be melodramatic Samual. In a couple of months you will have forgotten all about me and be searching other territory for another bride." He tried to protest but she hushed him up, "Now don't spoil it Samual, don't rush me. I have my plans. I will think about it next trip home and following the next trip I may marry you. But in the meantime, if you happen meet another woman, I will fully understand. I am not tying you down."

After an hour they returned to the house, receiving knowing smiles from the women folk and suggestive grins from the men.

"Come on Samual, it's time for getting back. We have a fair old way to go and Miss Polly and Mrs Pilgrim want a good day out tomorrow."

"If you are going on horseback Mrs Pilgrim I will leave the little mare, Polly is used to her now."

"That's very kind of you Samual. We should be finished by mid day. We shall have a ride to the river's edge."

Again woken by the kookaburras' laughing serenade, Polly was on the verandah dressed in trousers and blouse and watching the sunrise when Mrs Pilgrim joined her.

"That was a lovely dinner party last night Beatrice."

"Oh yes, the best I ever had and it was all down to you. Poor little Kathleen her eyes were nearly popping out of her head. She was two hours past her usual bed time."

After breakfast they mounted the horses and rode away.

"Samual took a real shine to you, Polly. Tell me, did he make any improper suggestions?"

"Good heavens. No! He asked me to marry him, pushed it rather hard, suggesting I stay behind and we get married in a month's time." For a fleeting moment Mrs Pilgrim's eyes shaded over.

"Well, be very careful. Samual is a nice young man. Very athletic and good looking but he does have a roving eye for the women. It is believed that he bedded a convict woman, or rather a convict girl. She was rather good looking and worked in their house. She was instantly dismissed and sent back to Sydney by his mother, so I do think I should tell you."

"Aren't all men the same? Believe me, if he had tried anything with me he would have been greatly disappointed, but I am very pleased you told me. I admit I was sorely tempted, but don't worry I am not ready for marriage for a few years yet. The truth is I am still in love with Aaron. I was hoping that one day we would be married, but in my own heart I know it can never be. I am a wealthy woman now with ambitions. So at the moment I don't want any commitment."

They stopped by the river. Beatrice had brought a lunch and they sat in the shade where it felt very cool. They lay back, eyes closed but something disturbed Polly and she heard the undergrowth rustle. At first she ignored it, but a few seconds later it happened again, Beatrice noticing it too and looking around. Suddenly two white men, unshaven and filthy, leapt out at them. One grabbed Polly and held a knife at her throat, the other grabbed Mrs Pilgrim. She tried to scream and he put a filthy hand over her mouth. Polly remain silent.

"Why don't you behave like your friend here, Mrs Pilgrim. Be like her and you won't get hurt." The man spoke with

an Irish brogue. He released his grip on Polly but still held
the knife near her throat, "One move my little darling and
this will go straight into your pretty little gizzard."

Beatrice stopped struggling and the other man loosened
his grip. She was still shaking, "Are you escaped convicts?"

The Irishman laughed, "Convicts – are we convicts?" He
touched his forelock, "No madam, we are men of leisure
and at the moment my leisure is you. Ah, I don't do these
things normally, but you must be the most beautiful
women we have seen for a long time. Struggle or fight and
you are both dead women."

He pushed his hand between Polly's legs and she whispered, "Not here, not in front of the other two. I want to
enjoy it too," she lied, "But tell your friend not to touch
Mrs Pilgrim, she is a happily married woman. Tell him I
will be willing to go with him too. It's much better than an
unwilling partner."

He laughed, his grin revealing two rows of yellowing
teeth, "You're right lady, but why?" He looked at her curi-
ously.

"Don't call me lady, my name is Polly. Because I enjoy it,
that's why. Now don't stand here talking – let's go somewhere on our own and tell that ugly mate of yours to leave
Mrs Pilgrim alone or he gets nothing."

He went over to his mate and whispered in his ear. He
looked at Polly, grinned and shook his head. Polly, now
having the man's confidence, led him to into the dense
undergrowth and away from the eyes of his friend. She
started lowering her trousers and he was hypnotised by
the sight. A woman who really fancied it. His luck was in.
His eyes were still on her but the only thing he saw was
her pubic hairs. Polly had handled men like him for years,
and she made as if to stumble. As he reached forward, she
let out a fierce kick that landed squarely between his legs.
In too much pain to squeal out he doubled over and tumbled towards the river. As he tried to stand, wincing, she
put her foot on his bottom and he went into the river head
first without hardly a splash. Quickly, Polly picked up the
knife he had dropped and went into the river after him.
She stabbed him several times holding his head under the

red-tainted water before he slowly rose to the top and floated away. Now she had to get back to Mrs Pilgrim.

Unseen, she dropped into the river again, and under cover of the river's edge slowly made her way back. Mrs Pilgrim was sitting down, the convict behind her, the knife still in his hand, but he looked relaxed and was eating some of the left-over meal.

"Paddy must be enjoying himself," she heard him say, laughing heartily, "Some friend you have there Mrs Pilgrim – she knows how to handle a man – pity you are not so co-operative."

'Keep him talking, the filthy bastard.' Polly was praying. When she was a couple of hundred yards beyond them, she got out of the water, the knife in her hand and stealthily, under cover of the undergrowth, made her way back towards them. She heard them talking, Mrs Pilgrim pleading with the convict not to hurt her.

"If Paddy doesn't hurry up you will be getting it Mrs Pilgrim. I don't think I can hold out any longer. Why the hell didn't he let me go first?"

"Look I know you are escaped convicts. If you let us go free I promise I will not say a thing. Name the place and I will leave you money, food and clothing, and two horses."

He gave a laugh that sounded more like the devil himself. "Let us free..." he mocked, "We already have your two horses and when I've had that delicious friend of yours, you will both be..." He made a gesture that meant he would cut their throats.

Beatrice started to struggle, and he held her down by throwing her on the ground. This was just what Polly wanted as he now had his back to her. She dashed forward, the knife held in a stabbing position. The man managed a startled look as the knife went into his back, right up to the hilt. He pitched forward and was already dead when he reached the ground. As Polly rolled him over, he was still wearing the startled look.

Mrs Pilgrim was kneeling over. Her forehead almost touching the ground and sobbing, "God Polly, you have killed him. He *is* dead, isn't he?"

"Yes Beatrice, as dead as mutton. And his mate is floating

down river. They won't try and rape any other women, that's the best place for them."

"How did you do it Polly?" She said in between sobs, "However did you do it? You knew of course that they would kill us afterwards."

"After they raped us, yes. Of course I guessed they would. Don't worry, I have handled men like that before. I went along with him; told him I really enjoyed it and made it clear I wanted it in privacy. When I started to pull my trousers down he was so pre-occupied he dropped his guard. And believe me he didn't see a lot, I kicked him between his legs and he dropped his knife. Before he had time to think the knife was in him. I pushed him into the water and held him under."

"My God Polly, you are very brave." Beatrice put her arms around her and hugged her tightly. "You have saved my life Polly, and I will never forget."

Mrs. Pilgrim quickly regained her composure, "I will have to warn Samual about you. Are you sure you won't stay longer?"

"No Beatrice, I have to get back to the ship, and in a hurry, before you start telling everyone about it."

Chapter Forty

When they reached the homestead, Michael had left to work on the land and wouldn't be home until nightfall. This pleased Polly for on their ride back, Mrs Pilgrim had never stopped talking, and between sobs and smiles she had kept on saying, "I owe you my life Polly, you are the bravest woman I have ever known. They had every intention of killing us once they had their wicked way with us."

Polly just smiled – as a small-time prostitute, she had been handling men of that calibre all her life. She had been beaten, robbed and assaulted by all types of men and had learned how to look after herself. And learned the art of self-preservation.

"I will get back to the ship now, Beatrice."

"No Polly, not until you have seen Michael. There has to be something he can do for you. I am sorry Polly, I cannot allow it. You cannot leave me on my own."

The argument continued for almost an hour, but eventually Polly won and Beatrice gave in, "Well, I insist on driving you there."

Polly laughed. "Oh no, we are going to return on horseback. You can lead the little mare back. I just want to see Aaron's face when I ride a horse to the ship. He will never believe it unless he sees it for himself."

She packed her clothing, leaving behind the one dress, "This is for Kathleen. She has fallen in love with it."

Most of the crew were leaning over the ship's rail when

323

they came riding along the wharf. They gave Polly a rousing cheer and Sam ran down the gangway to take her package from her. She quickly dismounted and gave Aaron a wave.

A convict standing nearby took the horses' bridles and touched his forelock. They both ran up the gangplank and before Polly could stop her, Mrs Pilgrim was pouring the story out about the two convicts.

Aaron put his arms round Polly's shoulder. "That's my Polly." Admiration in his eyes, he kissed her forehead.

They said their farewells at the quayside, tears in Mrs Pilgrim's eyes as she hugged Polly, "We will remain friends Polly to our dying days. I will never forget you and when you return I will get Michael and Samual to take you to those damn mountains you are so anxious to see. I may even come with you. Goodbye my dear Polly." She gave her a last hug and kiss.

But it wasn't the last time she would see Polly. The next day Mr Pilgrim, Samual, Mrs Pilgrim, and Kathleen were waiting on the quayside. Mr Pilgrim was the first up the gangway and took Polly in his arms, "What can I say Polly? If you hadn't been there I would no longer have my Beatrice. Is there anything I can do for you, anything at all?"

She shook her head.

"Oh yes there is. I understand you are having a shop built here." He pointed to the warehouse, "I will take full responsibility for it. You will have the greatest shop in the colony. Samual, as you know, has a contract with the government to supply timber. He will select the best for you."

With this Samual came forward and took her in his arms, "My brave little Polly. I will be waiting for you Polly, and your final decision."

Finally Kathleen came forward and put her arms round her, tears in her eyes, "Must you go?" Polly nodded. "Thank you for that beautiful dress Polly, I will keep it forever."

Polly said to Michael, "If you insist on taking over the job of building my shop, the agent next door has the plans. While you are here I insist you must stay for lunch."

They were shown into the large cabin and Kathleen became overwhelmed, "Oh Polly, this is so beautiful. I never realised it would be so large!"

They stayed for two hours and old Sam, the negro, was given the privilege of showing them the rest of the ship.

"I would love a trip home in this ship Sam, it's so large." Kathleen fingered all the shining brass work and inspected every corner.

She was overheard by Polly who laughed, "Well, it's not so pleasant when there are dozens of children running about and the ship is rolling, pitching and tossing. And the food gets very monotonous when you have been at sea for a few weeks. Then we have rough seas, and someone is sea sick over the decks, which have to be washed down with sea water. Believe me it can take the romance out of sea journeys – sea sickness is one of the worst things. I suffered terribly for the first few voyages. It was murder and you wish you could die prematurely. On the *Golden Falcon* they had to tie me in the bed so that I didn't fall out and injure myself. She was not so large as this ship."

They said their last lingering farewells as the ship prepared for sea. Then Mrs Pilgrim, dabbing the tears from her eyes, joined Kathleen and Samual, himself sulking badly and fighting against shedding tears. They all stood on the quayside waving until the ship was out of sight and passing through the heads.

It was a hard voyage. After passing through the heads the weather took over completely and it rained incessantly, the ship rolling and pitching like a rickety old stage coach over uneven roadways. By some twist of fate, the part of the voyage where the sea was most likely to be turbulent, the notorious Bay of Biscay, turned out to be as calm as a mill pond. In the English Channel they suffered the worst weather they had ever experienced and it was with great relief that they reached the Thames estuary. The tide was in their favour and they didn't have to wait long before they returned to their own berth. It had been a very profitable trip, completely full on the outward journey and half filled with passengers for the return trip.

Aaron's London agent had seen the ship heading up the Thames and was waiting to board the minute the ship tied up, a broad smile on his face as he held his hand out to Aaron, "Captain, I have a letter for you."

He handed Aaron an envelope that looked like it had been in his pocket for months, "We have had a young lady here asking when you were due back, a pretty little thing with blazing red hair. She came here every month."

But the agent was less interested in the Captain's private affairs than the business of the day, "We have a full passenger list and cargo for Australia, Captain. I believe it would pay you to have your ship converted to take more passengers. I could have filled this ship ten times over."

After the agent left Aaron sat down by the great window and began to study the letter. It was the most passionate letter he had ever received, bettering some of the erotic French novels he had read. It finished with a final sentence that sounded more like a command, "Do not forget to come down to Esher the moment you arrive back. I have a very pleasant surprise for you; and my brother is still out in the West Indies."

The next morning the hostler was on the quayside with a grey mare, already bridled and saddled, "She is a nice quiet horse just as you ordered, but she can be fast and canters well."

Polly was on deck as he rode away. As Aaron turned in the saddle and waved, a sense of uneasiness stirred in her stomach and she sucked the tip of her index finger thoughtfully. They had never parted so quickly at the end of a voyage – he used to give her a farewell kiss full on her lips, but this time he just brushed his lips on the side of her cheek.

He turned into the drive at Esher, noticing that the trees were all bare. It was mid winter and a layer of frost spread over the ground, faintly painting the trees with a silver lining. Nearing the house Elizabeth saw him from the window and ran out to meet him. He sprang from the saddle and swept her up in his arms.

"I have been watching from the window every day, my beloved Aaron, hoping this would be the day you arrived. I

326

also went down to see your agent every month. The last time I left a letter. Did you receive it?"

A groom came running from the side of the house and took the steaming horse. Aaron had ridden it hard for the final few miles. She caught his hand and lifted her long dress up a few inches from the ground, running up the stone steps leading to the house and leading him into the drawing room.

He felt as if he had only just left. A log fire, smelling of pine, was blazing in the hearth.

"Oh Aaron, I am overwhelmed at seeing you. My mother warned me never to fall in love with a sailor. 'You never know when they will be back, or if they ever will be back'. She was quite right. So when you go away I have to start all over again; worrying if you are safe and if you are coming back at all."

She poured out two glasses of his favourite brandy and rather mysteriously said, "I think you should have a great drink of that before you see my next surprise." She vanished from the room while he sipped at his brandy, wondering what it was all about, but even he wasn't prepared for the next shock. He heard the door open and close and the next thing he knew she was behind him and touching his shoulder. He jumped, the thick carpets had deadened her footsteps. She stood looking down at him, holding a baby wrapped in a silk shawl, "How do you like your little daughter, Aaron?"

He jumped up quickly, "Do you mean..." But the words trailed off, "When, where?"

He wanted to say more, but the words failed to form in his mouth. The scar on his face turned a bright crimson as he took the shawl away from the baby's face and gasped. There was no denying who had fathered the child. His hands shook as he held out his arms to take the baby from its mother. His mouth and throat dried as he croaked out, "She is so beautiful Elizabeth, I mean, how, why?" The wrong words tumbled from his mouth. "I just don't understand."

She burst out laughing, "How? We slept together. Why? The same reason every baby is made."

He sat down again, his eyes straying from the baby to Elizabeth. It was several minutes before the implications of the association hit home. She was a young wealthy widow, he a small time ship owner and former smuggler. In her position she would be ostracised from society. Then, what of Polly? She had been his constant companion for many years, had stood by him through thick and thin, shared his troubles and shared his joys. He just couldn't throw her away like some old dish rag.

He handed the baby back to Elizabeth, "I think we must sit down and talk this over."

She took the baby and left the room. It was ten minutes before she returned. She went to pour him another brandy but he put his hand over the glass, "No Elizabeth, I must keep a clear head. That was the greatest shock of my life..." Aaron then promptly changed his mind and asked for another brandy, "... What do you want to do Elizabeth? I mean we are from two different backgrounds. I have never mixed with society." Marriage was at the back of his mind but he considered it would never be, "I would feel a freak in their company."

She placed her tiny hand over his mouth, "I knew it would be a shock to you Aaron." She giggled like a school girl, "I can tell you it came as a great shock to me. It must have been three months before I realised I was with child. There was no one to talk to, my brother and myself and some distant cousins are all that is left of the family, and my brother is out in the West Indies. I hoped and prayed each day that you would soon be home – but it was over a year before you returned. As for my society friends, I don't give a tosh for them." She snapped her fingers to emphasise her feelings, "I have little doubt that I was the centre of the gossip when the word got out, yet not one of my so-called society friends have enquired after my health. And after all Aaron, you have no worries or obligations to me, it was I that seduced you. Yes, I have been in love with you since the very first time I met you at the opera."

"I know. I have also felt the same way about you Elizabeth, dear. So if you can stand the gossip, we must marry straight away."

"That is an extremely gallant proposal Aaron. Are you not going to get down on your knees and beg my hand in marriage." Amidst her giggles he knelt down before her, kissed her hand and asked her to marry him.

They sat on the magnificent sofa, her arm around his, "The first time I met you at the opera house, with my brother, I knew there would never be another man in my life, Aaron. I was in love with you long before I met you." He looked at her and frowned, "When my brother returned from the war I was just a child, but he hardly every spoke of Trafalgar and the other battles. The conversation was always about you. You were his idol and you also became mine. I would picture you, aye, and on occasions, dream about you. But my brother had given me such descriptive details of you that when we did meet you were exactly as I imagined. I would dream about your exploits as a smuggler, and how you showed no fear when you released the prisoners."

Aaron turned further towards her and spoke softly, "I have to tell you now Elizabeth, Polly has been aboard my ship for a good many years. I mean..." he could hardly look her in the face, "It has been a man and wife relationship. Wherever I was – she was. Always beside me."

"Oh Aaron please, my husband was a seaman and my brother is married to the Navy. There is not a lot I don't know about seafarers. I didn't think she was there to make up a game of cards." They both laughed. "Will you tell her Aaron?"

"Without the slightest doubt Elizabeth. Polly is quite an intelligent girl and capable of looking after herself. She is also now, wealthy and a good business woman. She will take it hard at first, but I must tell her the truth."

"Now about this wedding, do you wish to get married straight away or wait for a few weeks. I can delay my sailing for three weeks or you can wait until I return from the next voyage to the colony."

"No Aaron, I feel I cannot wait another twelve months – the sooner the better. The local priest will have no objections, he relies on the family for his stipend."

"I agree. If your brother returns suddenly and finds I am

the father of your baby, born out of wedlock, he may challenge me to a duel and I am no good either with guns or swords. You would be a widow before we start."

There was a slight tap on the door and the young maid put her head round the door. "Shall I put the baby to bed now ma'am?"

"Yes Lucy, but bring her back in and let her father kiss her goodnight."

The maid's eyes shot up in surprise and looked straight at Aaron, bewildered. She was still staring at him as she backed out of the room, the baby in her arms.

Elizabeth was smiling when Aaron turned, "Now all the servants will know who the father is. It will be around the servants' quarters by morning and around the whole town by lunch time. Believe me Aaron servants are the greatest ones for tittle-tattle."

"You don't seem to mind Elizabeth."

"Why should I? I now have the man I love – the rest can go to hell."

Chapter Forty-one

The wedding took place a few days later in the weathered old ancient church in the nearby village standing on the edge of the family estate. It was conducted by an equally ancient vicar who constantly managed to get Elizabeth's name wrong, insisting on calling her Eliza. The congregation was quite small, consisting mainly of her servants and distant relations, half of whom she failed to recognise having only been a child when she last saw them. They attended not from a sense of duty, but out of curiosity. To them Aaron was a tradesman, albeit a ship owner and a Captain. He owned just two ships and was now marrying a wealthy widow with vast estates.

Elizabeth was attended by her sister in law, Captain Saunders' wife.

After the ceremony they returned to the house, and while the servants were celebrating below stairs, Elizabeth was trying to establish a relationship with her guests, many of whom she hardly recognised.

"By the way Aaron, there is someone here you should meet." She pointed to an elegant woman, in her mid thirties, one of the most beautiful women he had ever seen. Elizabeth took his hand and led him across the room, "Lady Medlam, I would like to introduce you to my husband, Captain Jacobs."

The lady turned and smiled, "Ah, so you are the daring man who rescued my husband." She held out her hand and he brushed it with his lips.

331

"And how is your husband, the Admiral?"

Her smile changed to a picture of hatred and she almost felled him with her answer, "I hope the old bastard is dead and rotting in hell." She smiled sweetly as she saw the look on Aaron's face, "Believe me Captain, you did me no favour by rescuing him from the French prison. Oh, don't look so worried Captain, we have not been as man and wife for several years now. When our paths do cross we squabble. If you should ever come into contact with some-one who likes him, please let me be the first to know."

"His father... he gave me five hundred pounds to rescue him."

"You should have told me of your intentions – I should have given you a thousand pounds to let him stay in that filthy jail and rot. I heard he rewarded you by wanting you put in chains for being insubordinate. That is my hus-band – he would cheerfully have had you hanged."

"Nice lady." Aaron whispered to Elizabeth as they drifted away to mingle with the other guests.

"Well Aaron, I did tell you what a monster that man Medlam was."

Polly had stayed aboard ship and went daily into the city to do her business, totally unaware that Aaron's secret romance had gone so far. She was making herself very busy, and had other important jobs to do. Firstly, there was the glazier. She handed him a list of the sizes of glass the agent had requested, then she had ordered two magnifi-cent brass oil lamps and several smaller brass wall lamps. Another trip to the dressmakers where she was served eagerly by the same assistant, Jenny, "You must be one of our best customers now madam?"

"Yes, my dresses soon get snapped up by the lassies in the new colony. They are waiting at the quayside when the ship arrives. But now I am opening a shop out there – it will be the first shop exclusively for women."

"Oh you are so lucky madam, I would love to go out there, but I am scared about all the convicts. My husband was talking about it the other night, saying how warm it is out there."

"I didn't know you were married Jenny." The assistant

went a bright red and put a finger to her lips, looking furtively round the shop, "Don't tell madam, please, she doesn't like married women working for her."

"That's very silly Jenny, what does your husband do for a living?"

"He is a saddle maker Madam, but he can make anything out of leather." She lifted her skirt a few inches and revealed a pretty ankle, "He made these shoes madam."

"Well he would have no problem out there, and I could give you a job, married or not. I need a dressmaker, in fact I need two. Actually I am soon going to Portsmouth to find two girls."

The assistant's face brightened, "Madam, may I talk it over with my husband? I really would appreciate the opportunity."

"Well, it's Sunday tomorrow, why don't you bring your husband to the ship."

Polly wrote down the name of the ship and where it was berthed, "If you come down some time in the afternoon, tell the man on the gangway who you are and he will bring you aboard."

But it was Aaron that arrived first that Sunday morning. Polly was still in bed in the great cabin and he gently woke her. She sat up sharply, throwing her blonde hair back and rubbing her eyes, "Oh, it's you Aaron. You've been gone quite a few days... anything happen?"

"Get up, let's have breakfast and you will hear all about it. I have something very important to tell."

Polly, still half asleep and rubbing her eyes, said, "Let me tell you. You have been and gotten yourself married."

Aaron was startled and caught her shoulder gently, "How in the hell did you know that Polly?"

It was Polly's turn to look startled, "You haven't, have you? Aaron..."

He nodded his head. She turned a fiery red and sat down. Aaron poured her a brandy, but she refused, "I knew something had happened to you the last trip Aaron. I guessed you must have met someone and I guessed it would be the fiery little red head we met at the opera. Well Aaron, all I can say is, I wish you all the luck and happiness in the

333

world."

"But you haven't heard the best part Polly. I also have a little daughter, a sweet little thing called Katherine."

"Bloody hell Aaron, that was quick. Married and become a father all in one week. Don't tell me – it was a miraculous virgin birth."

He laughed, in spite of her disappointment she hadn't lost her sense of humour, "I hardly think so Polly, she also has a son who is six years old – David."

"Oh yes that's right. She is a widow." Polly stood up and kissed him, "Well Aaron, those children couldn't have a better father. Good luck to you. I shall move my personal things from the cabin if you want me to."

"That is entirely up to you Polly, but I trust we will always remain very good friends, as you will always remain a part of my life. We have had some very good laughs Polly and you are a very beautiful lady. One day you will meet someone who is worthy of your love."

"With my background Aaron? Who will have the likes of me? I am seriously thinking of settling in the colony – I am looking for staff for the business and have a young woman and her husband coming to see me this afternoon. She is a dressmaker and could manage my shop; he is a saddle maker. If they do decide to settle over there, I suppose it will be alright with you if I offer them a passage?"

"You know Polly, you don't have to ask. If they want to go, find them a nice cabin and most nights they can dine with us. Little Tommy can be their cabin boy."

This somehow relieved the tension of the situation. Polly had taken it far better than Aaron had imagined. She had expected it sooner or later, and was now more than ever determined to make a go of her shop and would give Samual's proposal serious consideration during the voyage back to Australia

With the worry of informing Polly off his mind, Aaron concentrated more on his business.

"Mr Feltham left a message with the lawyer in Portsmouth," he told her matter-of-factly, " he has a vessel for sale, a French corvette which he has converted into a small passenger ship. By some coincidence it is named the

Golden Pheasant. He reckons it's a very fast ship, and I shall go down in the morning to view it. Do you want to join me?"

She gave it some thought, then shook her head, much to Aaron's relief. Polly knew he would want to call in at Elizabeth's house, "I don't think so, Aaron. I will go down later next week."

Polly interviewed the Hudsons that afternoon and found Jenny's husband, Bill, to be a very intelligent man. He had turned leather-working into a fine art.

"Until you find your feet in the colony, you can stay in my shop that is being built. It has two bedrooms and a large kitchen. I was going to use one of the bedrooms myself but it doesn't matter, I have a good friend out there who would only be too pleased to accommodate me."

She showed them around the ship and the cabin they would use for their voyage. It was the brightest and best cabin for the passengers, "I think you will be very comfortable here. Tommy, the cabin boy, will be looking after you. He's a bright little boy and if there is anything you need just ask him."

After a hard ride to the South Coast, Aaron found his way to the shipyard in the New Forest and Bucklers Hard. The ship was anchored in mid stream and Aaron fell in love with it even before Mr Feltham pointed it out and took him aboard. He inspected it from stem to stern and a price was negotiated straight away.

"If you are looking for a crew Captain, I have a first class shipwright and a sail-maker. I don't really want to part with them, but work is very slow at the moment and they are very good men. The sail-maker is ex Royal Navy and can turn his hand to anything. Both of them are single men."

Aaron interviewed the men immediately and told them to be at his favourite tavern next morning. He then remounted and made his way towards Portsmouth where he stayed at the George Hotel. Next day he interviewed men for a new crew, reading out his rules and how he punished offenders, "I haven't lost a man in years, so every man eats at least one citrus fruit; you are paid from the minute you sign on until such time as the ship returns to port. Any allowance you make will be paid by my lawyers in the Hight Street. He doled out two pounds to each man. You meet me here in two weeks to sign the articles and you will receive your wage from that date, so if there is anything you want, best to get it now."

He called at Esher that night. It was dark when he rode up the pathway and Elizabeth did not run out to greet him. She was fast asleep in bed. He rang the chain hanging beside the great oak door. In the silence of the night it sounded more like the great bells of St. Pauls as the echo reverberated through the house. It was several minutes before the old butler came to the door wearing a long white nightshirt and sleeping cap, carrying a lighted candle in one hand. He held the candle high, "Oh, it's you Captain, do come in." He swung the heavy door wide open, "Madam will be pleased to see you."

He made no noise climbing the heavily carpeted stairway and he opened the bedroom door slowly. The front door bell had not disturbed her and he slowly undressed, creeping in the sheets beside her. She woke with a start and tried to scream, but he put his hand over her face, "Ssshh, it's only me," he whispered.

"Oh Aaron, you fool." Her breath smelt of brandy and it was no wonder she had not awoken – her speech was slightly slurred.

"Surprised to see me Elizabeth?"

"Surprised... and exceedingly happy."

They went into a deep embrace.

336

Chapter Forty-two

The two days he intended to stay with Elizabeth and the children turned into a week. The thought of parting distressed them both and when Elizabeth realised that the parting was inevitable she became morose and began to drink heavily. At dinner the night before he left, Aaron watched her down the third glass of brandy and became concerned, "You don't need that stuff Elizabeth."

"Oh, now the dutiful husband is finally starting to tell me what I should or should not do. My Aaron, you catch on very quickly."

He picked up his half empty glass and went to the large fireplace. He threw the remains of the brandy on the fire and it exploded with a large flash, "Just imagine what that stuff is doing to your insides. Moderate drinking is quite in order, but you are ruining your health. Please Elizabeth... I have to go in the morning, please don't let me go seeing you in this state."

He put his glass back on the table and tried to give her a disapproving look but her eyes melted his heart. He held her tightly in his arms, "Good night my dear."

As Aaron walked to the door, she ran after him clinging tightly.

"Oh please Aaron, please don't go, stay another day."

"Don't be foolish Elizabeth, you know I have to go and prepare for sea. Waiting another day will only make it worse. We shall just go through this same routine again."

He lifted her in his arms and carried her to the bedroom.

Aaron was up bright and early the next morning. She followed him downstairs and they ate breakfast together. His horse was brought round. He went with Elizabeth to the nursery and held the children in his arms, kissing them then handing them back to the maid. Elizabeth was crying quite openly as they walked down the wide staircase, arms around each others waist. They embraced at the doorway and she kissed his face all over.

"Promise me dear, you will leave that damn brandy alone. I shall make the passage as fast as possible."

The cargo and stores were already aboard, stacked safely away and that afternoon the passengers were starting to arrive. At mid day Polly arrived back at the ship with a girl she had recruited in Portsmouth. She was introduced to Aaron, "This is Maud, Aaron – my new shop girl."

Maud couldn't be described entirely as shy, having been a prostitute since she was thirteen. Now in her mid twenties, she looked older – the ravages of her profession and the booze had taken their toll. She was to prove to have more than one endearing feature. She turned out to be a good conversationalist; had a good sense of humour and she didn't speak like a Portsea gutter snipe. Beneath her drink ridden face she had once been very pretty. She was placed in the women's dormitory.

Mr and Mrs Hudson arrived later that afternoon carrying several pieces of baggage. Polly greeted them at the top of the gangway with a smile, "Welcome aboard the both of you. We won't be sailing for another day so make yourselves comfortable and walk around – get to know the ship."

Aaron had one last job to do in Portsmouth and knew it would be hard having to pass within a mile of the house. But it was a job which had to be done, and the ship would be sailing within twenty-four hours. He looked longingly at the path leading to the house but forced himself to ride on.

As arranged the crew were waiting at the tavern. He interviewed them one by one; rejected three and signed on twenty men and two boys. An ex-naval officer was waiting for him with a letter from Lieutenant Saunders, introducing him as a potential Captain for one of his ships. Aaron noted there was no word about his sister apart from the usual, urging him to visit her if he should be passing that way, so his wife could not yet have told him about the baby.

Aaron shook hands, "Well, Mr Gilchrist, it seems that our luck is in. I have just purchased another ship and I am looking for a good Captain. It's a French Frigate captured in the war, she is being converted now. I must tell you immediately – I will have none of that stupid naval discipline. No rope's end and no flogging. That doesn't mean I am soft. Any breach of discipline and the offender is removed from the ship at the first sight of land. You buy in stores of citrus fruit at the Canaries, from a large fat Spaniard there. Ignore the prices he first asks, halve them, and give each man aboard one orange or lime each day. I know some of you officers don't approve, but I have proven that it works. "

"But I do approve Captain. I have already heard about your record and Captain Saunders has told me about the French episode. It will be an honour and a pleasure to work for you."

"Right then Mr Gilchrist, bring your gear aboard my ship as soon as possible, and you can sail with me until we reach the Channel, where you can take the ship over, I would like to see you handle it. I will drop you off at Portsmouth and you can prepare the new ship for sea. It is laying in Bucklers Hard."

The two days it took to reach the Solent, Aaron got to know Mr Gilchrist, who turned out to be a very pleasant man. There was nothing for Aaron to worry about, for the man had resigned from the navy because he couldn't stand the violence meted out to the crew.

Reluctantly, at Portsmouth Aaron parted with Willie and Gibbons. Willie was to act as Gilchrist's number one and Gibbons as his chief.

"I am sorry to part with you Willie, but I can't wet nurse you all my life. It's time you started taking command, for no matter what you say, you will be taking over the next ship. Mr Feltham is keeping his eye out for another. You have taken in everything I can possibly show or teach you. Now let Mr Gilchrist show you a few things I may have forgotten. Goodbye Willie, we are sure to meet again soon."

Willie did not answer. He was sure if he did speak he would break into tears. They shook hands and Willie threw his two bags over the side and into the boat that had been lowered. Polly came out and put her arms round him and hugged him close, "Goodbye Willie, it's been great knowing you." She whispered in his ear, "Next time, you leave them women passengers alone. Tell me honestly Willie, did you pay them?"

A tear came to his eyes, "You shut up Polly."

Willie quickly put his leg over the ship's rail and climbed down the ladder and into the waiting boat. The passengers stood at the ship's rail watching the small boat pull away, some realising it was their last link with the old country, for most of them would never see it again. Willie sat in the stern of the small boat with his back to the ship. He never looked back. Polly stood at the ship's rail her vision blurred by tears, for Willie had been, along with Aaron, her constant companion. They had laughed together and she had teased him dreadfully in his younger days. He had moaned when she first came aboard the lugger to stay overnight, and he had been relegated to the sail locker. But in spite of everything they had remained the best of friends. She would sorely miss him.

They had just reached the West African coast when a familiar sail came into view, "Sail on the starboard bow sir." The call came from the mast head.

"I see it." Aaron recognised it straight away, "Make towards the ship." Within the hour they lay near the Golden Falcon. Aaron and Polly were rowed towards her and were greeted by Hargreaves as they stepped aboard. His wife was standing next to him, a baby in her arms.

"I see you have wasted no time Hargreaves." Aaron nodded towards his wife.

"No sir, another boy." Aaron looked at the baby and Polly took it from Mrs Hargreaves' arms.

"Oh he is lovely, how old is he?"

"Seven months." She smiled and looked at Aaron, turning a deep red, "We named him Aaron after the Captain, for without him we would never have had another baby."

Aaron was flattered. "Well, look after him and I will hold you responsible for his care and safety."

He retreated to the cabin with Hargreaves and took his report, "By the way Captain we had to pull into the West African port where you had the trouble with the slavers. A tall African came aboard and asked for you. I could hardly tell what he was saying, but a Portuguese man who was with him – I think he was a slaver – said the man had been told to wait for the Captain, and to identify himself with this. A big piece of stone, that's what the Portuguese said, but I know different. The African had stayed around the docks for two years wouldn't go back to the village until he had contacted you. Apparently, you were to go back with him."

"Poor chap – is he still here?"

"As far as I know. He is living there with his wife, and he has three or four little kids with him."

"Well it seems he hasn't been wasting his time, either."

Aaron gave Hargreaves a sardonic look and both grinned.

"I read your reports at the agents, Hargreaves. I was very pleased and it looks like I chose the right man. I have a new ship just being fitted out and a new Captain has taken over, an ex naval officer. He was recommended by my brother-in-law"

It was Hargreaves turn to look startled. For he knew Polly had no brothers, "It would appear congratulations are in order then Captain. Good luck."

"Oh yes, and I also have a daughter and step son."

"Then it seems that you, too, didn't waste any time. Do I know the lady, Captain?"

"I don't think so Hargreaves. When you return to England stay there until we get back. Pay the men off, it will give your wife a chance to visit her relatives again. By the way, how is she taking to the sea life? She seems happy enough."

"It's been the happiest days of her life sir, and she loves it in Australia. Mind, she had some bad days with sea sickness, but has quite settled down. And like Polly, she has taken to wearing trousers and shirts – the old boy at Cape Town is quite indignant when he comes aboard and sees her dressed like that. Nelson loves the job too. He is learning navigation and coming along fine, mixes with the men quite well. Mind you they give him some stick being the Captain's son. But he give them as much back, they don't argue too much with him – he must be the tallest member of the crew. I just don't know where he puts his food. I think he has hollow legs."

They walked back on deck where Nelson had taken over the wheel duties.

Aaron came and shook hands, "You were not kidding when you said he was tall," and jokingly said in a most official manner, "... I want this man's rations cut down."

He patted Nelson's shoulder, "Glad to see you are doing a very good job Nelson, keep it up and who knows, one of these days I may give you a ship of your own." They shook hand, "Keep an eye on that little brother of yours Nelson, and see he doesn't start eating as much as you do."

They all walked to the ship's rail and Aaron turned to Captain and Mrs. Hargreaves, "Goodbye the both of you, and keep up the good work. I will see you in London on my return."

The light was failing by the time both ships were under sail and within the hour all they could see of the Falcon were the dim lights vanishing towards the far horizon.

That night they entertained Jenny, her husband, and Maud to dinner. Bill proved to be a very intelligent man, a good craftsman who obviously worked with pride.

"I think you have chosen wisely Bill. They must be very short of saddlers in Australia for I have brought over several saddles for various customers. I don't know how the leather situation is over there but if you need any we, of course, will be happy to carry it over for you."

"I don't know about that Captain, I am afraid I will have to work for someone else. I have no capital."

"Don't worry about that Hudson. What would you say if I put up the money to get you started and bring whatever you want from England."

Mr Hudson put up his hand in protest.

"Oh don't worry Hudson, I won't do it for nothing. Let's say I want to buy an interest in your business – I put up the capital for say a twenty-five percent share."

Hudson looked at his wife, hardly believing his ears, "That is extremely generous of you Captain, what can I say. I would be foolish to refuse." They shook hands.

"You are not the first I have staked Hudson. A brewer sailed out here with us three years ago and now has a very good brewery going. Didn't you see thee crates of bottles we loaded? They are all his."

"I wondered what they were. They must be stowed near us for when the ship rolls we hear them rattle."

"Yes, the brewer is doing very well. All they seem to have in the colony is rum. It's almost legal tender and I understand it is run by the New South Wales regiment, a corrupt lot of buggers, so I am led to believe. Now I give you a toast ladies and Mr Hudson, to a very successful partnership." They clinked the glasses.

Maud was clearly out of touch. Aaron's best Madeira was stronger than the wine she had been used to and she had been drinking it like water, her speech blurred and uncoordinated, "I think it is time for our dear Maud to retire, Polly."

"I think you are right Aaron. Will you give me a hand with her, Jenny?"

Chapter Forty-three

The remainder of the voyage was uneventful although it was a great relief to Maud and Jenny when they passed through the heads and realised the voyage was over. Both of them had been tortured by severe sea sickness that came on whenever there was the slightest roll of the ship. The women, a pale shade of green, leaned on the ship's rails as they sailed slowly into the calmer waters of the great bay and towards the anchorage. Polly joined them and put a sympathetic arm around their shoulders.

Maud, her mouth so dry they could hardly understand a word she was saying, stuttered out, "I will have to put up this place Polly," she sighed deeply, as if she was trying to clear her throat, "I would never make a return voyage. There were times when I really thought I was dying and would gladly have welcomed death."

Polly was very eager to return to Sydney and was equally relieved when the ship turned toward its anchorage. She borrowed Aaron's glass and sighed with relief as she saw her new building next to his warehouse, and pointed it out along the busy waterfront to the two women, "That will be your new home ladies."

For once, during the tormenting voyage, they both smiled.

But the port was getting far too busy and in spite of the ladies of the colony having influence, they lay at anchor for two days.

Polly and Aaron were rowed ashore and were greeted by

the agent, "Good news Captain, your ship is almost fully booked with passengers for the return journey, and we also have a good cargo." He turned to Polly, "Your shop is finished now Miss Polly, apart from the glass and inside furniture. That Samual fellow selected the best timber and brought it here personally. He has laid the floorboards, all a delightful red wood."

"Yes," Polly answered, "since we have laid off at anchor, I haven't been able to take my eyes off it. I feel like a young schoolgirl."

"And so you should, it will be the finest shop in the colony."

He led her inside and showed her around both the shop and the living quarters, "As soon as the ship unloads we will get the glass fitted and you can move in."

"I won't be moving in – my two assistants will. By the way, her husband is a saddler. Will there be any work for him?"

"My God," the agent slapped his forehead, "a saddler, why the man will make a fortune. Does he do any other leather work?"

"Yes, I understand he makes shoes, and bags... in fact anything to do with leather."

The agent again slapped his forehead and Polly thought he was having a bout of apoplexy.

"Alright Mr Abrahams, take it easy. Just you look after him – his wife and the other lady will get settled in."

The ship tied up at the wharf and the invasion of the ladies began. Much to their disappointment, however, no dresses were laid out along the ship's rail as they usually were.

"Sorry ladies, they are deep down in the hold but have no worries, I have bought plenty this time. And shoes and hats and very good news – my shop will be finished within the week. Then you may come and choose whatever you wish, without any hurry."

Polly watched the cargo being unloaded and sighed with relief when the packing cases carrying her glass were securely put ashore.

"Good for you Aaron, they all sound in one piece otherwise

I would have had your balls for dinner."

"Now, is that a very nice thing for an up and coming business lady to say?"

Maud and Jenny came ashore, and in spite of their violent sea sickness they now looked a picture of health. Especially Maud who had lost her Portsea tavern paleness. Jenny had re-styled her hair, now a streaky blonde – no doubt brought on by the tropical sun – and in a new dress, she looked a picture of English beauty. As they walked daintily across the cobbled stones, the men and convicts stopped work and stared at them. They entered the shop where the workmen were putting the finishing touches to the building.

"It's magnificent ..." Maud said as she was shown her small but comfortable bedroom and came to kiss Polly on her cheek.

But Polly pulled her head away, "Now ladies, there is something I must say to you straight away. First, whenever the customers are here, you will address me as Miss Polly. I don't wish to sound snobbish, but this will become a ladies' meeting place. Alone, you can address me as Polly, and the customers will always be addressed as Madam. If their husbands are with them they must be addressed as sir. The shop will be entirely in your hands Jenny."

She turned to Maud, "And you must address Jenny as madam while the customers are here. You will be living together and I want you to remain friends."

That afternoon Mrs Pilgrim came by, and after alighting from her carriage, ran into the shop, "Polly!"

She ran towards her, arms outstretched and they fell into each others arms, "Oh Polly, it's so nice to see you again."

Polly took her through the living quarters to the sitting room and poured out two glasses of port. They sat opposite each other.

"I don't suppose you have heard the news yet have you Polly?" Polly shook her head, "It's about the two convicts you killed – the authorities are going to reward you. The men were notorious highway men, both wanted for murder. They killed a trooper and a settler's wife and had her jewellery on their bodies. Apparently she'd caught them stealing food from her house and they raped her and killed her. Then they ransacked her house – they would have been hanged, so you have saved the authorities money and got rid of two notorious criminals. How much more have you to do here?"

"Not a lot, the girls can handle it, I will come with you to the homestead, I have been looking forward to that. How is Samual these days?"

"Like a lovesick schoolboy, for heavens sake. Put the man out of his misery, Polly, every time he comes to the house he asks how long I think it will be before you get back."

When they arrived back at the homestead, not only Mr Pilgrim but Felix, his wife, and their daughter – as well as Samual – were waiting to greet them. She was kissed by each in turn.

"Ever since you left Polly the whole colony has been alive with your exploits, they intend to hold a civic reception for you."

Felix said, "My Polly, you have got some guts." And they all chorused the same feeling. A meal had been prepared and they sat talking until darkness fell, then retreated to the verandah.

"What do you think Polly, my parents said I can return to England on your ship. I am only sorry you will not be returning with us."

Polly frowned and looked at Kathleen, "What do you mean Kathy?"

"Well I understand you will be marrying Samual and staying here to open your new shop. I know all the preparations for the wedding are completed."

Polly turned sharply to Samual and he looked sheepishly back at her. She indicated a walk in the paddock, and as he slowly rose from his chair he went to take her hand but she snatched it away, out of sight. Kathleen's mother looked at her daughter, "Good heavens Kathleen, now you have let the cat amongst the pigeons."

They could hear Polly's voice right across the paddock, "You have no bloody right to tell them anything, Samual. I told you I would give you my answer after this trip. Now you can go and bloody well tell them it's all off. I wouldn't marry you, if you were the last man on earth. In fact I don't ever want to see you again. I am a free woman Samual, with my life before me, and a business to establish. I was ready to give you my answer tonight, but I will give it to you now – the answer is no."

Samual roughly took her hand and pulled her towards him, "No! You don't do that to me, you cow. It's that damn Captain – you sleep with him and act as man and wife. I suppose you want to marry *him*?"

She laughed in his face, "If only I could Samual – he is a real man with feelings for his fellow human beings. But I am afraid that has been denied me. He has married some-one else. But I will tell you this Samual, I *am* still sleeping with him and will do so until he tells me to get off his ship. You are not half the man he is and you will never be."

In the darkness Polly couldn't see Samual's face, but she felt the tension rising. He caught hold of her and threw her to the ground, viciously pulling at her dress.

"Take it easy Samual... if you make so much noise, they will know you have raped me."

She quietly undid her clothing and lay back, "Enjoy your-self – because it will be the first and last time. You are not the first man that has raped me. I was raped when I was a young girl of fourteen."

Half an hour later they were walking back to the house, "I'm sorry Polly, I shouldn't have done that. It was both cruel and crude of me. Please forgive me Polly and don't say a word to them."

"Don't worry Samual, your parents are too nice to be hurt. I wouldn't want them to know you are a rapist with your heart set on every nice looking woman in the colony, including Mrs Pilgrim."

He caught her arm and stopped her, "Who told you that?"

"No one Samual. I have watched you looking at her, I would know that glance anywhere. Oh yes... I have been around this world quite a lot and met your sort in every port. Now just listen to me, if when I get back here and you have made any further advances to my friend, every-one will know the truth about you. When we return to the house, act normally and when I leave here in a couple of days you can tell your parents that the wedding is off. Whatever excuse you use I will go along with, so long as you leave Mrs Pilgrim alone."

Polly was smiling as if nothing had happened when they returned to the verandah and she sat down and sipped at her port. But Mrs Pilgrim was no fool and sensed that something was not right. She wrongly blamed Kathleen for spouting her mouth off and hurriedly brought the party to a close.

"Well Kathleen, if you do wish to return on our ship I shall arrange it as soon as I get back and see Captain Jacobs. We will find you the best cabin on the ship."

The next morning Mrs Pilgrim and her husband, with Polly, went on a long horse ride across the open bush. They saw Ju-Ju and her baby walking towards the homestead, devoid of all her clothing and without her tribe. Michael walked his horse over to her and talked to her in the same gibberish that Samual had used during the last trip.

"You will be the death of me one of these days Ju-Ju," said Mrs. Pilgrim, a smile rising on her lips as the girl laughed loudly treating life as one big joke, "Go on, get back, and give that lovely baby some fresh milk."

Ju-Ju put the baby on the ground and it walked steadily towards Beatrice, who caught its hands and lifted it on to her horse. Beatrice shook her head, "What the hell can I do with them Polly? It looks like I am stuck with them for life." She gave the baby back to her mother and they turned towards the homestead.

The days passed quickly. Although Polly had been looking forward to seeing Samual, she now knew exactly what and how he was – and was greatly relieved to have gotten rid of him.

"I suppose we had better return to the ship now Beatrice, we will be sailing in a couple of weeks and I still have plenty of work to do. I love it here in this country. Now it is finished between Aaron and me I may think of settling down here. I still have to make arrangements with my suppliers in London to send the dresses, shoes and hats I need to keep me in touch with all the latest fashions. Getting them here will be no problem now that Aaron has three ships and hankering after his fourth. Believe me it won't be very long before he has a ship landing here every month."

Beatrice rode with her to Sydney. Polly was proud that she was now a very competent horsewoman and had to admit to herself that she had become a bit of a show-off.

She slept on the ship every night, but at dawn every morning was back at her shop. Already the women were beginning to flock there and using it for their daily tittle-tattle.

A messenger arrived, with suitably headed notepaper, requesting her to attend on the Governor at two o'clock that afternoon. A deputation was waiting to greet her. The governor looked at her when she came into the room, surprised to see how slightly built she was – astounded that she had been able to deal with the two notorious convicts. After a brief speech and description of how her deeds, there was an applause from the small gathering. The governor handed her a small purse of gold sovereigns.

"Madam we are delighted that you have taken it upon yourself to start a business here, and we all wish you the very best of luck."

When she left Government House and was making her way back to the ship, a carriage slowed down beside her. Kathleen was with her father, "I have brought you a passenger Miss Polly, please look after her."

The girl's travelling bags were unloaded at the ship and Felix took a sorrowful parting from his over excited daughter.

Chapter Forty-four

Polly made sure her two ladies were comfortably settled in. Jenny was proud of the fact that she now had her own shop to manage without an owner standing over her watching her every move. For Polly would be sailing any day now, and Maud, who never had never known what it was like to spend two nights in a row in the same bed, couldn't believe she had a room to herself alone. Looking back she saw that part of her life, patrolling the dark streets and alley ways of Portsmouth touting for customers, as like looking back on a living nightmare.

When the news got around that Bill was a saddler – and fresh news flew around the colony faster than a bush fire – he was inundated with work. The agent rented him a small shed at the back of his premises and he began repairing and taking orders for new saddles. He needed large supplies of leather from England, and gave Aaron a list of his requirements. Luckily, he had brought most of his tools with him.

Polly left the layout of the shop and its goods to Jenny. The girl's years of experience, from the tender age of twelve, had taught her a way with customers; making each one feel as though they were contributing towards the new shop. So when Polly rejoined the ship for the homeward bound journey, she felt far more contented. When the *Golden Eagle* pulled away she stood at the stern with her arm round Kathleen's shoulders, comforting her and handing her a small silk handkerchief to wipe away the tears.

The girl's mother and father had come to see the ship depart but there was no sign of Samual. As always, Mrs Pilgrim was there, waving and dabbing her eyes.

Kathleen remained depressed for the first few days. The first time she had been away from home and she was on her way to the other side of the world. But soon her zest for life returned and she happily watched the antics of the dolphins amid the thousands of flying fish. The ship ran side by side with a school of whales, and she couldn't believe the size of them. One especially large whale, only a hundred yard away, rose to the surface as if in defiance and raised its gigantic tail, slapping it on the water with a loud crack like a heavy gun being fired. She kept a diary and every night, under the dim flicker of an oil lamp, wrote vehemently about the wonders of the deep.

Several weeks later they anchored in Table Bay, where Polly changed into her tightest pair of trousers and a light, revealing blouse waiting for the horrible little Boer to board the ship. She winked her eye at Kathleen and asked her to sit down beside her, "Just watch this hypocritical old bugger, Kathleen."

She nudged her as he came aboard and stepped over the taffrail. He gave Polly a look that would have made one of his Kaffirs prostrate himself with fear.

"Have you no shame, you hussy?" Polly stood up and walked away from him with an exaggerated swing of her hip and bum.

She paused, turned and stopped before tickling him under his chin, "Hello darling," he pushed her hand away quickly as she invited him, "taking me ashore?"

He fumed and sweated when he saw Kathleen trying her best not to laugh aloud, and stamped his foot pushing Polly away, "You damn hussy."

Quickly he completed his business with Aaron, quite aware he was the centre of amusement for Polly, Kathleen and the other members of the passengers and crew.

Polly quickly changed into her cabin boy shore gear and, arm in arm with Kathleen, Aaron and a crowd of passengers, spent the next couple of hours ashore with the black lady, buying the fresh fruit and vegetables from her friend.

"One of these days Polly you will really rub that old man up the wrong way and he will catch you ashore. It's not the done thing in this country to dress up as a boy."

"Oh tush to him Aaron. More like one of these days I will throw the little bugger over the side and feed him to the fishes." They stayed at Cape Town two days to take on stores and water and allow the passengers to feel firm ground under their feet once more.

The weather deteriorated and two days out of Cape Town the ship tossed and rolled and pirouetted on the huge waves. Most of the passengers refused to leave their cabins and beds. Tommy the cabin boy had a permanent grin on his face – indifferent to the discomfort felt by the passengers, he at the same time sympathised with them. After all, it meant more food for him. Kathleen had turned out to be a good sailor and took it all in her stride, never missing a meal.

The poor weather continued until they reached Madeira where they took on a shipment of Madeira wine and port. Now in calm waters the passengers lined the decks watching the barrels being swung aboard. A lucky few went ashore until the ship sailed.

The weather had moderated and the seas eased off a bit when they again set sail but not enough to stop the passengers retiring once again to their cabins and beds.

Several passengers joined Aaron for dinner and Kathleen looked the picture of health. Tommy, serving dinner, offered the girl her third glass of wine, "Tomorrow we'll catch a glimpse of old England, but it won't be the famous white cliffs you have been on about Kathleen – they are on the other side of the channel." Starry eyed and a little unsteady on her feet, she attempted to make her way to the cabin.

Aaron nodded to the boy, "You had better follow her Tommy, see she doesn't stumble and hurt herself."

A few days later the ship tied up alongside their own berth and started unloading. The agent came out to meet them, a broad smile spread across his face. He held his hand out, "Good news Captain – I have a full compliment of passengers and a full cargo. Your new ship sailed three weeks ago, she looks very elegant, if it's possible to describe a ship that way. She was full both with passengers and cargo."

Polly came on deck dressed in her best dress and bonnet and Aaron saw her to the carriage. He held the door open and gently kissed her, "This will have been our last voyage together Aaron. When the cargo has been organised I suppose you will be off to see your family." She held her hand out and he kissed it, looking straight into her blue eyes.

"I will miss you Polly, we have been in some tight spots together, and have had some good times."

She gently slapped his head with her glove, "Shut up Aaron, you rotten sod, before I start crying." She jumped into the carriage and ordered the driver to her destination.

It was to be the following day before relatives arrived to collect Kathleen, and Aaron could not leave for Esher until he was sure she was safe.

Kathleen was impatient, wanting to inspect London, and that night Aaron took her to the opera. She sat throughout starry eyed, and in the foyer after the performance she watched the ladies in their beautiful dresses and their escorts in various bright uniforms and colourful clothing. The foyer itself was brightly illuminated with magnificent glass chandeliers throwing out thousands of sparking lights.

Apart from three members of the crew, there was no one else on the ship. They ate a supper of cold mutton washed down with wine, before Aaron showed her to her cabin bidding her goodnight.

It was dark and cold and Aaron was wrapped up in blankets, fast asleep in his cabin when he felt a movement in his bed. Someone was climbing in beside him, "I didn't expect you back tonight Polly." There was no answer as she snuggled down beside him. She put her arm round his waist and rubbed her face between his shoulder blades, her hand wandered down to his thighs, "What the hell are you doing Polly? You know I will be with my wife shortly." He sprang up and raised the wick in the lamp. A mop of red hair was spread over his pillow, "Kathleen! What the hell are you doing here? Please get out."

She was completely naked, "But Captain, you have been so good to me on this voyage, I wanted to repay you. To be honest I have been wanting to make love to you since we left Sydney. I love you Captain."

"Now don't be a silly little girl. Go back to your cabin. You have drank too much wine tonight and it's gone to your head – you know I am a married man."

"I know you are a married man, Captain – but it doesn't stop Polly from sleeping with you."

"Polly is different, she has been with me for a very long time."

Kathleen stood by the bed, completely naked, her breasts firm and proud, "You are still a child, Kathleen... and also my wife knows the arrangement with Polly... please go back to your cabin. You will feel different in the morning."

"I won't Captain! I have felt like this since we left Sydney, surely you must have noticed. I am not a child and I am not a virgin. I have a lover back home who threatened to kill himself when I left."

"A lover!" Aaron looked surprised. "How could you have had a lover? There aren't that many single men about. Who the hell is he?"

"One of the convicts. We have been lovers for two years now, he is quite young and handsome. I was swimming in the river one day, completely naked. He hadn't seen me and had stripped off, and was swimming towards me." She laughed, "You should have seen the look on his face, he didn't know what to say. He just looked away, frightened – but I smiled at him and before long we were making love on the river's bank. We have made love twice a week ever since. I thought I was in love with him until I met you."

"Now, come on Kathleen, don't put me in this terrible position. I've given my word to your parents that I would look after you, I would never be able to look your father in the face again." He got out of bed and put a blanket around her then led her back to her cabin. At the door she turned and kissed him passionately. Aaron slapped her bottom and closed the door behind her.

It was mid-day when Sam knocked at his cabin door, "A

355

carriage has just pulled up at the bottom of the gangway
sir, I think they have come for Miss Kathleen, sir."

"Thank heavens for that Sam. Please tell her to get ready,
I will be out in a few minutes."

Parting with Kathleen hadn't been the sweet sorrow he
expected. during the voyage she had been the life and soul
of her shipmates, helping to bring excitement to what had
been a dull and monotonous voyage. But now that Aaron
knew the hidden secret of her life, she no longer appealed
to him. While he hadn't led a blameless life himself,
Kathleen, who was the apple of her father's eye, yet hid a
secret life. At the gangway he bid her goodbye and held his
hand out, but she quickly reached up and kissed him firmly on his lips. He gently pushed her away, "Behave yourself
Kathleen."

Surprised at her actions the previous night, he stood at
the top of the gangway and watched the carriage rattle
over the cobblestones and out of sight, greatly relieved.

His own carriage was waiting for him. He completed his
business with his agent before visiting the old jeweller
and handing him the valuable diamond that Hargreaves
had given him. They discussed it in his private office cum
showroom, "Don't do anything with it just yet, I have been
invited to meet the African chief and will do so on my next
trip. Keep it in a safe place until I return." They shook
hands.

Aaron felt he could visit the shipbuilders after he had
seen Elizabeth and his family. As usual she was waiting
for him by her favourite window. She ran to meet the carriage and Aaron jumped from it and closed her in his
arms. She smothered his face and neck with kisses, "It
seems like these departures are getting longer and longer."

As he returned her kisses, her face was wet with tears
and she sobbed gently in his arms. He stayed the week and
promised he would stay another few days before he sailed.

After a visit to Portsmouth he went to see Mr Feltham at
Bucklers Hard. He had a sixty-five foot ship almost completed on the stocks, and immediately Aaron took a fancy
to it, "She is beautiful Mr Feltham, and I bet she is very
fast."

Mr Feltham stroked the newly varnished woodwork on the taffrail lovingly, "Yes Captain, it has been designed and built for speed. It will be out on its shake-down cruise next Thursday. Why not come out on her?"

Aaron agreed and the next Thursday, accompanied by Sam, he joined the new ship with its owner, Mr Feltham and a scratch crew made up from his workforce. They raced the ship as far as the Solent and Aaron immediately fell in love with her.

"Right Mr Feltham, start on one for me, the fastest you can possible make it. Have a contract ready and be at my lawyers in the Hight Street at mid-day tomorrow. You know Harris, don't you?"

"Yes Captain, about one year from now it will be ready."

Back at Portsmouth, in his favourite tavern Aaron asked Harry to prepare another crew for the following year.

"And this time I want a skilled Captain, and a couple more officers. You know how I run my ships Harry, make sure they know – no flogging or rope's end."

Harry passed Aaron a tankard of brandy and sat facing him talking about the old days when he had hidden from the press gangs; and they talked about Polly and how she had risen in the world, "She was always a clever girl Aaron."

"Yes, and a bloody rich one now."

"How many ships do you own now, Aaron?"

"This will be my fourth, but I want at least ten, maybe more. Good healthy ships and good healthy crews – that is the secret – and passengers' quarters scrubbed and cleaned every day, weather permitting."

Chapter Forty-five

Aaron spent the final week before sailing, with his family. It was late summer and very warm. Most days they spent on the river bank that ran through the estate, fishing and swimming, but most of the time was spent in each others arms. Some days Elizabeth looked despondent and would often weep softly. Other days she felt buoyant, without a care in the world, as they raced each other on horseback around the vast estate. But it soon had to end and on the last day she was in tears.

"Why not stop for just one trip Aaron? Surely with three ships and a fourth on its way you could stay ashore occasionally and really get to know your family. We all miss you terribly when you are away. David keeps asking when you will return and your daughter hardly knows you."

"Well Elizabeth, I may stay a little longer next trip. I will only be taking my new ship to West Africa. Then I will be handing it over to a new Captain and I can stay for a couple of months."

The news partly cheered her up, but she started sulking again at the time of his departure, almost fainting when she heard the carriage returning to take him away.

"Please Aaron, darling, don't stay away too long, try and make it as fast as possible." He held her close in his arms and stroked her red flaming hair as she sobbed, "I know you are married to the sea and I have accepted that. But you must also remember you are married to me and you now have a family here, so try and spare us a part of your life."

The ship was almost ready to sail, passengers and crew were safely aboard. It was the same crew as the previous voyage and Aaron called them together, "I want as fast a trip as possible this time men – I want you to give me the best you can."

There was a bit of a rumpus on the gangway and when Aaron and his first mate went to investigate, Polly was struggling up the gangplank with two enormous boxes. They went to help her, "Bloody hell Polly, more stock?"

"Shut up you bloody old miser. You are getting as tight as a duck's arse, Aaron."

"Now that isn't ladylike Polly. I have just been down to Portsmouth and boasted to everyone how you have changed into a lady. Some lady, using that language."

They sailed with the tide and lady luck was with them, for they made a very fast passage everyone enjoying the sunshine once they passed the Canaries. They took on a cargo of Madeira wine filling the holds completely. Much to the delight of Aaron's Madeira agent who was finding new outlet for the famous wine in the new colony. It seemed like Aaron had gained the Midas touch; for everything he touched appeared to turn to gold. Polly, too, was eager and excited to reach the colony. Impatient to see how her new venture was going, she had plenty of stock in the holds.

They stopped at the Cape only to replenish the water and stores, and much to everyone's relief Polly didn't put in an appearance on deck as the old Boer came aboard to carry out his official duties.

The last leg of the journey went without mishap apart from two days of being becalmed, and Polly was delighted when the heads loomed up. The passengers lined the deck, some quite amazed to see a thriving town looming up before them, with brick buildings and a church. The anchorage was crowded with ships of every description and they had to wait for two days before they could tie up at the jetty. But both Polly and Aaron had been rowed ashore within an hour of dropping the anchor.

As Polly entered the shop several customers greeted her, and Jenny excused herself, "Why madam, I am very pleased to see you and I hope you have brought plenty of stock."

"Oh yes, plenty – but where is Maud? Surely she should be in the shop at this time?"

Jenny lowered her voice and said, "I think you had better go to her room madam. I am afraid there has been trouble. I will join you as soon as I have finished with my customers."

Polly entered the room and Maud was lying on the bed, her face buried in her pillow, "Why hello Maud, aren't you feeling very well? Have you a fever?"

"No madam." She slowly sat up and Polly staggered back a few steps.

"My God Maud! Whoever did this to you?"

Maud's face was covered in bruises and both eyes were blackened. As she reached out, Polly could see her arms were swollen and badly bruised. Maud tried to talk but no words came out. Fortunately at that moment, the customers having left the shop, Jenny came in. Polly turned to her and asked, "What's happened Jenny?"

"After you had left Madam, a man kept coming into the shop. He reckoned he was a friend of yours, a rather tall handsome man. He started taking Maud out, and after a few weeks she surprised me by saying she was going to marry him. First his father comes bursting in the shop, forbidding the marriage and shouting he had just lost his own daughter and wouldn't see her for two or three years. She was away in England and he didn't want to lose his son..."

Here Polly interrupted her, "This man wouldn't be named Samual by any chance? A large blue eyed and handsome blonde?"

Jenny looked surprised. Wide eyed she answered, "Yes madam, do you know him?"

"Yes I know him alright. I was going to marry him myself, but he started taking over my life before we started. What happened then, to Maud?"

"Well it seems that his father ruled the roost and his mother didn't want him to marry a shop assistant; so Maud told him it was all over. Of course he wouldn't take no for an answer and kept pestering her. Really, she was head over heels in love with him and they kept walking out together. Eventually she became pregnant and that was when the real trouble started. One night it was very dark and he came here banging on the door. Unfortunately, it was Maud that went to the door, he caught hold of her hair and dragged her out. Bill went after them but he kicked Bill and hit him, knocking him to the ground. By the time he got to his feet Samual had Maud across his horse and was galloping out of town with her. I shouted to the troopers, but they just laughed and said he was only having a good time. Next night, the man knocked at the door and Bill answered, he threw Maud into the shop. We thought she was dead. She told us later that he had taken her out to the bush, raped her several times and said he was going to get rid of the baby. He stripped her, laid her on the ground, or rather knocked her to the ground, and punched and kicked her repeatedly jumping on her stomach. She had a miscarriage about a week ago. See her now, you can imagine how she'd looked then."

"Why the bastard! Have you seen a magistrate? The man could easily have killed her. I will go to Government House today."

But Maud stirred, "Please Polly, don't do that."

"Has she seen a doctor yet?"

Jenny shook her head, "We sent for a doctor, but he was drunk when he arrived and hasn't been here since. He gave her some medicine, but it hasn't done her much good."

"Right, I will be here for two weeks. I will get this settled up – Samual won't be bothering us again."

Next day Polly went out to see her dear friend Mrs Pilgrim. It was apparent that the news was not about that Samual had beaten up Maud. Mrs Pilgrim was over the moon that she could spend a few days with Polly. They sat down to dinner the first night and eventually the talk got round about Samual.

"I'm sorry about you and Samual Polly. I really thought you would get along well."

"Yes I know Beatrice, it was just a silly thing really." Polly

361

lied, "I am rather sorry it happened – still, never mind."

Beatrice's eyes lit up, "Oh, in that case I will invite him over and you can make it up, I would be happy to see that."

The next night Samual arrived with his family for they were anxious to know if Kathleen had settled.

"Yes Felix, she loves London. She was amazed at the size of it, and has visited all the sights and been to the opera."

Polly suggested a walk with Samual and they left the house hand in hand, "I am sorry Samual I reacted the last time." She wanted to put him at ease, "I shall never forgive myself for treating you like that. I must make up for it." She pulled him to the ground and they made love there and then.

Two hours later they returned to the house. Samual a happy and contented man – Polly satisfied she now had him under her control. The mood he was in, she was sure there was nothing he would not do for her. Sitting on the verandah, the talk got round to her shop and staff.

"Of course you know one of my assistants was beaten up by a convict and raped. There really are some animals about. At least... she thinks it was a convict."

Quite convinced now, that he was beyond suspicion, and that Maud hadn't told anyone who it really was. Safe in the knowledge that she wouldn't dare accuse the son of one of the colony's leading families, he became bolder, "Why the damn fellow wants horse whipping before they hang him."

"Yes and I would like the privilege of hanging him myself if ever they catch him."

To allay any suspicion, Polly spent most of her time with Samual, hiding her hatred for the man, laughing and joking and regularly making love. But each time it took supreme effort to stop shuddering as he touched her.

"No, I shall be staying here now arrangements have been made in London for my dressmaker to send me regular supplies."

Alone that night Samual said, "Does that mean we can settle a date for our forthcoming marriage Polly? Should we tell my parents?"

She placed her hand on his arm, trying to hide her loathing of him, and looked directly into his eyes. From a certain angle, he looked evil.

"No Samual, not just yet. Let us carry on like we are for a while. We don't want to rush things, it will give us time to get to know one another much better." He tried to argue but she put her fingers on his lips, "Not now Samual, you know I don't like being pushed."

A few days later Polly was ready to return to Sydney and asked Samual to escort her. He jumped at the chance, and brought the small quiet mare round the next morning, laughing and joking as Polly showed off her prowess as a horsewoman. Polly stood up in the stirrups and turned waving frantically at Mrs Pilgrim, who enjoyed seeing them together so happy and contented.

Aaron was on deck, and welcomed them both aboard, shaking hands warmly with Samual. Polly led him to the main cabin where he nodded towards the double bed, "I see you still share a cabin with the Captain."

"Oh yes, I wouldn't do otherwise. It's a long and lonely voyage between here and England." She giggled like a small girl, "I don't wish to shock you but we do try out various ways."

Samual was far from shocked and became very interested, his evil eyes lighting up as he licked his lips, "How do you mean, various ways?"

He was sweating profusely, as Polly tried to act demure, bowing her head, "Well I can't tell you... but if you like, I will show you our favourite. Lie on the bed."

Polly locked the cabin door before sorting through several drawers, "Spread-eagle out – but first, undress."

Eager to comply Samual quickly undressed and lay out on the bed. Polly, after tying his wrists and ankles to the bed post corners, sat on the edge of the bed.

"Now my fine gentleman – I understand you raped my assistant, and knocked ten different kinds of shit out of her to destroy the baby you had put inside her." Her eyes widened as she looked down at his naked body, "I see you have lost interest in sex. I am sorry I have no horsewhip, but I do have this cane – perhaps it may hurt more. You did say *you* would like to horsewhip the culprit, but now we have him I can't let you do it. *You* would only give light strokes."

She brought down the cane at an angle across his belly, and he let out a loud groan. Polly tut tutted and warned him not to scream out too loud or Aaron may come in.

"And when I tell him what you did to Maud he will lay into you."

Polly moved to the other side of the bed and brought down the cane, hard across his abdomen, leaving another red weal, "I understand you jumped up and down on her stomach. Is that right?"

He was too surprised to answer, and Polly punched him. "Is that right? I will know if you are lying!"

He nodded his head.

"Like this?" Polly jumped on the bed and began jumping up and down on his abdomen, as he tried to move his body to throw her off. She then put her foot straight into his face — but she didn't want to mark him to much.

"You said you would help to hang him too."

She took a knife from a drawer and pressed the point against his throat, "Well, you know I have already killed two men for trying to do the same thing to me. I can't hang you, or cut your balls off, but I can do worse..."

Polly picked up a feather, that had dropped from a pillow and sitting down beside him she started to tickle his genitals.

"Oh dear dear, just look at this — rising to the occasion. We will have to settle that." She picked up the cane and slashed him across the penis. He squealed out loud.

A few moments later there was a knock on the door and Aaron shouted, "Are you alright Polly?"

She laughed and opened the door.

"Bloody hell Polly, what is going on? I thought you were enjoying yourselves."

"Well I am! But I don't think dear Samual is. He meted out this punishment to Maud while we were away. He put her with child — then kicked and beat her until she miscarried. She is absolutely terrified of him. Just look at him there Aaron, you wouldn't think butter would melt in his mouth. Now he is absolutely terrified. Do you think we should castrate him Aaron – Maud has not been his only victim."

Samual writhed and twisted on the bonds that held him securely to the bed.

"I think we could recommend him for a job with the church choir with a nice high voice."

Samual was now so terrified that he began to wander off into long lapses of silence, followed by a violent struggle to escape from his bonds.

"Why don't you stop struggling Samual. You forget I have been at sea for many years and I know how to tie knots. The more you struggle the tighter they will get. Look your hands and feet – they are turning blue."

Aaron turned to leave the cabin, "If you do kill the wicked bastard Polly, please throw him overboard."

The torture, both physical and mental, lasted for three more hours. At times Samual was blubbering like a baby.

"Now Samual," Polly was twisting a sharp knife in her hands, "I have watched you squirm here and plead with me. I should kill you, for there is no telling what you have done to Maud. But I shall cut your bonds free and I will tell you this. If you come anywhere near Maud, or any of my girls again, I really *will* kill you. I am writing a confession for you here, admitting that you raped both Maud and myself. Now if I ever hear again that you have raped another woman I will take it to Government House. Is that clearly understood?"

Polly sat at the desk and wrote out the confession. She cut his right hand free and stood over him with the knife at his throat. He didn't say a word but his hands were shaking as she cut him loose.

"Now get dressed and get out of my life forever. Don't come near my shop, or else I promise – I will kill you."

Samual didn't say another word as he dressed and slunk ashore and away from the ship.

Chapter Forty-six

It was a sad farewell as Aaron stood at the stern of his ship and Polly stood on the quayside dabbing away her tears.

All alone now he could hardly take it in. Willie, who had been his faithful companion from the time of his smuggling days, was now on another ship. And now the owner of three profitable ships with another on the way, Aaron would not be happy until he ran a fleet of ten ships or more – happy in the knowledge that he had a well fed, well paid, and contented crew. What was taken for granted in other ships, and particularly the Royal Navy – flogging, hanging and bad food, Aaron would never accept. He continually sent reports to the Lords of the Admiralty, but no doubt they were put aside with only the lowly clerks ever looking at them, never to be seen by the high and mighty themselves.

Four days out of Sydney they came in contact with a small fleet of British men-o-war, a three decker and four Frigates. Aaron was hailed from the flagship, and ordered a member of his crew, "A small boat is coming alongside with a high ranking officer. Please prepare to take him aboard – doubt they have mail for home. See that it is safely stored below."

"Aye aye Captain."

A bosun's chair was lowered and the naval officer was hoisted aboard. As he set foot on the deck, Aaron ran to meet him.

"Saunders, how the hell are you? My God this is a pleasure." They shook hands warmly.

"Well Aaron, I have waited years for this, and I believe congratulations are in order. I suppose I can say we are now related and that you went straight to work and made me an uncle for a second time. What are the chances of your giving up the sea?"

"Very little hope for that, I am afraid – not in the immediate future – however, my fleet is growing steadily."

"Oh yes I have heard all about that. I am sorry in some ways I didn't join you, but one couldn't possible say no to Lord Nelson. Still I have made my mark in the Navy. I suppose one day I will become a grumpy old Admiral suffering with gout and a bloody big red nose, telling all and sundry how I served with Nelson."

They retired to Aaron's cabin and carried on talking for the next two hours, finishing a bottle of brandy between them.

"I hope you treat your men better than most of the naval officers I know, real brutes some of them." Aaron went on to relate how well he got on with his own men, "I put in a report to the Admiralty about the medicinal values of citrus fruit. I only wish you could help, it would drastically reduce scurvy. You must have some real influence now. I have another report prepared – could you possibly see that it is read by the right people?"

"I will do my very best Aaron, but I doubt if I will see England for another three years at least. But we do have some mail to go home, and Elizabeth sends her deepest love should I bump into you. She said your regular run was Australia... I don't think she has any idea of the vast size of these oceans, but we are lucky we met. I will have to say my farewells now." He held out his hand. "Goodbye old chap."

Saunders was hoisted in the bosun's chair and lowered into his small boat as the gap between the two ships widened. Aaron watched from the deck until he was safely hoisted aboard his own vessel.

The interlude had cheered him enormously, for without Polly to talk to and Willie, he had been down in the dumps since they left the colony. Every night he invited several passengers to dine with him, but somehow it wasn't the same without Polly. She could always keep the conversation going when he tired out. One of the passengers, now a rather old man, an ex-convict who had done his time but liked the country, had decided to stay behind and make his fortune. He had succeeded and now was intending to settle back in a small village in Dorset to spend his last few years.

"It's a good country, but hard Captain. If you are willing to work, and don't mind hard work, you can make a fortune."

"I know, I own half shares in a brewery there and my partner can't make the beer fast enough. He calls it Jacobs Ale, do you know it?"

The man burst out laughing, "Know it! Why, what I spent on that booze probably made you a rich man myself. Not a bad drop of beer that Captain, better than that gut rot they call rum."

Several days out of the Cape and much to Aaron's annoyance, for so far they had made excellent time, they lay becalmed. There was not a wisp of air and the sea was like a sheet of glass. Several sharks circled the ship, their slender bodies gliding effortlessly just below the surface of the water, their dorsal fins gliding just above. The children amongst the passengers became very excited and their parents shuddered with fear.

Suddenly there was an almighty splash and a woman screamed, "My boy!"

Sam, without any hesitation or fear for his own life, dived overboard and caught the boy under his chin, his face deeply etched with fear. Aaron seeing what happened rushed to the ship's rail and told everyone to make a noise and catch hold of anything they could to cause splashing in the sea. At the same time he lowered a rope overboard to Sam, who grabbed the boy with one arm and the rope with the other. Aaron rushed to his cabin and returned with several guns, dropping them on the deck before firing at the shark's fins, as a crew member carried out the reloading. Sam was pulled aboard and quickly deposited the boy on the deck, who ran squealing to his mother's arms. Sam became the hero for the remainder of the long haul home.

There was cheering from the stern and all the passengers rushed to see what was going on. A crew member had caught a shark, about eight feet long and was clubbing it with a belaying pin and shouting "Eat one of our little boys would you, you bastard, now we are going to eat you! Anyone fancy a nice shark steak?"

The passengers looked at the crewman in disbelief. How could he eat a thing like that? As if in answer to their unspoken question he took a knife from his belt and sliced through the shark's skin and ate a slice.

"It's lovely and better still when it's cooked."

The passengers turned their backs on him and walked away, some looking as if they were going to be sick.

That night the guests who joined Aaron did not realise that they were dining on the very same shark, "How did you enjoy the fish, ladies and gentlemen, much to your liking I hope?"

"Very nice Captain."

For the remainder of the voyage the boy never left Sam alone. He followed him everywhere until he eventually became such a nuisance that Sam threatened him time and time again, "If you don't stop following me around Jimmy, I will throw you back to the sharks."

But all Jimmy did was laugh and run up to Sam throwing his arms round his legs. It came as a relief to Sam when the ship finally sailed up the Thames to its usual docking space.

It was also a relief to Aaron, who lost no time in contacting his agent. But this time he was not greeted with the usual smile, "I think you had better get down to your home Captain, I have had urgent messages that it is vital you should go there the minute you dock."

The agent could not enlarge on the message and Aaron sent a crew member with a message for the hostler to fetch the fastest horse he had in the stable.

The horse, a white hunter covered in a lather of sweat, with Aaron astride galloped up the long path leading to the house. He jumped off and ran the few yards to the great doors. Something was the matter, for Elizabeth did not run to meet him like she always did. He banged on the door and pulled the great iron chain at the side. The bell inside clanged like a giant cathedral bell around the great building. Aaron pushed the door, but it was firmly bolted from the inside.

It was ten minutes before he saw a young groom come from around the corner. He ran to him and caught the boy's coat, pulling it to him, "What's the matter here? Where is the butler and the maids?"

The boy stammered and stuttered, with fear on his face. He shook his head and managed some hardly intelligible words, "You are choking me, sir."

Aaron let the boy go, he knew he was frightening the boy and would never get an intelligent answer from him until he calmed down.

"Where is madam boy?" His voice had quietened down, "Where is she?"

Something was really wrong.

"Don't you know sir?" The boy's bottom lip quivered, "Madam died sir."

"When boy? Where!"

"About three months ago, sir. She took the small pox... It went through here sir, like a knife through butter."

"And my children, where are they? Who's in charge of them?"

"Your children too, sir. And the butler and two maids, sir. There was no stopping it. They were all dead within two weeks."

Totally subdued Aaron found a side door in the lower part of the house opened, and walked in. As if in the middle of a nightmare he walked up stairs and into the lounge. It was just how she had left it, a half glass of brandy on the side table and an unfinished bottle, corkless, by its side. He refilled the glass with brandy and sat down heavily on the armchair and stared in space. He drank glass after glass of brandy and when night fell he was drunk and completely out of his mind. He lay there completely unconscious until the light, streaming through the windows, woke him. Unshaven and unwashed, still completely under the influence of the brandy he staggered to the window and looked

out. A young serving girl was picking flowers. He lifted
the window and called her over. She ran to him and covered most of her face with her scarf.

"What's the matter girl?" She mumbled something. "I
can't hear you girl, take that thing from your face." She
lowered the scarf and he winced and turned his head away.
Her face was a mass of scars, a victim of the dreaded small
pox.

"My God, girl, is this what happened to your mistress?"
She curtsied and answered. "Yes sir, she was badly
scarred. She didn't want to live sir. She told Mrs Duncan,
the housekeeper, to take the children away and look after
them and they wasn't to come back to the house. Madam
wouldn't kiss them goodbye, and just waved from the window. But it was too late sir, they already had the pox and
died two days after their mother – then Mrs Duncan and
the butler and half the staff as well. What shall we do sir?
Where can we go?"

"Well, you must stay here. I will get food sent to you. For
now, you must tell me where Madam is buried, and the
babies."

He could feel his heart pulsating through his body as they
neared the churchyard. He sank to his knees at the foot of
the grave. The girl had brought the flowers and now put
them in a vase sunk into the earth.

"That was very kind." He frowned, "What's your name?"
She curtsied again and answered, "Nancy, sir."

"Ah, that's right, I remember now."

He remembered her alright, a sweet pretty little thing
with blonde hair and a little turned up nose, now completely disfigured with the small pox scars. If Elizabeth
was like that he was sure she *would* rather be dead. But it
was Nancy that answered his thoughts.

"I wish I had died too, sir. Now no one will want me with
a diseased ridden face like this." She lowered her head
and whispered, "No one will want me sir."

He didn't answer for he knew it was true. All that the
lower class girls could look forward to was marriage – a
hope that they could find a decent man who would look
after them. Now all Nancy had to look forward to was to

371

grow old and unwanted, looking like an old witch with the kids all shouting after her. No wonder she wished she were dead.

Aaron patted her shoulder, "Now don't you worry Nancy. You stay here as long as you like."

He tidied the grave and picked up the dead leaves, then bent and kissed the headstone, whispering a prayer, "I shall love you always my darling."

Nancy was crying, "She loved you Captain. Yes, she really loved you. Sometimes I would go into her room to comb her lovely red hair and she would be staring into her mirror, tears flooding her eyes and she would say, 'I love my husband Nancy. How I miss him'."

Aaron's throat seemed to constrict and quietly he gasped, "Did she suffer for very long, Nancy?"

"Well, sir..." She hesitated, but he assured her he was well composed and wanted the truth, "Well sir... when her daughter died and then her son, she seemed to go down fast. She said to me, 'All I have now is my Aaron, how I wish to God he was here beside me.' Then she asked for a mirror, I was dreading her seeing herself, her face was covered in large blistering sores. She shed no tears, sir when she looked into the mirror but from then on she rapidly went downhill. She wouldn't eat and would only drink sips of brandy and saying, 'I can never let my beloved Aaron see me like this'. She was so ill sir, no one would go into her room, even the doctor was afraid to go. And when she called for her lawyer he would stay near the door. It was just my lady and myself at the end. The last night sir, she drank nearly a full bottle of brandy. She didn't wake up the next morning, I really think she poisoned herself sir, she had no will to live." Nancy burst into a flood of tears.

"Well Nancy, as I say, you must stay at the house for as long as you wish – at least for her brother to return and take up residence – it will be his house now."

"Oh no sir, the house is yours. It has been left to you and everything in it. This was agreed by her brother when he first heard you had married. And when the lawyer called, when my mistress was dying, I witnessed her signature. It's all yours sir."

"Oh no it isn't. I don't want the damn thing. Fetch the damn estate manager and you can stay here. I could never sleep another night in this house. It holds too many memories."

After arrangement were made with the estate manager to run the estate and house until the return of Commodore Saunders, Aaron had his horse brought round and in the company of a stable boy, returned to his ship. As he rode away he never looked back at the house again.

They rode in complete silence, the stable boy mounted on a grey mare and Aaron on the white hunter. The boy looked at the ship and whistled through his teeth.

"She's a biggun sir." It was the first time Aaron had smiled through the whole of the episode.

Chapter Forty-seven

Aaron was welcomed aboard his ship by Sam and another crew member. They looked rather doubtfully at each other for they hadn't expected the Captain back aboard for at least a week. He went straight to his cabin and poured himself a liberal glass of his favourite brandy; kicked off his shoes and lay down on his bed. He downed the brandy in one go instead of sipping it slowly and savouring its warm glow.

But sleep would not come, and he stared blankly at the ceiling of the cabin for the first time in his life he felt like crying. Unsteady on his legs he made his way across the cabin to the door, opened it and bellowed across the open deck, "Sam! Make sure I am not disturbed for the next two days!"

He took out another bottle of brandy and uncorked it and without bothering to get a glass, downed half of it straight from the bottle. He again threw himself on to the bed and with one arm hanging over the side clutching the half filled bottle he fell into a deep sleep.

He saw Sam come into the cabin through a drunken haze and lifted his head. He felt as if he had been struck by a thick wooden post, "I told you I wasn't to be disturbed..."

"But Captain, that was three days ago." Sam bent down to pick up the several empty brandy bottles, "Look sir, you have been shouting and raving for three days. What is the matter?"

"The matter Sam? I'll tell you what is the matter. before

our last voyage I had a family; two children and a beautiful wife. Now I have neither Sam, they are all dead. Strange Sam, I have fought for years to keep fever and scurvy from my crew and passengers and now my whole family is wiped out by disease. Ironic isn't it? All these years and I have never lost... not one crew member or passenger then I go home and find my family wiped out."

Unsteadily, he walked across to the cupboard where he kept his liquor and took out another fresh bottle.

Sam went to say something, looked at the Captain, and changed his mind. To Sam, as to everyone he came in contact with, Aaron was a hero. Sam knew he'd had a dreadful shock. Why not rid himself of it with the effects of drink?

"You don't approve Sam? Then why don't you say something?"

"It is none of my business, sir. But Captain, we shall soon be getting ready for sea and your agent knows you are back. He wants his orders, and a runner has arrived from Portsmouth with messages from your lawyers."

"Alright Sam... fetch me some hot water. I will shave and clean myself up, I suppose life has to go on, but nothing is the same. Polly is gone, and Willie has gone, now my family is gone."

"You better let me shave you Captain, your hands are shaking so... you will cut your bloody throat."

This brought a shadow of a smile to Aaron's face.

"Would that be a bad idea Sam?"

Aaron returned to the deck an hour later; washed, clean shaven, and changed into a fresh uniform. He called for the messenger from Portsmouth, read the note then clenched it in a ball, "Damn, damn, damn!"

He threw the ball of paper over the side, "Now my bloody lawyer has gone and died. What the hell is the matter with me Sam? Am I cursed or something?"

As the agent stepped aboard he was greeted with, "I thought you may have died too." The agent looked at Aaron, a deep frown on his face, but Aaron shook his hand, "Don't take any notice of me, I've been having something of a bad time."

"I understand you are having a small but fast ship built, sir. I can assure you, we will have no trouble filling her with passengers that want a sharp run to the colony. As it is I think we are over-sold for this."

"I did intend to visit the shipyard today and see the progress." said Aaron desperately trying to concentrate his mind on the business in hand, "As soon as it's finished I will put it on the Australian run... at the moment I just cannot think straight. I feel my sea days are almost over, there is far to much for me to do in England. I never thought when I first nurtured ambitions to own a fleet of ocean-going ships that it would ever curtail my going to sea. It's like a large serpent – tread on it's tail and eventually it will strike at you, and yet it feels good and I doubt if I will ever stop building ships – if eventually I have to stamp on the serpent's head. I want you now to find me a crew. I can't go down to Portsmouth, not just yet, it will mean passing Esher and my wife's house. It holds too many memories for me, fresh memories that only time will diminish."

"Getting a crew will be no problem Captain," answered the Agent softly, "I know of many good seamen and one very keen Captain. Mind you he is getting on a bit – had his own ship once, but lost it on the Scillies during a great storm. There was only him, another officer and three men saved, but he's a likable chap."

The new Captain came aboard that afternoon, a giant of a man well over six feet, with a swarthy complexion that told anyone he had spent his life at sea. Most of the lower part of his face was covered in a luxurious growth of snow white hair. Like most sailors he wore a gold earring in his right ear. When he spoke it was quiet and musical, but when he laughed as he often did, his mighty chest rose up and down in unison with his belly. But his eyes were his most fascinating feature – dark brown, lined at the corners and against the backdrop of his white beard they looked almost black but kindly.

Aaron shook hands with him and his grip was firm and steady like a man with nothing to hide. They retreated to the great cabin and the old Captain looked around with relief. "I see you have a large double bed, does your wife travel with you?"

Aaron shook his head, "No, not any more, but if you have a wife you are welcome to take her with you."

The great man gave a belly laugh that shook the cabin, "No, Captain, I have never been a man to settle down to one lady. I have several wives in many ports from the Cape to Cairo and beyond. On occasion I've thought I may find myself one and settle down but something in me takes over and advises me differently."

Aaron poured two glasses of his best brandy and shoved one across to the old salt.

He shook his head, "Never touch the stuff Captain, I did once and it started controlling my life. I found out that one glass was too much – and ten glasses, not enough. I had delirium tremors and that was it. Fifteen years ago, I threw all my drink overboard and haven't touched it from that day."

Aaron was taking a liking to the man with every word he spoke, "I understand you lost your own ship. How did it happen?"

"About two years ago we had a violent storm off the Scillies and she smashed up against the rocks. We had a full cargo of wine and fruit from the Canaries. No one has given me a ship since – and I've been sailing, man and boy, for over forty years. The only mishap I ever had..."

"Well I am willing to give you a chance, but you have to abide by my rules. First and foremost I want no tails or canes – any disobedience and you put the culprit ashore at first sight of land."

Aaron went on to spell out the other rules, "A happy ship is an efficient ship. Look after the men and they will follow you to hell and back. You will be sailing, two weeks from now. For the time being I will be using this cabin. There are two men to interview, one of them an officer. I will leave that to you. The ship is a bit sluggish, but it's a good sea boat.

"It will be strange seeing this ship going down the channel without me aboard. I will sail with you to Portsmouth, then she is all yours. I take it you agree with me about the treatment of the ship's crew."

He touched his forelock, "I do sir, wholeheartedly agree with you." They shook hands.

At Portsmouth Aaron handed over the ship, satisfied completely with the way the new Captain had handled the ship from Wapping, "Sam are you ready to go ashore?"

"Yes sir." He handed the baggage down to the two sailors in the small boat and followed the baggage in. Then Aaron climbed down beside him. The small boat returned to the *Golden Eagle* and they watched from the shore as it upped anchor and sailed.

It was an emotional experience for Aaron that left his throat dry and a lump slowly raising in it, "Come on Sam, let's go and find ourselves a bed for a couple of nights."

They returned to Aaron's favourite tavern, and spent several days going round the old haunts. They visited the ship builders in Bucklers Hard, where they were welcomed by the owner who thought at first he was in for an order to build another ship.

They walked to the top of the hill that overlooked the great naval harbour, "That's a sight to behold Sam."

Captain Jacobs walked back a few yards and dug his heel into the soft sand, taking another look over the harbour.

"That's where I intend to build my new house Sam, away from the hub-bub of the town and yet near enough to visit it whenever I want a night out."

"Yes sir," answered Sam. The great smile had once again blossomed on his face revealing the two rows of pearly white teeth.

A visit to a builder well known for constructing beautiful houses was arranged for the afternoon of the next day. They met on the site and Aaron described exactly what he wanted, with an emphasis on the windows of the main rooms looking out across the great harbour and town.

The builder touched his forelock and said, "Six months Captain, and you will have a house that will be the envy of every person in Portsmouth."

Six months to the day, and Aaron had finally decided to swallow the anchor. He would do the run now and again, for his fleet was growing fast.

In another five years it grew to seven ships, with another being built. Using one large room as his office where he held meetings with his agents from London, Bristol and Portsmouth, Aaron kept extremely busy, but he still yearned for the sea.

One day Sam answered the door to an urgent knock and a tall elegant naval officer stood there. Aaron heard the mumbling and went to investigate.

"Saunders, come in man, come in." They shook hands warmly, "When did you arrive in port?"

"Two days ago – I went down to Esher, but all the windows are boarded up and the place has gone to rack and ruin. I'd heard the news about Elizabeth when I was in Australia. I am so sorry Aaron, I know how much you loved each other and those dear children – fate deals some bad blows."

"I couldn't believe it myself," answered Aaron wearily, "to think I should never see them again – it broke my heart. It was months before I could even go near the place. I do pluck up the courage now, every month and tend to the graves. When I'm there I feel much closer to them."

Aaron poured two glasses of brandy and passed one to his friend, who gulped it down in one go.

"Why didn't you take the place over Aaron. You know she left it all to you, lock stock and barrel. The furniture, everything – and there is a great deal of money."

Aaron shook his head, "I could never live there, it holds too many memories. The only thing I wanted was the oil painting of her." He pointed to the large oil painting above the fireplace and stared hard at it, "She was so beautiful."

Saunders put his hand on Aaron's shoulder, "Yes, she was beautiful. At least, Aaron, take the money she left you."

But Aaron shook his head, "It's not mine – you have it, give it to your children. I have all the money I need. We can go to the lawyers tomorrow and I will get it signed over to them."

"Stay for dinner now. Sam is just preparing it and believe me, he is a great cook. I am leaving for Australia in a few days time, but not as Captain – it will feel strange. My ship the *Golden Drake* holds the record for the Australian run."

All through dinner they talked about old times, "... and Admiral Medlam, do you ever come cross him these days?" asked Aaron, "I seen him once, at the George Hotel, but made out I never knew him."

"No I have never seen him since, and we shall never see him again. His ship was lost with all hands a couple of years ago."

"His wife will be pleased. I met her at the wedding, and she said she would have doubled the reward if I'd left him there to rot."

"Poor woman, the family were distant relatives – his wife is such a beautiful woman."

The conversation drew well on into the early hours, and the Commodore was given the spare bedroom. The next morning it was arranged for the estate and all its contents to be made over to the Commodore's son.

Two days later Aaron sailed aboard the *Golden Drake*. Occasionally he would take over the wheel at the Captain's invitation, relishing the opportunity to experience at first hand just how fast his ship really was.

"Have you much cargo for Miss Polly Captain?"

"Oh yes sir, every voyage I make. Her business is one of the busiest in the colony."

As they passed through the heads Aaron could feel his heart thumping as the familiar places – and many more unfamiliar – loomed into sight, "My God this place is growing fast Captain. You should have seen it when I first came here."

Then Polly's shop loomed up, all freshly painted. The ship dropped anchor and Aaron was rowed ashore.

He walked into the shop expecting Polly to throw her arms around his neck, but Maud was serving two ladies and Jenny came over to him. It was several minutes before she recognised him and her lower jaw dropped.

"Where is Polly, Miss Jenny?"

"Oh my God!" Her face lost its colour and Aaron expected to hear the worst, "She has gone back to England sir. She heard you lost your wife and family a time ago and had been wanting to go ever since. I suppose you must have crossed paths – she will be wild."

"Not as wild as I am this very minute. What about her friend Mrs Pilgrim, how is she?"

"Very well sir – she has had two children since you were here last. One of them, a girl, is named after Polly. They are very close friends."

"I will go and see her before I go." He called to Sam who was standing at the shop door, "Go and tell the Captain we will be returning with the ship Sam. Miss Polly isn't here, she has gone to England."

Two weeks later Aaron was back aboard his ship bound for home. The only hope he had of seeing her was that the ship she was sailing on was the slowest in his fleet. But fate was playing her worse hand, they were dogged by bad winds and lay becalmed for several days – piling on the agony for Aaron. He walked the decks day and night and drowned his disappointment in the bottle, convinced that by the time they reached England Polly would have left. By the time Aaron did arrive at his home in Portsmouth he felt a shattered man.

Some nights later he was sitting in front of a roaring fire, smoking his long pipe when there was a slight tap on the door, "Door Sam! Whoever comes visiting this time of night and in this bloody weather, must be mad!"

Sam, his hair now grey, almost white and shuffling badly, went to the door. A lady stood there, a long velvet coat stretched to the ground and her head covered with the hood. She turned slowly and dropped the hood, Sam looked surprised and was about to say something when the lady put her finger to her lips and walked across the carpeted floor.

Aaron had his back to her.

She kicked off her shoes and softly crossing the floor whispered in his ear, "Drop me kecks for sixpence sailor," in a broad Portsea gutter accent.

Aaron dropped his long stemmed clay pipe and glass of brandy, "Polly! You old bugger! What the hell are you doing here?"

She fell into his arms, at the same time her heavy cloak dropped to the floor, "Aaron." And she kept repeating it over and over again, kissing his face, his ears, his lips.

"Oh Polly, I am so pleased to see you again after all these years!"

"Now that you are a great ship owner I thought you wouldn't want to see me. I was at the tavern last night and heard you now have twelve ships and this new house." She looked around her, "It is so beautiful, Aaron."

He called for Sam, "Look who's here Sam, Miss Polly!"

"Yes sir, I saw her. Have you come to stay Miss?"

"Never mind about that now, go and prepare dinner for the both of us Sam!"

Sam left, his eyes dimmed by tears, for this was the first time in years that he had seen the Captain happy.

"I thought you would come over and see me again Aaron, and I kept waiting. But when Captain Hargreaves and his wife came ashore last time they said that with the size of your fleet it was unlikely you would ever go to sea again. So I decided to return with him."

After dinner Aaron told Sam to go to bed, "Miss Polly and I have a lot of talking to do."

They sat on an enormous sofa talking and catching up on all those lost years, "I was so sorry to hear about Elizabeth and the children, Aaron." She ran her fingers through his greying hair.

"Yes, it took me years to get over it. She was so beautiful. She left me everything. Her brother was in the navy and hated farming, but I couldn't take it, so I signed it over to his son. After all, it's been in their family for several generations and that's where it belongs."

"But let's talk about you Polly. You are looking as beautiful as ever — age has certainly not taken its toll on you. You are still the beautiful girl I knew so many years back. You never did marry then, Polly?"

"No Aaron. When I couldn't have you there was never going to be anyone else. I did have hopes for Samual, but after he raped me that was it. Marriage and children was a thing of the past — all my hopes were shattered."

It was past midnight when sleep finally overtook them. Aaron lifted her to her feet, "Sam has made up your room, Polly." He pointed to a door, "There's a nice fire going."

382

"Do you think I have made this long journey to sleep alone, Aaron?"

He put his arm around her, "Let's start where we left off, twenty odd years ago."

She snuggled up to him as he closed the door behind them.

The End